A Lily in the Light

A Lily in the Light

A NOVEL

KRISTIN FIELDS

LAKE UNION
PUBLISHING

Text copyright © 2019 by Kristin Fields
All rights reserved.

Published by Lake Union Publishing, Seattle

www.apub.com

Amazon, the Amazon logo, and Lake Union Publishing are trademarks of Amazon.com, Inc., or its affiliates.

ISBN-13: 9781542041690 (hardcover)
ISBN-10: 1542041694 (hardcover)
ISBN-13: 9781542041683 (paperback)
ISBN-10: 1542041686 (paperback)

Cover design by Philip Pascuzzo

Cover photography by Laura Andrea Harris

Printed in the United States of America

First edition

For Mom, Dad, Michael, Jenna, and Emma,
who inspired this story through and through
For Rob, who followed every word of this journey
with love, support, and hope

PART ONE
QUEENS, 1997

Chapter One

"Ladies." Amelia clapped, and all ten dancers stopped moving. The air went still. "Find a seat."

Esme found a place on the hardwood floor. A grapefruit candle burned in the corner. The air smelled fresh even though there was fog on the mirror from a room of sweating, heaving dancers. Afternoon light spilled through the windows in angular shards and threw a warm triangle over Esme's leg.

"Let's talk about pointe, ladies. Slippers off. Tights rolled up. I need to see your toes."

Esme inched closer to Amelia, close enough that Amelia's sheer cranberry skirt grazed the top of Esme's big toe as she moved toward the other side of the room. Pointe was the next step to professional. Esme kicked away her faded pink slippers, the bottoms black with use, and fought the urge to hide her sweaty, stinky feet. She waited, breathing shallowly, hoping. One day when she was famous and had done thirty-seven turns on top of an elephant in China like Anna Pavlova, she'd think back to this day and know everything had started with pointe.

"Some of you are ready," Amelia said. "Some of you are not. On Monday, this class will officially become a pointe class. If you're not selected, we'll make other arrangements for you."

Amelia moved from one girl to the next, lifting a foot for a closer look or walking past them altogether. Esme was at the end of the row, last. The sun was hot on her face now, blinding. She felt like an ant under a magnifying glass. She turned away from the window, blinking until she could see herself in the mirror again, legs splayed, ribs a shadowy outline beneath her black leotard, the youngest in the class. She looked so much smaller in the mirror than she usually felt.

If she didn't make it this time . . . no. She pushed the thought away, but there was always next year, just like Anna Pavlova. Whoever had thought she'd looked too sickly when she'd auditioned for the Imperial Ballet School must have felt really stupid about it later. Anna Pavlova had been anything but.

"Think about it this way: It doesn't matter how much you hope it will snow on Christmas. We can't control the weather, and today, nothing you say will affect the outcome. The decision's been made. If you're not selected, it doesn't mean your career is over. You'll leave here like a professional, not a little girl. No drama. No crying to your mothers on the way home. You'll work harder instead. Understood?"

The girls mumbled agreement, but Esme only nodded. She'd tried to say yes, but her voice had caught in her throat. Amelia knelt before Esme, lifting her foot from the floor. Her fingers were cold and sent a chill through Esme's leg, still warm from dancing. Maybe she was imagining it, but it felt like Amelia lingered longer with her than she had with the others. She searched Amelia's face for clues, but her lips were pressed into a line, eyes focused on Esme's foot. Esme had the strange sensation that Amelia was looking at the bones beneath her skin, unaware that Esme's foot was connected to her at all.

"Let's look at Esme's foot." She called the other girls closer until they'd made a half circle around her. Esme balled her hands into fists and waited. Amelia ran her finger along the tops of her toes so gently it made her shiver.

"Esme's toes are boxy and equal in length, which means if she dances en pointe, her weight will be distributed equally. She would not have to compensate and compromise form because one of her toes is longer than the others. And the same goes for her arches." Amelia balled her fist and fit it under the arch in Esme's foot to show its curve. "Esme's feet are just right for pointe work."

Esme's eyes widened. Did this mean . . . ?

"I'll see you in class on Monday." Amelia smiled finally and lowered Esme's foot to the floor. "Liz, Rebecca, Sophia, and Jenna, I'll see you on Monday too."

"Thank you," Esme whispered, feeling as shaken as a soda bottle. She might have fizzled over if not for the five other girls gathering their bags and sweaters from the back of the room, huffing into the lobby like a swarm of angry wasps, blurring the joy Esme felt for pointe shoes with pink ribbons, custom made for her like a real dancer's.

Esme waited until Amelia was alone in the studio, sweeping under the wall of framed newspaper articles. Some of them were about Amelia, but most were about her former students. Esme envied the girls who'd traveled to Paris and Italy and danced on old, old stages and who'd already mastered things like the thirty-two fouetté turns and fish dives. She wanted to know what it was like to let her partner catch her when her nose was only inches from the floor. She imagined it would make her cross-eyed, but she'd have to smile because the audience, one big, breathing animal, would clap as wildly as her heartbeat.

"But it's a little different, isn't it?" she asked. The unfairness wavered in her chest under those articles. Amelia listened as she swept. "People didn't make weather, so we didn't make its rules, but people made ballet and its rules. We could change them."

The broom handle rested on Amelia's shoulder. Amelia stretched her arms over her head and yawned. Her arms floated back to her sides. Even yawning looked like dancing for Amelia. Esme promised she'd never yawn again without making it look like dancing.

"In Russia," Amelia said, pushing the little dust pile forward with the broom, "every little girl wants to be a dancer. Every family hopes their daughter will, too, and many of them try, but most don't make it. That makes it more special for the ones that do. Someone made rules, yes, but it wasn't you or me. Working toward something that seems impossible makes it more of an accomplishment. Think of it this way: even if we could control weather and make it snow every single Christmas, eventually that wouldn't feel special. If everyone made pointe, would it feel like such an accomplishment right now? Remember that."

Everything Amelia said sounded important.

Esme packed the last of her things and stepped into an oversize pair of gray sweatpants, pushing back damp hair wisps before her mother could see what a mess her bun was. Amelia waved goodbye as she put a cassette into the tape deck and hit play. Esme wished she could watch Amelia alone in the studio: Amelia, who'd made NYCB at only sixteen, who'd leaped across the front page of the *New York Times* in grand jeté as the Firebird, her long hair sweeping behind her like inky wind. People had whispered the word *prodigy*. But now, Amelia danced in the studio alone. If the lighting was just right, the long, jagged scar down the center of her knee showed through her tights. Amelia never talked about the accident that had ended her career at twenty-one even though everyone knew. Sometimes Esme wondered if Amelia was hiding in Port Washington instead of living and teaching in New York City, if being close to Lincoln Center would be too painful a reminder of what she'd lost.

The first few tinkling notes of "Clair de Lune" eased the empty studio awake. The last thing Esme saw as she closed the door behind her was Amelia's triangular back at the barre, fingers softly resting on the wood, her long braid hanging behind her like a rope.

In the lobby, Esme's mother, Cerise, wound her measuring tape around her fingers. Her clipboard with measurements was tucked under her arm. Lily was sitting behind a folding chair, her head just beneath the backrest. A crayon sign was taped to the backrest that read Kissing

Booth Five Cents. Lily giggled wildly, cheeks scrunched, lips puckered, waiting for Esme.

Esme hid her smile. Cerise rolled her eyes. "She's been waiting."

"Kissing booth? Five cents?" Esme said, taking heavy steps toward the chair. "Let me check my pockets. Mom?" Esme paused dramatically. Lily giggled even harder, shaking the folding chair until it rattled on the linoleum tiles. "Mom? Do you have five cents?" She crept closer to the chair, close enough to smell Lily's strawberry shampoo, to see a tiny cookie crumb in the corner of Lily's mouth.

"No? Then I'll just have to steal them!" She covered Lily's face with smoochy kisses and pulled her through the hole in the chair and onto her hip. Even with her coat unzipped, Lily was a ball of heat. Lily's arms wrapped around Esme just far enough to loop her fingers at the end. It was easy to forget that Lily was only four years old.

"You owe me five cents." Lily nestled her head on Esme's shoulder, heavy from so much waiting. Esme understood that feeling. She was only eleven, but there was already so much she wanted.

"Yeah? What would you buy with five cents?"

"A train ticket," Cerise said. "Let's head over." She zipped Lily's coat and opened the door, passing the **SORRY, NO MOMS** sign outside. The door swung shut behind them.

Cerise was the only mom allowed in the studio lobby, but only because she made costumes for their company. Even so, after Cerise set up her sewing supplies, she wasn't allowed to watch classes. The studio door was always closed. It was a little sad that the most her mother heard between measurements was Amelia clapping to keep time.

The sign was for the Moms. The Moms clustered around the studio like gnats with thick thighs and teased hair, stinking of hair spray. They hovered for Amelia, waiting to ask about their daughters' future, a word their blotchy, lipsticked mouths dragged out like a wet secret, as if the future were a glass ball Amelia could stare into and read while the Moms decided if they liked what it said. If Amelia did get caught in a web of

Moms, she'd always give the same clipped answer. *I'm still teaching her, aren't I?* The Moms would scatter then because they'd heard about girls who'd been dismissed. Esme imagined there would be some very upset Moms at the studio next week.

Today, the cloud of Moms had cleared by the time Esme's family left the studio. They wandered through rows of parked cars toward the train station. Seeing the cars pulling in and out of spots under a sky of moving clouds was like watching a dance of its own—a boring one, but it had its own rhythm. There was rhythm in everything really. It helped her understand what was coming next, a quiet part or a crashing part, like in a symphony. Playing with Lily in the lobby had been a quiet, resting part of a symphony. Carrying Lily's little warm weight was a quiet part as well, so a loud crashing part with cymbals and drums and brass instruments was coming soon. Like Amelia's rules about weather and ballet, this was a rule too.

"You know," Cerise said as they waited for the train on the empty westbound platform, "you shouldn't challenge Amelia so much. You should just listen and learn. I'm sure she doesn't want to hear your opinion on everything all the time."

So her mother had heard the thing about weather. Esme rolled her eyes at Lily, still on her hip, who stared back wide eyed, a sponge absorbing things she didn't understand but filled with sympathy for her big sister. Esme squeezed her tighter and paced the yellow line on the platform. **WATCH YOUR STEP**, it said.

"I don't have an opinion on everything. Just some stuff, and Amelia doesn't mind." She turned away from her mother, wishing Cerise was more like the other moms, who signed their daughters up for more classes and made them practice before school or got passes to meet principal dancers at Lincoln Center so they could ask about career stuff. Those moms wanted their daughters to stand out and sharpened their edges like knives, ready to cut through all the hard parts of life, while her mother told her to be good. *Don't make trouble. Do as you're told. Be patient.*

Wind rustled the trees, which were turning from green to yellow and orange to red. She picked up an acorn and handed it to Lily. The cap was cracked, but Lily didn't mind. She folded it into her palm and held it there.

"Be careful," Esme whispered. "If your hand gets too hot, that thing might sprout a branch."

Lily squeezed tighter, trying to make it sprout. Esme traced the scar on Lily's hand from the time she'd burned it on the radiator. It was long healed, but it shouldn't be there. Babies weren't supposed to get hurt.

In the distance, train lights fell over the tracks like two white eyes staring out from the dark. The air was crisp, and the train was far enough away to be silent, but soon it would roar into the station, and Esme would lean against the wind it made.

Cerise huffed and pulled her coat tighter around her. The sewing basket hung at her side, the wicker faded and out of place on the concrete platform.

"Think Mom has Toto in that basket?" Esme whispered to Lily. Lily's giggle was lost in the whirl of the train.

"I'll say one more thing." Cerise pushed wind-whipped hair away from her face. She sounded annoyed but didn't seem to want to argue. "She could have picked any of those girls, but she picked you. Try not to push your luck. If you're too difficult or she thinks you won't want to do certain things, she'll ask someone else. That's not what you want."

No, it wasn't. Esme picked at her cuticle and pulled it away in one long line like a thread from a sweater. The skin underneath was a soft pink. She shifted from one foot to the other, easing weight off the new burning blister on her toe. Her finger and toe made her all the more aware that her body was constantly changing, growing and shifting. What worked for her today might not work tomorrow. Her mother was right, but when she thought of girls who'd been dismissed because a toe

9

was too long or an arch was too flat or their boobs were too big, she figured opinions didn't matter if something unchangeable could knock her out no matter how hard she worked or how much she wanted it. It was probably better not to want things too much just in case her place on Amelia's wall never came.

But it would, Esme reminded herself, certain that if she pulled back the imaginary curtain between now and the future, she'd see herself on that wall. She felt as sure about it as she did about breathing.

"Will you show me the orange thing now?"

The doors slid open. Esme stepped inside and sat down, hugging her sister closer, thankful for the weight on her hip, a teddy bear she wasn't embarrassed to carry around.

"Where is it?" Lily bounced in Esme's lap, pulling herself closer to the window.

Her pink sequined shoes sparkled against the faded navy seat. Cerise was sketching on the back of an envelope, an intricate pattern of beads for a wedding dress. Esme didn't have the heart to tell Lily they were on the wrong side of the train, that they wouldn't see the orange thing today. It was only a washed-up construction cone, but it was shockingly orange against the marsh grass and the blue of the Little Neck Bay, making the eleven stops from Woodside to Port Washington just a little more interesting. *Lily would like this*, Esme had thought, and the mystery of the orange thing had begun.

"I want to see what it did today." Lily's foot grazed Esme's thigh and left a dusty smudge.

"Keep looking," Esme said, even though they wouldn't see it.

Cerise looked up briefly from her drawing. "Congratulations, Esme," she said. "I should have said so earlier, but don't let it go to your head. You still have a long way to go."

Esme nodded, watching the back of her sister's red corduroy coat. She closed her eyes and pulled Lily into her lap, listening to the sound of her mother's eraser and the conductor announcing Murray Hill, then

Flushing, and waiting for the long stretch without stops that would bring them home. Next week, she'd lift onto pointe shoes for the first time. The weight would be crushing, but she imagined there was something weightless about it, too, like floating or flying. If it hurt, she could always invent something specially for her feet to make them hurt less like Anna Pavlova had done.

The Little Neck Bay had passed. It was only houses now, faded bricks with bars across the windows and awnings as colorful as M&M'S dotting empty streets.

"I guess it didn't want to come out today," she told Lily. "Maybe next time."

"Maybe it went to the store," Lily said, "for Oreo ice cream."

"I think you're right," Esme said, imagining the construction cone walking to the supermarket. "Remind me when we get home that I owe you five cents."

"OK." Lily shuffled and settled into place with a heaviness that made Esme feel centered. They spent the rest of the ride in silence, the calm before home, the slow part of a symphony, just strings and maybe little bells, as the train swayed quietly beneath them.

~

"So it doesn't just sit there?" Lily pulled wrinkled clothes from Esme's dance bag. A pile of tights collected at her feet, Lily's pet snakes.

Esme pointed to the black leotards. "Clean." She pointed to the pile of tights and leg warmers. "Dirty."

Lily gathered the pile and walked it to the hamper, dropping it into the wicker basket. Esme was surprised Lily didn't press her hands together over her head and sing her snake charmer song, hoping Esme's tights would lift themselves out of the hamper like cobras.

"It can move?" Lily asked again, still fixated on the orange thing.

Even though Esme liked this game, she had a test the next day, and her leg was aching. She balanced an ice pack on her knee, a heating pad on her shoulder, and an open textbook across her lap. Her stomach rumbled. And it was her night to cook dinner. Why, why couldn't her mother just go to church once a week on Sundays like everyone else?

"Yes, but it just sits there when I see it."

"But sometimes it can move, right?" Lily put the clean clothes back in Esme's dance bag.

"Sure," Esme mumbled. She skimmed her textbook for words in bold. The Emancipation Proclamation stared back at her. Jim Crow, Union, Confederate States, Abraham Lincoln, Robert E. Lee. Her shoulder throbbed. The ice pack was melting. Water trickled over the side of her knee and onto the bed. The wet spot spread.

"Maybe it can float away and come back when it wants to. Maybe it's a fish named Marley, and it has a tail you can't see."

Lily crawled onto the bed. Dark hair fell over her face in tangles, and her weight shifted the ice pack until it fell. She stumbled into Esme's textbook. The words blurred, and she lost her page.

"Lily, I have to study."

"After?"

"Yes, I'll tell you after." Esme sighed.

"No, study *after* you tell me." Red spots rose on Lily's face. Her fists balled. Lily's heat pressed against Esme's thigh.

"No," Esme insisted, lifting Lily from the bed to the floor. "Later— go play. Or go get your book and read next to me, but you have to shut up for a little while. No talking."

Lily kicked the side of the bed once, twice.

"Stop it," Esme warned, but on the third kick, Lily stubbed her toe against the metal bed leg. She shrieked.

"I warned you." Esme pressed her eyes closed.

"Oh my God, shut up!" Madeline burst through the bedroom door, glasses balanced on her head, PSAT book thrown over her arm. Her face was still flushed from running, pink dusted from mile after mile with her long black ponytail chasing behind her like a lost shadow. Even her cheekbones looked pushed back and chiseled from wind against her face. Unstoppable. People told her she looked like Jessica Biel from *7th Heaven*, the pretty one, which seemed especially unfair because Madeline didn't care about being pretty. *At least I'm the graceful one*, Esme thought as Madeline thumped across the room.

"I can't concentrate!" Madeline whined. Lily screamed louder.

"What do you want me to do?" Esme yelled over Lily, face flushing. "I'm studying too."

Madeline pointed at Lily, still wailing and holding her toe. "Well, now no one is!" Madeline pulled Lily by the arm into the living room and slammed the door, leaving herself and Esme alone inside the room. Esme forced herself back to her book. She was breathing faster. States in rebellion. The whole house felt like a state in rebellion on the nights Cerise went to stupid church.

Madeline flopped onto the bed, stomach down, her shirt riding up to uncover her lower back, the same place she wanted a tattoo of a root chakra one day. "Why the hell can't Mom deal with her? Why is this our problem?"

Lily quieted. She knocked on the door. Esme softened at the sound of Lily's whimpering and got up to let her in. "Maybe she's over it," she said.

"Doubtful," Madeline mumbled, attention drifting back to the text in front of her. When Esme opened the door, Lily was watery eyed and holding two books. She'd coiled her hair around her thumb and was sucking it again, which Cerise said she wasn't supposed to do anymore, but Esme didn't say anything.

"You can come back in, but you have to be quiet."

Lily nodded, but her eyes narrowed toward Madeline.

"No baby stuff." Madeline glared back.

The whimpering stopped. Esme settled back on the bed and adjusted her heating pad, the ice pack, and her textbook back into place. A page turned. Lily inched closer to Madeline's bed, running her hands over the purple comforter, pulling herself forward slowly. Static popped on Lily's striped skirt and her green butterfly tights. For a moment, there was silence. And then Madeline screamed.

"She spit on me!" Madeline wiped the slick spot on her face. She sprang off the bed and after Lily. A flash of Lily's blue striped skirt disappeared into the living room. Esme held back a giggle.

"What is wrong with you? You're an animal!" Madeline shrieked. "The devil child!"

Lily screamed, a sonic, angry blast, full of everything she didn't have words for yet. If Esme went out there, she could pick Lily up, turn her away from Madeline. She could make Lily stop crying, tell her Madeline was being a bitch, set her up with books or something to color, but she didn't feel like getting up.

Why didn't Madeline realize she was only making things worse? Esme shifted her weight, ready to get up, when her father's bedroom door opened. Heavy feet shook the coffee table, the TV stand, rattling through her bedroom wall. He wasn't a big man, just a coil of muscles wound tightly together from years of boxing before Esme was born. Thank God, a real parent. The screaming stopped. Lily tried to catch her breath.

"Knock it off," Andre mumbled, voice thick with sleep. "She's only four."

"She's seriously like the worst kid ever," Madeline hissed. "It was better without her." The bathroom door slammed shut. The shower started. Pipes rattled in the wall behind Esme's room. That wasn't fair. She hoped Lily hadn't heard her.

"Don't listen to her," Andre said, turning on the TV for Lily. *Full House*. "She's in a pissy mood, and she doesn't mean it."

Esme got up to close the door and stared at the *Saved by the Bell* poster over Madeline's bed, thankful to have the room to herself. Zack, Jesse, Slater. None of them had to watch siblings or cook dinner. They just got to be teenagers in California, eating in diners and riding around in cars, pulling pranks, but that was TV.

Her mother should have been home by now. Esme heard the murmur of her father's voice. He knocked softly on her door, and Esme sighed. It was time to make dinner. She slammed her textbook shut.

"Would you mind?" he asked. She shut off the bedroom light and headed for the kitchen. Lily was tucked into her blanket cave under the coffee table, full of pillows and stuffed animals. Esme thought about crawling through the little entrance and telling Lily she was sorry, but it was finally quiet, and Esme sensed it would erupt again soon enough, so she left Lily's hideout alone.

Cerise had left two boxes of spaghetti on the counter. Esme fixed pots of water and added salt. She set the table and defrosted sauce in a skillet while she grated Parmesan cheese and waited for the water pitcher to fill up. The living room was quiet except for the TV, where Uncle Jesse, Danny, and Joey were singing a lullaby to baby Michelle. Esme was mildly jealous that people didn't actually do that stuff in real life, but then again, it would be a little weird if her whole family sang her to sleep. What would they even sing? Her father would pick Sinatra, and her mother might pick Gloria Estefan, and both seemed too ridiculous for lullabies. She made a salad and an egg for herself. No pasta before auditions.

The front door opened, and Cerise hummed her way from the hall closet to the kitchen, breezing in with the October chill still stuck to her hair and cheeks, humming "Amazing Grace" and "City of God," stinking of incense. She sprinkled salt and pepper on the food Esme had made without asking what she'd missed while she'd been gone or how her being out had affected anyone else. It was pointless. Esme left the spoon in the pot for Cerise to finish stirring. "I deserve a night out," Cerise had said once. "I do enough for the rest of you. You can do this for me."

"Time to eat," Cerise called through the living room. The TV clicked off. Without TV noise, Esme felt the tension in the house. Madeline dragged her chair out from under the table and sat down heavily, not looking at anyone as she piled salad and spaghetti onto her plate, her wet hair wrapped in a frayed towel. Andre took his place at the table, waiting patiently while Madeline kept the serving spoons balanced on the edge of her dish.

"What time are you leaving tonight?" Cerise asked Andre. Under the glow of the overhead light, her father's left arm was still summer tanned from resting on the open taxi window while he drove, his right arm a pale olive color.

"An hour." He shrugged, looking tired from interrupted sleep. He'd come home tonight after everyone else in the city had gone to bed, before the newspaper trucks threw papers on doorsteps, when no one else needed a ride. "You never want the ones out when no one else is. No good," he'd said, shaking his head from side to side.

"Put them back so someone else can use them," Esme mumbled, irritated everyone had to wait for Madeline to sprinkle grated cheese over her pasta. Madeline's eyes narrowed, but Andre snapped the spoon off her plate.

"Be considerate," he said, his voice tinged with annoyance. Madeline pressed her lips into a thin line. The argument was over. Even though Esme'd won, it would only start up again as soon as they closed their bedroom door tonight, stone quiet and tense until they both fell asleep. She was too ticked off to care.

"Where's your brother?" Andre looked up as Nick slid out of his bedroom, baggy jeans hanging just under his waist, covered in Wite-Out marks and frayed fabric. Nick slouched in his seat, black hoodie pulled over his head, a rash of dark stubble and shadows spread over his face. Quiet, solemn. He reminded Esme of a wraith now that he was seventeen and didn't care about anything except Metallica and Kurt Cobain—and farting and watching as everyone realized it. That he still found hilarious.

"Take that hood off at the table," Andre grunted, pulling the back of the hood off Nick's head. "None of that Beastie Boys shit at the table."

Nick rolled his eyes and filled his plate. *Be someone*, Esme could almost hear her father saying, disappointed with his son who'd become a baggy-pants-wearing C student wasting time in McDonald's or the park after dark. She stared at her brother as he poured extra sauce on his plate, unnerved by how quiet he always was.

"Where's Lily?" Cerise paused, holding Lily's empty plate. The faded *Lion King* characters balanced Simba over Pride Rock, Lily's favorite, but her seat was empty.

"Lily?" Cerise called into the living room.

"No wonder it's so peaceful," Madeline mumbled.

"I'll get her." Esme pushed back her chair. The living room was empty. Lily wasn't in her blanket cave. Esme tried her bedroom next, but the beds were as they'd left them. *Where the Wild Things Are* and *Take Me to the Zoo!* sat on the floor in a heap. She looked underneath the beds, shifting Madeline's bins of old shoes and winter sweaters, and in the closet, closing the door behind her. She tried her parents' bedroom and Nick's and even pulled back the shower curtain in the bathroom, but Lily wasn't there. She walked back to the table confused.

"I can't find her."

"What do you mean you can't find her?" Andre asked between mouthfuls of food. "How big is this place?" He retraced her steps, and Esme followed while Cerise checked the hallway closets, digging through the winter coats Lily liked to hide in. Cerise opened the front door and called Lily's name down the hallway. Everyone was looking now, pushing things aside under beds. Nick even looked in the kitchen cabinets.

"She wouldn't have gone out alone." Cerise repeated a rule Lily knew well, but Lily wasn't home, so she must have broken it. "Go knock on doors," Cerise told Nick. "See if she went next door."

"Lily! Enough!" Her father's voice boomed. Silence. Esme's heart beat faster. She glared at Madeline waiting in the living room.

"This is your fault," Esme hissed, but instead of protesting, Madeline furrowed her brow, worry lines creased. Madeline was nervous. *Life was better without you*, Madeline's words echoed. Esme's mouth tasted like she'd licked a lemon. If she'd gotten up and defended Lily instead of leaving her alone in the living room with bitch-face Madeline, she'd probably be at the table now, twirling spaghetti around her fork and calling them worms.

"Come on, Lily," Esme called. "We're having worms for dinner." Silence.

"I'll look outside," Esme said. Cerise was already putting her coat and boots on. Esme pulled on her sneakers. Lily's shoes were missing. She froze, then dug through the closet, tossing aside everyone else's shoes, coats, and the aluminum baseball bats at the back of the closet until she was certain Lily's pink sequined sneakers weren't there.

Lily's red corduroy coat with the pink buttons was missing too. They should have heard her leave. How could they have missed it?

"Mom?" Esme's voice came out higher than she'd expected. "Mom? Lily's coat and shoes are gone."

Cerise stared back.

"Mom? Lily's coat and shoes are gone." The closet door hung open. "I heard you. Andre? Get your coat."

"Maybe she put it on the back of a chair instead?" Madeline scurried back toward the dining room to look, but everyone already knew it wasn't there. Cerise sent them to check the other floors of the building, the playground, Lily's preschool. Her hand closed around the phone receiver as she shouted directions through the open door and dialed.

"Who are you calling?" Andre asked, his arms and legs jittering at his sides in the same way Esme's were, like waiting in the wings. The nerves in her body were reacting to everything—the feel of her clothes, a phone ringing next door, the smell of onions frying down the hall—as if they knew she'd need them at any second, coiled and ready to spring. She wiggled her fingers to calm herself, but it didn't work.

"The police," Cerise said. Her voice was calm and even, but the lines in her face were drawn tightly. Esme's stomach rolled. Cerise moved closer to the window and looked down at the street below. Andre stared down the hallway, where Halloween skeletons and scarecrows hung from doors.

"She can't have gotten far," he said and started off down the hallway.

Esme couldn't move, even though it was all she wanted to do.

"Go!" Cerise urged, still staring at the empty street below.

Esme's legs shivered awake. She meant to walk down the stairs from one floor to the next but found herself running. The hallways were empty. The roof was empty. Birdman's forgotten pigeon coop looked murky brown in the darkness, but she made herself look inside just in case. It was filled with old mail crates and black plastic garbage bags that shook behind the chicken wire. It gave her the creeps. The roof door slammed shut behind her.

The hallways filled with neighbors in winter coats over pajamas, echoing Lily's name. Nick knocked on doors, asking if anyone had seen Lily, but no one had. His scalp looked eerily white in the hall light, freshly buzzed that morning in the bathroom, dark eyes lost under thick black eyebrows. If he wasn't her brother, if their neighbors hadn't known him since he was born and remembered him catching ants on the stoop with paper cups, would they have opened their doors for him if they saw him through the peephole or pretended no one was home? She pushed the thought away because he was Nick, bug killer extraordinaire, hider of Slim Jims and Rice Krispies Treats, lock picker, collector of scary stories. As Esme left the fluorescent glow of the lobby for dark streets and cold shivered through her clothes, she wished Nick was with her.

She jogged as fast as she could to all the places Lily liked: the playground, her preschool, the store on the corner that sold Warheads and Swedish Fish in plastic buckets, but the store was closed, the preschool gates shut and locked. Esme crunched through frozen grass to look inside the playground tubes, their colors muted in the glow of the streetlights. The plastic slides and tubes were cold enough to crack under the heat of her hands, but when she looked up the slides and under the rope decks and behind all the hiding places, Lily wasn't there, not even on the rope net where Lily pretended to be a spider. The swings swung slightly in the October breeze. Esme was alone in the park. In the summer, the playground was full of kids running and screaming through sprinklers, chasing each other in soggy bathing suits, stringy hair clinging to their cheeks and plastic shoes slipping from wet feet as they ran, but now the playground was empty.

Tomorrow, the sidewalks would be packed with trick-or-treaters dangling plastic jack-o'-lanterns over costumed arms. It would be the neighborhood Esme knew again, where parents watched their kids climb stoops and ring bells and everyone knew which kid belonged with who, but tonight, no one was watching. Esme was alone in a way she couldn't have imagined. She ran back to each place one more time, slowing down to look up dark driveways lined with trash bins and behind parked cars, hoping she'd spot Lily in her red coat and sparkling shoes, but every place was as empty as the playground.

She paused on the corner, not sure where to go next.

A bottle broke in the distance. It echoed between buildings. Every noise was amplified, even the silence of her unusually quiet neighborhood. There were no barking dogs, babies crying, car horns blaring down Queens Boulevard—only the smell of cold air and wood burning in someone's fireplace. She looked down the row of bars and storefronts. The supermarket had taken its baskets of fruit and vegetables in for the night and locked them behind a gate. The bank and post office were closed and locked. Even Cerise's church was locked, but the street was alive in a way she hadn't seen before. Broken glass sparkled in the moonlight. People collected beneath a red-lit bar sign, shivering with cigarettes in hand. The tips glowed in the distance. She'd never been out this late, not without her parents, not without Nick. A car lingered at a stop sign, a thin plume of smoke rising from the idling tailpipe, and Esme was convinced the shadowy outline of the driver was watching her. An acorn fell and grazed Esme's shoulder. She covered her mouth to stifle a scream and ran, her legs shooting out so forcefully she forgot to breathe until she remembered again, suddenly, and her breath rushed back in short, ragged bursts.

Lily would be home when she got there, nestled in blankets and sipping a thermos of hot milk, and she would feel silly for all the running and fear she'd felt. No way was Lily brave enough to stay out here no matter how mad she was. No way.

But when Esme rounded the corner to her building, her parents were outside, hastily wrapped in their coats and holding their arms across their chests to keep warm under the red-and-blue kaleidoscope of police lights. An officer was taking notes. Cerise was crying. How much time had passed? Esme was sweating and shivering from running in the cold. Her breath burned in her chest, and the ligament in her right knee was throbbing, but Esme froze. She held on to a parking meter, hoping it would calm her nerves like the barre did at the studio, but the chilled metal only made her colder.

Andre noticed her shaking in the streetlight and called her over. She tucked herself under her father's arm, rocking from one foot to the other to keep warm, wondering how a night that had started like any other, with spaghetti and homework and arguing like they always did, could end with swirling lights sweeping over buildings, parked cars, her neighbors' faces. Calling the police was something people did when they couldn't do anything themselves. The sour taste crept back into her mouth.

We wouldn't have had to call them, Esme thought, staring at a sliver of moon through the buildings with a bright star next to it, *if I'd just told her about the orange thing. Yes,* she now wished she'd said, *it is a fish named Marley, and he can swim away and come back whenever he wants to, but only when the moon is full. If it isn't, he has to wait and eat marsh grass and horseshoe crabs even with those crunchy shells and pointy tails until he can swim again.* That's what she'd tell Lily when she came back, what she should have told her already. That was the next part of the story.

"What was she wearing?" the officer asked. Cerise described Lily's striped skirt, the pink sequined shoes, and corduroy coat until Lily sounded like a doll in a Mattel box and not a person.

Andre pulled her closer. The pressure broke through Esme's thoughts, as swirling and jumbled as the red-and-blue lights, until all she could do was cry in the streetlight.

Chapter Two

The police started on the roof and spiraled down to the basement. They knocked on every door. They called the super and made him come all the way from Eighty-Third Street with keys because they wanted access to locked closets, the boiler room, and the maintenance office. Lights snapped on and off in the windows above. Heavy boots filed through the front door with German shepherds on leashes. Voices melted together into white noise so loud it felt like she'd been on a Tilt-A-Whirl, spinning and spinning as more cars pulled up with flashing lights. Officers blurred into outlines of noses and chins, nodding heads, moving legs. Esme felt like she was looking from her side of the stage to the other, lights blinding everything into shadowy shapes.

Every light in the building was on except Birdman's. It gaped like a missing tooth.

Detective Ferrera spread a map over the hood of a patrol car and marked streets with a red Sharpie. The ink stained his thumb and looked like blood in the streetlight. Lily would be in so much trouble when she came home.

"Spread out, starting here, block by block, until you get here." His finger looked heavy and bloated against the delicate line that marked Queens Boulevard and the tiny boxes that surrounded it in every direction: houses, apartment buildings, big giant things that didn't seem anything like boxes in real life. It felt like a complicated, grown-up game of hide-and-seek. Esme wondered how they'd ever find someone so small when the city spread out in every direction, above the street and below.

Hours passed. The neighborhood was its own kind of symphony now: barking dogs, helicopters spinning, a chorus of voices calling orders over steaming cups. Someone brought Esme a coat. She didn't remember slipping her arms through the sleeves or tucking her hands in the pockets. She only realized, suddenly, that she was warmer, that the shivering had stopped, and she was so still she felt more asleep than awake. It scared her. She shook her arms and legs to wake the nerves under her skin.

"You." Esme's head snapped up. Detective Ferrera was pointing at her, walking quickly toward their house. "Come with me."

Her parents were huddled side by side. Her father's shoulder was much higher than her mother's, asymmetrical, like a fever dream she had had once where her fingers were too thick or too small to pick things up. Cerise's fist was pressed against her lip. A helicopter hovered in the distance, throwing light circles over the city. Her parents looked like they'd woken up from a nightmare and were waiting for it to ease away before going back to sleep. Esme followed Detective Ferrera. While her parents looked lost, Detective Ferrera buzzed, like he enjoyed this and Lily was an excuse to push around dogs and toys as big as helicopters.

Inside the lobby, Mrs. Rodriquez was standing in the corner, wearing her husband's old camel coat. It came down to her bare ankles, where a web of blue veins met a leather slipper. It was odd that she still had her dead husband's clothes. She had rosary beads wrapped around one wrist, and the cross at the end swung wildly as she shook her fist. Madeline was listening, chin pointed, eyes narrowed, pale but determined.

Mrs. Rodriquez wasn't even five feet tall, but she had sharp, beady eyes that darted from place to place until she found a target. Mrs. Rodriquez didn't walk like other people did. She swooped, landing in a rush of air and latching on like a hawk, spitting opinions on all the scurrying prey beneath her.

"You understand?" Mrs. Rodriquez glanced between Madeline and Detective Ferrera, wild hair pushed back with a headband where a rim of gray hair under dyed black poked out. Madeline nodded. Mrs. Rodriquez reached her small hand forward. Esme thought she was going to make the sign of the cross on Madeline's head, but she pushed her forward instead.

"Go," she whispered. Like magic, the cross stopped swinging at her side.

"Mrs. Rodriquez." Detective Ferrera stopped. The lights in the lobby were unusually bright. He was so much taller than Mrs. Rodriquez and made a point of looking down at her. He threw one hand on his waist casually, but it was enough to pull back the gray suit jacket and flash the holster attached to his belt. "How is our friend Denny?"

Mrs. Rodriquez stared back, lips pressed tightly together, tipping her chin up to glare at him. If she'd been sleeping on the sidewalk in that old coat under a pile of cardboard, she'd look more at home than she did now, eyes puffy and shiny with night cream. Esme sensed she might spit right onto Detective Ferrera's suit jacket if it wasn't for Lily.

"My son is just fine," she shot back instead. "Clean and sober."

But Esme didn't think sitting on the stoop and drawing new tattoos with pen ink on the backs of his hands was an especially clean thing to do, even if she wasn't sure about sober.

"Want one?" Denny'd snickered from the stoop recently while Esme had fumbled with her keys. "Of course not. Not for the precious princess who's going to dance her way out of this shithole." He'd thrown his arms over his head in mock ballet, and Esme had slipped inside without answering.

Esme stared between them, curious who'd turn away first, wondering if this was the cop Mrs. Rodriquez had been ranting about months ago, arms flying, ice cream melting in Cerise's grocery bags while she'd told them about some cop who'd dragged Denny out of a warehouse and broken his arm. "To make a point," she'd said so fiercely Esme had worried she would crack the mug she'd been holding. "No one gives a shit about kids who make mistakes."

Esme didn't understand how robbing a bodega was a mistake, not in the same way spilling milk was or coloring out of the lines, but Mrs. Rodriquez clearly thought so. How could anyone rob a store by mistake?

They wouldn't send the same cop, not for someone so small. Someone so good.

"Glad to hear it," he said, turning toward the elevator, footsteps echoing on the marble floor. Madeline's eyes were wide and glassy, darting between Esme and Detective Ferrera's back. The hem of Madeline's pajama pants dragged behind her. Her hair was pulled into a knotty, lopsided ponytail from not being brushed.

"What?" Esme mouthed, knowing Madeline wanted to tell her something, the way she always knew, even late at night when their bedroom was dark.

Detective Ferrera leaned against the wall while they waited for the elevator, hands on his hips like a superhero. Esme half expected he'd rip his button-down shirt and flash a Superman S underneath.

"Who's older?" Detective Ferrera asked as the door opened. It should have been obvious. Madeline was taller. She wore glasses that made her look like a real grown-up, but Madeline was scrunched into the corner of the elevator, arms folded across her chest. She didn't look older. She just looked scared.

"She is," Esme said. "She's fifteen, and I'm eleven."

"And your brother? How old is he?" The elevator dinged at the fourth floor.

"Seventeen," Madeline mumbled.

Where was Nick? Esme hadn't seen him since they'd passed each other in the hallway. She didn't even know what time it was. The elevator dipped into place. Lily always said, "Whoa!" when it did. It must have felt like a bigger drop than it actually was under her little feet. The doors slid open.

"Lead the way." Detective Ferrera moved aside even though he knew where they were going. Esme didn't argue. She led the way to their apartment and pushed the door open. Another officer, a woman, was already inside, sitting at the table with a briefcase and the phone from her parents' bedroom. The phone was upside down, and the officer was unscrewing the bottom with a screwdriver. The cord dangled over the edge of the table. The receiver rested on the rug.

Esme fought the urge to put it back in place. "Why is she doing that?"

The woman looked up briefly, then away, and no one answered. There was a thin layer of dust on everything now. The woman at the table was wearing bright-blue bags over her shoes. Lily's blanket cave was gone now, folded neatly into a stack of pillows and blankets, erased. Esme's house was a mirror version of its real self, the rabbit hole version. Her hand lingered on the doorframe, painted gray steel like it had always been. What would happen to her if she passed through?

"Sit." He gestured toward the couch. Why would he offer them a place to sit in their own house? His gray suit and shiny tie looked out of place on the recliner chair, where her father should have been in his pajamas, slippers poking out from under one of the fleece blankets, instead of a gun in a holster on Detective Ferrera's waist.

Outside, he'd had a plan and had known what to do to find Lily, but after Mrs. Rodriquez, Esme wasn't sure. He reminded her of the dogs on the corner behind the double fence, with eyes dark as marbles and tails that never wagged, the kind that looked like any other brindle pit bull until someone walked by on the sidewalk. Then they stopped moving, eyes fixed, holding one foot up still as wood until they snapped awake and sprinted, jumping and snarling, spit spraying through the chain-link fence. "They'll rip you apart," her father had told her once, crossing to the other side of the street. A tuft of fur had blown past

Esme's sneaker. Both dogs had been sleeping, spread out on the concrete where the sun was the warmest, but they'd been watching her anyway, even with closed eyes. The wind had been a traitor, carrying her scent to them in their sleep. Detective Ferrera wouldn't be the best person to find Lily if he was like those dogs.

Esme sensed that he had to talk to them but wasn't expecting to learn very much, like he was talking to cardboard cutouts instead of real people.

"So you were both in there when your sister went missing?" He pointed to their bedroom door behind them. It was open, but the lights were off. Lily's crayon drawing of the three of them eating birthday cake with pink candles was taped to the outside from Madeline's birthday last month. The edges curled.

"I was in there," Esme said. "She was in the shower. Then I went to the kitchen to make dinner."

"There'd been some kind of disagreement with your sister?"

They nodded. Esme swallowed. Madeline's hand found hers. They hadn't held hands since Esme was old enough to cross the street by herself. Madeline's fingers were thin and cold. Esme squeezed them, wishing she was still young enough to trust that Madeline could look left and right and guide her home safely.

"And you didn't hear anything after that? You didn't hear the door open, didn't hear the doorbell?"

Esme opened her mouth to speak but exhaled instead. She cleared her throat. "I was cooking, and the TV was on. My dad put it on for her."

"So your mother was at church, your father was out here with Lily, and where was your brother?"

"In his room," Madeline said. She looked at Esme, eyebrows narrowed in question. Had he been? Across the living room, Nick's bedroom door was open. It spilled light onto the closet and into their parents' bedroom, but Esme couldn't see inside.

"Or our parents' room, but he wasn't out here," Esme said, remembering him yelling to shut up.

"OK." He nodded slowly, and Esme could almost see him thinking. She shifted her weight and tightened her hand around Madeline's.

"Tell me about your brother's relationship with Lily."

Something in the room shifted. She looked at Madeline, but Madeline glared at Detective Ferrera like she did when the high school kids drove around the block in borrowed cars, slowing down, then flying over speed bumps, windows down, laughing while kids scurried out of the street.

"It's fine, I guess. He's not around much," Madeline said. "He's seventeen and out with his friends a lot."

"Would you say Lily and Nick spend a lot of time together?"

"Not really. He'll play with her when he's home, but it's not like they really do stuff together."

"He takes her to the park sometimes," Esme added, wanting Detective Ferrera to see that Nick was a good brother, not the kind Madeline was describing, but Madeline pinched her thumbnail into the flesh between Esme's thumb and forefinger. Esme did her best not to flinch, but she'd obviously said something wrong.

"When our mom asks him to," Madeline added.

"How often is that?" he asked.

"Not often," Madeline shot back.

"What kinds of games do they play at home?" Detective Ferrera was leaning forward now, resting his arms on his knees. Esme pressed herself into the back of the couch. The springs pushed her forward, toward the recliner. The holster rubbed the leather chair and squeaked. The gun made her house feel dirty.

Esme pressed her lips together. Nick and Lily made up their own games. Once he'd rolled her in his comforter so she could wiggle out of the world's biggest burrito. Another time he'd hidden her toys in his room so she could find them. Once, he'd ripped the last page out of

29

Lily's book because it was a stupid ending and she could make a better one. Then he'd let her draw on the inside of his closet. Actually, the inside of his closet was covered with Lily's drawings. Esme shivered. Someone like Detective Ferrera would think he'd locked her in there, not that he'd been on his bed watching, smiling, throwing her new crayons with pointy tips, covering her drawings with Metallica posters so Lily wouldn't get in trouble. She'd never thought about it much before, but she doubted Detective Ferrera would think those games were very nice.

"Nothing special," Madeline said. "I don't really remember."

Detective Ferrera looked from Madeline to Esme. "Do you remember?"

"Not really," Esme said. "No."

"Neither of you can think of anything they played?" He leaned forward a little more.

"He was teaching her to ride a bike," Esme said. "On my old bike with training wheels."

"Yeah." Madeline's hand squeezed Esme's. That was good. "He put neon spokes on it, too, so she'd be less scared to ride it."

"Lily didn't really pedal too well," Esme added. "So he mostly pushed her along."

Well, he'd pulled her. He'd tied a rope to the front of Lily's bike and attached it to the back of his, pulling her down the block until Lily's bike had hit the maple root that lifted the sidewalk and she'd scraped her knees and palms. Cerise had slapped him for it. "She's a baby," she'd yelled. "What's wrong with you?"

Detective Ferrera nodded slowly. The officer at the table was screwing the bottom of the phone back into place. The receiver was back in its cradle. The briefcase was open, and there was a mess of wires inside, like a bomb. Esme looked away. She didn't like the way Detective Ferrera was watching her, searching her face, so she looked at her foot instead, a foot that on Monday would wear a pointe shoe for the first

30

time made of soft pink satin instead of the rubbery sneaker with dirty laces she had on now. *If,* her brain reminded her. *If this goes away.*

He gestured toward the birthday cake picture on the door. "Why do you think he's not in Lily's picture?"

It was just the three girls, holding huge forks with big bites of cake, each a little bigger than the next like nesting dolls with matching ponytails. They'd made the real cake together and poured cherry juice into Cool Whip for the frosting. Lily had stuck her fingers in the jar and jabbed cherries, licking them like lollipops and popping her fingers in for more. "That's disgusting," Nick had told her, prying the jar from her hand and tossing it into the trash. "Really puke worthy."

"I don't know." Esme shrugged, but her face flushed from lying. "Maybe because he didn't help with the cake. We made it together."

Detective Ferrera drummed his finger against the arm of the chair. Esme was sickeningly aware that he was missing half a fingernail on his pointer finger. Pink skin showed beneath the jagged nail. *Just stop,* Esme wished.

"How about the bottles?" he said finally.

"What bottles?" Madeline asked.

"We heard a story about Nick dropping glass bottles off the roof with your sister and the kid down the hall. Someone on the sidewalk almost got hit."

Madeline and Esme looked at each other, confused.

"Do you think that's a great game for a toddler to play with her older brother? Dropping bottles off the roof?"

"We never heard that." Madeline's voice had an edge to it now. "Obviously it's not, but that's assuming it's true."

"Sure," he said. "Assuming it's true. It's not a game I get the sense you'd play with her. In fact," he said, turning to Esme, "I hear a lot of nice stuff about you and Lily. I hear you play all kinds of games with her and walk her to school sometimes. That must be a lot considering all the stuff you do outside of school."

31

Esme squirmed. She didn't deserve that compliment, not now, not after she couldn't even tell Lily the story of the orange thing. It took so little effort to make Lily happy, so little it almost made her feel guilty when Lily drew picture after picture about how much she loved the cookies Esme brought home from school or some cast-off costume Esme let her play dress up in, but she hadn't even found two minutes to tell her a story that night. Two minutes would have stopped all of this.

Esme's throat squeezed. She couldn't find words for Detective Ferrera, but Madeline's breathing was shallow and quick. She hadn't heard what Detective Ferrera said last, hadn't heard the accusation hidden behind a compliment. Madeline rushed on.

"If you heard that bottle crap from Denny, if that's the 'kid down the hall' you're referring to, he's a junkie. Ask anyone. Why would you believe anything he says about Nick?"

Madeline was spilling secrets to help Nick, the connection between them twinlike, all their earliest memories blurred together because they were so close in age. "He was always there," Madeline had said once. Esme didn't really understand, but mostly, she was jealous she'd been left out. "That's how Lily will think of you," Cerise had explained when Lily was born, pulling Esme closer to the red-faced baby swaddled like an insect while Nick and Madeline traded words without talking in the corner. Esme didn't think it'd be the same thing at all.

Madeline's arms crossed over her chest. Esme's palm was cold where her sister's hand had been. Their secret code was over.

"All right," Detective Ferrera said, lowering his voice into something more soothing. "Let's let that be for now." His gaze shifted toward the mannequin. "How about your mother's business? People were in the house all the time. Did any of them make you uncomfortable?"

In the corner near her mother's sewing machine was a mannequin with a sheet over it, wearing a half-finished wedding gown. It would be a long gown with a train, but Cerise always did the bottom half last. The top had an open teardrop back surrounded by beads. All those beads sat in little tubes under the sewing table, as pearly white and iridescent as snow and ice, waiting to be used. The mannequin's fabric head curved under the sheet, still and faceless. Esme pulled her knees to her chest, feeling that this dress would never be finished, though she couldn't explain why.

The brides had manicured nails, crossed their legs, and wore shiny diamond rings. They were mostly women Cerise knew from church, but they glowed in the living room like new stars, throwing all their happiness over the dull furniture while Cerise sketched dresses for them, and they nodded yes or no. The pencil strokes darkened with every yes and the eraser moved with every no until there was a drawing of a dress, and then those new brides almost always cried pretty tears, the kind Esme was sure could wake a winter garden. "Who needs a vase of flowers when we have happy brides?" Cerise joked. "Nothing brightens a room like a happy bride."

"No," Madeline and Esme said together.

The woman at the table snapped the briefcase shut and carried the phone back to the bedroom, her blue-covered shoes leaving oval dents in the carpet.

"How about anyone else in the building? Did anyone make you feel uncomfortable? Maybe they never did anything bad exactly but gave you a bad feeling."

The woman found her way to the bathroom and came out with Lily's Little Mermaid toothbrush in a plastic bag.

"If you need her pajamas," Esme said, thinking the officer was packing Lily an overnight bag, "they're in the bottom drawer. She likes the ones with the blue stars and the slipper feet."

The woman froze, her face a plain white blur. If this was a dream, Esme could've rearranged the woman's face with her thumbs like clay, smearing it into something else. The woman opened her mouth and closed it. Ariel was lying on her side, red hair streaked with toothpaste, her mermaid tail caught in a plastic net. The bag was labeled "Evidence."

"She'll need that when she's back." Esme's throat throbbed. Her voice caught. Hadn't she just lifted Lily to the bathroom sink this morning, pulled her up under her armpits to let her spit? Hadn't they just hummed "Yellow Submarine" together this morning because Dad said that was how long they should brush for?

"Did you find her?" Madeline's voice was a whisper. "Do you already know what happened?"

The beeper on Detective Ferrera's waist lit up with green numbers, but he ignored it. Esme hugged her knees tighter, heart beating so fast it pounded in her temples. Heat flashed to her face. Her chest was tight.

"Listen," Detective Ferrera said gently, shooing the other officer from the living room. The front door closed quietly behind her and Lily's toothbrush. "We don't know anything yet, but we're trying, and this is how we find her. I need you to think very carefully. Can you think of anyone who made you feel uncomfortable? A bad feeling?"

The Golden Rule Cerise loved so much crept into Esme's thoughts: *Do unto others . . .*

It blurred into Mrs. Rodriquez in her camel coat, Ariel's smile through the plastic bag, and another memory, less fresh but so vivid it made Esme sick to think about. "If there was someone, would you tell them we said so?"

"No," he said, meeting Esme's eye and cocking his head to one side. "But we'd look into them further."

"What happens to them?"

Detective Ferrera paused and looked toward the scattered pile of Lily's toys and books. *A Bargain for Frances* was on the rug, spine creased and cover bent. He picked it up and closed it, putting it gently on the table.

"It depends what they did," he said. "If it's bad, the court decides on a punishment."

Esme bit her thumbnail. It tasted bitter and left a film in her mouth so sour she couldn't swallow it away. She could feel Detective Ferrera's eyes. The house was stiller than it had been before. *Please just come home*, she prayed to Lily, silently begging her to climb out from behind the couch or unravel herself from one of the winter coats in the back of the closet so she wouldn't have to tell Detective Ferrera something she wasn't sure made sense.

"Just say it," Madeline whispered, her hand finding its way back into Esme's.

"Birdman," Esme said, picking up the stone in her chest and handing it to Detective Ferrera. "The only person whose light wasn't on tonight."

With that, Detective Ferrera pulled his notebook from his pocket and started writing.

Chapter Three

Five Years Ago . . .

It was August, and Cerise was meeting a bride. She sent Nick, Madeline, and Esme outside with a bucket of sidewalk chalk and a jump rope. "Come back in an hour, unless I yell down sooner." They knew the rule: no one in the house when Cerise was meeting a bride for the first time. It was too distracting, and she wanted to make a good impression. Esme thought an impression was like Ash Wednesday smoke, but the brides never left with a smudge on their foreheads. They held purse straps tightly as their heels clicked down the street.

That day, heat rose off the sidewalks in waves so thick the air wiggled. Somewhere in the distance, an ice cream truck tinkled "Pop Goes the Weasel."

"We could find it," Esme suggested, wanting to stand on tiptoes under the truck for something cold with sticky syrup. Nick ignored her. Madeline said it cost too much money. Then Denny wandered out in cut-off jeans and an undershirt, oblivious to how hot the concrete was under his bare feet. Madeline abandoned the lazy stars she was drawing, comet trails dragging, and hid the chalk in her fist.

"He looks like Jordan Knight," Madeline whispered, her voice watery and full of giggles even though nothing was funny. Esme knew they were going to get in trouble.

"Punks," he said, straddling the stoop. "I'm bored as hell." Sweat beaded on his lip. He pulled a lighter from his pocket and lit the flame. It burned in the sunlight. Why would anyone make the air any hotter? It seemed especially stupid. Esme slid to the other side of the stoop.

"Scared?" He smirked.

Nick snatched the lighter and swiped twice before the flame popped up. Dripping air conditioners left raindrops on the concrete. Birdman's was the noisiest. It sputtered and left a puddle on the sidewalk.

Kids made up stoop stories about Birdman between hopscotch skips and tag. Birdman's mailbox was always full. Neighbors grumbled as they gathered spilled junk mail and dumped it in a heap by his door that grew and grew until it disappeared and the whole thing started over. He'd had a pigeon coop on the roof with birds that flew to Staten Island and back until the super had shut it down. That was a fact because her father said it was true. He'd seen them fly with little messages tied to their legs while Birdman waited up there in a plastic lawn chair, watching the sky until they came home.

On nights when the weather was warm enough to sit in T-shirts and sandals, even grown-ups told stories. They said he was homeless and had gotten his apartment after his mother had kicked the bucket or a former marine who'd almost eaten a poisoned orange in Vietnam, but mostly they tipped back imaginary cups and clucked their tongues as if that explained everything. Kids should not talk to Birdman or go near his door or his pigeon coop. That was a rule.

Birdman's air conditioner dripped a bad idea right into Denny's head.

"Let's steal his mail," Denny said, dark eyes squinting in the sun. "Whoever gets the most and doesn't chicken out wins. Then we'll know his real name."

"That's stupid. How's it brave to steal from a mailbox?" Madeline's forehead scrunched in the sun. Esme slid closer.

"Not from the mailbox." Denny patted the side of Madeline's head like a dumb pet. She turned red and as wide eyed as a Pac-Man ghost. "From his door."

"Extra points if you knock and don't run away," Nick added. A car passed on the street. The window rolled down, and something bright flashed quickly and then exploded at their feet. A water balloon. *Yes!* Esme thought. This was so much better than the mail thing.

"Let's get 'em!" Esme's fingers itched to wrap a water balloon around a spigot and feel it swell. Water dripped down her leg. Denny laughed as the car swung around the corner. Madeline laughed, too, but it sounded forced and fake: her new grown-up laugh. Madeline was wearing mascara, blinking and playing with her long dark lashes, bold as butterfly wings. Esme wished she could rub it off with the back of her hand. Maybe then she'd see how stupid Denny actually was: Denny, who painted plastic army men with Wite-Out and set them on fire, who stole cans of beer from his father's cooler and poured them on slugs, who drew skulls with shaving cream on car windows and watched from the stoop empty handed while Nick got caught adding bones but said nothing. Denny, who did not look like Jordan Knight at all.

"Let's go." Nick stood. The rush of cold air from the lobby made Esme follow, even though it was a stupid idea.

They crept as quietly as four kids on a mission could, a hush of stifled giggles and noisy tiptoes, closing the hallway doors slowly so they clicked instead of slammed. Birdman's door was gray like the others, dim under a fading light bulb. A pile of glossy cards and newspapers sat where a welcome mat should have been. The peephole stared back like a fish eye. Nick was first, looking smaller than usual next to Denny's long legs and hunched shoulders. They tucked envelopes into their waistlines. Madeline stuck important-looking long envelopes with typed addresses under her arm, but Esme lingered behind. They looked like hens pecking at seeds in the dirt. She didn't want to be a hen, but being left out was worse. She crept closer, picked up a postcard with three waxy pepperoni pizzas on it, and folded it into her pocket.

"Let's go," she whispered.

"Shush." Madeline pressed a finger to her lips.

Denny stopped. Envelopes bulged unevenly under his shirt. He threw his fist against the door and hammered. They froze. There was a shuffle on the other side, and Denny took off running, Nick and Madeline behind him, scraping the backs of each other's heels. Mail scattered like leaves. Something caught Esme's foot. She landed with a thud on her back, crushing a package beneath her, shaking the welcome wreath on the door across the hall. The ceiling was an endless white. She tried to breathe, but jagged, high-pitched sounds came out instead. Of course she'd slipped. She was the stupid one who still needed to be watched, too young to join the over-ten club, too slow to keep up on bikes. Now she'd proved those points ten times over, coughing and wheezing, stunned and staring at the ceiling.

The door swung open. Esme rolled off the box, trying not to make those awful animal sounds. Her hand landed on something soft and familiar. It was hair. Rows of different-colored hair, shiny and tied into neat ponytails without a head. Esme stared at the red ponytail in her hand, more orange than red, and felt sick. Had it come from a real person? She dropped it into the crushed box but couldn't hide. Birdman's bald spot shone in the light, his eyes puffy behind milk-bottle glasses, lips cracked. A scar gashed across his bare chest, long healed but thick as rope.

Run. But her breath kicked out in wheezes so powerful they made her shoulders heave. Madeline and Nick thundered down the staircase. The pain in her chest echoed the hopeless feeling in her stomach. They'd left her behind. Her hand slid around the carpet and touched envelopes. Birdman watched her carefully; then he knelt and pulled her up by the shoulders. She looked away from him, embarrassed by the red-brown nipples, the scar, the thin, spidery hair on his chest.

"Can't breathe?" he asked gently, quietly, as if he were afraid one of the other doors would snap open and someone would take her away. His hands were hot weights on her shoulders and smelled like plastic and glue. Esme stood very still. His thumb moved in small circles, rounding her shoulder like clock hands, ticking away trapped time. She shook her head.

"It'll come back," he said. "Just stay still." Through the open door, Esme saw a plastic arm on a table, its fingers curled gently, the forearm as long as her own. She stared at the small shoulder, the connecting piece to a plastic doll torso. She was able to breathe now but felt light headed, dizzy, her heart oddly still. If she fainted, would he take her ponytail? She pictured it chopped off and in that box, clean and brushed, a stump on her head where it used to be. His hands weren't tight on her shoulders. She could shrug them off and run after Nick and Madeline, but something about Birdman's colorless eyes behind those thick glasses made Esme think he'd squeeze tighter if she moved.

"OK?" he asked in that same whisper. She nodded. His hands slid from her shoulders to her waist, pulling the hem of her shirt to straighten it into place.

Get off, she prayed but said nothing. Her throat burned. Her chest ached. If there wasn't so much burning, she'd feel a scream building. He took a deep breath and sighed, blowing peppermint toward Esme. She wanted to press her hands over her mouth and hide.

"What a mess," he said. Envelopes scattered the hallway, legal-size ones and colorful postcards with pictures and prices, *Pennysavers* in red plastic. He kicked things through the open door, where the doll arm was on the table. His spine curved into spiky disks as he bent for one piece after the next. Esme backed away, forgotten. She walked until she reached the stairs, shoulders shaking where his hands had been, and then she ran, thundering down the concrete steps so loudly she hoped everyone would open their doors to see what the noise was so she'd have lots of people to hide behind.

Outside on the stoop, Nick sniggered, waving his pile of mail like a trophy. "Couldn't keep up?"

Madeline sorted envelopes by size, lining the corners neatly over each other.

Where were you? her siblings should have asked. *We were worried about our third musketeer.*

"They all have different names," Madeline mumbled instead.

"What happened, *baby*?" Denny sneered, spitting the word with such force Esme felt like he'd knocked the wind out of her again. Only this time, she wasn't wheezing. Her fist sliced through the thick air and left a heat trail behind it, cracking Denny's nose. She wished she could've hit Birdman, broken those glasses in two, leaving him small eyed and blind in his pile of fake mail. Hot, wiry pain shot through her arm and numbed her elbow. Tears sprang behind her eyes, but she stuffed them back into her sore chest and grabbed her elbow, rubbing it the way her mother would have done if Esme had fallen off a bike.

"What the fuck?" Denny's voice was shrill and muffled behind a mess of blood and fingers.

I did that, Esme thought stupidly. Red spots spread on Denny's T-shirt. It seemed impossible. Not her small fist. Her knuckles were a blueish purple. Nick caught her hands behind her back just as Cerise's bride opened the door.

She stood in the doorway, hair braided neatly, lilac blouse tucked into her skirt. Her new diamond glittered in the sun as she pressed her hand against her cheek, eyes narrowed in concern. She hovered by the door, unsure if it was safe to walk past these kids. Esme saw herself as the bride saw her: hands behind her back, chest heaving, red faced, hair shaken loose from its ponytail, sweating and angry in the hot sun. Her shoulders fell.

"Sorry," she mumbled, stepping aside to let her pass. Cold air hit Esme's face hard as she pushed through the lobby. Her fingers throbbed when she pressed the elevator button for the fourth floor. As the light dinged from one floor to the next, the first wet tear splashed the marble floor, small enough that she could rub it away with her toe.

"What happened?" Cerise lifted Esme like a baby. Esme's hands and feet dangled, thoroughly exhausted. Later, she'd have to explain— if her mother didn't figure it out first. Later, she'd be punished. She'd have to apologize to stupid Denny, but for now she cried on her mother's shoulder, who made soothing sounds, and pretended there wasn't a Birdman or a kid with a bloody nose and that her chest didn't hurt so much.

That night, Esme stuffed her shirt into a ball and shoved it to the bottom of the hamper, pushing away the peppermint smell and those circling thumbs. But the hamper wasn't far enough away. She carried the shirt to the bathroom and locked the door, letting it fall on the white tile like a hot-pink stain. It was her favorite. Madeline had bought it for her at the church basement Christmas sale. Bugs Bunny, Foghorn Leghorn, and Wile E. Coyote leaned over the pocket as Tweety tumbled toward the hem. She loved it, loved how Speedy was tucked inside the pocket, only visible if she peeked inside. There had been so many Saturdays with bowls of Cinnamon Toast Crunch watching *Looney Tunes* with Nick and Madeline before they thought it was boring. The tears she'd stuffed back plopped onto the hem as she made the first cut through dried blood. It was hard to see against the hot-pink fabric, but it was there, along with all the invisible marks from Birdman's hands.

She cut strips and then small pieces, pulling the threads apart, but stopped at Speedy. He hadn't seen anything, but he'd felt her heart beating. It hadn't been the same kind of beat as when she raced down the sidewalk, bike streamers flying, or when she double dutched, legs high and feet floating through swinging ropes until she couldn't believe how long she'd jumped, and the light-headed, big-smile feeling made her skip a step. No, today's heartbeat made her sick, as gross as dried piss on a toilet seat. She cut Speedy in half and stuffed him down the kitchen garbage, burying him under crumpled paper and salad scraps so he'd never tell anyone what had happened.

~

She'd been only six then, a soon-to-be first grader. She'd never danced or read a book without pictures and didn't know she could make up stories for Lily by pulling a world out of thin air like a magician, but the shame still stuck years later. It echoed as the hard lines around Detective Ferrera's eyes softened. She tasted that bitterness all over again, so strong she couldn't look at her sister.

"Why didn't you tell me?" Madeline's leg was shaking, bouncing against the couch cushion while Detective Ferrera watched them both. Esme felt heavy now, deflated.

"Because you would have said it was my fault." Madeline would have been right. It was a fact. The hurt feelings from years before rolled away with it.

"No, I . . ." Madeline stopped and looked at Esme, but it was true. *The sun and the moon*, Andre called them sometimes. *Two halves of the same thing, even if it feels like you have nothing in common.* The lamp threw dark shadows over Madeline's face. *Sister.* Esme rolled the word around in her head like a marble.

"Now what?" Madeline asked Detective Ferrera. "What does that do?"

"It gives us something to work with." He turned to Esme. "Keep thinking of stuff like that. Even little things, things that you don't think are very important, can make a big difference. Did you ever see him do anything strange like that to Lily? Or anyone else?"

If Amelia had told Esme she'd done well, she would have jabbered on about it at dinner between mouthfuls of salad. Then she would imagine what it meant—dancing where Paloma Herrera and Anna

Pavlova had one day, that a choreographer would fall madly in love with her and make new ballets just for her—but when Detective Ferrera told her she had done well, she didn't feel very good at all. She felt the way she had before the dentist had pulled her back tooth, when he'd pricked her finger and told her to count backward from one hundred, and she'd only made it to ninety-seven before the office had wavered and gone black. She wanted to sleep now, but Madeline's leg was bouncing, and Esme's stomach felt queasier than it already had because Madeline was thinking something over.

"Everyone always said how cute Lily was," Madeline said slowly, "but one time, there was a replacement cleaning guy, and he was looking at her kind of strange."

"How?" Detective Ferrera asked.

"Like he was measuring her or something. Do you remember?" Madeline turned to Esme. "The guy with the scar under his eye?"

"No." Esme forced her eyes open and shook her head. The back of the couch felt like a hand against her head, soothing.

"He kept complimenting her outfit and her hair and how pretty she was. Just lots of stuff. Dad must have thought it was strange, too, because he picked Lily up and carried her the rest of the way."

"When was this?"

"A few weeks ago, I guess."

"Have you seen him before? Did he work here often?"

"No." Madeline shrugged. "I only saw him once or twice."

Someone laughed outside. It startled Esme.

"All right." Detective Ferrera snapped the notebook closed. "Thank you. I'll be outside. You can stay here or come outside with your parents. There will be an officer outside the door or inside with you. Her name is Officer Rivera, but you can call her Jean. If anything bothers you, just let her know." He stood from the chair and stretched, arching his back gently at the waist.

"Punching Denny. That's how I got ballet," Esme said quietly, so softly only Madeline heard, thinking of that bride stepping over the tangle of them on the stoop in her perfect peep-toe sandals. If it hadn't been for that bride, Andre wouldn't have said they needed something constructive to do with their free time.

"Not a bad punishment," Madeline whispered. She reached for one of the fleece blankets behind the couch and pulled it around them both, tucking the top of the blanket around Esme's shoulders before folding her legs into the empty space where Esme wasn't. They were a nest. Two baby birds. The busy hum outside could have been a rare Saturday night when Cerise and Andre went out to dinner and they could stay up late watching SNICK or *Tales from the Crypt*, microwaving popcorn and making heaping bowls of ice cream because no one told them not to, not their parents, not Mrs. Rodriquez down the hall, whom they could go to if anything, *anything*, went wrong. This wasn't the same kind of excitement. It felt lost, something they weren't supposed to know. The clock chimed in the corner. Midnight. *Come back*, Esme prayed to Lily, thinking of her sister riding home in a pumpkin carriage. Madeline's foot twitched under the blanket. Esme let her heavy lids close. In the morning, it would be over.

"I'm sorry," Madeline whispered. "I wish you'd told me."

Esme didn't answer. She closed her mind around it and kept it safely there.

~

In the morning—well, no, it wasn't morning, not the usual kind—she opened her eyes and squinted against the living room lights. Every lamp was on, throwing yellow light over all the furniture. The sky was a violet blue. It could have been early morning or just past sunset. Pain shot through Esme's neck from sleeping without her pillow. Madeline was gone. Her mother was at the end of the couch, resting her chin against her hand, as delicate and gray as a dandelion puff.

A Bargain for Frances was on the table next to a pile of photo albums open to Lily's last birthday, when Cerise had made a cake that looked like Flounder. That had been the day Lily had dragged a step stool to the kitchen and scooped her hand through Flounder's face when no one was looking, skipping away blue mouthed and happy. "No yelling on birthdays," Lily had said when Cerise had served a headless cake. Now, there were dried glue marks where some of the pictures had been. Esme's throat tightened. She couldn't remember the missing pictures.

Lily's corduroy coat wasn't hanging by the door. Cerise held rosary beads between her fingers, but her lips weren't moving. The beads were still. The crucifix rested against Esme's foot, metallic and cold. Lily wasn't here. Someone had cut away a piece of time. They were suspended like dust in the air, rolling over and over slowly. Last night she'd told Detective Ferrera about Birdman. It flickered painfully through her head. Had he told Cerise? Esme swallowed, throat dry.

"Mom?" Esme whispered. She wanted to inch closer and rest her head against Cerise's shoulder or feel her mother's fingers through her hair, always cool and comfortingly sharp against her scalp, but Cerise stared upward as if she were talking to someone on the ceiling. *She knows*, Esme thought. *That's why she won't look at me.*

"Mom?" Esme tried again, louder, her voice raspy. Cerise turned slowly toward the sound, eyes red rimmed and puffy.

"It's OK," Cerise said, mouthing the words so quietly Esme had to hold her breath to listen. "They're still looking. The news is outside."

"What news?"

Cerise's hand rested absently on Esme's foot. The rosary beads left circle imprints on her arch. It was wrong for a holy thing to touch the bottom of her foot. Esme inched away and wandered toward the window. Outside, news trucks with big antennas and poles with swirling cables spanned the block. Seven, Four, One, Two, Five. All the main channels.

"We're on TV?" Esme was shocked. They were the bad news, the sad things that happened to other people. They were the *Do you know where your children are?* people, with kids' faces and lots of numbers about them cutting between whatever show they were watching. "Of course," Andre would tell the TV. "They're all right here."

Cerise had a couch cushion pressed under her back the way she used to when she'd been pregnant with Lily. Except now her stomach was smooth instead of beach ball round, and Cerise didn't have to pace with her hands on her lower back, holding the top half of her body to the bottom. Esme wished she could slip her hand over Cerise's stomach and wait for Lily's quick jabs from inside. It was incredible that something had lived in the same place Cerise stored the food she ate. Cerise had always known what the baby was thinking or feeling even though she couldn't see it.

"How do you know it's even alive?" Esme had asked once, her head pressed against the taut skin of Cerise's stomach, listening to the watery world inside. "If you can't always feel it moving?"

Cerise had smiled and rubbed her hand over Esme's ear, holding in all the seashell sounds a covered ear made, something Cerise called human magic. "A mother always knows when something is wrong with her baby, no matter how old it gets or how big it grows." Was it the same thing now that they were waiting in a different way? It felt almost the same, Lily missing and Lily yet to be born, only there was more Lily-ness now. She'd grown into the alphabet of their family in a way she hadn't before she'd been born, when she was an idea of a baby, possibly a boy, possibly a girl, a no-name thing without a voice or a face instead of someone who made trails of peas on her plate to look like *The Very Hungry Caterpillar* and fed him first before she tasted her own food or who listened to Esme's heart with a Fisher-Price stethoscope when she was sick.

"Mom?"

A woman on the street below powdered her face and retied the belt on her blue coat, pulling strands of blonde hair into place and steadying herself in front of their building. Esme had seen her on TV, but she looked smaller on the street than she had on the screen.

"Is it the same thing like you said before Lily was born? That you always know what we're feeling and thinking even after we're born?" If it was true, then she'd know this would be OK, and it didn't matter if all the news stations in the world and more cops than she could count swarmed the street if Cerise still had that umbilical connection with Lily.

Cerise stared at Esme without blinking. She looked like she wanted to fold into herself and roll away like a pill bug. The lights flickered overhead, and the room was washed in gray. Esme wanted to shake her. Was it true or not? What did any of this mean? She wanted to snap the rosary in half and let the wooden beads roll out everywhere because praying wasn't the same as doing. It felt like a *nothing* something.

"Get dressed," Cerise said finally. "Someone's coming to help us."

"Who?" Esme asked, desperate for something.

"Someone Mrs. Rodriquez thought could help. Someone who can see things other people can't."

Esme doubted anyone Mrs. Rodriquez thought could help would be any less strange. She wondered where her father was and whether he'd agreed to whatever Cerise had planned, if he knew about it at all.

"Go," Cerise urged, gesturing toward the kitchen. "There's peanut butter and apples."

And if only because Esme thought it might make her mother a little bit happier, she pulled herself away from the window where the camera was pointed at the woman in the blue coat and found her way to the kitchen, where the fruit bowl was empty and there weren't any apples after all.

Chapter Four

When the doorbell rang, Cerise abandoned the list of names and phone numbers she was making. She flew toward the door in such a rush that Esme was sucked up into it, too, and followed at her heels. Esme felt her mother's disappointment when the door opened and it was only Mrs. Rodriquez and her friend.

"This is Annette." Mrs. Rodriquez stood in the doorway, one arm hooked through Annette's like little girls on the playground. "She's found my Denny more times than I can count in places no one could imagine."

Annette didn't look like the sidewalk psychics that sat under ten-dollar palm-reading signs. Those women were wispy thin with inky hair and dark eyes. They smelled like a garden after a rainstorm. Annette had gray-streaked temples and a thick mole under her right eye. She looked like a mom waiting outside school at three o'clock or in line at the supermarket with a cart full of potato chips and skim milk. She didn't look very magical.

Esme kicked at the rolled-up newspaper by the door. It was Friday. It should have been a school day. She'd missed the test she'd been studying for, but it didn't seem to matter. Pointe shoes on Monday. They should have been celebrating that. She looked down at her feet in purple socks, so threadbare the curve of her nail showed through. She flipped into first position, then traced a rond de jambe with her right foot even though there wasn't much space between her and Cerise, pushing away the pit in her chest telling her that things wouldn't be better by Monday. If Lily hadn't made all this trouble, Esme would've been examining shanks and boxes. Amelia would've matched her foot with a perfect shoe. Then, she'd hold the barre while Amelia told them to roll onto relevé, and finally, she'd let go and stand en pointe for the first time for five or ten seconds. And summer programs auditions were in January. She was finally old enough. Maybe, maybe if she asked nicely and promised to keep it short, her mother would let her call Amelia to explain. She felt guilty for worrying about ballet and what Amelia would think if she wasn't there on Monday when Lily was . . . when Lily was where? The sour taste came back full force. Why hadn't she just told her the stupid story about the fish?

"Stop that," Cerise snapped. Pain shot through Esme's toe where she'd kicked her mother's calf by mistake. She thought of Lily's stubbed toe in her sequined shoe. Cerise rubbed her hands over her eyes. Esme balled up the frustration she felt in her core and pretended to squeeze an orange between her stomach and ribs like Amelia had taught her. *Use it*, Amelia would say when someone fell out of a pirouette after three when they wanted four. *Take that feeling, and try again.*

"She doesn't mean it." It was the same whisper their mother would have used, only it came from Madeline. Before Esme could answer, Mrs. Rodriquez pushed past the circle of dining room chairs set up in the living room and unpacked two candles from under her arm, one brown and one white, and a bottle of oil that made the room stink like black licorice.

"It's a candle spell," she mumbled. Lily's name was scratched into the wax in neat script. "To bring back something lost. No matter what"—she flapped her old finger at them—"don't blow out the brown one."

Oh my God, Esme thought, still smarting from Cerise. Mrs. Rodriquez wasn't a psychic—she was a witch.

"Thank you, Teresa." Annette nodded approvingly as Mrs. Rodriquez lit the candles. They flickered and jumped as she walked toward the door.

"This always worked for Denny." Mrs. Rodriquez sighed. "And Annette, well, we met when Denny'd been missing for about a month. She had a dream about him in some warehouse by a river and four numbers she thought was a phone number. She looked through the whole phonebook until she found me, and then we found my Denny." Mrs. Rodriquez smiled at Annette, the kind of smile she'd give a fireman who saved a kitten from a tree. Esme rubbed the little dent under her chin from when Denny had thought it would be funny to pull the lobby rug out from under her, wondering if some people should just stay lost. The bodega owner Denny had stolen everything from probably felt that way too.

"I'll leave you to it," Mrs. Rodriquez said, placing her hand on Cerise's arm. "If you need anything, I'm down the hall."

Andre placed the last dining room chair in the living room, counting to make sure there were enough even though there were too many. He didn't look tired and gray like her mother did. He reminded Esme of the popcorn maker they used to have, where the kernels rolled over one another in slow waves while the whole thing got hotter and hotter and popped all at once. Annette rummaged through her purse, but she didn't pull out a crystal or a pack of tarot cards. It was a wad of crumpled tissues. She pressed them to the red tip of her cold, flushed face.

"I'm sorry," she said. "This weather always gets me." To Esme's horror, she threw the used wad back into her purse and extended her hand toward Andre.

"Annette," she said. Andre's big hand closed around her small one. He'd said once that the street psychics were gypsies who made up stories people wanted to hear. If he didn't approve of Annette, he didn't show it.

"Sit," he said, guiding Annette away from the door.

"Tea?" Cerise's hands were shaking. She pressed them against her leggings, stretching her fingers like she did after a long day of sewing.

Esme's heart beat a little faster. She recognized the look in her mother's eyes. It was the same look dancers had when they leaped for the first time, running delicately, thinking so much that it showed in tight lines around their mouths, hoping they'd land correctly instead of crumbling. Her mother looked more likely to crumble.

"No, thank you." Annette stared into the flickering candle on the table. Esme wondered if that was how it happened, if images of Lily jumped out of the flame and Annette read them back like reading a newspaper. Annette's purse fell beside her feet, open, dark, and gaping like a hungry mouth.

"All right." She sighed. "Did Teresa explain the process?" She turned toward Cerise, already settled into one of the dining room chairs. Annette's Keds looked uncomfortably tight around her feet. Esme wondered if loosening the laces would make air hiss out, but she pushed the thought away because if Annette really could read Lily's thoughts, she could probably read hers too.

"Yes." Cerise nodded. If Esme wasn't so nervous, she might have laughed at how serious everyone was.

"I need something of Lily's, something she used often, and then I'll share what I see."

Used. The word made Esme bite her tongue sharply and taste blood. She rolled the word around in her head until it lost its meaning.

Cerise turned to Esme. "Es, why don't you pick something? You know what she likes."

It was an apology, a small stab at normalcy. Esme accepted. She made her way to the bathroom for Turtley, Lily's sponge pet with googly eyes. It was just a bath toy, but Lily took Turtley to bed, even when it was still wet. It was the fastest swimmer of all the bath toys, faster than scuba man and tugboat. The world's fastest turtle. Lily held up its drooping head to talk to other stuffed animals. Turtley told them how he used to be a real turtle with a gold shell and lived in the ocean, not a dumb bathtub. She had tucked it in her backpack and taken it to preschool because Turtley had never been to school, but he'd only gone once because it was boring. Turtles didn't have to read anyway, Lily explained. There were no turtle books.

Turtley was on the edge of the bathtub, his front arms hanging over the lip of the tub, long dry since Lily's last bath. Why would Lily leave him behind? Esme didn't want to touch him. Turtley should stay exactly as he was, but nothing else would work better. She picked up the floppy turtle and silently promised Lily that nothing would happen to him.

In the living room, Annette's voice was muffled. "Are you sure?"

"Yes," Cerise said. "I'd like them to be here." The pain and decision in her voice were almost tangible.

"Let them decide," Andre said. "They're old enough."

Annette smiled sadly.

Were they?

Esme put Turtley on the table between the two candles and settled into her seat beside Madeline. Nick hovered by his bedroom, slouched against the doorframe. No one moved. It was the most "yes" anyone could offer.

Annette pulled a tape recorder from her pocketbook and slipped a new tape into the open receiver. She pressed play and record. Esme glanced at Madeline quickly. How many times had they waited by the radio together for some song they wanted to tape, squealing as the first few notes started and they slammed their fingers down on play and record? Madeline pulled her knees to her chest and hugged them close. She looked like she wanted to vomit. Esme didn't blame her. Everything was real and not real, nauseatingly so, like wearing someone else's glasses.

"This is yours to keep. What we hear may not make sense today, but it might later. When we start, it'll sound like I'm talking in my sleep. I'll talk to you through Lily's words. You can ask questions, and we'll see what answers we get."

Nick lingered in the alcove between his bedroom and the living room, eyeing Annette carefully. If she'd been a person on a late-night infomercial telling them to call now and get answers, Esme knew he would've laughed. *Anyone who falls for that crap is an idiot*, he would say.

"How the hell does this work?" Nick interrupted, frustration oozing off his skin in waves as thick as radiator heat. "How do we know you're not just making shit up?"

"Nick!" Cerise's voice was so harsh Andre jumped up from his chair. Then he stood there, wavering.

"No, really. How do we know? She's not a cop. There's no pictures or evidence or anything that's actually real. She just makes stuff up and goes home with a fat check, and who cares? It's not her problem, is it?" Nick matched Andre's height. "Dad, c'mon. You don't believe this shit, do you?"

Andre's hand tightened on the back of the chair. His wedding band made a clicking noise on the wood. He couldn't believe it, Esme thought, torn between wanting to know what Annette saw and wanting her to leave. Nick glared at Andre, shifting from foot to foot silently until he looked away.

Nick snorted. "Figures." Some kind of boy code had been broken, but Esme didn't really understand.

Annette jumped in. "I'm not taking money for this."

Nick's forehead furrowed deeper; he was now more suspicious than he had been. His fists were balled up in his pockets, but his knee bounced in his jeans, an old habit. He'd done that when he was younger, bouncing before taking his place at bat, waiting for the pitcher to make a move, waiting for their father to find out he'd stolen forty dollars from the food money in the drawer or been caught with beer on the roof. Lily's drawing was still on the wall without Nick. Was Detective Ferrera right?

"I don't take money from anyone. I do this because I see things other people can't, things I shouldn't or couldn't know any other way. When Teresa told me about your sister, I wanted to help."

Annette paused, sifting through words. "How does it work?" She laughed. "I'm not sure. I've been waiting my whole life for someone to explain it, but here's what I know. When I see pictures of people, I see things that happened to them. I might think a certain thought or feel a sensation and know it isn't mine. It happens when I'm awake or asleep, like stepping out of myself and into someone else for a little while."

Annette stared into the corner of the living room, eyes glazed as if she saw something other than where the walls met and the lamp stood with its cord wrapped around its base. *Just be the regular living room,* Esme prayed, watching the same corner carefully. Annette turned her attention back to Nick.

"In one of the visions I had about Lily, I was running in a playground, and someone was chasing me. I was laughing and having so much fun I didn't notice the wall ahead until I ran right into it. I didn't understand how I got from running to staring at the sky. My head felt funny, and the next thing I heard was . . ."

Good job, dummy, Esme remembered, shocked. That was what Nick had said, and she'd slapped him for being so mean.

"You let her wear your Mets hat, the one with your initials on the brim."

Nick always wrote his initials under the brim with a Sharpie. It had started when he was a kid and wanted to pitch for the Mets when he grew up. He threw balled-up socks against targets Andre set up for him in the house, but Nick hadn't done that in years. She had no idea what he wanted to be instead. She'd ask him later, she decided. Maybe that little boy was still in there.

"And you carried her home on your back. That's what she liked most."

She'd forgotten about that day in the park, but she wished now, deeply, that she hadn't. Memories drifting into forgottenness seemed unspeakably sad. The photo album with missing pictures had been put away. A lump throbbed in her throat as Nick wiped his face with his sleeve. It was the first time she'd seen him cry in a long time, and she wanted to tie him back together like undone shoelaces. Maybe that was what Annette could do.

"She wore that hat on her first day of school too," Annette said softly. Nick nodded, not meeting her eye, and stuffed his hands back in his pockets, where they sat in two balled lumps. "Because you said it was good luck."

There was a pause. A lock clicked in the hallway. Everyone swam in private thoughts, treading water as one thought rolled in after the next. Annette's voice guided them back to the living room.

"Why don't you join us?" Annette gestured toward an empty seat. "I don't always understand what I see, but you might because you know your sister in a way I never will, and hey, maybe I am making it up. Sometimes it feels that way for me, too, but you can be the judge of that." Annette smiled softly as Nick took a seat. It seemed like Annette understood how hard the past day had been more than anyone else. Esme tried not to think about anything. She would just listen.

Annette reached for Turtley and held him between her hands, forming a new shell.

"I think we're ready," Annette said as she closed her eyes. Her head tipped slightly toward her right shoulder. Andre lowered the lights. Annette sighed deeply. If Annette could step out of her old body and into Lily's young, elastic one, it must be a relief. The peaceful look on Annette's face must be Lily shining through.

It was quiet for a long time. The flickering candles in the darkness reminded Esme of a birthday cake, only no one was singing, and no one moved. They sat in half shadows and waited. Was it working?

Annette's voice was thick and dreamlike, sleep talk forgotten by morning.

"I see a thousand rainbows flickering over the walls and floor. If I try to catch them, they're on my foot instead or the back of my hands. My name is strange. Here, I'm called Elizabeth."

"That's her middle name." Cerise slid to the edge of the chair, her back pin straight, as alert now as an antenna. Annette's eyes rolled back and forth, up and down behind her eyelids, looking at another world where there should have been dark, wet skin. Esme wished she could press her thumbs against those eyes to make them stop moving. It unnerved her. This wasn't like watching light shift behind her eyes from orange to yellow to red when she was going somewhere in a car or dozing in the sun. This was a cross between make-believe and scary.

"Two, three, two," Annette said. "I see the numbers two, three, two."

"Is it an address?" Cerise was having trouble keeping her hands in her lap. They darted toward Annette, like touching her could pull Lily back from the world on the other side of Annette's eyes. Cerise drew them back.

A long pause filled the living room. Esme watched Annette's face carefully. Had she fallen asleep? She shifted her weight, feeling suddenly heavy, unsure if she should tap Annette.

"I can see the moon," Annette said finally. "Only half of it."

"Through a window?" Cerise asked. "Or from outside?" Outside, it was dark enough to need lights. The light was fading, but there was no moon. No stars. Maybe time was different where Lily was, but Lily couldn't read clocks with hands yet. Was 232 the time?

"From a window with a red tree."

"Lily," Esme asked. "Does it say 232 on a clock?"

Annette shuffled; her fingers twitched. Lily did that sometimes in her sleep. Annette didn't answer. Lily had caught her attention elsewhere.

"What else can you see?" Madeline asked.

"A tree house with a bird."

"Lily?" Cerise called her back. "Is this happening now, or did it already happen? Is this place real or something you saw on TV?"

"The dog is real," Annette said, still shuffling, feet bouncing. "It barks all night."

"Is it barking now?" Esme asked, still thinking about the moon.

"No." Annette's brow furrowed deeper like she was trying to push away a headache.

"How'd you get there, Lily?" Andre asked.

"I see a car," Annette said. "It's tan and dark on the inside."

"Who are you with, Lily?" Madeline jumped in, leaning forward.

"Elizabeth likes red," Annette said.

"Why do they call you Elizabeth?" Cerise asked.

Annette's breathing quickened, short, shallow breaths. She shifted in her seat. Her back straightened. The peaceful look was gone. A thin line of sweat beaded on her forehead. Annette pressed her eyes farther shut. Her lips were one long line of blueish white. Oh God. Was she in pain?

"Elizabeth is dead," Annette said, finally.

"All right, enough!" Andre said. He jumped up so quickly his chair fell backward. Esme pressed her eyes closed and tried to focus on the light behind her eyes. Yellow, black, yellow. She squeezed harder, but all she saw were prisms throwing half-moon rainbows on everything. A little girl looking at the moon.

"Enough," he said again. He walked toward the door and held it open.

Annette blinked slowly, dazed. Whatever she'd seen was over now.

"But she's not finished." Cerise was a pile of dandelion wisps again.

"Yes, she is." The decision in his voice was final.

The peaceful-sleep look Annette had had during the trance was gone. The lines around her eyes were creased and tired again like a worn glove. Esme deflated, as if someone had opened the oven and all the heat had rushed out. Annette didn't answer. She gathered her things and let one hand rest briefly on Cerise's shaking shoulder before turning to the door. Annette's quiet was eerie. Was it kinder not to say anything if there was nothing to say?

Annette paused by the door, hazel eyes almost brown, almost green, shifting color but holding Esme's gaze steady. Esme emptied her head and thought of black space like the universe so there'd be nothing for Annette to read.

"She'll know you," Annette said, looking like she'd broken a rule. "She'll know you without knowing you."

"OK." Andre pushed the door closed and bolted the chain into place.

"What does that mean?" Esme asked. The back of her neck burned. There had to be more. She couldn't just leave them with nothing. Esme looked at her parents. Was she the only one who didn't understand? No, Cerise was biting her thumb, eyes closed, rocking gently back and forth. The cassette tape sat on the coffee table next to Turtley. Esme picked him up and cradled him in her hands, covering his eyes.

"Call Detective Ferrera," Cerise said, still biting her thumb. "Tell him what she said."

"Tell him what exactly? Some random numbers and shit about rainbows?" Andre's voice was ragged. "What the fuck would that do?"

Esme winced. He never used that word. Not ever.

Andre rounded on Cerise. "Have you lost your mind?" Andre was pacing now. The floor creaked beneath him. Esme stared at a crack on the ceiling. The peacefulness of the rainbows was absurd now. But they were real. Lily saw them.

"What a fucking idea, Cerise. Just great. Really wonderful. You want to be useful? Finish the list they asked you to make. Call the numbers they gave you. Make a fucking poster instead of listening to this shit."

"Maybe it means something," Cerise whispered, but Andre wasn't listening. He knotted his hands into fists, squeezing hard and fast, before throwing one through the wall. The picture frames shook. Plaster scattered over the carpet. Cerise strangled back a sob.

The door slammed shut. The candle flame jumped. Nick flashed across the room. The door slammed behind him, too, leaving Esme alone with her mother, Madeline, and a gaping hole where the wall used to be a smooth, boring beige.

The phone rang in Cerise and Andre's bedroom. It rang and rang, and soon it would be picked up by the thing that looked like an answering machine but wasn't, and everything would be recorded alongside their real answering machine. *Hello, you've reached the Bellerose family. Please leave a message after the tone.* A garbled voice left a message Esme couldn't hear. Outside, the 7 train rumbled to a stop. The clock ticked. Cerise picked up the half-finished list of names and held it in her lap.

Madeline was very still, staring at the lines on her hands. A love line. A life line. How many times had they traced those lines and made up stories for each other? *You'll have three husbands. You'll live to be one hundred.*

"They let her see where she is," Madeline whispered, rubbing her thumb over her palm where her life line would be. She looked like she'd been kicked under the ribs, crushed. "That's not good."

"What do you mean?" Esme asked. Slowly, the unfairness settled in. You couldn't just take someone who didn't belong to you. Esme thought of the tan car Lily had seen. You couldn't just pluck someone out of their real life and drop them into another one like a doll in a dollhouse. What kind of person would do that?

Les Sylphides. Swan Lake. There was almost always an evil something pulling strings so people would see the wrong thing. Was that what Annette was?

She hadn't seen it right. Not all of it. That day in the park, Lily had been running because Nick had said there was a ghost in the slide.

He'd slid halfway down and held himself inside the tube, banging on the plastic and screaming that he was being eaten alive, and Lily had bolted. The birthday cake picture fluttered on the door. Why wasn't Nick in it? Why wasn't Nick in any of Lily's pictures?

It was too much. Esme felt like the last dead leaf on a tree, afraid the wind would blow too hard and knock her into a gutter. She held the seat of her chair until her fingers ached, pretending it was the barre at the studio. In only a minute, the music would start, and Amelia's voice would follow. Her body would do what it was supposed to do, and she wouldn't have time to think about tiny rainbows on Lily's fingers or a tree with a tree house or her father throwing holes through walls.

"Come on," Cerise said, gathering herself and brushing away the wet spots on her cheeks. "We have work to do."

Chapter Five

On Sunday just before dawn, a flock of crows landed on the street. They covered the phone wires, walked on parked cars, perched on side view mirrors, and covered the stoops, sipping from icy puddles and scratching through garbage scraps. The air was flapping, heavy with the sound of bird wings. Esme wondered if Anna Pavlova's backyard with its pond full of swans would've felt like this and decided it wouldn't have. Swans were too graceful to be noisy.

"You have a message." Madeline shook Esme's shoulder. She hadn't heard her sister's bare feet on the carpet and wondered if she'd been asleep, if the crows were a dream, but she looked out the window, and they were still there.

"There's a bunch of crows outside," Esme said. Maybe Madeline knew how to interpret them, but she was pacing, freshly showered, the only one who'd kept to an almost-normal schedule, and didn't bother looking out the window.

"You have a message," Madeline said again. A notebook was balanced on her arm, the same way she did when she studied and paced. "I'm a kinesthetic learner," she'd explained, but it was an annoying habit. The crows were weighing down the telephone wire. It sagged. How many birds would it take before the line snapped and the birds scattered? It wouldn't matter then if they'd kept the line free or not. It already felt like it didn't matter considering no one important had called. *Do you remember,* she wanted to ask Lily, *all those numbers we practiced—our address, your phone number, your tricky zip code—and how to spell your name, first and last, in case you were ever lost?* Maybe the birds had a message for her like Birdman's pigeons.

"Esme?" Madeline tapped the pen on the notebook. The plastic clicked against the spiral wires, shattering the snow globe world outside the window, where people had left things on the street: balloons, open Bibles, stuffed animals.

"Stop it." Esme snatched the pen from Madeline's hand and threw it across the room. It hit the wall and left a blue streak.

"Asshole," Madeline hissed. "Don't even *try* to ask me who it was later." Madeline stomped back to their bedroom and slammed the door. Esme pulled the blanket tighter and leaned her head against the window. It was cold. Her breath fogged the glass. She drew a little *L* and wiped it away. Lily would have thought the birds were special.

Cerise had covered the hole in the wall with a black plastic bag and relit the candles. The room smelled like black licorice again. She missed the grapefruit candle Amelia had in the studio. That was a friendly candle, unlike this one. Bundled shapes left things on the sidewalk below. *Who are you?* Esme wondered, but she was most curious about the person who hung prisms and built a tree house in a red tree, whatever that meant, assuming it was true and that it meant anything at all.

"And it's not a 'bunch of crows,' dumbass. It's a murder," Madeline yelled through the bedroom door. Esme watched until the birds took off as suddenly as they'd arrived. She heard them faintly in the distance but couldn't see them. After dawn, it was as if they'd never been there. Not even a feather was left on the street. It meant something, like all the plagues God sent in the Bible. It had to.

Esme sighed and gathered herself in her blanket. She could check the message. The machine in her parents' room was quiet. No blinking lights. No new messages. Her parents' unmade bed didn't have the warm sleeping smell they usually left behind, a smell that made her want to crawl in between her parents on Sunday mornings like a little kid, like Lily still could. Lily's bed was made up in the corner, stuffed animals lining the place where the bed met the wall. They were just matted fur and floppy heads without Lily's puppet work, hand-me-down castoffs from Esme and Madeline. They were supposed to get bunk beds soon—then Lily's little bed and all her things would move into the big-girl bedroom. Maybe they could set it up before she came home. *Look*, they'd welcome her back, *you're one of us now*.

If she came back. Annette hadn't seen that, hadn't promised them she'd be back in a week—or at all. Esme pushed the thought away and flipped through messages until she found the one for her.

"Esme, it's Amelia. I heard about what happened and just wanted to say how very sorry I am."

Amelia's voice in her parents' bedroom was startling. She straightened her slouching spine, pushed wisps of hair away from her forehead. *What you do when you're not here counts as much, if not more, as what you do when you're here.* That was one of Amelia's favorite sayings. Esme'd been poked with a stick, reprimanded from far away, and it didn't seem fair, not with how things were.

Esme's finger hovered over the delete button. She did not want Amelia's pity. There was a pause. *If you need anything, you know where to find me*, she imagined Amelia would rush on, the same way everyone else shrugged off other people's problems to move on with their own day.

"Pointe shoes are tomorrow if you can make it," she said instead. "If not, do last week's barre, as much as you can remember. Stay focused."

Esme hit rewind. Yes, she'd said everything Esme thought she'd heard. *Stay focused.* The audition was in January, the one that would take her to San Francisco for the summer (hopefully!), where she'd live in a dorm at the top of a huge hill for the first time with a stranger instead of Madeline, and her roommate would be a friend and competitor at the same time, Camargo to her Sallé. And maybe she'd have a cute pas de deux partner and sneak her first kiss in the studio after everyone else had left. She'd ride cable cars to the studio every day like on TV. That dream felt like someone else's plan now. *Stay focused.* Esme laughed, and the sound didn't make sense next to the big bed where her parents slept or the little bed where Lily slept or the dresser cluttered with piles of clothes and a mirrored tray full of dusty jewelry and a bottle of Tabu.

She laughed again, joyless, but the vibration jolted her dream awake. She did want to see the Golden Gate Bridge, to walk under swaying red and gold lanterns in Chinatown. She wanted to sneak down to the dorm lobby in her pajamas, where she'd sit with other dancers and talk about how scandalous it was when Sallé let her hair down or Camargo took the heels off her shoes and Taglioni figured out how to dance on her toes or, ew, how Degas's beautiful dancers were really prostitutes, a word she couldn't say at home, not in front of her parents, but could in a dorm after hours of dancing and sore feet and a scalp rubbed raw from bobby pins keeping her bun in place.

The rest of the message played through. "Stay focused. If you can dance through this, Esme, you can dance through anything."

Esme's stomach sank. Was this the worst thing that could happen ever? Was there nothing worse? Through anything. This wasn't like her bike slipping out from under her because she'd ridden over wet leaves, knowing forever after that she should slow down and steer around them. She didn't want this to be something that made her stronger or smarter. It wasn't fair to Lily, who was a person, somewhere, and not a pile of leaves she could outsmart.

Outside, keys jingled in the lock. The door opened and closed. Esme hit delete, but the message stayed with her. "Does fog taste like cotton candy?" Lily'd asked once, standing on tiptoes to see Esme's picture of the Golden Gate Bridge. "Because it looks like cotton candy. Or marshmallows?"

There were heavy feet in the living room. Nick and Andre. Esme crept toward the door and watched them pull off boots and coats and leave them in a heap on the floor. They were windblown and early-winter raw, but the most striking thing was Nick's eye. It was black and blue, shiny and swollen. It watered and ran down his face. If she were invisible, she could creep closer and look at the shades of blue and purple, poke that spongy skin because she'd never seen a real black eye before, but mostly, she wanted to know how he'd gotten it. A reason that made sense would make everything feel less like her looking glass world.

"Where's your mother?"

Esme jumped. She wasn't invisible after all. The open door rattled the plastic over the hole in the wall. Andre was looking right at her.

"Church." The word squeaked out. She opened the bedroom door wider. Andre turned toward Nick.

"Take a shower," he said. "Then go to bed. Don't let your mother see that yet."

They'd been out all night. Her father's hair stuck up in spikes, and the bottoms of his jeans were black with dirt. So were Nick's. Where did people go when they stayed out all night? Where was there to go that wasn't home? Esme's head pounded. Their normal world was hiding here somewhere, a lost sock in the dryer. Things didn't just change this fast.

"Dad?" He should know about the birds. It seemed important somehow, but Andre looked so tired. The half-moons under his fingernails were black. The flickering candles on the table woke him up momentarily, long enough for him to cross the room with purpose and blow out the flames. A thin line of smoke traveled toward the ceiling. A puddle of wax sat in its place.

"But she said—"

"Get rid of this shit," he said. "And wake me up when your mother gets home. Don't let me sleep for more than an hour."

Nick slumped on the couch, his reflection shadowy in the dark TV. Water rolled from the corner of his eye down his cheek, but Nick wasn't crying. There were traces of blood on his hands and face, brown and dry in the early-morning light. The candle smoke roiled Esme's stomach. Her knuckles ached where the red, cracked bruises on Nick's hand must have burned. Where was their brother who threw LEGO houses down the stairs to see how strong he'd built them? Esme swallowed, chasing the bitter taste away.

"Hey." Andre picked Nick up by his armpits and stood him on his feet. "Come on—let's clean up."

The tenderness in Andre's voice surprised her. She thought he'd be in trouble for whatever he'd done, but instead, something had shifted between Nick and Andre. Andre helped Nick to the bathroom. The water started. They were both too big to be in that small room together. Water splashed over the sink. She heard soap between their hands. They were washing something away, a secret only the two of them understood.

"Get some ice on that." The bathroom was a mess of dirty clothes and black city dirt on the sink. Esme waited until they'd split off from one another, each finding his room, before scooping their clothes into the hamper. She wiped away the dirt from the sink and put their toothbrushes back in the cup with the others, minus the Little Mermaid toothbrush that was somewhere else now.

Then she filled a pot with icy water and carried it to Nick's room.

He was lying on his back. The swelling made it hard to tell if his eyes were open or shut. She sat beside him, careful not to rattle the ice cubes as she set the pot down on the floor, plunging her hand into the freezing water and bringing the washcloth up with it. It stung her hands. She shivered as water dripped down her sleeves but folded the cloth neatly and set it over Nick's face. It felt good to do something nice, to feel important.

Nick flinched. Esme pulled a blanket over him, the blue-and-white quilt Cerise had made when he was born. In sleep, Nick looked too young to be her older brother. It was strange to see Madeline and Nick look as young as they actually were, even rarer for her to help them instead of the other way around.

"I'm sorry, Mom," Nick mumbled.

Not Mom, Esme, she wanted to say. *Mom is sitting in a church pew praying to stupid statues and lighting squatty red candles for a dollar over and over again.* Esme wrung the washcloth, dabbing his eyes and wiping away the drops that ran down his face to his pillow. Their mom was supposed to do things like this. If she'd been home on Thursday night instead of at church, maybe this wouldn't have happened. And how could God let something bad happen while Cerise was at church, actual church, his house? If God rewarded good people and punished bad ones, then maybe something was wrong with her mother . . .

It was the first time she'd ever thought such a thing, and the hostility surprised her. It felt as wrong as drinking spoiled milk.

"It's Esme," she whispered finally.

Nick nodded. He smelled like damp earth, smoky and burnt. It made her nose tingle. She ran the washcloth over his knuckles and stopped only when she realized the water in the pot had turned a rusty brown.

She assumed he'd been hurt, but what if he'd hurt someone else too? The thought of her brother's fist hitting someone's face hard enough to rip their skin and make them bleed disgusted Esme.

"I'll get more water." The mattress sprang up without her weight, filling the space where she'd been.

Nick opened his eyes for the first time, flinching against the sunlight trickling through the blinds. "Stay."

Esme blinked, not sure she'd heard him right. She hesitated by the door.

"Just stay," he said again. She put the pot down and found a place next to his bed, resting her head on her arm. Nick put his hand near hers. It was weird to touch her brother.

"I didn't do anything wrong," he whispered. Esme stared at the things in her brother's room, things that belonged only to him: sweatshirts and baseball mitts, aluminum bats with missing paint chips, a bottle of Barbasol. She was jealous of the empty space on his walls.

"I thought I was helping." Nick's hand throbbed against hers like a beating heart.

"Where'd you go?"

"The depot." He coughed. "And a few other places with pictures of Lily."

Esme cringed at the thought of Lily in the depot. It was an old trolley barn. Sometimes Nick threw rocks at the windows. They all did. Only the highest ones were still in one piece, and kids got as close as they could, picking through the chain-link fence, stepping over old mattresses and torn trash bags. Homeless people lived inside with thrown-away things. The police had found Denny there once after he'd been missing for a while. Esme was too afraid to ask what it was like inside.

No, Lily was with another family, like in storybooks where kids walked through cupboards and into other worlds. They fought wars against animal people, sailed imaginary ships across oceans full of paper monsters, met kings and queens, and came back unscathed but smarter. Lily would love that. It was make-believe, but even pretend stuff was based on real things. Even the possibility was comforting.

"All those cops asking people in our building what they'd seen seemed stupid, and people will just walk past posters. No one really looks because they're so busy with their own shit. But lots of people see shit every day, and no one pays attention to them."

"What do you mean?"

"Homeless people, Esme. People who live on the street and watch everyone else all day. A lot of them sit in the same spots. They know what's normal and what's not, which kids belong to who. Dad thought it was a great idea, so that's what we did. We went to the depot, the park, the corners, under the train, wherever we could think of. Now they're looking. They're out when no one else is, and everyone thinks they're invisible, so they see stuff."

It was a good idea, surprisingly good from someone who didn't bother with school or homework or studying for tests, who didn't have a "constructive" hobby and hung around with Denny. She felt stupid in comparison.

"How'd you think of that?"

"Es," he said, "when shit like this happens, you have to think outside your world."

She thought of Cerise praying at church, hoping Lily would reappear when she opened her eyes, or her own small world at the studio, how just going there almost every day was her portal to the next part of her life.

"How do you do that, though?" She felt especially stupid, something else she needed him to explain. Ice melted in the pot. She wanted him to keep talking.

"You already know how to do it," he said. "You've already figured out that dancing's how you'll do stuff no one else will. Think about it, Es. Everyone else your age is studying the same stupid crap as everyone else, writing the same answers on paper for bullshit grades and being told how special they are."

That's what Madeline was doing. School was so easy for her. He was calling Madeline a sheep, but he wasn't entirely right about ballet.

"I just do what I'm taught in class," she said. "I'm just learning things other people already figured out."

"So? That's how it starts. You learn words one by one before you string them together."

He was right. Anna Pavlova had done it, eventually moving away from what she was taught and creating her own, but Esme didn't understand how it happened.

"Yeah, but . . ." She trailed off. How could she explain that learning things that had started centuries ago was like staring at the sky? She felt big and little for being part of it, even though none of that was helping now. It didn't even feel important anymore, not in the way it had last week, but the thought of Amelia's studio—its grapefruit smell; the feel of the floor under her feet, solid and polished and squishier than regular floors; the chill on her bare arms before she was warmed up—made her miss it bone deep. The thought of it filled her lungs with the right kind of air in a way that felt selfish now. She pushed it away.

"What do you think it means?" She changed the subject to Annette and everything she'd said the day before, debating whether to float her theory of Lily living with another family. "All that stuff about prisms and the tree house."

"It's a nice story, I guess." He sighed and pulled his hand away from hers, tucking it under the quilt. Someone knocked on the front door. Cerise, maybe, back from church having forgotten her key.

"You should get that," he said, rolling away from her. His back was a thick lump under the blanket. "And wake Dad up soon."

No, she wanted to say, feeling more alone now that he was quiet. Someone knocked again, louder this time. Esme left to answer it, feeling as bounced and disoriented as a Ping-Pong ball. It wasn't just a story. It could be real, as real as she was. She pinched the place between her thumb and forefinger. The pain felt good, refreshingly real, but the feeling left when she saw Madeline by the door and Detective Ferrera in the doorway. Andre spilled out from his room, as ragged and loose limbed as a puddle. Detective Ferrera's gaze flickered toward the garbage bag taped to the wall, but he said nothing. It couldn't be bad news, Esme thought, not if he was wearing a faded old Champion sweatshirt. Bad news came in suits.

"All right," he said, closing the door behind him. "I have updates. Is Cerise here?"

"No." Andre's voice swam to the surface. "She's at church."

"Anthony Santos, Birdman as you call him, has an alibi. He was in Atlantic City on Thursday night and has been there since early last week. The maintenance man Madeline mentioned was working another building. We have surveillance footage of him in the building all night."

"Which leaves us with no one," Andre finished. His voice was flat, reciting a fact. Esme waited for the *but*. When God closed a door, he opened a window. Wasn't that what Cerise always told them?

"Not necessarily." Detective Ferrera opened the front door and pointed down the hallway. Esme leaned forward to see. It was full of casserole dishes smothered in plastic wrap, flowers, stuffed animals, fruit baskets, balloons, a jumble of things wrapped in cellophane and tied shut with ribbons. A bizarre kind of Christmas without a tree, like all the boxes wrapped in mismatched wrapping paper for the giving tree at church, but they hadn't posted any ornaments asking for things they couldn't afford. Or the kind of dressing room she hoped to come back to one day after an amazing show, full of appreciation from fans. The astonishment she felt for a hallway full of presents turned sour with hopelessness, stacked with every dish and basket of waxy fruit.

"Carry it in, and make a list of everyone who sent something. I want to see that list every day, especially if someone sends more than one thing or if it's really expensive or someone you don't know. And if there's anything without a name, like a card or a gift, and you don't know who sent it, save it for me. The same goes for any of the stuff left outside." Detective Ferrera looked to Andre and back. "Esme, maybe you could start the list?"

It seemed like too big of a job for someone who was only eleven, but she nodded. How wrong could she be? It was a list of names.

"Anyone who volunteers to help should also be on that list. We've contacted Border Patrol, the Coast Guard, and the National Guard and put out an APB with Lily's description, and there's also a tip line in place. We need copies of her medical and dental records. And there's one other thing . . ."

His voice trailed off. He shifted from one foot to the other and rubbed his thumb over the frayed edge of his sweatshirt even though his gaze was level with Andre's. A pit worked its way into Esme's throat. He didn't want to say what he had to next. She could feel it.

"The two suspects outside your family check out, at least for now. We need you, Cerise, and Nick to come in for a polygraph. The sooner you do it, the quicker we can move forward with other leads."

"A lie detector test." Andre's voice was a flat line, but the anger spilled off him in waves so thick Esme wanted to cover her head.

"The sooner we rule out the possibility, the better. How about this afternoon?"

"Fine," Andre snapped. He ran his hand through his hair, pulling at the roots. The skin on his scalp moved with it, upward into a small tent of skin that made Esme want to puke.

"No one here has anything to hide from a bullshit science experiment," Andre said. "Carry that shit in. Start the damn list. Do some real work." His footsteps shook the living room. The TV rattled in its stand. His bedroom door slammed behind him. *Fee-fi-fo-fum*, Esme thought, *the giant is angry*. If Lily was here, she would have whispered it to her, and Lily would have laughed, but there was only a pile of stuff in her place.

"I'm sorry," Madeline whispered to Detective Ferrera. Her eyes were glassy, ready to break and spill over. "He's just upset."

"It's OK," he said. The harsh lines softened around his face, and he looked as tired as everyone else did. Esme wondered if he had a family, too, if he had kids who were home watching TV or playing with toys and waiting for their dad to come home, if they ran to the door when he did and hugged him tight, if he'd rather be there with them instead of here. He shuffled toward the door, picked up the first few things in the hallway, and carried them to the table. They worked like ants until the hallway was empty and the table was full. Esme's stomach rumbled at the waxy fruit, at the perfect Snow White apples behind cellophane. She hadn't realized she was hungry.

"Why do we have to do this?" Esme stared at the pile of things on the table. The first card was from Father O'Brien.

"Well"—he sighed—"sometimes people do nice things because they feel guilty. Like if you had a fight with your sister, maybe you'd do something nice to make up for it. This is similar. Keeping a list tells us who might feel guilty."

The signed names under x's and o's were suspects. She wished he'd just drop it all in evidence bags and carry it to the police station so she wouldn't have to wonder about people she knew. She'd heard once that crazy people mailed exploding boxes to strangers, and now all the food, cards, and baskets felt like that too. There was a small bakery box on the table tied shut with red-and-white twine. Peppermint string. The little card was from Annette.

Esme handed the card to Detective Ferrera. "This is the psychic who came yesterday. She came for free to help."

Detective Ferrera paused by the door. "How'd she find you?"

"Mrs. Rodriquez."

"What's her name?"

"Annette." Madeline crossed the room, pulled the little tape from the recorder, and handed it to him. It might not be the right thing to do, but Esme wished she would pack the candles too and send the whole night away with it.

"I'll listen to it," he said, turning to leave.

Esme wondered what he would do after this. "Hey," she called after him. "Are people mostly good or mostly bad?"

He paused by the door. She felt very small next to the pile of stuff.

"What do you think?" he asked.

She shrugged. Only days ago, she would have said mostly good, but now she wasn't sure. He would know better. He'd seen more things. The chain lock swung on the door. He stopped it with his finger.

"Think of it this way," he said finally. "Good people can do bad things, and bad people can do good things, so maybe it depends on the choices we make. Even good people can do bad things for good reasons."

"Like stealing to feed hungry kids."

"Exactly. Everyone can be both. It just depends on how we look at them. Sometimes how we look at people is decided by law or religion. Bad things wouldn't be bad if we lived in a world where they were good, right?"

That was too much to think about. It was the kind of grown-up answer she usually wished her parents would give but didn't want today. She just wanted a yes or no answer, something clear and uncomplicated, and he'd given her a whirling headache instead. Disappointment spilled into her hands and fingers. They felt thick and heavy as she picked up the pen and clicked it, as she opened the notebook he'd given her. She should just shut up and do what she was told, stop thinking about confusing things. Write the names. Show him the list. It was easy enough.

"Esme." He pointed toward the pile of stuff on the table. "Most of those people are good, if not all of them, OK?"

"OK," she mumbled as she opened Father O'Brien's card, the priest who'd dunked her baby head in a baptismal font and put a communion wafer on her tongue every Sunday. How could anyone be good if Detective Ferrera didn't even think her parents were innocent? Or her brother. The door closed behind him. His peppery smell hung in the room, and Esme found it strangely comforting. She wrote the first name on the list, then the next. He might be wrong, but at least he had a plan.

Chapter Six

The skeleton wreaths and jack-o'-lanterns had changed to cornucopias and bouquets of fiery leaves. There were bunches of colorful corn in reds and yellows, oranges and brown. Flint corn was Esme's favorite, especially the blue kind. She'd taken a walk with Lily last year in their building looking for blue flint corn. "Why is our corn only yellow," Lily had asked behind her web of hair. "Why don't we eat the colorful ones?"

Christmas music was already playing on the radio, and twinkle lights hung in store windows. It was *Nutcracker* season. She could watch the dance of the snowflakes over and over again because it was her favorite. When the curtain rose and those snowflakes filled the stage, it was the best part of Christmas. But she didn't want to watch *The Nutcracker* this year. Two weeks had passed, and even though she kept the list of names and brought it to Detective Ferrera every day, there were fewer cards now, fewer dishes outside their door, the gift baskets rummaged through. People were already forgetting.

Someone from Connecticut had donated a trailer. It sat outside their apartment building, parked on the street like a cave, the kind of clubhouse they would have wished for when they were younger, but this one was for Cerise and Andre.

"I thought you might like to use it as a command center," he'd said. "We lost our son twelve years ago, and someone brought it to us. It helps"—he sighed—"not running things out of your house."

His name was Joe. His son's name was Joe too. Esme didn't have to ask if they'd found him. She could tell by the way he'd folded into himself, like origami stuffed in a pocket for too long, that the answer was no. The walls of the trailer were covered in pushpin holes as thick and heavy as a sky of stars. Cerise spent most of her time in the trailer now, a shadow moving behind faded plaid curtains.

Old ladies whom Cerise called advocates flocked to the trailer and talked about rewards and second phone lines. They made more flyers and sent them places Cerise said were helpful. They said the FBI should be involved and rattled off names of organizations with weird combinations of letters, like a bowl of Alpha-Bits. They also talked about everything Detective Ferrera had done wrong: *The police should have used bloodhounds instead of German shepherds because they have sixty times the tracking power. German shepherds can't smell the air if a child's been carried. Everyone knows that. Why didn't they polygraph faster? Why wasn't the media more involved? Why didn't they put out the APB sooner? Where was the FBI?*

They whispered things Esme wished she hadn't heard: that bodies dumped in rivers floated up in the spring when the weather was warm, that police had to stuff them in body bags before taking them out of the water because they fell apart otherwise, that missing children who weren't found within twenty-four hours usually never were. She overheard things about bodies found in burlap sacks on the beach, about a little boy in a drainpipe. She only heard a sentence or two before someone realized she was there with hands full of mail or thank-you cards or baskets of food, and there was silence again.

Not Lily, she wanted to say. *She's in a room with rainbow prisms and a tree house outside her window*—but she didn't think the old ladies would believe her. They enjoyed whispering too much. Esme stayed out of the trailer, except when she had to, and she slammed the door every time she came in or out so the old ladies would know when she was there and when she wasn't. They could do whatever they wanted with their maps and pushpins, but she didn't want to hear the rest.

It'd been two weeks without school, two weeks without dance, two weeks without Lily. The mirror version of life was sickening, like being upside down or walking on your hands for too long. Two weeks of milling around without any kind of time. Today was no exception.

"Mom and Dad are back," Madeline said, looking through the shade in the living room.

Esme and Nick slid off the couch. No one wanted to help, usually, but now they were thankful for something normal. Downstairs, Andre's cab waited at the curb, hazard lights flashing, the trunk filled with grocery bags.

They passed Cerise on her way in. She held the lobby door with her back, eyes red rimmed and blotchy. She'd been crying. The way she looked carefully over her shoulder and into the hallway behind them told Esme she didn't want them to know.

"Mom?" Esme asked. Anxiety tightened her chest. Was there something new? Madeline slipped her fingers under Esme's elbow and pulled her through the door.

"Come on," she whispered. "If she wants us to know, she'll tell us."

Cold air slapped Esme's face and stung her eyes. She looked back at her mother's sagging shoulders, head hanging, grocery bags on either arm. If the bags weren't so heavy, Esme suspected her shoulders would've been shaking, arms wrapped around her torso to keep herself in one piece. Cerise was carrying more than usual. Esme wondered if she'd taken more than she could carry to distract herself from whatever she was feeling.

Andre was waiting with the car. He handed two bags to each of them and slammed the trunk shut.

"I'll be up in a minute," he mumbled, his voice thick and gruff. He'd been crying too. Esme shivered in her sweatshirt while everyone orbited each other, boxed into their own private worlds, swirling with unnamable emotions. They were looking at each other through glass cages at the zoo or aquarium tanks, together and not. What were they now, she asked, studying how they paced and fretted. Madeline was a horseshoe crab, dragging along the bottom of her tank. Nick was a betta fish, fine alone but ready to attack a mirror. Nothing had changed in two weeks. No news. Her parents were the worst. They were fish who'd forgotten how to swim.

The grocery bags cut into her hands and left red, hot marks on her skin. Her mother was upstairs. She'd be back in her bed again soon if she wasn't already or locked in the trailer. Everyone else would tiptoe around, clock ticking, refrigerator humming, listening to TV sounds filtering through the walls, smelling other people's food cooking, the squeal of the 7 train. She couldn't move. She'd suffocate if she went back upstairs. The wind blew down her collar. Her throat was tight, covered in a thousand pressing hands, smothering the delicate bones in her neck. She opened her mouth and screamed.

It was a shrill sound. It echoed against buildings on either side of the street. She ran out of air, then filled her lungs and started again. Short screams, louder, punching the world in shrill bursts. Her throat was raw, and the effort doubled her over. The driver's door burst open, and her father ran out, calling her name but too afraid to touch her. Madeline watched from the doorway, openmouthed. Esme didn't care. She screamed, standing in the exhaust plume while the car idled. Her father stopped asking what was wrong and held his head in his hands, walking in small circles. It was almost funny, them staring and staring while pigeons flew overhead, disgusting birds with stupid purple-pearl eyes, molting feathers and shitting on the sidewalk. Something white flashed on the stoop. She pressed her eyes shut and started a new scream.

Nick's hands were on her shoulders now, shaking hard. Her brain bounced against the bones that held it, and her voice faltered. She tried to shrug him off, but he held her shoulders tighter. His fingers dug into her skin.

"What the hell is wrong with you?" he yelled into the wave of a scream. "Knock it off."

Esme stopped screaming. She stared at her brother. Would he hurt her? If he'd shaken Lily's little shoulders as hard as he'd just shaken hers, Lily would have snapped. Nick didn't look like a kid anymore. He looked more like a man now, lanky and stretched, stubble blistering his cheeks and chin like a rash under his purple-green eye. Everything was changing. His grip loosened, but his hands stayed in place, the only warm spot on her body.

"Stop it," he said. How long had it been since he'd looked at her so intently? He wasn't trying to hurt her. It was his boy way of soothing her. She'd broken his glass box. If they were in aquarium tanks, water would flood the street, and slimy sea things would flop in puddles. She forgot about the grocery bags and wrapped her arms around him because he couldn't be bad, not her brother. He wasn't a betta fish after all. She hugged her untouchable teenage brother, breathing in his smell: Irish Spring soap, Head & Shoulders, and sweat. She was done, but when Nick led her toward the house, the screaming feeling came back.

"I'm not going in there," she said. Red bricks hovered over her. The windows stared down like eyes. Esme wanted to throw things at its cold, boxy face. Tears prickled the backs of her eyes. This building had seen everything happen and just kept standing. The blinds in Birdman's apartment flicked, and rage bubbled in her chest. He'd been watching the whole thing.

"I'm not going back in," she said again, convinced.

"Let's take a walk," Nick said. The first tears spilled over. She didn't want to pass the signs with Lily's face on telephone poles, curled up from water and wind, or see people who'd smile sadly and ask if there was any news. She didn't want to be here. She'd light a match if she could and set the whole place on fire just to watch it disappear and fly away like a firebird.

"Why don't you get in, and I'll drive us around?"

Her father's voice startled her. She was trapped between them now, her father and her brother. The building loomed from its hole in the sidewalk. She'd broken one box and created another. Her chest heaved, short, quick breaths that felt like choking.

"We'll go wherever you want." The pleading in Andre's voice made it harder to breathe. Where would she go? She felt panicked with choices.

There was an empty space where Madeline had been. She was probably upstairs, telling her mother everything like a good little snitch. Lava pooled in Esme's chest. Only when Madeline reappeared a few seconds later, she was carrying Esme's dance bag. It looked out of place on Madeline's shoulder, confused. *Don't touch that*, she wanted to scream, but Madeline looked determined. She pushed the bag into Esme's hands and turned to Andre.

"Her class starts at four o'clock. If you leave now, she'll make it." The bag flopped unevenly in Esme's hands, like a dead cat. She hadn't been to class in two weeks. Everyone had pointe shoes. Dance was something she'd done once but couldn't remember anything about.

"Just go." Madeline was not asking. She opened the passenger door and led Esme to it. The seat belt was rough against her neck, sharp. Andre's cab smelled like other people—it always did, a jumble of lingering perfumes and food, crumbs on the floor. Andre sighed and took his place behind the wheel. Nick and Madeline watched them pull away, two small shapes in the side view mirror. Maybe they weren't just worried. Maybe they wanted to go somewhere too. Andre turned right at the stop sign, and they were gone. It was too late now. She didn't want them to come anyway. Without them, she could pretend to be normal again. Her shoulders throbbed where Nick had grabbed her, hard enough to leave a mark. As the road spread the distance between them, she couldn't shake the look on Nick's face, that fading bruise. Esme slumped in her seat, hugging her dance bag like a pillow.

"I'm sorry," she said, and Andre nodded.

"Have some water." He pointed to a bottle in the cup holder. "Your throat must hurt."

The water burned. She was embarrassed now, thinking of the neighbors who'd probably heard and run to their windows, shaking their heads behind vertical blinds and curtains, but her father didn't ask for an explanation. What had it looked like to other people? As the Long Island Expressway rolled past, her anxiety about home was replaced with worry about walking into the studio. She wouldn't know the new stuff. She hadn't practiced, didn't have pointe shoes; her muscles were soft instead of sore. Amelia would think she was lazy, unprepared.

She didn't know if the right things were in her dance bag. *Oh God*, she thought. Lily had sorted the things in this bag. She hugged it closer. She couldn't unpack it now.

"Just turn around," she mumbled, regretting the tone in her voice, addressing him like a passenger with a no-name driver. "What's the point?"

Andre kept driving. He flipped the signal to change lanes and slid to the right. As the car rounded the exit, Esme wasn't sure she could dance even if she wanted to. Her body felt like she'd been buried in sand.

"If you don't want to go in, we'll just watch through the window," he said. He didn't want to go home either. That made her feel better. At least she wasn't the only one.

Andre pulled into the parking lot. There were so many things she hadn't noticed before: the speed bump by the entrance, the hole in the sign above Sal's Pizza, how the line of cars waiting for spots looked like a vein. She hadn't noticed when the geraniums in the flower boxes had changed to purple and green cabbages. Just behind the studio was a tall tree with red leaves. It was no one's tree, forgotten when concrete had been poured to build this busy place. The leaves moved in the breeze. It was pretty but too tall for a tree house. What good was a red tree without a tree house? Esme pushed the thought away. It was a nice story, Nick had said. Maybe that was all it was.

"There it is," Andre said of the studio, as if he was showing her a favorite toy she'd played with when she was a baby and forgotten about. Minivans idled at the curb, blocking the glass windows. The curtains were probably shut anyway. The whole idea of Amelia hiding her studio in a shopping center was ridiculous. What kind of former NYCB star had a studio between a pizza place and a nail salon instead of near Lincoln Center? It felt like a fat, elaborate lie that meant minivans could drop kids off every day, and it didn't matter how good anyone was because they'd be minivan-driving people eventually, towing kids around and telling them how good they were. This was stupid. Coming here was stupid. Worrying about the right kind of tights was stupid. Not being allowed to dance because her bun wasn't in the right place was stupid. Spending so much time in a studio staring at herself in a mirror with a tennis ball between her ankles was stupid. It was another make-believe story, and she was stupid for believing it.

Andre parked and shut off the engine. If she was looking down from a cloud, she would have seen one bumblebee-yellow car and the strange looks people gave the unlit taxi. Andre was quiet for a long time, watching from his own cloud.

"Go ahead," he said quietly. If this had been any other time, he would have been mad for driving all this way if she'd refused to move. Wind swayed the car slightly. "I'll be right here when you're done."

Her hand closed around the door handle. The door opened. Cold air rushed at her face and stung her eyes. It swirled through the car and pushed her toward the studio, toward the red tree. Her bag weighed her right shoulder down. Little quartz pieces in the concrete sparkled in the sun. People chattered around her. *We need eggs. I did Tiffany Blue last time; I want something darker this time. I don't understand him. Ask your mother. The dog's in the car. No garlic knots before dinner.* It twisted together into a weird kind of poem. At least people here were alive and moving and full of things to do that seemed important but weren't. They were happy because they didn't know how dumb it was. *Hey!* she wanted to scream. *Everything's fine until something important is snipped away from your life like a magazine cutout, and then everything you ever did will feel like air, and you can just blow it all away.* She wanted to pretend she was dumb and happy for a little while, so she pushed the studio door open and stepped inside.

The kissing-booth sign was gone. Had that ever happened? Her mother with the sewing basket was a ghost, something she'd imagined. The inside door to the studio was closed. The younger girls were in there.

"And two, three, turn, three, four," Amelia called over the music, clapping when their feet should touch the floor. They were waltzing from one diagonal corner to the other. She couldn't see them but knew exactly what those ten girls in black leotards and pink tights looked like, all evenly spaced and waiting for their turn. Soon they'd stretch, the studio door would open, and they'd find forgotten water bottles, taking long sips with pink faces as Amelia swept the studio, changed tapes if there wasn't a pianist, and relit the grapefruit candle to cover the sweaty smell while older girls in pink tights and black leotards took their place at the barre. They were an infinity band of arms and legs rotating in and out of the studio. Esme leaned against the door. It was cool against her cheek. Just knowing what the next two hours would be made her dizzy with relief.

She wandered into the changing room, stepped out of her sweatpants, and left them on the floor in a heap. She pulled her legs through her tights and felt like Giselle, unburied from a bed of soil in the forest, thankful no one else was here. There weren't any marks on her shoulders now, just soreness where Nick's fingers had been. It still made her squeamish, but she pushed the thought away because he had only been trying to help. She yanked a hairbrush through her hair, raking knots. It was easier to make a bun when her hair hadn't been washed. The painful pull of hair against her scalp felt good. In the mirror, she was skinny and a little duckfooted but Esme again.

Footsteps overhead meant the studio was open. Girls spilled out of class. Shoes were changed, coats and sweatpants thrown over leotards. She stretched in the changing room where it was empty, not ready to see anyone just yet. Seeing people made her skin feel cold and still, like waking up at night and seeing a spider on the pillow. She'd go up eventually, but for now, the blood rushed to her head as she touched her toes and hugged her elbows, swinging gently in an upside-down world.

The footsteps overhead quieted. It was time. She climbed the stairs, unsure of what she'd say to Amelia. *I'm sorry I've been away, but my sister.* No, Amelia already knew. *I promise I'll work hard to catch up.* She would. Maybe she didn't have to say anything. The lobby was empty; the studio was not. Amelia's back was to the door, facing the stereo and changing tapes. Esme took her place at the barre, wishing she could wipe her reflection out of the mirror so she wouldn't be seen. The other girls were stretching, lost in their own world of hamstrings and obliques. She'd been gone, and now she wasn't. She wouldn't say anything at all. The first few notes of Tchaikovsky's Serenade in C started, her favorite. The barre was inward time. That was what she wanted.

Amelia passed by in a breeze of black fabric, smelling like fireplace smoke. She took her place at the front of the barre, modeling for them before drifting away to make corrections. It was the same barre it always was: pliés, slow and fast tendu, slow and fast dégagé, ronds de jambe, fondu and développé, frappé, grand battements. Esme lowered into demi-plié. Did Serenade always have such long, lonely strings? Those first few notes had always been the blue stage lights and diamonds part in her memory. Her muscles warmed. She lowered into grand plié. There was too much tension in her shoulders. She lowered them and lifted her chin. Her knees felt swollen and heavy, pushing her up when she wanted to go down. Amelia's knee brace bulged over her tights, and Esme was sorry for all the mean things she'd thought about her earlier.

She hadn't meant them. Tears prickled behind her eyes, and she wished the music would change to the Waltz Girl part, quicker, lighter, not so sad. If it would just change, she'd feel better, but Tchaikovsky was taking his time, and Amelia was behind her now, her hands on Esme's waist as light as butterflies, assisting Esme into a deeper plié, the kind she could have done on her own two weeks ago when her body was cooperating.

"Welcome back," Amelia whispered, just loud enough for Esme to hear. Amelia's hands moved to Esme's hands, correcting her index finger, then the height of her elbow. She lifted Esme's chin just a little higher, adjusted the tilt of her head. She was glad Amelia was watching her through the mirror instead of looking directly at her. It was safer when it was only mirror Esme. Real Esme was afraid to blink, afraid the tears she was holding back would spill over. It felt good to be corrected, inspected, to have someone look carefully at all the littlest things she was doing and make them perfect again. *You're still here*, Amelia said but didn't say.

Real Esme wanted to undo all the little corrections so Amelia would stay with her and fix them again, but mirror Esme held them perfectly. Amelia moved on to someone else. All the little places she'd touched felt cold now, silvery. *If you can dance through this, you can dance through anything.*

Chapter Seven

Nick's spoon dinged against the cereal bowl, a mix of Frosted Mini-Wheats and Cinnamon Toast Crunch so full it spilled onto the table in milky puddles. His black eye had gone from black blue to purple green to a fading yellow strip, and any trace of the broken boy Esme had nursed a few weeks ago had faded along with it. Being around Nick was like waiting for a stink bomb.

When he wasn't in his room with the door closed or out with Andre at night, he was gone for long, silent hours without a call or a note explaining where he was or when he'd be back. He was already thinner, and the shadows under his cheekbones stood out. He stank like cigarettes, but no one said anything. Lily missing was an excuse for Nick, an opportunity to disappear too. She rolled the word *permission* around in her head. Before, he would have had to ask permission, but now no one cared. It was unfair that Nick could tumbleweed from one hour to the next while she and Madeline were at least trying to follow the same rules as before.

"Where does he even go?" Madeline had said to no one in their dark bedroom one night. Esme hadn't answered. She didn't know.

Madeline stomped into the kitchen, opened and slammed cabinets, looking for nothing in particular. Esme sat across from Nick, legs dangling, watching her brother through a maze of gift baskets wrapped in plastic, wishing today was a talking day for Nick, but it wasn't.

"Where do you go?" Madeline blurted, arms crossed against her chest, bouncing her foot like an angry parent. "I mean, really, why is it OK for you to do whatever you want, and we're just stuck here? Well, maybe not *her*." Madeline stretched the last word and pointed her chin at Esme. "She gets to do whatever stupid dance shit is more important than being here, but what's your deal?"

Nick looked up from his cereal long enough for Esme to realize he wasn't bothered or jabbed in the same way Esme was, face burning, too angry to form a sentence.

Nick shrugged. "No one's holding you hostage."

"Yeah, but it isn't right." Madeline's voice rose and broke into something shrill.

"That's your opinion." Nick slurped the last of his cereal and refilled the bowl.

"What's wrong with you?" She stamped across the room and shoved Nick's shoulder. "What is wrong with you?"

She was screaming now. Nick pushed her hand away, and it hit the table with a thud, tossing his bowl over. Milk spilled off the table and onto the rug, landing soundlessly. Esme got up from the table and stood against the wall. *Like a fire drill at school*, she thought absently. Didn't they all have to line up in the hallway sometimes, abandoning notebooks and pens, sentences half-finished on the page, or was that something she'd imagined from before? The molding cut into her spine. The scream feeling sat in her chest like a pit, but she was stone quiet, too exhausted to do more than shiver inside. In three hours, she could go to dance. She pressed her eyes shut and imagined her legs cocooned in tights, Amelia's cranberry skirt brushing past, the back of someone's bun ahead of her at the barre.

Andre thundered from the bedroom. "Knock it off."

Madeline scratched an angry red line on Nick's arm. Andre pushed between them, stepping in the milk puddle on the floor, but he didn't notice. The table slid.

Cerise crept into the room, barely aware of Andre, Madeline, or Nick. She smelled like the dust and old pond water from the trailer. She was holding papers in her hand, stapled in the top left corner. It could've been someone's test or a failed report card that needed to be signed and returned, but it wasn't. Cerise had rolled into the room as quietly as a dropped ChapStick forgotten on the floor. She was not the ball of energy she used to be, the mom who could stitch swirling bead patterns into a gown while dinner cooked in the kitchen and check homework over her shoulder or stop a fight with one look, all without losing that swirling pattern. Now, even holding papers seemed to take every ounce of effort, worse than when she'd had the flu and disappeared into her bathrobe for a week until she'd emerged again, throwing open windows and scrubbing everything until it was dizzyingly light and hospital clean. No, her mother could crack and scatter into dust and blow away with the wind. It might even make her happier to be gone. Esme stared at her new mom. There wasn't enough glue to piece her back together. Esme curled quietly into herself against the wall, ignoring the pain in her spine where the molding pressed against her bones, and checked the clock again. Three hours. Then the music would start, and her whole head would swim with it.

"Nick, what is this?" Cerise's whisper cut through the room. Everything stilled. The paper in her hand shook slightly.

"What is that?" Andre reached for it, but Cerise snatched it to her chest, then let it fall.

"Nick, what is this?" she asked again. "You weren't in your room."

Nick stared back. The rest of his face had somehow disappeared, and he was only blinking eyes, empty and blank.

"Why did you say you were, Nick?"

"Is this what the police asked you?" Andre picked up the papers and flipped from one to the next. They looked especially fragile in Andre's big hands.

"He lied," Cerise said. "Everything he said isn't true. So what is true, Nick? What is true?"

Cereal dripped onto the floor. It made a soft sound as it landed on the carpet, but no one noticed. It made her stomach sick.

"So maybe he wasn't in his room. What difference does it make? He was here."

"Was he?" Cerise stared at Nick. It struck Esme that he'd once been as small as Lily, too, a bread loaf that'd fit in Cerise's arm. The first and only baby for a little while. He hadn't been disappointing then. He could've been a lot of things. Now, he likely wouldn't be an astronaut or a mathematician or cure cancer or do whatever Cerise had hoped for him. Cerise couldn't hide her disgust. Esme hovered against the wall. What if she couldn't be the dancer? Would her mother look at her like that too?

"I want to hear it from him."

"We don't even know if this is real, Cerise."

"Of course it's real," Cerise snapped. "Yours is fine. Mine is fine."

Andre moved closer to Nick, the only boy. "How do we know they're not just pinning this on him because it's easier that way?"

Nick's knee bounced. The paper was a jumble of up-and-down lines and tiny text.

"I wasn't in my room," Nick mumbled.

"Where were you?"

"On the fire escape."

"Doing what?"

Nick looked away and fumbled with his sleeve, twisting the fabric between his thumb and forefinger until it popped back open again.

"Smoking."

"Smoking," Cerise repeated. There was a time when this would've been bad enough, but now Cerise wanted worse. She was tired and rabid, and Esme could almost feel her mother's angry heart beating in her own chest, so angry it pumped mean cold through her whole body, keeping her as still as a lion waiting in the weeds.

"What else, Nick?"

"That's it. Just smoking."

"What else?"

"Cerise—"

"Stop it, Andre. Just stop! You were here. You were here, and you had no idea—none—what was really going on, and here we are. So stop defending him, and let him speak."

She wasn't just blaming Andre. Esme felt the hot tar hit her too and stick to her skin.

"Nick, every day that passes, every second this gets colder and colder, the less likely, the less . . . if you know something, Nick, even if you were too afraid to say it before, please, Nick, please tell us now." Cerise's voice fell away. She turned her head to the side and looked away from them all, like she couldn't stand the sight of these four people who'd let this happen. Disgust rolled off her in waves. And then it broke.

"I wasn't here," Cerise sobbed. She looked down into her open palm. "Her little head used to fit right here." Cerise wasn't talking to anyone now. "I just want to see her."

Her mother's shirt was on backward. The neckline climbed her mother's throat and dipped in the back, but her mother hadn't noticed. This wasn't Mom. No matter what, even if Lily came home, her mother would never be the same. Esme could never unsee this mom, telling an imaginary baby in her empty hand that she was sorry.

Nick stared at the ceiling. His eyes were red rimmed, but Esme couldn't tell if he was crying or angry. He was somewhere in between, knee bouncing, fist opening and closing at his side, lost in his baggy clothes. Esme wanted to tell him it was OK, but he would've pushed her away. *Alone.* The word floated through her head. He was alone.

"I didn't"—Nick started, and then he flipped—"*do* anything! I was just on the fire escape, and why is it always me? Look at her . . ." Nick pointed at Madeline and rushed on. "She tells Lily that she's the worst baby ever and throws her hissy fits, and no one says anything to her, but me, me, I must've done something, right? Nothing *I* say is true. What would I even do, Mom? What would I even do?"

Nick paced in little circles. He found the cereal bowl on the table and flung it. It smashed somewhere in the living room, and then the front door slammed behind him. He was gone, but the air was still charged where Nick had been. Madeline stared back like a ghost, and for a quick second, Esme hated her for being so mean and blameless.

"C'mon," Andre said softly, stepping toward Cerise. The palm of his hand closed around Cerise's shoulder, ready to lead her away to the couch or the bed. *Put her away*, Esme prayed, *so she'll stop mumbling to no one.*

Cerise pushed his hand from her shoulder. "Don't touch me," she hissed. "This is your fault."

It was a poison-apple bite. There was an odd stillness where Esme's heartbeat had been. Her blood stopped flowing. Her mother hadn't spoken to her, but she had. She should've gotten up that night, put away her textbook, joined Lily in her pillow fort, and told her about the orange thing before the whole thing escalated. But she hadn't, and now the thought of Lily's tipped-back face smiling at her big sister felt like the worst punishment because she'd never deserved any of Lily's I-love-you drawings or best sisters or special kisses because she was not the good person Lily believed her to be. She was just lazy and selfish, and Lily knew that now, wherever she was.

Her father turned to stone.

"You were here, Andre, and what were you doing? A mother always knows," she was babbling now. "I would've known, and we wouldn't be here."

Esme could not take it. She slipped around the side of the room like a shadow. She made a breeze too small to notice but enough to rattle Lily's drawings on the wall. Were they laughing at her? Pointing paper fingers. Madeline had said so many mean things that night, but Esme had not gotten up. Esme had not told Lily the story of the orange thing. Esme had not left her bed when everything had been happening in the living room, too annoyed to do anything but wait until it was over, desperately craving quiet—and now she'd gotten that.

But Lily. "Pretend she's an egg," Cerise had explained on Lily's first night home from the hospital. "She's very delicate." She'd put Lily's head in the crook of Esme's elbow, and Esme had finally understood. An eight-pound caterpillar had stared up at her with milky-blue eyes. Her arms and legs had moved freely, so unlike the stiff limbs on the plastic doll Esme'd practiced with. A real baby was tiny bones and fresh skin, a peach fuzz of warm hair on a soft skull, not blinking doll eyes that never wrinkled or watered. A doll never balled its hands into little fists and screamed. There was room for mistakes with the plastic doll baby, but not with Lily. She'd been as fragile as a seashell, and Esme had only just forgotten.

That same fragility was still there, waiting behind every tantrum. If her baby swing was moving, she'd cry until it stopped. She'd spit her pacifier in and out, crying for it, then pushing it away. That was still Lily.

Once, she'd wanted to play soccer like Madeline, but on her first practice, she'd refused to wear shin guards and had sat in the dirt drawing pictures with a stick until practice had been over. Then soccer was stupid. Or jeans. She would not wear jeans because they squeezed her legs, but tights were OK. And school. She liked preschool mostly, but there were days she would not go. No amount of coaxing could get her out of her pajamas and into her clothes or her hair brushed and teeth cleaned. She would push breakfast off her plate and onto the floor until

Cerise gave up and let her stay home. Lily wanted things her way. There was very little room for anything else.

But she couldn't blame Lily. She was only four.

The door closed behind her. The door between her and her parents was almost magical. Out here, she couldn't be pierced by bitter bullet words. She was Rapunzel. She'd thrown down her hair and been saved. Now she was floating free in the hallway, weightless, like Anna Pavlova on top of her elephant. She held the doorknob so she wouldn't float toward the ceiling. Lily might have felt like this that night, relieved to leave them all behind and wander the hallway, stepping from one carpet square to the next, finally alone and content in her own head. Would this have happened to any other kid, or was it Lily's fault somehow, just by being Lily?

There was a light bulb out in the hallway, and the whole stretch was green gray without it. Before, her father would've fixed it. She would've taken a chair into the hallway and held the new bulb while he unscrewed the old one. Then the new one would pop into place and throw bright light over everything, but that was before. This hallway was a dark lifeless stretch, the kind of a place a child could disappear from.

She walked the hallway in little Lily-size steps, following the old gray rug, and tucked herself into a corner. The row of closed doors stared back.

The door to Mrs. Rodriquez's apartment opened and closed. Mrs. Rodriquez was in her ugly camel coat and slippers again, fumbling with the lock while a bag of trash bulged unevenly at her side, but instead of swooping toward the elevator, she stood stock still and tipped her head toward Esme's door, where her parents were still hurling muffled, angry words at one another.

Another door opened, and another neighbor popped out. Jeannette had her baby strapped to her chest. Its arms and legs dangled like a marionette without a string. The top of its head was covered in a knit yellow hat. Esme couldn't tell if it was a boy or a girl, but it stared at her with wide, blinking eyes, a silent watcher. Its mother turned toward the muffled voices and shook her head slowly from side to side, making big sad eyes at Mrs. Rodriquez.

"What a sin," Jeannette said softly. "No family should have to go through that." She kissed the top of the baby's head, like counting a blessing. Esme curled further into herself, an invisible lump in the hallway.

"She was a beautiful girl," Mrs. Rodriquez said. "Just beautiful. When I think about it, my heart breaks."

"They seem like a nice family too."

"The oldest is a wild one." Mrs. Rodriquez rolled her eyes. "Like my Denny."

Why were they talking about Nick?

"That's what happens with too many kids." Jeannette wrapped her arms around the baby. "I was one of five. My parents were just too tired . . . the things we did . . ." She shook her head and tipped her chin toward Esme's door. "Between that and all those people she had coming and going, it's no surprise. I never liked that business running out of there. God knows who's coming in your home. Our home . . ." Jeannette threw her hands in the air and waved them around like a wild bird. "Once they're in, they're in."

She couldn't be talking about the brides, not the ones with pretty hair and perfect makeup. How could she think they were dangerous? Esme wanted to stand up, to rustle herself so they'd know she was there and stop talking. It would feel good to see their faces turn red in the gray-green light and their eyes dart wildly, trying to figure out how much she'd heard, but she was too stunned to move. How could the same people who'd left sloppy tuna casseroles in glass dishes say these things about her family?

"I don't know what they were thinking." Mrs. Rodriquez sighed. "Letting that little one take the train to Long Island by herself sometimes. Unbelievable. The things that can happen to girls . . ."

Esme froze. Mrs. Rodriquez was supposed to be their friend. She was one of the few places it was safe to eat Halloween candy from without her parents checking it first. Esme had never liked her, and she was probably a witch, but her mother had liked her. She'd even sewed a black lace shawl and a hat with a black web when Mrs. Rodriquez's fat husband had died. Cerise hadn't even let them laugh when she'd told Andre that Mrs. Rodriquez's husband was so big they'd had to nail two coffins together, because it was disrespectful. But Mrs. Rodriquez didn't care about being disrespectful, not here in the hallway where she thought no one could hear.

Shut up, she prayed silently. *Shut up, shut up, shut up.*

"I just hope that little girl gets a second chance," Jeannette said finally.

Something broke in Esme's apartment, something glass. They both froze. The screaming stopped. Esme didn't want to hear any more. She jumped to her feet and slammed against the push bar on the stairwell door, not caring if they finally realized she was there. She ran to the roof, feet pounding on the concrete steps, leaving a trail of echoes in the empty staircase behind her.

The sun was blinding. It turned all the tar lines and silver vents into a blur. The 7 train peeled to a stop behind her. She pushed the door shut and didn't care if she was locked up here. It didn't matter. There was nowhere to go. She wiped at her eyes and flipped into first position, second, third, rounding her way through this week's barre and every piece of choreography she could remember for as long as she'd been dancing until she was warm despite the cold or the clouds over the sun or the fact that there was no music, only notes that echoed in her head, drowning out all the ugly things she could never unhear.

Chapter Eight

"Esme? May I see you for a minute?" Amelia was standing in the doorway, blocking the door. Esme was the last student in the studio again, still practicing the choreography Amelia had taught earlier, a series of chaînés and piqué turns set to Tchaikovsky for summer program auditions in five weeks. The tendon between her neck and shoulder ached. Her left ankle was already swelling, pushing against the ribbon and elastic in her technique shoes.

All she wanted was to run the combination one more time before she packed up and raced through the parking lot to make the train, but now she couldn't. She could run it anyway and make Amelia wait, but she'd miss the 8:35 p.m. train she'd promised her father she wouldn't miss, and she couldn't risk her parents not letting her come back, so she walked duckfooted toward the door, heels thumping in disappointment.

"Why don't I make us tea?" Amelia asked.

"No, that's OK," Esme said, annoyed that Amelia didn't just come out with whatever it was.

"It's a conversation we shouldn't rush, and there's something I'd like you to see." Amelia moved slowly, deliberately, pulling mugs and tea things from her desk with care. The back of Esme's neck tensed as if she'd been cuffed like a bad puppy and carried off to the corner. She'd been back for a week and had done everything Amelia asked. She'd gotten up every morning to do the homework her teachers dropped off, do at least half an hour of Pilates, and practice as much choreography as she could in the living room. She drank disgusting, chalky protein shakes midmorning and afternoon to keep her weight normal even though she weighed eighty pounds every morning, consistently. She was at the studio by 3:30 p.m. every afternoon and danced until 8:15 p.m., only stopping when Amelia closed the studio. Her applications for summer programs were almost done. She hadn't done anything wrong. She could dance through anything.

Amelia filled two mugs with hot water and dropped tea bags in each one. She bobbed them up and down, but rushing the brewing process didn't make Esme feel better about the time. Amelia's face was thin and drawn. She tossed the tea bags into the trash, steadying herself as she passed Esme a mug and sat beside her on the waiting room chairs. *Please don't ask about home*, Esme prayed. *Just tell me I've done well.*

"So." Amelia cradled the mug between her hands. "I have an interesting proposition for you."

Esme glanced at the clock out of habit, unsure what a proposition was.

"I've already spoken to your parents, and they think it's a good opportunity if you're interested. How would you feel about living with me now that you're beginning auditions?"

Esme was stunned. The mug wavered in her hands. She was sure she'd misheard. "Live with you? Here?" It sounded ridiculous.

"Yes," Amelia said simply. "Well, not here at the studio. In my house. You'd have your own room, and we can arrange correspondence classes for school. You wouldn't have to travel every day, and you could use the studio when it's empty."

"My parents are OK with this?" Why didn't they want her at home? It was for dance, but wouldn't they miss her? Losing someone else should have been unbearable. Even her father must have agreed. Esme felt dizzy with choices. Her own room, no school, the studio to herself, a house that wasn't painted with sadness, covered with sympathy cards and hints of what life used to be. She thought of her mother in the trailer, hanging maps and finding new places to contact, new packages of Lily's picture and flyers to send to some new part of the world, something no one had thought of yet. Or Detective Ferrera's list. How could she help if she didn't live there?

"They think it would help you. You'll have to live away from home for most of the summer programs you're applying for. This would be a good test."

Amelia watched her carefully. Esme's gaze flickered to the framed articles and pictures of Amelia dancing. If Amelia were young, considering options most teenagers didn't have, what would she say? When Amelia was eleven, she hadn't known her career would start in five years. Every choice mattered when things happened quickly. Lily wasn't even five. Lily was four, cut free and untethered, floating in space like an astronaut while everyone else tried to figure out what to do next. Did leaving home mean she was giving up? A lump formed in her throat. Esme didn't know what to say.

"Why don't I drive you home? I can show you my house on the way, and you can talk it over with your parents when you're ready."

Her family only used words now when they couldn't be avoided. The thought of talking things over was ridiculous, but Esme didn't say so.

"OK." Esme leaned forward to pick up her bag, forgetting about the tea. It spilled all over her tights. The peppermint smell turned her stomach. Amelia handed her a paper towel. Esme was mortified. She should have been calmer, honored Amelia would offer this and weighing the offer carefully like a real professional. Instead, she felt even younger than eleven years old, afraid she'd miss her room or Madeline sleeping in the next bed, and yet she wanted to see Amelia's house. Esme had read everything about Amelia, watched videotapes of her as the Firebird, Juliet, and Esme's favorite, the Swan Queen, graceful as the feather-white swan and terrifying as the Black Swan. Amelia liked apples and handfuls of almonds, but Esme didn't know anything about Amelia's real life, the one people didn't see.

Esme threw sweatpants over her damp tights. She packed the pointe shoes she wasn't allowed to use yet and spread the tongue of her sneaker, widening the laces to ease her swollen ankle into her shoe, then tightened them fiercely to control the swelling. Amelia waited by the door, arms carefully crossed over her chest.

"I don't live far." The car beeped. It echoed through the parking lot as the headlights flashed. Clouds rolled over the moon, and the air, cold and heavy, tasted like snow. Somewhere in the distance, a dog barked. Esme wondered if Amelia had a dog.

The car smelled like coffee. There was a stain on the dark carpet near Esme's foot, and clothes were scattered in the back seat. Esme was a little disappointed that Amelia's car, world-famous Amelia's car, was so ordinary.

The radio switched on when Amelia turned the key. It wasn't classical music but a talk station. The man on the radio was talking about the weather. Six to ten inches, enough to close school. That would have made her sleep with one eye open before, checking for small serious flakes all night, but that was the Esme before Lily. New Esme didn't care if it snowed or not. If it did, maybe Lily's new family would take her sledding.

A pair of pink ribbons dangled from the rearview mirror, Amelia's first pair of pointe shoes, maybe, or a first performance, but there was no date on the ribbon, so Esme couldn't be sure. It was another of Amelia's secrets.

The road to Amelia's house ran alongside the train tracks Esme took to and from the studio every day. Slowly, the streetlights dwindled until there were only headlights and window lights to guide them. Porch swings swung silently in the darkness. If Nick saw this, he'd say it looked like a neighborhood from *Unsolved Mysteries*. Robert Stack would step out of the shadows where houses disappeared and the woods bloomed to tell them something awful had happened here.

But that was the old Nick. Now, the buzzed parts of his hair were growing back in patches. He never washed his clothes, and the cigarette smell circled him, leaving a trail wherever he'd been. Esme didn't know what he was anymore, but she was relieved when he was not home. When he was, it was hard to look at him, even if he was still her brother, even if she still missed the good things about him, like his jokes, but he'd been cut away from her too. It made another reason Amelia's house would be a relief.

Woodsmoke filtered through the car, making it smell like a fireplace. Perfect houses with gas lanterns threw light over potted plants and wicker furniture. Mailboxes dotted the street. Esme wanted to cry. Real people didn't have fireplaces or live in Christmas-card houses like these, where they couldn't hear other people moving and cooking in the spaces above, below, and beside their own sounds and smells.

"This is it." Amelia pulled into a gravel driveway. It crunched beneath the wheels. Amelia's red-painted house wasn't as big as the others, but electric candles glowed behind lace curtains, and a big evergreen tree grew in the front yard. This house would be beautiful covered in snow. The candles in the windows were so unlike the concrete stoop at home and faded welcome mats in the hallway. Her heart sank. She didn't deserve to live here, not even temporarily.

Esme followed Amelia up the walkway. Keys jingled as Amelia found the right one and placed it in the lock. It only took one key to open the door.

"That's it?" Esme was shocked. Her front door had three locks. "One key opens your whole house?" The woods were dark behind them, empty and thick with silence. Anything could be in there. Anything.

"That's it." Amelia smiled. The front door creaked open. Food was cooking, meat and potatoes. Her stomach rumbled. She pressed her hand against her stomach to quiet it.

"Look around." Amelia dropped the keys on the hall table and hurried to the kitchen. "The bedrooms are upstairs; the living room, dining room, and kitchen are down here. I have to check the Crock-Pot."

What was a Crock-Pot? Exploring on her own was uncomfortable even if Amelia trusted her to. A spoon tapped against a pot. A lid clattered. If she closed her eyes, she could almost pretend the sounds were coming from her mother's kitchen, but that home seemed much farther away than just eleven train stops now. Esme stepped into the living room and ran her hand over the books on the shelf, VHS tapes, a tiny Eiffel Tower, a white spiral seashell the size of Esme's head, and masks, not costume pieces or the Halloween kind but little ones carved from pink stones with eyes, noses, and mouths so boxy they were barely human.

There were also framed pictures of Amelia dancing, not as an adult but as a child and a teenager. Amelia was maybe seven or eight in the youngest picture, dressed in a hot-pink tutu with a diamond-studded leotard and a tiara. She was only in technique shoes and first position but smiling so brightly that Esme knew ballet was her favorite thing. It must have been so hard for her to stand still when all she wanted to do was dance in her beautiful costume.

In another, Amelia was sixteen or seventeen, posed at the barre in leg warmers with a baggy sweatshirt covering most of Amelia's frame. One leg was stretched over the barre. Amelia stared into the mirror, wisps of hair escaping her ponytail and framing her face like a halo. Her reflection stared back, unaware that someone was taking a picture. *I will get you there*, the real Amelia whispered to mirror Amelia, holding a perfect pose. The intensity was so great that years later in Amelia's living room, Esme shivered.

"You must be starving," the real Amelia called from the hallway. "How about some soup?" She'd already set a tray of soup, a plate of crackers, and two water glasses on the coffee table.

Esme found a place beside Amelia, surprised it was OK to eat on a couch as nice as this one. Amelia lifted her spoon and blew on it a little, sending steam in Esme's direction without noticing how carefully Esme's bowl and spoon were balanced. She wouldn't spill anything, not on this nice couch. But Amelia was so relaxed that Esme relaxed too, taking a first spoonful and blowing steam in Amelia's direction. *Let's evaporate*, Esme's steam said to Amelia's. The two mixed together and floated away. Esme's throat tightened. Lily would've liked that one.

"I always try to have something ready when I get home. Does your mom use a slow cooker?"

Esme shook her head.

"They're great," Amelia continued. "All you have to do is set it up in the morning, and it cooks dinner while you're gone."

"It wouldn't start a fire or something?"

"No." Amelia laughed between bites. "It's safe."

Was she really eating here? Red and white flowers chased each other around the rim of the bowl. How could the woman she idolized so much do something as ordinary as eat soup on the couch with her legs tucked beneath her?

"My mom said electric blankets start fires, like Christmas tree lights. That's why we don't have either." That probably sounded too strange, like she was afraid of simple things.

Amelia would change her mind about Esme living here for sure, but Amelia only nodded and said, "That's true."

They ate the rest of their soup in silence, except for when one of their spoons dinged against the bowl. Esme pretended that eating dinner in Amelia's house was normal, that she could do this every night. Esme wondered what her family was eating, if they'd made her a plate and set it aside for when she got home. Madeline might have. Madeline. Could she sleep without Madeline in the next bed? She'd fallen asleep to the sound of her sister breathing every night for as long as she could remember.

"Amelia?" She waited for her to look up. "Would the other girls know I'd be living with you, if I did?"

"Well, it wouldn't be a secret."

"But would they think it's weird?" It would look odd, like she was being favored. But Esme was already the weird one from Queens who took the train and didn't go to the same schools as the others, so maybe it didn't matter. Amelia considered this carefully, placing her bowl on the table and turning her full attention to Esme. Esme wasn't used to being listened to or looked at so carefully. She took nervous sips of water until the glass was empty.

"Lots of students live with their teachers, and no one thinks it's strange, especially if their circumstances make it difficult to focus otherwise."

Esme felt as if someone had pressed a cold finger against the back of her neck. She thought of the dirty dishes and the tiny apartment, headlines with Lily's name and picture all over newsstands, and hoped Amelia didn't think of her as someone who needed a better home.

It was quiet. The candles flickered in the windows. There were real candles on the coffee table. Wax had dripped down the sides and stuck there. She'd made something like that at home once with crayons in a tuna can. They'd baked it in the oven until the wax had melted into one multicolor crayon. It had been a present for Lily's third birthday. She'd loved it.

"Did I ever tell you," Amelia started slowly, "about my accident?"

Esme stilled. Of course she knew about the accident, but she didn't really know. She'd seen the jagged scar, wondered about it, but she'd never asked. And why would Amelia want to tell scrawny Esme, who imagined herself dancing on an elephant in China like Anna Pavlova but hadn't done anything yet?

"I was in a car accident. The details don't matter now, but they told me I'd never dance again and I'd be lucky if I walked without a limp. But Esme"—Amelia shook her head from side to side—"I didn't accept that. So I danced on it anyway, before it was healed. Well, I tried," she said. "But it was broken forever. I knew it the first time I walked into the studio and tried to dance but couldn't. The studio was so quiet, almost like it was waiting for me to realize I didn't belong there anymore."

Amelia paused. "The other driver was drunk, and we went to court. I 'won' enough money to buy this house, but it didn't matter. It felt like

I'd lost my whole life, and I wished, more than anything, that I'd just died in that accident."

Amelia's eyes found Esme's, brown and sad. Esme thought of the teenage girl in the picture on the shelf. That was Amelia before the accident. Intense and focused. This was Amelia after. She'd always known Amelia after.

"Do you understand why I'm telling you this?"

Esme couldn't speak. She knew exactly what it was to live in a shadow of a world that used to be comfortable and safe but wasn't anymore. She nodded.

"Sometimes"—Amelia sighed—"I still dream about dancing, and it feels like I've lost it all over again."

Esme looked at the beat-up toe of her sneaker that was holding her swollen ankle at bay. Lily wasn't gone, not when she could still hear her laughing sometimes, not when all Lily's things were exactly as she'd left them, when Turtley was waiting.

"It gets different," Amelia said softly. "Not necessarily better, but different. You still have the world ahead of you, Esme. I promise."

Esme stared at the masks on the shelf, wishing she could hide behind that smooth, pink stone and look at the world with new eyes. Then she wouldn't feel like she'd caused what had happened because she hadn't even finished a simple story for her little sister, and now she never would.

"Come on," Amelia said, standing. "Let me show you upstairs before it gets too late, and then I'll drive you home."

Esme wiped her eyes with the backs of her hands. It was time to be professional Esme. If she really wanted to live here, she'd have to be.

The stairs to the second floor were dark. It was strange that one person living alone would have a house with two floors. Esme's family only had one. Picture frames lined the steps. Esme wished it were brighter so she could see, curious about Amelia's brothers and sisters, her parents, whoever Amelia loved enough to frame. At the top of the stairs, Amelia flipped the light switch on and pointed to the first bedroom.

"This would be yours." The door creaked open heavily. The room smelled like cedar and emptiness. There was a bed with a wooden frame and a dresser with a lamp and a mirror, all the same honey-colored pine. The windows were covered with long white lace curtains. Esme imagined they'd billow when the window was open. The room was full of space. It wasn't filled with posters on the wall or Madeline's stuff. It had only the things a bedroom needed. Living here would be like living in a magazine room. She wanted to slide beneath the checkerboard quilt and know what the green and lavender squares smelled like, if the blanket felt as soft against her face as it looked, and fall asleep to cricket sounds instead of car horns and bus brakes whooshing past the stop sign on the corner. In the morning, she'd wake up to birds. She didn't know for sure what she'd hear, but she thought she'd burst if she didn't find out.

"OK," she said. "I'd like to live here."

But where do you belong? It was only a little voice, but it chased back the guilt.

Amelia smiled, arms folded over her chest in the doorway, watching Esme the same way Cerise used to watch Lily sleep, like Lily's sleep was restful for her too.

"It's a big decision, Esme. I think you should talk about it with your parents."

It was time to go. Amelia walked downstairs and locked the front door. Candles flickered in the window as the car backed onto the street. Esme didn't want to leave. She wanted to count the candles in the windows. She didn't want to go home and was ashamed to admit it. Her tongue stuck to the roof of her mouth, heavy with the thought of her parents orbiting each other from one room to the next like lost planets, waiting for Lily. This was the wrong thing to feel, so she closed her eyes and imagined the checkerboard quilt, wishing she could trace the pattern with her fingertips until she fell asleep, listening to the sounds of a new house while shadow cars chased each other soundlessly along the ceiling.

Chapter Nine

Esme waved goodbye as Amelia drove away from her building, wishing she was still in the passenger seat. The neighborhood echoed with cold. Sounds escaped closed windows and washed away with the wind: laughter, bottles being dropped in recycling bins, a baby crying. The windows were a blur of blue television glow. Garbage bags stacked on the curb spilled into the gutter. This place was not magical, not compared to Amelia's candlelit windows or the whispering forest across the street.

She squeezed her eyes shut as she passed the teddy bears and dead flowers left on the street, the dark trailer. Soon, she wouldn't live here anymore. She couldn't quite imagine it. She'd always known this address, this phone number, the hallway smell of lemon and bleach, the way the key caught in the door. There wasn't any other home. She took the stairs instead of the elevator. The burn in her legs felt good. It slowed her down, gave her more time to think.

Mom? Dad? Are you sure you don't want me to stay? I can be helpful.

She was, wasn't she? Hadn't she put up flyers and carried things to the trailer and made every list she was supposed to make? Hadn't she always made dinner on her night and done her own laundry on Sundays or helped with Lily or vacuumed or whatever they'd asked her to do? She didn't always want to do it, but that couldn't be enough to send someone away.

Wouldn't she leave another hole in their lives, a paper doll cutout where their Esme used to be? Or was she less somehow, not smart or the first girl like Madeline, proof that they were good parents, or the only boy like Nick, who kept everyone tipsy with nerves? *We love you all just the same and just as much*, Cerise had promised once, but now it wasn't true, not if losing one person brought out so many other lies. She hovered in the hallway, guilt smacked, wondering if she'd betrayed her parents somehow or if they'd betrayed her, sending her away for her own good. This was supposed to be her home, the best place for her, her broken-in shoe. Maybe she wouldn't have to say anything, and they'd bring it up. She'd take a long shower and hide for a little while, then sleep. She held her breath and pushed the door open.

But Detective Ferrera was there. His smell prickled her nose. It wasn't a smell Esme could identify like she could with her father, matching medicine cabinet bottles to the scent on his skin. Being close to Detective Ferrera triggered something as complicated as a smell: hope, fear, anger, sadness, frustration. Feelings Esme could name and ones she couldn't mixed into something she blamed on him.

He was standing very still in the living room, hands folded over the bottom of his stomach. His badge was clipped to his belt. Esme wished the tarnished silver numbers matched their phone number or address or someone's birthday, a sign that this would be OK, but they didn't. Whatever she'd planned to say about living with Amelia stuck to the roof of her mouth. He was wearing a suit. He smiled sadly when he saw her. Suits meant bad news.

"There's no easy way to say this." He sighed. "But at this point, we have no further leads. Anthony Santos has an alibi. No one saw Lily leave the building, and no one's seen her since."

A cup of coffee sat on the table, untouched. An oily sheen floated on top, changing colors in the light as Detective Ferrera spoke.

Cerise was in her forget-me-not-blue bathrobe, an ice pack pressed to the back of her neck for the same headache she'd had yesterday. They were all in pajamas, and it didn't matter. Esme's dance bag slid to the floor.

"What about the psychic?" Cerise leaned forward as if she might latch on to him but stopped. "Maybe there's something in there to . . ." Her voice trailed off. Her fingers curled around the sleeve of her bathrobe, lost in the thick terry cloth.

Detective Ferrera's right foot turned toward the door. In dance, the direction of Esme's feet always determined where her body would go. His foot was a clue. He didn't want to help them anymore. Or couldn't. Esme's mouth felt dry. Was it over? Her body was heavy enough to sink through the floor.

"It isn't concrete enough." The lines around his eyes softened. "Even if it was, we don't have evidence to substantiate her opinion."

"So what you're saying is there's nothing else you can do?" Andre pressed his fist to his chest as if he were holding his heart inside.

"For now," Detective Ferrera said. "If anything changes, call me right away. If we hear anything, we'll do the same. I'll send the case file over. Go through it. Something might click that didn't before."

"What are we supposed to do?" Cerise's voice broke in the middle. Andre peeled his fist from his chest to let it rest on her shoulder. She pushed it away. "Just pretend she never existed? Give up? There has to be something else." She looked between Detective Ferrera and Andre, begging. "What else is there? Just tell us, and we'll do it."

She was crying now, slow tears that beaded on her collar. Detective Ferrera sighed and stared at the floor. Madeline picked at her cuticles, peeling away bits of white skin and letting them fall. Nick's foot kicked against the bottom of the couch. His eyes met Esme's across the room, an invisible bridge. This felt final.

"You could hire a private investigator. They have time and resources we don't. I can give you a name." He fished a card from his pocket and handed it to her father. The glossy letters held the light. No one moved. Staying still would make the bad news go away like a seeker in hide-and-seek.

"Think it over," Detective Ferrera said. "We'll be in touch if anything changes."

He let himself out, footsteps echoing down the hall.

"We'll be in touch." Cerise laughed, a thick, bitter sound that caught in the back of her throat. "Like it's poker night. And you." She rounded on Andre. "You're letting him leave?"

Andre looked young, small. "Why don't you lie down?" he suggested quietly. Cerise threw the ice pack. It hit the wall near Esme's head and landed with a thud, waterdrops flying.

"I'm done lying down." She grabbed the card from Andre's hand and stomped across the room, slamming the bedroom door behind her. The lock clicked. Cerise punched the phone number so hard they could hear it through the door. Esme stared at the carpet. She didn't want to look at her father, hands hanging at his sides, or the drawings under the window, Lily's thick crayon marks already fading.

She dug her nail into the tender skin between her pointer and thumb to see if it hurt, but it didn't. She didn't know what to do, so she curled up on the couch with a blanket, tucking her head underneath to breathe into the warm space. Her father knocked on his own bedroom door, begging Cerise to open it, but Cerise was already involved in a muffled conversation with someone on the other end of the line.

The couch shifted, and Madeline's feet worked their way under the blanket. They were cold on Esme's leg, but she didn't mind. She listened to the noise outside the blanket, pretending it was a TV channel she could change if she didn't want to watch anymore.

I have a sister named Lily, she thought. *She's four years old. When she grows up, she wants to be one of Santa's helpers, and if she can't do that, she wants to be the Tooth Fairy's assistant. When no one's watching, she climbs to the freezer and fills bowls of ice cream. She likes clothes that don't match. Her favorite is a royal-blue-and-teal-striped skirt because she likes the way it circles when she twirls. Without Lily, I'm the youngest, the cookie part of the Oreo. With Lily, I'm the cream, and she is the cookie. She was born in September on the first day of school. Lily was pale when she was born, like the inside of a flower. That's how you got your name, Lily.*

What would Anna Pavlova do? She would just find another way. That was what she always did. Rigid feet, make a new shoe. Make your own company. Make your own ballet. Hide away in a country house with a pond full of swans and a secret husband.

It's sad because you're here, Anna Pavlova whispered. *And things aren't the same anymore . . . but if you just left . . .*

Amelia's house was waiting; she could make a new life. But she couldn't make a new sister. That was just impossible.

~

The house was smoky. Esme opened her eyes and realized she'd been dreaming of smoke, of a fire that had started at the foot of her bed, jumped to the *Saved by the Bell* poster on the wall, then Madeline's bed, but there were no flames now, only the faint smell of cigarettes and Madeline's glassy eyes in the darkness.

"Did you hear something?" Madeline said.

"No." The clock blinked midnight.

"I heard the front door." Madeline kicked free from the blanket. "And someone closed our window."

She threw it open again. Cold, fresh air circled the room. Outside, the air was wet with snow. Thousands of tiny flakes drifted past the streetlight. The quiet part of a symphony. Esme tried to follow the same flake but lost it every time.

The living room shook. Her father. Soon he was a shadowy outline in their doorway, looking from Esme to Madeline. It occurred to Esme slowly that somehow she'd moved from the couch to her bedroom without knowing it.

"Your mother's not in here?"

"Why would she be?" Madeline crawled beneath her covers again. Andre lingered in the doorway. It made Esme sad to ignore him too.

"We thought we heard the door before. Maybe she went out."

Her father's face shifted from worried to determined. He crossed the living room, and Esme followed, watching as he put one arm through each coat sleeve and stepped into his boots. His pajama pants looked funny beneath his coat. The door slammed shut behind him.

The house was quiet. The clock ticked on the wall. But the quiet didn't last long. Through the window, Esme saw Cerise in her bathrobe and slippers, hair wet with snow, collecting teddy bears and flowers, Bibles and balloons, candles, some lit and others out cold, and shoving them into a black trash bag with a hole at the bottom.

Cerise threw a candle into the trash. The bag dragged behind her in the streetlight.

"Stop it!" Her father was trying to keep his voice low, but it came out loud. Lights clicked on in other apartments. Cerise dropped a candle in a glass jar, and it shattered in the snow. Andre reached for a pink teddy bear with a white stomach and put it with things Cerise hadn't touched yet. She kicked it. It landed on its side. Cerise stopped trying to stuff things into the bag and threw them instead. They landed on the street, on parked cars, setting off a car alarm and flashing lights. In a few hours, the plows would come and push broken things into a pile of snow. No one would know they were for Lily.

The last of the candles made shadows on the snow. Andre sat with his head on his knees. His back was shaking. Her father was crying. She'd never seen him cry, not ever. The sounds he made were horrible, a broken machine. Esme hated her father like this. Part of her was disgusted that he couldn't be the person he had been before he was her dad, the one who walked into boxing rings without being afraid. Cerise carried what was left of the bag to the trash can on the corner.

Her parents were dollhouse small on the street below. She watched them break separately, and for the first time in her life, Esme imagined her parents apart. She'd seen people who used to be married but weren't anymore sitting alone in church, hanging back to kneel on church pews during Communion because they'd broken a sacrament. It was an old rule, and not everyone followed it, but her mother would. The thought of her mother folded onto a kneeler while that slow line wandered to the altar without her made Esme unspeakably sad. How many times could God punish a person?

And her father—what would he be without her mother? He didn't eat or sleep or wake up without Cerise prompting. *Andre, it's time for dinner. Andre, you should get some rest. Andre, the toilet's leaking,* or *We're out of milk,* or *You have work in an hour. When's the last time you spoke to your son?* Her mother's voice must be a running script in her father's head, an echoing conscience that left little room for his own thoughts. Without Cerise, her father reminded her of a bath toy left in the tub, floating aimlessly while the water got cold around him.

"She isn't coming back," Madeline whispered, sliding in quietly beside Esme, eyes wide. "She isn't coming back."

Esme pressed her eyes shut. Goose bumps prickled her skin. "That's not true."

They were both shivering. Her parents disappeared from the window. The street was empty.

"Why did I say what I said?" Madeline sobbed. "Why did I say those things?"

The bag on the living room wall billowed, but Madeline's eyes darted to everything as it'd been that night before she slammed the bathroom door and washed her hair and shaved her legs while Lily disappeared. Esme said nothing.

Madeline picked up one of Lily's books and stared at the cover, where three pigs sat on a bus bench. "I should've read to her more. She always asked, and I always said no."

Madeline's eyes glazed, face red, nose running, a baby version of her teenage self. It made Esme sick. *Stop it. Everyone just stop.*

She led Madeline to their room and closed the door. "Lie down," she whispered, wrapping a blanket around her sister.

Madeline shivered beneath her blanket. "I'm sorry," Madeline sobbed.

Esme could not bring herself to say it was OK. She stared at the ceiling, careful not to look at her sister, and tried not to think about the things Cerise had thrown away. The sidewalk was a kind of altar where people kept hope, but now it was gone. She prayed that the tree house and the red tree and the prisms were real. It was a kind of heaven she could imagine, where Lily was safe and still Lily even if they called her Elizabeth. Maybe she even liked it better there. If it was really so bad, wouldn't Lily call home and ask to be picked up? Maybe Lily was OK wherever she was.

Could she leave too? She didn't want to admit how much she wanted to live with Amelia. But if Nick was lying and her parents were broken, then who did Madeline have? It wasn't supposed to be that way either. Madeline was supposed to go to college and leave Esme and Lily behind, and they were supposed to count the days until they could finally, finally slide their stuff to Madeline's side of the room, take down her posters, and turn Madeline's bed into a couch for their friends. The thought of Madeline alone in their room made Esme as sad as watching her parents through the window. Everything was wrong. Little sisters weren't supposed to leave first.

Hours later, Madeline's sobbing had stopped, but she was still awake. Esme knew it the same way she always knew when Lily had been in her drawers, even if nothing was out of place.

"Madeline?" She almost wished her sister wouldn't answer, but Madeline's muffled voice swam through the blankets.

"Yeah?"

"Do you think Nick's lying?"

It was quiet for a long time. She waited for Madeline to say something like *I don't know* or *of course not*, but her sister was silent. The blankets rustled. Madeline sighed, and it filled Esme with a push-and-pull feeling in her chest so strong it made her sit up and wrap the covers around her.

"Do you remember what Detective Ferrera said about people doing things to help because they feel bad about something?"

"Yes, but what does that have to do with anything?"

"Maybe that's why Nick's out every night with Dad." Madeline's words were measured, unsure how much to feed Esme before she'd spit it out. Her voice was still hoarse from crying, but there was an edge to it now, unlike the broken thing it had been before.

"Maybe he's out because he loves Lily and wants to help."

Madeline laughed in the darkness. It sent a shiver through Esme's bones. "Yeah, OK." Her sarcasm called Esme an idiot. Esme's hand balled into a fist, and she punched it against the bed. "Just think about it, Esme. When's the last time Nick did anything because he wanted to help? Something Mom and Dad didn't force him to do. I bet you won't think of anything because I can't think of one thing. So there's that.

"That's the problem with you, Esme. You're so deep in la-la land all the time. The only reason you're not pissed and angry about all of this is because you probably believe everything that fucked-up psychic said, but that's stupid, Esme."

"That's not—" Esme started.

"It is true," Madeline cut in. "You're delusional. It was cute, I guess, when you made up stupid stories for Lily, but it's insane to actually believe them. The irony is . . ." Madeline made a dry, huffy sound. "You'll probably be just fine because you can't see it, and the rest of us will go crazy."

Esme felt stung. Madeline's words leaked through her. What couldn't she see? Lily's not being here was bad, of course. Just the thought of it gave her a cold, shivery feeling on the inside, and Esme couldn't go near it. She just couldn't.

Esme's head pounded. When Madeline finally spoke again, her voice was softer. Madeline rolled over, putting her back between them like a wall. "It's probably better that way. Don't let me ruin your delusional world."

Esme pressed her eyes closed and replayed all the nasty things Madeline had said sentence by sentence, floating each one away on a newspaper boat, but the loneliness stuck. She wished she could float away, too, but she was stuck on the same bed and the same room she'd slept in for her entire life. Neither felt like home.

"You should watch what you say," Esme said finally, hovering on the edge of tears, braver with the promise of Amelia's house waiting for her. "Just in case your bitchy words are the last thing someone hears." She stomped out of their room dragging her blankets behind her, hating her sister in that moment.

She wandered into her mother's room, wishing she could curl up beside her. The door was closed but open enough for a triangle of light to fall over the foot of the bed. Her mother was sleeping, a single, uneven heap beneath the comforter. There was a new bottle of pills on the nightstand, an orange bottle with a childproof lid covered in red and yellow flags. A glass of water sat beside it.

Her mother should've rolled over and asked what was wrong in her half-asleep whisper. She could always feel them standing there somehow, but not tonight. Esme sat on the foot of the bed and pulled her knees to her chest, imagining the checkerboard pattern on Amelia's quilt, the smell of lavender, dinner cooking in the kitchen downstairs, wishing she could bring those things here to make it feel like home again, but she couldn't. She could only bring herself there instead. The thought rolled through her, and the relief was so overwhelming it carried Esme back to her hostile room, where she counted every ballet she could think of until she drifted off to sleep in the only bed she'd ever slept in.

~

In the morning, the world was white snow. It'd blown through the open window and covered her dresser in watery patches that dripped onto her bed. The whole room was crying, melting in puddles. She closed her eyes and pretended she was watching through a watery world, where laundry floated on the floor like limp fish stabbed by rays of sunlight. It was peaceful to watch her world instead of live in it. Would living with Amelia feel like this too?

The sound of her feet on the floor surprised her. Energy dangled in her fingertips.

"This isn't about boxing." Cerise's voice was a harsh whisper on the other side of the door. "This is not the same thing."

Esme held her breath. They were talking about her. She could feel it.

"It's not?" It wasn't a question, at least not the kind her father expected an answer to, and yet he sounded so sad. She'd heard the story a million times: how he'd been training to debut at Sunnyside Gardens, but he'd just met Cerise, and she'd begged him not to fight. He'd been so in love, so awestruck, that he'd thrown down his gloves and walked out just to make her happy. There was a Wendy's where the arena used to be. He pointed it out every time they passed it.

She'd never seen her father box but imagined he wasn't the type to throw the first punch. No, he'd bounce from foot to foot, dodging blows until the other person was tired; then he'd strike and end the whole thing quickly. She couldn't prove it, but she'd seen him like that with her mother, dodging, sidestepping, watching with quiet intention until he found his window and the whole thing had run its course.

"Not her too." Cerise's voice was a broken, muffled whisper. Esme knew her mother was biting her nails, an old habit. "You can't take her away from me too."

"But you will lose her, Cerise," Andre said softly. "Just not in the way you're thinking."

But they weren't losing her. She would only be at Amelia's house, but the weight of it hung in the room like the ice outside the window. It didn't make sense. Living with Amelia should've been her mother's idea. Her father probably knew she was on the other side of the door. He wanted her to know. It made everything clearer.

She opened the door without looking at her parents because it was too sad, so she talked to their two hunched shapes at the table instead.

"Mom and Dad." She took a deep breath and drew another line between them. "I want to live with Amelia."

Chapter Ten

On Esme's first night at Amelia's house, she hovered at the top of the stairs, listening to the hum of the TV, deliberating over how to say good night. Should she go downstairs, or was it OK to yell from upstairs? She rubbed her thumb over the smooth wood of the banister. "Good night!" Her voice echoed in the new space. She closed the bedroom door behind her, embarrassed. Maybe when two unrelated people lived together, they didn't have to say good night at all.

It was Sunday night. At home before Lily had gone missing, they would've watched *Touched by an Angel*, except Nick, because angels coming down from heaven and impersonating humans just to help them didn't make sense. He was probably right. If there were angels, now would be a good time to help her family. Her pajamas dragged along the hardwood floor instead of the worn white carpet at home. They looked out of place here. She wondered who Roma Downey was helping this week.

Her suitcase, the one her mother kept in her bedroom closet stuffed with old clothes, was worn and faded next to Esme's new bed. Esme wondered if it was excited to be on a journey or if it missed the top of the closet and all the familiar clothes and smells. Soon it would be shoved in a closet again, where it could talk to unworn shoes and forgotten eighties clothes about what it had seen. Lily would've liked a talking, bragging suitcase. Esme pushed the thought away and decided to read instead.

She had the Chronicles of Narnia, but Madeline said the only one worth reading was *The Lion, the Witch, and the Wardrobe*. The thought of her sister made her mouth taste sour. They hadn't even said goodbye before she'd left. She peeled the bedspread back into a triangle and ran her hand over the green and pink flowers on the flannel sheet, her new grown-up bed.

It was a stupid book, but it distracted her from the lavender-scented sheets, unusually soft against her cold feet, or how for the first time in her life, Madeline wasn't in the bed next to hers. She'd never once fallen asleep in an empty room. It should have been wonderful, but it felt lonely instead. Esme fought the urge to tiptoe down the hall to call home. *It's only your first night*, Nick would snicker. Was that better or worse than her father telling her she'd be fine or that he could pick her up if she wanted? She closed her eyes and imagined Lily was tucked into the space beside Esme, warm as a potato in her slipper-feet pajamas.

"Lily?" Esme whispered. "I'm scared."

"It's OK," Imaginary Lily whispered back. "It goes away."

Before Esme could ask how she knew, Imaginary Lily had vanished too.

She tried reading again, but the story was about four bored brothers and sisters. She slid it under the bed. That was too familiar and also not, something she remembered but couldn't relate to anymore. Downstairs, laugh tracks and Helen Hunt's voice whirled through the house. Real houses were supposed to be quieter. Sounds stayed in one room instead of traveling everywhere, changing shape as they went, but that wasn't true after all. Amelia was quieter than her family, but Esme didn't know what it sounded like when she shuffled to bed at night or tossed her feet over the side of the bed in the morning, whether she wore slippers, what it sounded like when she made coffee. She would learn eventually, just like everything else.

When she still couldn't sleep, she tiptoed to the closet. It was stupid, but she didn't want Amelia to know she wasn't sleeping. It wasn't something a serious student would do. Sleep was just as valuable as waking time. Her brain would process what she'd learned that day, organizing it into categories as tidy as moving boxes while her muscles healed and cells rebuilt, but the closet had been staring at her all night through its slanted wooden door and made her feel uneasy.

Even without opening the bulging garment bags inside, Esme knew they were costumes. She glanced at her bedroom door before unzipping the first bag. The pale-pink bodice was crisscrossed with beige ribbon. The sleeves puffed, and the skirt was long and mauve, longer in the back than the front. Aurora. Esme tried not to squeal as she unzipped one bag after the next. Juliet. Odette. Odile. The Sugar Plum Fairy. But it was the Firebird that intrigued Esme most. Amelia was famous for the Firebird, but it was shoved in the back of the closet.

The tulle was coarse under her fingers, and the whole thing was heavier than she'd expected. Beads swirled over the bodice like flames. The audience would only see a glimmer of this beautiful costume as fleeting as the Firebird herself. Before she could stop herself, she'd slipped out of her pajamas and into the costume. It was too big. She pinched the shoulders to hold it up in the mirror, disappointed by the messy-haired girl in dress-up clothes staring back at her. Her pajamas were curled on the floor like shed skin. She rose into dancer's pose and imagined it hugging her waist and chest. If. If she grew enough. If she was just the right size.

The TV clicked off downstairs. Esme slipped the costume back on the hanger and slid the garment bag into place. Next time, she'd try on the feather headpiece, full of hot-red-and-orange feathers. She'd look more like the real thing then. Her mother would have loved all that beadwork, but she wouldn't see these costumes. Esme felt guilty for sneaking through Amelia's things as she crawled back into bed, for not sharing something her mother would have loved, but it was a secret treasure, the kind she always hoped to find in dreams about secret doors that led to rooms with miniature carousels and Ferris wheels, secret attics with train sets above her head, only these costumes were real. She could look at them whenever she wanted.

Outside her window, a dog barked. Amelia climbed the stairs, heels thudding against the wood floor. Even though the room smelled like lavender and the pillow under her head was flatter than she was used to, Esme fell asleep counting details on the Firebird costume, the swirling beads as magical as counting stars.

～

Esme slipped her foot into her first pointe shoe. It closed around her foot like a second skin. She wiggled her toes inside the box. They didn't move as much as they would in her technique shoes, and she wasn't used to the extra weight, but Amelia said they were just right. She tied her ribbons and adjusted the elastic, smoothing the wrinkles in her tights. Her first few steps to the barre took extra thought, but then she was in first position, second, rounding her way through positions she knew so well but that felt new again with pointe shoes. She remembered suddenly Lily's first steps, holding Cerise's index fingers as she'd taken her tiny steps on wobbly feet. Esme's hands tightened a little on the barre. She checked the mirror for Imaginary Lily, but it was empty except for Amelia and her own reflection, which was a little more serious than usual now that she was focusing so intently.

"Ready?" Amelia asked. The first few notes of "Clair de Lune" started behind her. "Start in second, and roll very slowly into relevé."

Esme closed her eyes and placed her fingers on the barre for support. Shouldn't her father be filming like he did for special occasions, that boxy camera pressed into his shoulder, face scrunched behind the eyepiece? She was not used to doing special things alone, but the wood was there beneath her fingertips, cool and reassuring.

She rolled into relevé, muscles stretching, feeling the pressure on her toes from the box. How long had she hoped for this moment? She fought back the urge to smile and look down at her feet, but when she opened her eyes in the mirror, she was smiling—the happiest one she could remember in a long time now.

Amelia adjusted Esme's core, pressing down gently on her shoulders.

"Relax," she said softly. "And then let's do it again."

She lowered herself to the ground again, but inside, Esme was still floating, hovering above the ground by only a few extra satin inches, enough to make her feel new and alive again, as if she'd lifted herself over the same fog that floated above her Golden Gate Bridge and could see the sun again, shining and shimmering just for her.

~

"I have a surprise for you." Amelia flipped an omelet. It landed perfectly in the middle of the pan. Sunlight poured through the kitchen windows, especially bright against the snow outside. Seeing Amelia in anything but dance clothes was weird, but Amelia looked so comfortable in her gray sweatpants, and her hair was in the same braid as always, only little wisps escaped from sleep. Everything about the round white plates and the mug of spicy chai tea and the half-melted real candles on the table was new and exciting, as exciting as the costumes in the closet. She wondered how she'd managed to sleep at all.

"What is it?" Esme looked up from her tea, mouth ringing from the peppercorn and ginger floating in her cup.

"Well." Amelia slid the omelet onto a plate and cut it in two, sprinkling green stuff over the top, a half smile settling over her mouth. "It's *Nutcracker* season, but a few friends of mine are rehearsing *Serenade* for a private performance, and I thought you'd like to see it."

"Really?" Esme tried not to squeal. She'd only ever seen videotapes from the library. What would it feel like to watch that blue light fall over those diamond girls? All these new things made Esme's brain turn over in a way it didn't usually. Maybe it had happened to Balanchine when he'd first come to America, and that was why *Serenade* was so good.

"Mm-hmm. We can go this afternoon. It's a dress rehearsal. We'll be the only ones in the theater, and there's someone I'd like you to meet."

"Who?" Esme asked. Amelia had only been sixteen when she'd joined the New York City Ballet as a corps member. It was hard to believe Esme was only five years away from the beginning of Amelia's dance career.

"Paul Katzman, a choreographer. He's part of the judging panel for NYCB summer students this year."

"Oh," Esme said, mildly disappointed that Paul and NYCB were here in New York. She wanted to be farther away.

Amelia handed Esme her breakfast. Steam rose off the omelet next to a pile of mixed greens and sliced cherry tomatoes. This was fancy restaurant food. She couldn't remember not scooping her food from a big bowl her mother set out for everyone. This was the first time someone had made a plate with everything on it just for her. It was too perfect to touch.

At home, Madeline and Nick would be pouring cereal from a box and splashing milk over it. Why did she get to be here? And Lily. Did she have nice breakfasts in her new house? Someone who hung prisms in windows and built a tree house must make nice things. She hoped it was pancakes for Lily, the kind she loved with melted sprinkles inside so it looked like tie-dye.

"He's very well connected. He used to dance in San Francisco and does some work in Boston. I'll give you some info to read about him before we go. You should always know who you're meeting, especially when they can be helpful to you."

"Eat," Amelia urged.

Esme pushed away the lump in her throat. On Friday, she'd go home for two nights, but she had a whole week before that happened.

After breakfast, she showered, surprised there were only two shampoo bottles on the bathtub ledge, and changed. It wasn't an audition, but wearing a black leotard and pink tights felt appropriate, especially because she hadn't brought any nice clothes, and this was a ballet thing. She was fussing with her bun in the hallway mirror when Amelia walked in, heels tapping on the hardwood floor.

"Oh." Amelia stifled a smile.

The bobby pins pressed between Esme's lips tasted especially metallic. She didn't want to tell her she didn't have anything nice to wear, but Amelia was already rummaging through the closet. Esme finished her bun, pushing away how stupid she felt next to Amelia in her wool pants and leather boots.

"Here." She slipped a pale-gray sweater over Esme's head, adjusting the turtleneck so it draped in pretty layers. It was too big, but Amelia wrapped a brown braided belt around Esme's waist, and when she was finished, it looked like a dress.

"That works," Amelia said, stepping back to admire Esme. "It's cashmere. I shrunk it by accident, but I loved that sweater. Soft, right?"

Esme nodded, fighting the urge to snuggle into it. In the mirror, she looked like a mini grown-up. She felt like one, too, living here, going to the city to see a real company rehearse.

On the train, Esme skimmed Paul's history while a cat in a carrier hissed and scratched against its plastic walls. Its owner whispered soothing sounds. Paul had danced in San Francisco and Boston, organized dance festivals in Saratoga Springs and Prague. Esme wasn't sure where Prague was, but she knew all about San Francisco.

The theater was somewhere in Manhattan. The city was whirling. The rights and lefts were impossible to follow. People hovered next to buildings with cigarettes, pushed past with shopping bags, carrying children, walking dogs on leashes, while new smells came and faded: sugared nuts, salted pretzels, the faint scent of a fireplace, oil on a cooking grill, exhaust from idling cars. She looked at the smallest New Yorkers under heavy hats and hoods, walking hand in hand with their parents, hoping to spot Lily's brown eyes under her web of lashes and bangs, but she didn't. The usual disappointment worked its way between her thoughts and footsteps down the crowded sidewalk.

And for the first time, Esme wondered if those kids belonged with those grown-ups. How would she know if they didn't? How would anyone know by passing someone on the sidewalk if the little girl they were with wasn't really named Elizabeth after all and was really someone else? She looked up at Amelia, who was and wasn't really her own grown-up, and felt panicked for Lily, who was too little to make sense of any of it, especially if Esme couldn't.

"We're here." Amelia pushed open an unmarked door on the side of a building. It wasn't the kind of theater Esme had expected, in the circle of Lincoln Center or on Broadway with glittering lights and fancy signs, but this was for a private performance, so maybe things were different.

They found seats in the middle of the theater. Amelia waved at someone she knew. The stage was a mess of dancers stretching and talking, sipping coffee, sewing ribbons on pointe shoes. Others kicked the boxes of their shoes against the stage, slipping back to the wings for more rosin. Some practiced. The theater lights dimmed and rose, tracing broken patterns on the stage until the entire theater was bathed in blue light. Even Esme's hands were underwater blue.

The orchestra tuned strings and chords. The splashes of noise were comforting. The whole theater was charged in a way Esme couldn't have imagined from the videos she'd watched at home. The dancers wore plain white leotards and long white tutus. The simplicity of it wasn't as exciting as the sparkles and glittery fabrics her mother had made for her. No one wore those things anywhere but onstage, which made it more special to wear a costume at all.

"Places." Someone clapped. Esme searched the theater for the voice and found it in a tall, balding man dressed in a fitted black T-shirt and pants.

"That's Paul," Amelia whispered. He walked with his shoulders squared, ready to lift someone at any moment. His face was all angles, sharp cheekbones, and a once-broken nose. He reminded Esme of the Brawny paper towel man. His voice was so soft Esme couldn't hear the instructions he gave his dancers, but she wouldn't be nervous if he was judging her audition. If anything, he felt safe.

Dancers found their places, whispering last-minute instructions to each other. The lights dimmed. The corps formed two perfect diamonds, touching at the center. As the music started in long, slow strings, their right arms lifted toward stage right, where the lights were brightest. Esme wanted to shield her eyes like they did, brushing a palm against her temple gently, carrying that beautiful light to her face and letting it rest there like a kiss.

Esme mimicked the first few movements, imperceptibly repositioning her fingers as dancers moved on- and offstage. Soloists traced patterns between Balanchine's lines, every movement light and quick as air with Tchaikovsky's strings. Each dancer blended into the next in a blur of blue-lit tulle. She was spying on a secret world of women, not swans or mythical things, just beautiful women. The Waltz Girl was light and quick, impossible not to watch as she flitted between groups onstage, sharing a secret with Esme. Every off-centered geometric pattern, every movement was tracing a message for her on the stage floor. *You're one of us. This is where you belong.*

The men walked lightly, every muscle a ropy knot beneath their tights. These men wouldn't scream at the TV on Sunday during football season or sprawl on the couch, a mess of limbs and baggy clothes, blasting the Beastie Boys. These men accentuated everything the women did, stretching their legs longer and lending extra balance without any eye rolling or teasing, but it still felt like they'd intruded somehow, like they didn't belong with all those beautiful women.

And then the Waltz Girl fell over and over again. She fell until she couldn't get up, and her lover was led away with covered eyes. The men carried her away into the blinding light. The Waltz Girl leaned back, arms stretched above her head, reaching away from the light, but it found her anyway. Everyone followed behind like at a funeral, but there was one dancer in the back, head bowed, arms outstretched before her, who made something stop in Esme. She was the left-behind one, following like a rag doll, the Waltz Girl's only friend.

The stage and dancers were now a black spot. The music that was supposed to echo in her bones was gone. She pressed her eyes closed. Where were the flashes of white tulle turned blue, flowing and sweeping behind a trail of gracefulness? It was just over. The show was over, but worse than that, all the dancers would go home. The orchestra and Paul would go home. The message they'd been trying to spell out for her onstage would be wiped away before she knew what it meant.

Amelia watched her carefully. She could feel it in the darkness. It was hard to breathe. What had they said, those women in the trailer, about bloodhounds catching the scent of kids being carried off? It haunted her now. The Waltz Girl so willingly falling and being picked up, carried off to nowhere.

"What did you think?" Amelia asked. Her perfume was suddenly nauseating. Backstage the Waltz Girl was changing and laughing and doing whatever she did after a show, and it all felt false. That wasn't how it worked.

"Hey?" Amelia leaned closer, bringing that stinky perfume with her. "Are you all right?"

"I'm gonna be sick." Esme ran, her legs suddenly alive. She wanted to outrun Amelia's sweater. The borrowed belt cut into her waist and made it hard to breathe. She found a bathroom and forced her way in, ignoring the men's sign on the door, vaguely aware of footsteps behind her. She retched. The air around her was sour. Old air. Someone opened a window, and new air flooded in. Her eyes watered. There was no tree house or red tree or prisms in the window. That was all make-believe, just like the show.

Someone knocked on the bathroom stall. She hadn't locked it. It swung open, but Amelia stayed outside.

Esme wiped her eyes with Amelia's sweater. She choked back a sob. "What does it mean?"

"The show?"

"Were they supposed to be some kind of angels carrying her away?"

Outside the door, Amelia sighed. The lines between the tiles were cracked and gray. There was nothing pretty about it, but it held the floor together.

Esme wrapped her arms around herself. What held her together? "That's why the light is all blue, isn't it? Because they carried her into the sky. But why did they pick her? Why did it have to be her?"

"Oh, Esme . . ." Amelia paused, choosing words carefully. "That's the whole thing about Balanchine. His choreography isn't supposed to have meaning. He said once that *Serenade* was just 'a dance in the moonlight' and nothing more."

"That's impossible," Esme said. She thought of something she'd read in one of the cards someone had sent. *We don't always know why God makes the decisions he does.*

In the theater, the spell *Serenade* had cast was broken. Instruments were retuned. Strings stretched and ached as bows passed over them, sending broken sounds into the echoing space. The bathroom floor was cold. Esme pulled her legs in closer, wishing she could fold into something small enough to be carried away by the wind. It wouldn't matter then what she felt or didn't feel.

"But that's the beauty of it, too, Esme. If he doesn't tell us what it means, then we decide. So maybe that is what it means, if that's what it means to you."

Amelia shuffled. Fabric rustled. "And one day, if you're ever the Waltz Girl, you can project whatever emotions you feel into that role, and the audience will carry them away. In that sense, Esme, it means something different every time because no two dancers ever dance a part exactly alike. And no two watchers will ever see it the same way. What I'm trying to say, Esme, is that there's a place for everything you're feeling."

She thought of her mother alone in the dusty trailer, sitting outside their house instead of in it. Maybe that was her place for everything that was happening. And this was hers.

"Come on," Amelia said. "When you're ready, I want you to meet Paul."

Esme traced the netting on her tights with her finger. Everything Amelia had said made sense. The window closed. The breeze stopped suddenly, shocked into stillness. She felt stupid for sitting on a dirty bathroom floor in a borrowed sweater.

Like the Waltz Girl, lifted and carried into the dazzling light, Esme followed.

Chapter Eleven

It was easy to live with Amelia, even though there were so many choices now. "Chicken and vegetables tonight?" Amelia might ask, peering into the fridge, where their options were lit with one light bulb. At home, it was always the same rotating menu of spaghetti, tacos, lentil soup, minestrone, turkey meatballs, hamburgers—crowd pleasers selected from dozens of failed recipes, wrinkled noses, and pushed-away plates. Here, Esme didn't have to make her own meals on spaghetti night, and she always agreed with Amelia's suggestions because she didn't know the difference between arugula and romaine anyway.

Amelia showered in the morning, and Esme showered at night. There were no egg timers or panic when someone took too long or fists banging on the bathroom door or investigations about who used someone's shampoo. Esme's coconut Suave sat beside Amelia's TRESemmé like two old friends keeping each other company on a front porch.

From seven to nine in the morning, Esme did schoolwork, then Pilates for an hour before Amelia drove them to the studio, where Esme warmed up at the barre before Amelia reviewed choreography or technique if there was something new. For lunch, she ordered a salad from Sal's Pizza and slid into a plastic booth. Sometimes the pizza guys slipped garlic knots onto her tray and winked. The garlic smarted on her tongue for the rest of the afternoon while everyone else was at school, counting minutes from one period to the next, changing into gym uniforms, buying Famous Amos cookies at lunchtime while she danced all day. At school, she'd only been quiet, shy Esme, too skinny for boys to notice, too distracted to care. Here, she was everyone's pet.

At meals, Amelia's attention didn't spin to the loudest person. It was always Esme time. Something shifted inside, like a plant that didn't have to bend and twist in its pot for sunlight on the other side of the room. Everything she needed was here, without asking, and all she had to do was grow. At night, she watched videos of Anna Pavlova or Galina Ulanova, a reminder of the big picture, that all the right pieces were sliding into place. She fell asleep to Bach or Mendelssohn, to music she used now or would use one day, while her brain processed what she'd learned that day and sorted it into place.

"Let's talk about auditions, Esme. They're only two weeks away."

They were sitting at Amelia's kitchen table, next to empty breakfast plates. Esme's mouth lingered on the sting of fresh orange juice. It was still early, but Amelia was already dressed for the day. Amelia laid out the schedule in front of her. Auditions were highlighted on the calendar in bold pink. Most of the auditions were in New York, but San Francisco was marked in blue. She was too young to audition anywhere other than San Francisco for SFBS. If she really wanted that one, she'd have to travel.

"Talk to your parents about San Francisco," Amelia said. "Everything else we can manage. And the other thing is . . . it's time to really think about whether or not you're ready to go away. It's OK to do the summer program and come home in the fall, but if you're asked to stay for the school year, that's the real goal, Esme. That's the next professional step, but only if you're ready. I think you are, but I can't decide for you."

Amelia drummed her finger against the schedule. "It would mean not seeing your family until holidays, if even, and living with people you don't know. Your friends at school will also be your competition, and what you achieve determines whether you're asked to stay on. We've never talked about your sister, Esme, and how that might change whether you want to do this, but you need to think about it. I don't need an answer right now, but I'm trusting you to think this through and talk to your parents."

There were ten schools, but the only one she really wanted was the farthest away. Maybe that meant she was ready to leave them behind and start over. San Francisco. She wanted to know what real Rice-A-Roni tasted like, if it was really a San Francisco thing, and see the real house from *Full House*.

"And," Amelia said, choosing her words carefully, "it's very important that you're doing this for dance and not to . . . well, not to hide from anything else that's happening in your life right now."

"Of course it's about dance," Esme shot back. It hurt that Amelia would question her. No, she didn't want to see that sad, concerned look in Amelia's eyes begging her to open up and talk about the other stuff. She didn't want to talk about that here. She folded the schedule into her pocket. "I have homework." She gathered her plate and put it in the dishwasher, aware of Amelia's eyes on her back. Her homework was already done, but still. She had a schedule for a reason.

She curled into the wicker chair on the porch and tucked her legs beneath her. It was unusually warm for December; warm enough to forget that Christmas was so soon. There were twinkle lights on the trees and wreaths with red bows on front doors, but not at Amelia's, and Esme was glad. Christmas was for other people this year. The snow had mostly melted, but a few thick patches clung to the grass in gray heaps. The sun warmed the porch and the blanket Esme had draped over herself. In the forsythia bush next to the porch, there was a cardinal's nest. Sometimes the bright-red father would fly home to check on the dusty-red mother. They'd wait together for a bit before the father flew off again. Even though it was December, there were eggs in the nest, which Amelia said was very unusual, maybe even unnatural, but they were there. The babies probably wouldn't make it through winter.

She liked doing homework on the porch because it kept the mother bird company. Esme wanted to know how many eggs were in the nest, but walking too close might scare the mother off. She hoped she'd see the sticky baby birds poke through their shells, watch as they learned to fly, diving into the grass for seeds or worms. It was fascinating to see another kind of family in a twig house. Esme thought of herself as a guardian, ready to shoo away stray cats or vampire bats that ate bird eggs. *I'm watching*, she told the mother bird silently. *I won't let anything hurt you, even if you're in the wrong season.*

"You should study animals." The porch door closed behind Amelia.

Esme fumbled to open her math textbook, still annoyed by their conversation earlier.

"You'll have to dance a lot of them if you go classical." Amelia the swan, the Firebird.

"Did you?" Esme asked, curious.

"Of course! I watched swans in the park before I was the Swan Queen just to get a sense of where they live, what they think. The emotions in *Swan Lake* are human, but the birds are so magical we forget they're animals. I wanted to understand where the inspiration came from before I developed the character."

Esme would've watched other Swan Queens but wouldn't have thought of animals.

"It sounds crazy, I'm sure, but there's so much more than costumes and choreography to bring a character to life and make her your own."

No wonder Anna Pavlova had had swans in her backyard. What kind of dancer would she be if she didn't study animals?

"Watch that mother bird. Imagine what she's thinking and feeling, what she fears for her eggs, what she's looking at when she sits on them all day, what she ate for breakfast."

The bird cocked its head toward Esme and then looked away.

"She's beautiful." Amelia nodded, appreciating the rusty-red feathers, the muted tones that blended into the speckled brown bark at the center of the bush.

"The audience needs to live her journey. That's what we interpret. That's something you have to learn to observe and re-create beyond technique and form. So"—Amelia sighed, unfolding her arms from across her chest—"that's your assignment before auditions." She pointed at the bird. "Study her, and add her personality, fears, and desires to the piece you're learning. Understand?"

Esme nodded, feeling more responsible for the cardinal in the bush than she already did. Amelia disappeared inside, and Esme wondered how many twigs the mother bird had used to build a home safe enough for the lumpy eggs beneath her.

~

Her father picked her up on Saturday morning after class, one week after she'd moved to Amelia's. He didn't come to the door or ring the bell, curious to see where his daughter was living. Instead, the car idled at the curb, spitting gray smoke onto mailboxes and wreaths on front doors, his taxi stark yellow against the evergreens on the other side of the street. She stepped from stone to stone down the walkway, wondering if she should sit in the back like a passenger, if he'd notice or care that she hadn't taken the front, but she didn't want to hurt him. Even the shadowy outline of his face through the glass was enough to make Esme's throat tighten for the way things used to be. She slid into the front seat and closed the door behind her.

He hugged her with one arm, the other still on the wheel. The Long Island Expressway rolled past, but Andre didn't ask about her new life. Amelia's world slipped away with it. All that was left was dried sweat on the back of her neck, damp hair in a sticky bun, the faint smell of cinnamon.

"Your mother is so sad," he said. "She started working with a private investigator. Tom. He stops by often. He might be there this weekend. No news from Detective Ferrera, but what else is new? Don't tell your mother this, but I'll be surprised if there is at this point. It feels hopeless. I don't mean to sound heartless, but what are we supposed to do?"

He paused to change lanes. "The refrigerator's broken. Just stopped working. Everything's in coolers in the kitchen, so don't be surprised when you get in. I don't want to upset your mother."

Esme didn't respond. The more he talked, the more invisible she felt, like a confessional. When he paused, she wondered how many Hail Marys she should tell him to do.

"Dad?" She cut in during a long pause. "I learned a new piece this week for a show in February." It was a safe topic, the kind of thing she would've brought up at the dinner table.

"Oh, yeah?" He honked at a car in front of them, cutting into their lane. Red taillights popped up like two angry eyes. Esme waited for the distraction to end, hoping Andre would ask more about it, but he didn't. The seat belt pressed against her throat.

"I don't know what to do anymore." He sighed. The disappointment stung. Her father was lost in his own box of thoughts. She stared out the window, resting her head against her fist as the endless concrete wall rolled past, punctuated by metal bolts. She toyed with the zipper on her backpack, wondering what Amelia would do without her. Maybe she'd go on a date and wear one of the million pairs of high heels in the hallway, and the house would still smell like perfume when Esme came back. It was only one night, Esme reminded herself, confused by not wanting to go back to the home she missed.

When they pulled up in front of the house, Madeline was sitting on the stoop with a book. Her sister looked so small, knees pulled to her chest, hair windblown into ropy strands. Madeline wouldn't admit it, but Esme knew she was waiting for her. Esme hopped out, throwing her backpack over her shoulder, and slid in beside Madeline.

"Hey," she said. Madeline looked up, eyes bleary from reading for too long.

"Hey," she said, pulling a pile of glossy pages from the back of her book. "You can have these if you want." McDonald's scratch offs. "I stole them from everyone's bag."

Esme pictured her wandering hallways, stealing ads from *Pennysaver* bags, sorry she hadn't been there to help. It was almost an apology or at least a truce. Maybe it was true that she didn't want to see what was on the other side of the after curtain, but for now, she didn't have to.

They took turns scratching the silver smudges with a quarter. It didn't matter if they won a soda or fries or a Happy Meal. Anything would be enough, even if it wasn't a trip to Disney World or a car they couldn't drive. The chill of the stoop shivered down the length of her legs. Her muscles would cramp later. They already felt tight. She was supposed to drink water and have protein for muscle repair, but Esme was content to sit shoulder to shoulder with Madeline, scratching stupid ads in the cold. There was only a small window before she'd go upstairs and find her mother curled up with one of Lily's toys, face streaked with dried salt, and pretend her world with Amelia didn't exist. Esme inched closer to Madeline, thankful someone'd missed her enough to save scratch offs.

They finished the last ad in silence. They'd won fries and a soda.

"Keep them." Esme folded the winners into a square and handed them to Madeline.

"Fine," Madeline agreed. "You probably can't eat this stuff anyway."

"No." Esme sighed, thankful Madeline had acknowledged her new life.

"You're not missing much."

Esme knew her sister wasn't talking only about fries. Their father's cab circled the block for the millionth time. A plane passed silently overhead. Madeline stood and stretched.

Their window was a dark hole. If Lily was here, she'd be bouncing in that same window, hair flying, and there'd be a mess of scribbled pictures narrating everything Esme'd missed all week, but there wouldn't be any new crayon pictures upstairs. Esme followed Madeline anyway, hiding in her sister's shadow, praying for the right words to take her to San Francisco.

Chapter Twelve

"No," Cerise said. "Absolutely not."

San Francisco was over in three words. They buzzed through her head like flies, but she couldn't slap them away.

"Let's talk about this." Her father put his hand over Cerise's on the table—or tried to, but Cerise moved it away. Esme ignored the hurt on her father's face and the pile of pillows and blankets on the living room couch, her father's new bed. She wasn't sure when he'd started sleeping there instead, and she didn't ask why. It was too much.

"The answer is no. It's impossible right now." Cerise gestured toward the heap of untouched fabric on the sewing table. She slid her chair back and put her shoes on by the door. She would go back to the trailer and stare at the map on the wall covered in circles and pins.

There was only one dream for her mother now, a long-ago, half-forgotten version of the way life had been before. Everything that came after would always reach for it. There wasn't room for dance anymore in her mother's heart. There wasn't room for Esme. There wasn't room for anything except the void Lily had left behind.

Her mother used to brush Esme's hair into a bun and secure it in place with bobby pins and absolute faith that her daughter could do what so few people were able to. That was why she'd made costumes at night in between her real business, why she'd done everything she could to get Esme into Amelia's studio, why she'd gotten up before the sun to take Esme to auditions all over the city and hunted down the right ones for her. "You would be perfect for this," she'd say softly to Esme as she showed her a flyer, and Esme would believe her because her mother's faith was contagious.

Now, she had to believe it for herself. She wouldn't have that whispered faith from her mother anymore, but Cerise had planted it a long time ago, and it had been growing all along. Maybe Esme was wrong; it hadn't come from her mother at all. Her mother had only watered something that was already there.

Andre put one cold hand on Esme's shoulder. She didn't push it away even though the weight pressed into her sore neck. Her fist balled in her lap. She wanted to slam it against the table and rattle the dirty dishes loud enough that her mother would stop putting her shoes on and look at Esme, really look at her little dancer like she used to, and then say no, but the door had already opened and closed. Esme sat with a hot rage in her chest and her father's hand on her shoulder. It didn't matter how bad he felt if the answer was no.

"Next year," Andre whispered softly. "We can think about San Francisco when all this is behind us."

She climbed into his cab that next afternoon and silently waited for the ride to Amelia's to end.

But the next weekend, as Esme waited for the bathroom and mixed cold water into her oatmeal packet, wondering why the oats were floating in milky liquid instead of puffing up, she counted the hours before she could go back to Amelia's.

"You have to heat the water first, dumbass," Nick mumbled, poking her floating oats with a spoon. "It's not gonna work that way."

Her mother was in the trailer with the advocates. Who knew if she'd come out again before Esme left. Nick had the football game on mute in the living room. Little helmeted people ran across the green field. Her father circled the living room, staring out the window at the trailer below, pacing past Nick and Esme and the garbage bag over the hole in the wall until Esme was sure she'd lose her mind.

"Enough," he said suddenly, startling the two of them. The spoon clattered to the table. "Esme, get your stuff."

It was too early to go back to Amelia's. She couldn't just . . .

"But, Dad—"

"We're going to the airport. I'm not gonna lose you too."

He unzipped Nick's backpack and dumped everything inside onto the living room rug. A mess of crumpled loose-leaf paper, pens without caps, cigarettes, and a switchblade spilled out.

"We'll talk about this when I get back." He pocketed the switchblade and threw the cigarettes into Esme's oatmeal before dumping it into the trash. Nick stared from his slumped heap on the couch. Andre stuffed a change of clothes into Nick's empty backpack and slung it over his shoulder. *Go, Dad!* Esme silently cheered, so thankful to see her real dad again instead of the shadow version. She gathered her ballet things as quickly as possible, anxious to keep moving so her father wouldn't have time to slip back into his sad self. He stopped only once at the trailer, opening the door just wide enough to toss the knife inside, and then they were off.

At the airport, Esme watched in disbelief as her father pulled the emergency credit card from his wallet. The airport was a flurry of rolling suitcases behind quick footsteps. Announcements Esme didn't understand filled the empty air. There were lines of people and luggage everywhere. A plane whooshed past on the runway, throwing a shadow over the terminal. Esme wrapped her arms around her stomach. *We don't buy what we can't afford,* Cerise's words echoed. Panic boiled in the pit of her stomach as her father slid the card across the counter to the ticket agent.

"But, Dad . . . I might not even get in." It was true. It hadn't fazed her when she was tracing the Golden Gate Bridge with her index finger or imagining Chinese lantern tassels making shadow lines on the sidewalk. But at the airport with the emergency card swiped and her father's signature on the receipt, the hours he'd spend driving people from borough to borough while her mother stitched beads onto satin, working extra to cover this trip, made not getting in seem suddenly too real. It was wasteful and selfish, especially after Lily, but Andre was smiling. He folded the tickets, slid them into his jeans pocket, and gathered their two small bags.

"Look at me," he said. He looked so out of place without the backdrop of their house, his cab, their neighborhood. He looked like a different person. Had he ever even been on a plane before? *Oh my God*, she realized, staring at the planes landing and taking off through the window, *I've never been on a plane*. Her stomach lurched. What a stupid idea this was.

"It's not an option." His voice was calm, but every word buzzed as loud as a bee swarm. "No matter what it is, even if it's just an idea, everything starts with your head, and your head starts here." Andre tapped the place where his heart would be.

"Come on." He threw her backpack over his shoulder and reached for her hand. She would have been embarrassed anywhere else, but not here. Not today. He was the dad she remembered from before, and she'd do whatever it took to play along.

"Look at your mother. No matter how sad she feels, when she sews, only beautiful things happen. She makes a lot of people happy because of it. That's what's inside your mother, beautiful things, whether she always feels it or not. You and her are the same. There's only one outcome, Esme, because once you're in that room and the music starts, you'll do what your heart wants even if your head is confused, and it will be beautiful too."

Esme was surprised her father had so many things to say, more than he'd ever said about her and Cerise at home. How could he be so sure? She believed him but wished he could lift her to his hip like he did with Lily so she could see the world from his height instead of her own. If she could see things the way he saw them, maybe she wouldn't be so confused.

She nodded, pushing away the doubt she'd felt moments before. Her father rested his hand on her shoulder as they waited for security, backpack in hand. *There's only one outcome.* Was that true about everything, even things that didn't seem important? If one thing led to the next and tumbled the future into place, had he just tipped the first domino when he bought their tickets, or had it already tipped a long time ago, and she just hadn't noticed? Only last week, he'd said no. They couldn't go to San Francisco, not with everything, but now they were being scanned through an x-ray machine, and the answer was yes.

~

They stayed in the cheapest hotel Andre could find, but Esme loved it. Windows opened to a hallway full of real and fake plants. The rooms didn't have bathrooms, only sinks. It was fun to have just a sink, even if it was weird to wash her face and brush her teeth without the bathroom door closed, but Andre didn't pay her much attention. He opened and closed the windows and came back with a bar of sandalwood soap from the real bathroom down the hall and held it out for her to smell. It tickled the inside of her nose. The whole place was dark and wooden, a maze of meandering hallways that Esme was sure she'd get lost in, and everything shook a little when cars passed outside. She tried not to think about earthquakes.

"You're where?" Cerise screamed through the phone that night, so loud Esme heard her from the bed on the other side of the room. "How dare you leave me with *this*," Cerise rambled on the other end of the line, but Andre's voice cut over hers.

"We're here. We're fine. We'll work it out. She has to do this, Cerise." It almost sounded like a prayer. Andre hung up the phone, but there was already a separation between them that felt permanent, like the last day of school when you knew your teacher wasn't your teacher anymore. Esme wondered if her mother would call them back, but the phone was silent. Andre shut the light off. A shadow car drove past on the ceiling.

"Get some sleep," he whispered, and for the first time in a long time, he kissed her on the forehead. His mother's cross, the one he always wore, brushed the side of her face. She closed her eyes, focusing on all the love she felt, until she fell asleep.

She woke up before dawn. The city was quiet below. Her father was still asleep, one arm thrown over his eyes. It was too early, but she pulled on her tights and leotard in the darkness and curled up by the window, tucking her good-luck note into the top of her tights. *Bring me my swan costume.* Anna Pavlova's last words. It was Anna's ending but her beginning.

Outside, the whole world was slanted. Everything leaned with the hills. The houses were almost triangular, built into the slant, but everything was painted so beautifully. There were no boring brick buildings. If a house was blue, it was dark blue, light blue, sky blue, all in one, covering all the unusual shapes like costumes. Esme wrapped her arms around herself tighter. Was she colorful enough to live here too? Her father was a sleeping gray shape in the darkness. Soon she'd wake him, they'd leave, and she'd know for sure if she could ever live here or not. The world here was as off balance and tilted as she felt inside. It fit.

They took a taxi to the audition. Her stomach swelled with every hill. Everything outside the window flashed by in a blur. Her father offered her a muffin. She broke off a small piece, but it felt like sand between her fingers, and when she tried to eat it, the blueberries tasted sour. She sipped water instead. Amelia would have made her eat an egg or miso soup, something mild for fuel, but she was running on something else now. She knew the building before the driver stopped: blue glass and white stone. The sun was rising. The last of her nerves burned away with the morning fog. She was ready.

Inside, she registered, safety pinned her number to her chest, and waited to be called. She stretched, and when she was done, she sat up straight, thinking of the mother cardinal in the nest. One day, she'd left and never come back. There had been five eggs, one cracked; the rest were blue and speckled brown. She'd put them under a lamp in the basement and wrapped them in a blanket, but nothing had happened. In every ballet she'd ever seen, everyone lost something. The Swan Queen, the Firebird, Giselle, Sleeping Beauty. Esme looked around at the other eleven-year-olds in the waiting area. They might have the right technique, but how could they be something they'd never experienced? She could be the mother bird, the broken egg, because she'd lost something too. For the first time in her life, Esme felt older than her eleven years. *Anna Pavlova*, she prayed, thinking of her frail hero, *I think I understand now.*

~

"Dad?" They were sitting by the Palace of Fine Arts, watching ducks swim past on the pond, their feathers gold in the afternoon sun. He used to tell her stories about a golden goose when she was little. It was strange to remember that now, sitting on the curb with her audition number still pinned to her leotard. "Do you think it's a stupid thing to do?"

"What's stupid?" He bit his hamburger and put it down on the paper in his lap. The take-away bag rested between them. In-N-Out Burger, another of many things Esme had never heard of. Her head buzzed with jet lag. It was three p.m. here but would be six p.m. at home. The sun was still shining. At home, it had already set.

"Doing ballet instead of school."

He'd always said school was the only way to really succeed. One year, he'd given them a dollar for every point their report card grades went up, which Madeline had thought was unfair because her grades were already high.

He threw a crumb to a passing duck with a green neck. The morsel floated on the surface, pale and bloated, until the duck scooped it up and swam in circles, waiting for another.

"Well," he said at last, "you're doing both. Everything you learn about dance is something you'd never learn in school, so that's an education too. What I meant about school"—he paused, picking his words carefully—"was that I didn't want you guys to be like me."

Esme opened her mouth, but he held up one finger.

"I always wanted to go to school, but I had to work, and when you start working, it's very hard to stop. I rely on the work I get from one day to the next."

A water plant swayed with the wind. What would her mother say when they got home? Esme's tongue was acidic where the ketchup had been. She closed her eyes. Andre would have to find money for this trip. He'd work nights that bled into early mornings. Hours and hours and hours just for one audition. And that was if she didn't get in. What if she did?

Andre must have read her expression. "Don't worry about that now," he said. "Don't get caught in that cycle." He gestured to the park around them, to seagulls circling above the pond. "We should be able to do things like this while we can. That's what I want for you."

"But if I'm, like, sixteen when I start with a company, doesn't that mean I've done the same thing? Like I only have one option?" Her future already felt decided. The 207 on her leotard was etched into her skin, as permanent as a birthmark. It was important, just like all the street names they'd passed. Geary Boulevard. Divisadero Street. Fillmore. Chestnut. They might be important, but they blurred together until Esme couldn't remember why she'd wanted to come here so much. Home felt as far away as a forgotten dream.

"No," he said. "It's different. You'll have a skill very few people have. That's different from driving a taxi. Anyone can do that." Her father looked at the sky, dotted with feathery clouds. Cloud shadows rolled past the pond.

"Dad? When you were a kid, what did you want to be when you grew up?"

"A pilot." It was a quick reply, ready on his tongue.

Esme was sorry she'd never asked. "That's cool," she said, picturing him surrounded by tiny dials and a window full of clouds, night stars as clear as anyone on earth could see them. It was sad that he'd settled on navigating streets instead, listening to conversations as if he were invisible instead of radioing down to a tower for weather conditions up ahead, but that wasn't his life. He'd be a very different dad had that dream happened, flying from one country to the next while the rest of them did schoolwork and homelife and dance. She thought of all the recitals he would've missed, how she'd always expected him there, waiting afterward with a pink rose. She rested her head on his shoulder.

"I'm glad you stayed on land instead," she said, thinking of lightning strikes and the dips and swells of turbulence.

"Me too. I have much better memories because of it. But speaking of pilots . . ." He sighed. "We should go soon." He crumpled his wrapper into a ball and held out the bag to Esme, sending a whiff of french fries toward her. She wasn't supposed to, but she reached in. Salt melted on her fingers, her tongue. She hadn't even realized she'd wanted one until she tasted it.

"You already burned it off," he said, offering another, but she didn't take it. If she really were going to SFBS, she'd have to be very serious. Every choice had to make her a dancer, even one as simple as french fries. Across the park, a cluster of pigeons scattered into the sky, leaving a trail of feathers in their wake. Esme threw the last fries into the pond. The grease left an oily sheen on the water's surface.

"Don't tell your mother I had any either," he said as he stood. "You know what she'd say."

Esme nodded. She'd keep his secret. A plane passed overhead, trailing a long white cloud behind it. Was he sorry he hadn't become a pilot? Did he think about it sometimes? A bicycle bell tinkled, and a Rollerblader passed by as smooth as wind. He wasn't watching the sky. San Francisco Ballet was her dream company. She'd wanted it for so long she couldn't remember why anymore. Her father's hand closed around hers. He hadn't gotten what he wanted, but he had other things instead. It was impossible to have nothing.

Esme had one last question, one that'd been floating around since she'd left the audition and found her father shuffling pamphlets and promotional cards in the waiting area. "Dad? Are you happy?"

He looked down at her, surprised. The lines around his eyes wrinkled. Before Lily, he would have said something like, "Of course, why not?" Now, he was deciding which version of the truth he should give her. Esme readied herself for whatever he was about to say.

"We don't always choose our choices, but they're ours. Am I happy?" He sighed. "Look around. This is a beautiful place, the most beautiful I've seen in a long time. I'm here with you, and I'm happy to be. We can't be everything all the time. That just wouldn't be life."

Esme stopped walking and closed her eyes. If she didn't get in, she might never come back here. The breeze blew past her ears, freeing stray wisps from her bun. The back of her leotard was still damp, and the breeze made her shiver. They were under a row of eucalyptus trees, and the whole place smelled like earth. A black-and-orange butterfly flicked by overhead. A swan cried on the pond. It *was* the most beautiful place she'd ever seen, even more so because of what they'd left behind. She wasn't ready to let go of this version of her father for the one he was at home.

"Thank you," her father said quietly.

"For what?"

"We're here because of you." He put his arm around her. Her father was right; she'd been calm during the audition, and as soon as the music had started, she'd moved with it. It was more than just muscle memory. Dancing let her soul breathe. It had always been that way and always would be. She wasn't ready to leave yet. She wanted to touch the Pacific Ocean for the first time and follow a monarch butterfly along part of its migration. She wanted to ride on a cable car and lean out the window as it crept up a hill or hear fishermen shouting by the wharf. And worse, she felt like she was being plucked away from where she truly belonged. It was time to leave, but she would be back. She took one more deep breath to fill her lungs, collecting as much of this place as she could carry, wishing she could take it home with her.

~

Three weeks later, Esme took down the poster of the Golden Gate Bridge from above her bed because she didn't need it anymore. She'd been accepted, officially, and they'd even given her a scholarship. Soon enough she would see that real bridge every day, learning and dancing like Anna Pavlova and Amelia and every other great dancer had done. She took down one piece of her room every time she went home so it would feel less and less like the room she remembered until it was essentially empty, proof that her life was not here anymore in the empty shell home had become without Lily, but it was waiting for her on the other side of the only world she'd ever known.

PART TWO
PARIS, 2005

Chapter Thirteen

Esme felt like a wet leaf plastered to her sheets. The summer air was icy cold outside her blanket. Her arms and legs and muscles were wet-sand heavy. She was dehydrated and jet lagged, but she would not miss the opening night of *Serenade*. Not in Paris. Not with Adam.

Advil and electrolyte tabs were in the nightstand, a bottle of cold water on the floor. She swallowed the pills as the tabs fizzled in the bottle. She rubbed her temples in slow circles, repeating the same words she'd woken up to for the past eight years. *Today is a new day. I'm happy to be here*, the only remaining tenet of a grief support group she'd gone to once in a church basement. A chill spread through her bones as her feet touched the cold floor. Today it was true.

Esme left the hotel an hour later, head floating in the early-morning haze. Dull achiness crouched behind her knees. A woman in a blue apron swept cigarette butts into the gutter while a man set out café tables along the sidewalk. In the next shop, a girl placed orange madeleines and macarons in the window. The smell of warm chocolate and baking bread crept silently through the street. Murmured conversations she didn't understand made everything feel like a dream. She felt alive in a way she hadn't for a long time—and safe. Most importantly, she felt safe.

In San Francisco, her cramped apartment tottered on a hill, swallowed in morning mist and shaken occasionally when the earth shifted. It had lost its thrill a long time ago. She dreaded the uphill walk at night, the constant Pacific chill. It still didn't feel like home, not even after eight years, but then again, no place felt like home anymore. Neighbors shuffled across the street to warn her about a push-in robbery down the block or someone mugged at their car. "Please be careful, Esme," they said. "A woman living alone. What a shame that would be." She was not an exception. Anything could happen, and yet she missed the oasis San Francisco used to be before she'd realized, truly realized, how many bad things happened to regular people and wished San Francisco was still as innocent as a beautiful red bridge in the fog.

In Paris, everything was new again. Not understanding newspaper headlines was a relief. A scooter bounced past on the cobblestones. Her favorite building jutted into the street with a red door and a trellis of hanging flowers. Next was the theater with green double doors, carved flowers, falling leaves: a true fairy-tale door. But she didn't have to knock three times or wait for a keeper to slide away a hatch because she belonged there. It felt magically old, like everything in Paris.

And Adam was here.

As students, they'd had a choreographer once, Dontel, who loved working with Esme and Adam. He'd pull them into the studio when class was over and run through new pieces for hours, using Esme and Adam to physically visualize what he saw inside and bring it to life. "Beautiful, beautiful, beautiful," Dontel would say when things were going well, or he'd shake his head, scattering his hair in a flyaway puff, when it wasn't, and they'd start again.

"Esme," Dontel would say over the music, "you love him. He's leaving you. Let me see that." Or "Esme, you hate him. Hate him with all your heart." And Esme would conjure those feelings for Adam until she actually felt them and craved the intensity of it all. The rest of the day would be dull in comparison.

"The two of you," Dontel would say at the end of a particularly intense session, holding each of their hands in his. "Beautiful, beautiful, beautiful." It became a kind of secret between them, those after-hours sessions. The intimacy of the whole thing almost felt like a wedding, a new bride at the altar, full of expectation, knowing they'd be tied together and sent away into the world.

She'd hoped that Paris would be like that for them—that they'd finish performances and wander along the quay, finding picnic spots under the willow trees at Pont Neuf or lighting candles at Notre Dame, finding favorite espresso cafés and jittering for hours afterward, laughing, and she'd fill her soul with Adam like she used to—but it wasn't. There were other company members that he danced with every day, and Adam's time was split between them and his show. He'd grown into his adult life in the same way Esme wished she had but hadn't.

The courtyard buzzed with dancers in tights and leotards, T-shirts thrown over for cover, knotted at the waist, cigarettes in one hand and water bottles in the other. Limp ponytails hung down backs, jagged from sleep. Circles formed throughout the courtyard, a flower bed of like plants with like plants. These were New York City Ballet dancers, Adam's cohort, newly released from Saratoga Springs, using their break to dance in Paris. She was the only one from San Francisco. She didn't have a circle, but she didn't mind. She hovered in the corner alone, wondering why everyone was outside instead of in.

"Have you heard?" Ashley slid beside her, exhaling a plume of gray smoke that twisted Esme's stomach. At twenty-five, Ashley already had lines deeply etched around her mouth. She was a soloist, not the oldest or youngest but old enough that she should have been a principal already if she ever would be. How anyone could make it this far and be content with coasting in the middle baffled Esme. The other dancers didn't pay her much mind, and Ashley seemed grateful for an outsider to pair off with. It was almost refreshing to be around someone so content.

"Hear what? I just got here."

"Denise fell," Ashley whispered.

People fell, but it wasn't talked about unless it was bad, and Denise was a principal. She was the Waltz Girl.

"I wasn't there, but Adam's looking for you." Ashley raised her eyebrows.

Esme's breath caught. She'd shadowed Denise's rehearsals all week, running choreography while the sun burned from afternoon to night in the faraway world outside the mirror. The more she'd watched, the more she'd hoped she wouldn't have to dance it. She'd run the choreography through technically, but she didn't want to find the real Waltz Girl, the one who threw herself again and again against something that wasn't working until it broke her. No, Esme had pulled inward, closing against the possibility of those feelings, of that little-girl version of herself who'd cried on the bathroom floor of a theater. That little girl was in her somewhere, beating behind her grown-up heart, and Esme wouldn't let herself feel that way again.

Adam wouldn't pick her over people he danced with at home. "It's just a corps role," he'd told her apologetically weeks before, knowing she was a soloist with SFB, "but it's Paris." She was safe.

The studio door opened, and Adam's head popped out. He was eight years older than when they'd first met at school in San Francisco, but Adam was just as blue eyed and open faced as he'd been then. He reminded Esme of the Scarecrow in *The Wizard of Oz*, only instead of making him goofy, all that charm had blown him to the top of the haystack. He still looked surprised to be an NYCB star instead of fumbling with the wet plastic rubber of a life raft.

They'd been a kind of family once, Adam and Esme, finding each other after classes were done and slipping off for rush tickets to whatever SFB was running that season. They went night after night, and when the initial wonder had worn off, they analyzed technique, compared performances. They spent every holiday together, alone in the dorms after everyone else had gone home to their families. "It's just too expensive, Esme," her father had explained over the phone, "what with everything else. You could come home two weeks later for half the price or less." But she could not go home two weeks later because school was in session again, and after the initial disappointment had worn off, it was a relief. Esme had almost enjoyed holidays again. Esme and Adam watched movies in their pajamas and rode trolleys covered in twinkle lights or walked along the park under Golden Gate Bridge, looking for driftwood that would burn blue but never finding it. She didn't feel lonely or family-less when she was with Adam. It was what Amelia might've meant once when she said life after Lily would be different, not necessarily better, but different. Being with Adam was certainly different. Esme never told Adam about Lily. He never talked about his life in Cuba, but there was an understanding between them, a language of loss, better unspoken.

There was something about Adam that made her feel like she'd been part of his success, even if it wasn't true. Here, among his closest peers, she realized other people seemed to think that way about him too. It bothered Esme that *her* Adam feeling, the one that filled her with courage and made her feel unstoppable, wasn't hers alone.

"Esme." Adam spotted her from the door. "Got a sec?"

The courtyard went silent. Dozens of eyes avoided the girl from San Francisco, Adam's random friend. Why was she here? One girl in particular, Jennifer, glared at her through blue-eyed slits, arms crossed icily over her chest, but the look Jennifer gave Adam was worse. She stared, daring him to look at her. The feeling was so intense it made Esme shiver in the sun.

"Merde," Ashley whispered, squeezing her arm lightly. "Go ahead, Waltz Girl."

Esme ignored her. For the first time in her life, she did not want a principal role.

~

"You've probably heard about Denise," he said. The office door closed behind him. It was a forgotten office. There was only a desk with a thin gold lamp, a quiet rotary phone, a vase of lilacs. "Are you up for it?"

Esme hesitated.

155

"God." He shook his head. "I don't know why you're so against this one, but the way you're warring with it makes it perfect for you, Es. Don't you see?"

He didn't wait for her to answer. "I probably shouldn't say this, and I'm sorry for Denise, but I'm glad it worked out this way. You can't fake a Waltz Girl, Esme. The only reason—"

"It's OK," Esme rushed on. "It's really OK, Adam. I didn't expect more than a corps role. *Serenade* carries a lot of weight for me—it always has—but I'm happy to be here."

Was she? "Hey, Emerald," he'd said that day over the phone, her nickname from a bored night of internet searching name meanings on a computer neither had used before. They'd screamed when the dial-up sound had started. They'd broken it for sure. If she could have a little of that old life back, maybe she wouldn't feel so untethered. Paris was better than home or her empty apartment, but she hadn't felt welcomed. Adam was too busy now. Their time was too short. This whole experience was meant to be something else, but she wasn't sure what. It left her feeling disappointed in some forgotten part of herself.

"Well." He sighed. A small smile crept over his face, the same promising one that had held her together that first year in San Francisco. "Here you are. I need an hour or two to sort a few things out, but start without me, and I'll join you when I can."

He was all business. Where was the Adam who'd come to see her after her first performance as a soloist last year, surprising her in the wings with pink roses? Or the Adam who called her sometimes in the middle of the night, when it was midnight her time and three in the morning his, just to see how her day had been?

Esme lingered in the dusty office. The vase of lilacs, bright and purple and startlingly out of place, stared back at her. Something nagged inside. Adam leaned against the desk, staring out the window at the courtyard beyond, a sketch of lines and shadows in the flickering sun.

"Adam, why are you doing this? You know they'll give you shit for it." This was Adam's show, his first stab at producing. It was a small show, but still. There was no one to blame except him, no management or higher-up conspiracies. The others would be pissed.

Her mother used to say her children were always with her, even before they'd been born. Now, Esme felt her younger self, an eleven-year-old in a black leotard and pink tights, her first pair of pointe shoes, walking around in the dark, empty space inside herself, waiting to see what her nineteen-year-old self would do. There was so much that little girl didn't understand. Serenade in C ran through her head. It shook all her nervous places. She would panic when the Waltz Girl's oblivion ended. That was the part she could not do.

He shrugged and stared into the courtyard. The glass looked like it was melting slowly. Everyone outside was a blur of colors and limbs. Adam was solidly real in comparison, even in the dim office light.

"This is my thing, Esme. I don't have to explain."

She'd seen this mood once before. In their third year, they'd gone to see SFB's *Nutcracker*. He'd been regular Adam, skimming the program, sipping a Diet Coke, mumbling that the orchestra was slightly off tempo, but after intermission, Adam's mood had changed. He'd kicked the back of the empty seat in front of him, pulled loose threads from his chair, torn his program into shreds, littering the ground with black-and-white headshots. When the sled had carried Clara and the prince away, heat had washed off Adam in waves so thick she'd thought he'd explode.

"Are you OK?"

No answer.

"We can leave if you want to."

He'd stared at the stage as snow sprinkled the audience. The show had ended. The lights had turned on. Ushers had opened exit doors. People had slipped arms through coats, the sleeves snakelike in the dim lights.

"I can't believe how stupid this is," Adam had said at last.

Esme had pushed a glossy program piece with her toe.

"Do you know how I got here?" He'd laughed, coughlike. "My mother put me in a rubber boat with a father I'd never met and pushed us into the ocean. She waded out . . . she waded out in this dress she always wore with little white daisies. It floated up around her knees, and her feet looked so bloated in the water. She kept pulling at the strings on my life jacket."

Adam had been lost in something so personal that Esme hadn't been sure how much he'd meant to tell her. He'd rubbed the side of his neck, easing away ghost pain.

"She pushed me into the ocean for this."

Stagehands had swept fake snow into buckets.

"I never thought," he'd said, "I never thought that'd be the last time I saw my mother. It's not enough to just be here. It has to mean something. Or what's the point?"

Silent tears had trickled down his face. An usher had woven through the empty seats. "It's time to go," he'd say. Esme had wished he'd get there faster because she'd been speechless, lost in a melded memory of a boy in a boat and a little girl with rainbows on her fingers.

She'd been stunned that someone else felt that way too. Now, she wondered why she hadn't told Adam about Lily. That would have been the moment to say she understood, truly, because she'd never said good-bye, that she'd always wonder what had happened to Lily, about the person she would have become. She could have told Adam that Lily would always be a four-year-old girl preserved in time like an insect in amber, perfect and unchanging, or that it sometimes felt like Lily hadn't been real. But she hadn't told Adam those things because the Esme then had believed Lily was living in someone else's house, starting a new life. It must have felt false even then because it was too complicated to explain to someone else, but what else was there? She still didn't know what anything meant. Adam's voice snapped her back to now.

"Before I forget." He fished for something in his pocket and handed her a small piece of paper. "Your sister called. It sounded important."

Madeline had called here? It was only nine a.m., three a.m. in New York, and they hadn't spoken in weeks. They went through phases. Sometimes they talked for hours, a strange kind of confessional, because no one else would understand, or they went for months without a word because they were too much of a reminder of their broken life. It intruded on the delicate balance of a normal one.

He slid the phone across the desk. "Take your time."

Esme was already dialing when the door closed behind him, fumbling with country codes until she gave up and dialed the operator. Was it her mother, her father? It couldn't be a wedding emergency. Madeline wasn't a fussy bride, even if her wedding was only a week away. *Oh God,* she thought, biting her index finger so hard it left a mark. Her brother. Her mother's words echoed as the phone rang. "It's a good job until something happens," she'd told Nick when he'd made the police academy.

"Esme?" Madeline was breathless. Esme's skin prickled at the urgency in her sister's voice. "Where are you?"

"The studio. What's wrong?"

"They found a girl." Madeline's words rushed out in a jumble.

"What?"

"They found a girl Lily's age."

How many times had she imagined something like this? Her ears rang. Her body was a flyaway wisp. She grabbed the wooden seat for support and stared at the blue-and-white vase on the table, the purple lilacs. They turned to salt and pepper.

Inside, her little self was dancing furiously, pounding inside until her heart skipped a beat. Across the ocean, Madeline made sounds. Esme listened through water. It took seconds, a minute, until she realized it was her name.

"I'm here." Esme's voice broke. "Alive or . . . ?"

"Yes, in a house in New Jersey. Neighbors called in a bad smell and mail piling up, and when the police checked it out, the owner had died, but they found a girl in the basement. She's roughly the same age as Lily and matches her description."

New Jersey. Outside, people snubbed out cigarettes in the courtyard, laughing and disappearing as the studio door slammed shut behind them. Conversations echoed in the hallway behind her. The sun was brighter through the window now. Esme pinched the space between her thumb and forefinger until it left a painful half-moon, a reminder that she was still living and breathing.

"How could no one know she was there?"

It shocked her when someone was found in neighborhoods where people rode bikes or carried groceries from their cars to their homes, mowed lawns, where neighbors waved to each other when they picked up mail. How could some sick bastard hide people without anyone knowing? It poisoned all the nicest neighborhoods, all the smiling faces.

"Listen." Madeline's voice was serious. "They don't know who it is yet or what she's been through. No one's contacted us. It was just on the news. We don't know anything yet."

Lily would be twelve now, older than Esme when Lily had first gone missing. The tiny baby teeth Esme had helped her brush would be gone. Lily was not supposed to be in a basement, but that was the thing about having someone stolen. She didn't have a say over what happened. Someone else decided for them. The unfairness stung all over again. Even after all this time, she wasn't numb to it.

"I have a show tonight." Anger washed in. Why did Madeline have to call here, right now? The old immediacy of Lily missing, of Lily trumping every thought and every action and stunning them into comas, was so unfair. She was already panicked about the Waltz Girl. She didn't need this too. The thought of a costume, fake eyelashes, remembering choreography, and being the Waltz Girl felt like a joke.

"Why did you call me here? Why couldn't it wait?" Knowing now wouldn't change anything.

"Well." Madeline's voice hardened. "I thought you'd want to know. You're her sister too. And believe it or not, you're still part of this family, even if you pretend not to be."

There it was. *I stayed, and you didn't.* Esme was sick of apologizing for her life. She hung up.

The cord dangled. People moved in the hallway. A woman threw a red scarf over her shoulder in the courtyard. It was a magazine world where people posed but weren't feeling anything. Esme sat very still on the wooden seat, aware of her heart beating too fast, her skin too tight around her fingers. The elastic bra clasp circling her back was too tight; her shampoo smelled too strongly of lavender. She repeated her sister's words, rolling them over her tongue. "They found a girl." She said them again to hear them, really hear them, so that she might believe them.

It probably wasn't Lily, but hope bloomed like a spring bulb waiting through a silent winter. This was someone's daughter, someone's sleeping hope. Maybe Lily was out there too, reading books, doing laundry, watching the same sun rise and set.

She'd seen so many pictures of missing children, studied heights and weights, eye colors, nicknames. Those kids posed in front of laser backdrops with folded hands were part of her invisible family. They understood what it was to lose someone and not know what had happened, to never say goodbye without wondering if it was the last time. She memorized missing persons like a prayer, hoping people did the same for Lily. She doubted they'd ever find Lily, but maybe she'd recognize someone named Emily who was four feet tall when last seen on the corner of Forty-First and Second. *Who are you?* she wondered of the girl in the basement, smiling sadly at the thought of someone's life starting over, of a family getting their missing piece back.

But if it was Lily, what would she say to her for the first time? She'd written so many postcards and mailed them to nowhere. For every year she'd been dancing and traveling, someone had been living in a damp, dark basement. She imagined sleeping on an old mattress on the floor with a rag for a blanket, listening to footsteps overhead, while Esme had worried over pounds, blisters, auditions, contracts, missed flights. Lily hadn't deserved that; no one did.

I would hate me, Esme thought. *I would hate me.* She prayed this girl was someone else's. Eight years made them strangers. A world in a basement made them strangers.

Tears slithered free. People were whispering in the hallway, but she didn't care. She felt invisible. Madeline didn't understand. For as much as she pushed away, there was still a part of her that wished she were in their old bedroom, on Madeline's purple bedspread under her *Saved by the Bell* poster, a pile of tissues between them, but that life was over.

Finding Lily now terrified her more than silence. At least there was a new normal. Mom was a gray watercolor of her former self. Dad orbited Mom, catering to whatever she wanted, desperate to make things better by not making them worse. Esme danced, always, no longer expected home for holidays or birthdays or illness because she'd given herself a permanent excuse. And even when she did go home, she wasn't expected to stay for long. She was not necessarily happy, but she was not unhappy either. She was a seesaw caught in a straight line, and that was better than being catapulted upward unexpectedly, legs dangling, not knowing how long she'd be there. A girl in a basement changed everything.

Madeline answered on the first ring.

"I'm sorry," Esme said. "And I do want to know. I just . . ."

"I know." Madeline sighed. "There's never a good time, is there?"

"No," Esme said finally.

"Go light a candle," Madeline said.

"You should, like Mom." Esme laughed a little through the last tears, terribly sad that Lily wouldn't know what Mom sounded like. "And what about Mom? She must be going nuts."

"Yeah, well, no more nuts than usual," Madeline said. "She's hopeful, but you know."

Esme sighed. When this wasn't Lily, Cerise would coast along again like an airplane flying after the oxygen was gone, full of frozen, sleeping passengers.

"Call me if you need anything."

"You too," Esme whispered.

She knew the statistics. It was unlikely that Lily was alive, less likely that she'd ever come home or that they'd ever know what had happened. There were more stories about bones and teeth found in unusual places than missing children coming home.

She pressed her sleeve to her eyes, ignoring the teardrops on the chair, glassy half globes that magnified the wood. Crying made her head throb. She was ready to move, to feel the barre beneath her fingers, to be in the studio with her suitcase full of warm-up clothes and makeup, but first she had a candle to light. *I don't have to feel bad*, she reminded herself, *for living the life I was given.*

The sun had shifted. Paris was washed out. Blue doors blended into gray cobblestones. The boulangerie was empty, her nose too stuffy to smell bread baking or warm chocolate. The café on the corner was quiet. One man sat beneath the awning, cradling an espresso cup. She followed the street past the bastille in the roundabout, her sister's words swelling in her chest.

There was always a church in Paris brighter and bigger than the last, glowing with stained glass and marble statues that made real people look gross. She wanted one with heavy doors to trap her prayer inside so it could echo through high ceilings over and over again. She found one with gargoyles on the roof, throwing long, stretched shadows over the sidewalk. The door closed silently behind her. Her footsteps echoed down the aisle as she ran her hands along the pews. A Blessed Mother held a tiny lamb near the altar. Esme lit a red candle beneath it. It seemed right, a mother and a lamb. She made sure the flame was still flickering when she left, just because.

~

Their final school performance had been *Sleeping Beauty*. The wings had been a rush of fabric and fear, rosin and joy. She'd just finished dancing Candide, her favorite fairy because Anna Pavlova had danced her once. Esme had danced beautifully—one of her rare performances that had filled her with purpose. It had been the moment she'd left home for, why she'd sacrificed her childhood, and hers alone. She'd stared at the empty stage while the stage lights had cooled and the audience had chattered behind the curtain. She hadn't been ready to take off her costume and hang it up like an empty shell. She'd wanted to be Candide a little longer, who'd gotten Esme into SFB, an official corps member, on the edge of a new unexplored part of her life in a costume that smelled like hair spray and sparkled in the darkness.

Esme bit the side of her thumbnail until her skin was red and raw, unsure what the Waltz Girl would be for her tonight.

"Stop," Adam said, jolting her back from the memory. "Let's run it one more time. But this time . . ." He turned his back to the mirror, hands on his hips, then circled back. "Are you nervous? Where's the emotion, Esme? You're flat as hell."

His frustration only made Esme more panicky. Esme took a deep breath. She knew this piece technically, but she had less than an hour to find the real character.

Adam gripped tighter than usual when he lifted her, so hard it caught her breath. She couldn't tell him about the girl in the basement. He'd say she was too distracted, and she needed to be here, not alone in an empty hotel room.

"You're traveling," he said of her supported grand jeté. "And you're not leaping high enough. Just let me lift you. Just . . . let's try it again."

He took his position. Esme took hers, aware of his breathing behind her. She leaped, and he caught her, releasing at the height of her jump so she'd reach a little higher before guiding her gently down. He was right. She had been overjumping.

"That's better," Adam said. He took her hands in his. "You're gonna be fine. I know you can do this. Take a minute, OK? Find the emotion. Maybe it'll be easier if I'm not here."

Adam stepped away, checking the clock on the wall. "We should get dressed."

His jaw made a harsh angle just under his ear like the corner of a box. She'd danced with Adam for years. He knew she was restless and didn't ask why and still trusted that she'd do the right thing for his show tonight. His show. She flooded with gratitude. He was the reason she was here, in Paris, in this dark studio with concrete walls and a dusty mirror. He gathered his bag and headed toward the door. She reached him first and put one hand on his shoulder, raising herself en pointe to kiss his cheek.

"Thank you," she said.

"For what?" Adam looked surprised.

"For everything. I wouldn't be here without you." It was true.

Adam looked down. He squeezed Esme's hand. He was blushing. "I'm glad you're here," he whispered and let go. Her hand was cold where his had been. They'd never had a moment like this. Esme lingered in the doorway, watching Adam shrink down the hall.

There was a poem she'd read once about grief, the only one that got it right, that told the world to stop clocks and put away the stars and the ocean because life was over.

It was what her parents had become, moping in the glow of internet forums, posting and reposting old pictures, skipping her shows or Nick's graduation because they felt too guilty to do anything but search. When this wasn't Lily, they would rev up again, hire a new investigator, because someone had been found.

Esme couldn't stand the oil drop in water her mother had become, how everyone slowly scattered away from her. After the cards had stopped and there was no news, asking how Cerise was led only to angry rants about what the police had done wrong. Or worse, Cerise would say things about Lily coming home, like, "I hope Lily has Mrs. So-and-So for her kindergarten teacher next year." Then people pasted those dumb, polite, how-can-she-not-see-it sympathy faces on and listened patiently, sorry they hadn't crossed the street or busied themselves with coat zippers or the *National Enquirer* at the supermarket checkout until Cerise was gone and they weren't at risk for catching her sad life and bad luck. Esme hated to admit it, but she was repulsed by it too. Talking to her mother had become something she did out of obligation, like leaving flowers at a grave.

But Esme had realized a long time ago that she did not want to freeze life as her parents had. It didn't mean she loved her sister less. She'd done her share of internet searching, scouring missing persons threads and sites for lost relatives. *Hello, my name is Esme. I lost my little sister when she was four years old* . . . hoping it would ring a bell for someone reading, but it never had. It had taken a long time to accept that someone could just be gone.

Esme shut off the light in the studio and stood in the darkness. She closed her eyes and imagined blackness inside herself until she found her younger self sitting at the foot of her mother's bed, watching her sleep through a haze of pills. "Lily, go back to sleep," her mother had mumbled. She played it over in her mind until the first tears prickled behind her eyes, and then she moved her arms and legs and traced the first few lines of choreography, pushing against the heavy feeling in her chest.

Imaginary Lily was curled in the corner of the studio, fogging the mirror with her breath and writing little *L*s on the glass.

"Am I coming home this time?" she asked.

Esme did not stop to look because Lily was never there. She spiked through the choreography, playing the music in her head, turning it up to drown out Lily, ashamed of herself for imagining Lily now, of using her sister to find the feeling Adam needed her to.

"Did they find me?" she asked again and again.

She was charged now. There was no darkness. She finished the set and did it again until she was sweating and her heart was pounding in her chest, and she pushed back a scream. She wiped her face with the backs of her hands and turned on the light, flooding the studio until she was sure she was alone.

"No," Esme whispered to no one. "You're still gone."

She gathered her stuff and counted down the list of things to do before the show, before she'd have to think about the girl in the basement again. Alone in the studio, she was exorbitantly grateful for the world she'd stumbled into, for not stopping the clocks but pushing them forward instead.

Chapter Fourteen

That night, there was a fire backstage. It started in a trash can and caught a dressing robe on the moveable rack. The girls threw water over it until it went out. It ruined a box of pointe shoes but didn't catch the costume rack with seventeen tutus or ignite the cloud of hair spray that blanketed the room. Aside from the pointe shoes, the smell of burnt plastic, and a smoke smudge on the ceiling, it was over quickly. But it felt like an omen.

The smoke smudge looked like a crow and made Esme uneasy. She threw a wet paper towel at the ceiling. It stuck for a minute before dropping to the floor. The smudge stayed. The intercom in the dressing room crackled with static, but the message never came.

"Where would you go?" someone asked in the hallway, a passing conversation. She finished her makeup under the smoke stain and tapped her feet, hoping to shed the jitters.

No matter where she traveled, there was one family photograph she tucked inside the vanity mirror. It had been taken after her first *Nutcracker* as Clara. Esme had floated offstage, beaming and breathless, leaping into the wings while the audience cheered. They'd stood for her, a wave of faceless people rippling from front to back, a sea of clapping hands, until her cheeks had hurt from smiling. Her family had waited backstage, squished between costume racks. Her father had a bouquet of pink roses. Cerise had been wearing makeup and a floor-length black lace dress she'd made, a beautiful version of regular Mom. Lily had been on her hip in a red velvet dress, black beads swirling from belly to neck. She'd been staring at something in the distance, a dancer maybe, a costume. Her face had been flushed and sleepy. It was past her bedtime.

Madeline's arm threaded through Esme's, smiling brightly, suddenly proud to share her room. Her father and Nick blended into the dark wing. Nick already looked like Andre, with his chiseled jaw and dark eyes behind long lashes, a glimmer of the man he'd become. And Dad. He never smiled much, but he was smiling here, so much younger than Esme remembered. He'd cheered for her with his football voice, so loud she'd heard him onstage, chasing her dream with her, all five pieces of her family. Esme tapped the picture for good luck and kissed it gently in Lily's place.

~

Esme's hair is in a tight bun, held in place by an invisible net, perfectly in line with her cheekbone. Her eyebrows are drawn on, fake lashes in place, skin dusted with bronzer, pointe shoes stitched. She closes the door on her pointe shoes to soften the box and rubs them in rosin, thanking FG, her maker's mark, an anonymous, faraway person who's made her shoes for as long as Esme remembers. She's ready. She will take all her feelings about the girl in the basement and make them part of the story. The intercom beeps. It's time.

There are last-minute instructions. Esme listens, but she's thinking about the girl. If it's Lily, is there any of the old Lily in the new? There's so much of little Esme in her tonight. For as much as she's stayed away from her family, she hasn't really moved on, not really, not when she carries so much of them with her. The thought is comforting. Adam catches her eye and smiles. Her skin tingles with the thought of his touch. She shivers a little under his gaze and wonders why she's never noticed it before. She shakes the thought away. Tonight. She focuses on tonight, on the Waltz Girl.

Esme finds her tape mark on the floor. The audience is restless. It's a small show, a small theater. All of the audience sounds are magnified. The lights have not dimmed yet. Behind the curtain, they're chattering and finding seats, rustling ice in glasses, scrolling programs, listening for seventeen pairs of pointe shoes to thud into place. She is the center point of the diamond. She inhales, and her costume stretches with her skin. The stage smells of deodorant, powdery and soft. Nervous sweat. The line of light disappears under the curtain before it rolls away. Stage lights are as blinding as old stars. The heat and Tchaikovsky's long strings and the dark mass of cantaloupe heads moving and shuffling programs while Adam watches in the wing feel like breathing.

Esme reaches for the light on cue, shielding her eyes from the glow with every dancer onstage. She loves this part, even though it still reminds her of that day with Amelia when she saw *Serenade* for the first time, her hands bathed in blue light, and realized Lily was not coming home. Now she is on the other side of the audience, and all the dancers are the same, equal, their movements in sync. *We all come from the same place*, Esme thinks, finding a story in choreography that isn't meant to have one. *We write our own journey.* She's always written her own journey.

She is moving, puffing, breathing, counting steps, not thinking about what she has to do and letting her muscles remember. She is too focused to think about Lily now, concentrating too hard to look forward to dancing with Adam. For a quick moment, she fears when it will end and she'll have to think again, but there's still time. She glances at the floor occasionally to make sure she's reached her marks, checking tape lines that only she can see through a blur of fabric, lights, and limbs. Hundreds of miles away, the police question a missing someone, sorting through years of files and evidence, facts as small as fingerprints or strands of hair, looking for answers, searching for stars. All she has to do is dance.

The orchestra is too fast. She glares at the conductor quickly. What is he doing? His arms are waving, and the instruments are playing. He's not watching her, so she speeds up to keep pace with the music. She's convinced conductors do this when they don't like someone. *Shit*, she thinks. *Someone probably told him to. I'm sorry*, she silently apologizes to Adam. *I'm doing the best I can.*

She falls on cue, gets up, goes down again, struggling to control her heaving chest once she's stopped moving. It wouldn't be convincing without real pain, so she thinks of her mother, half-asleep, telling Lily to go back to sleep, but her mother didn't realize or forgot briefly that Lily was already gone and it was Esme. Her mother didn't see her or wanted to see Lily instead. Esme falls until the pain of being forgotten and unseen is real. Adam is led away with covered eyes while one outstretched hand searches the air in front of him. She can't see this but knows it's happening behind her. Tchaikovsky's strings tell her so. She's covered in Adam's shadow.

The piece is almost done now. Her hipbone juts against the floor. Her shoulder aches. *This must be what it's like to sleep on the floor*, she thinks of the girl in the basement, how painful it would be to do that night after night knowing she'd had a real bed once with pillows and blankets and stuffed animals.

She undoes her hair and lets it stream over her shoulders. Her back strains. They have her by the ankles, behind her knees, and lift her. Now that she's not dancing, her chest strains to breathe. Her costume pulls against her skin, keeping her lungs and pounding heart inside. She's carried away without a floor beneath her feet. She looks up and sees only stage lights and scaffolding. The girl in the basement would see a hanging light bulb, a ceiling with black mold. No, she closes her eyes and leans back, arms above her head. She imagines a swirling galaxy of glow-in-the-dark stars, prisms, and rainbows. That's what the girl would see, memories from her home before. That's what she would pray for, what would keep her breathing, hoping.

The curtain falls. They lower her to the floor. The audience is applauding. She waits in the wings for the curtain to rise again and the corps to bow and holds back real tears. She hasn't thought about that night with her mother in years and can't shake the shivery feeling it's caused or how fragile it makes her feel. She is ready with an excuse about the orchestra, but when she sees the smile on Adam's face, she knows she doesn't need it.

~

"Esme!" Adam rushed toward her, arms outstretched. He wrapped them around her and lifted her from the floor. His heart beat against hers. "You were amazing! Everyone's talking about it. What happened tonight? That was incredible."

Hadn't he said those same words after *Sleeping Beauty*, just before he'd blurted out his offer to NYCB and she'd blurted hers to SFB, the realization slowly dawning that a curtain had fallen between them?

"I don't know," she lied. "But I woke up with a fever this morning. Did I tell you?"

Adam blinked, laughing. "Shut up."

"Nope," she said. "It's too late to be mad at me."

The corps stepped backward. It was their turn. Adam lifted her hand and walked her to center stage, his hand chalk dry under hers. The lights were strong enough to make her see stars. They walked forward together, four long steps, Adam a step behind, and curtsied. He held his right hand to his heart, stepped forward to escort her back. Someone threw flowers. She pulled one long white stem from the bouquet and handed it to Adam. She was doing everything she was supposed to do, smiling in all the right places, but the whole thing felt wrong. Imaginary Lily was behind her, stomping her foot into the stage. *You used me*, Imaginary Lily hissed. *Why do you only think about my sad stuff for stupid dance?* The curtain came down one last time. Her head was spinning as the adrenaline eased away. It bothered her that she hadn't known she'd done well until she'd seen Adam's face. When would she ever know for herself? She smiled past everyone congratulating her to gather her things, ready for a shower and maybe a glass of wine before bed to muffle anything else Imaginary Lily had to say.

~

She'd done well. Soon people would whisper loud enough for her to hear, and reviews would pick her apart. She walked home past empty shops, turning in the opposite direction of her hotel just to pass Notre Dame. It was late, but she sat on the bridge and looked at the church, built of light and shadows. Streetlights sparkled on love locks along the Seine. Late-night dinner boats passed on the river, full of candlelit tables and shadow shapes. Esme felt like she was floating somewhere between real life and all the things in her head.

A street seller passed with headbands of jasmine flowers. A wreath of little white flowers would look pretty in Lily's hair. She wondered if Lily's hair still had red-gold streaks in the sun, if she still sneezed when the sun got in her eyes. Esme bought a string of flowers. The girl in the basement might not be Lily but could be. That was enough for now. It was nice, Esme realized, to think of Lily as a person again and not just something that had happened to her family.

She wandered slowly along the river, kicking cigarette butts with the toe of her sneaker. Her legs were ready for an ice bath. Heat pushed through her jeans. She was sore and tired, in need of Advil. Her stomach was unsettled, nauseous with possibility when there were only two: it was Lily, or it wasn't, like pulling flower petals. *It's Lily, it's Lily not.* The jasmine smelled more sickly than sweet. She tossed them into the river and watched them float away. A rat scurried past on the cobblestone quay. It was peaceful to be alone in the city, like a prayer. She enjoyed the possibility of not knowing and tried not to let "what if" ruin the dream of "maybe."

Chapter Fifteen

It was eight o'clock in New York. Madeline would be filling out seating cards. It was going to be a small wedding, fifty people and a ceremony at city hall followed by dinner in Chinatown, where Nathan and Madeline had had their first date. Too shy to admit she didn't know how to use chopsticks, Madeline had stabbed a dumpling through the middle and eaten until it had splashed onto her plate. Nathan had made her a pair with rubber bands and shown her how to hold them, and Madeline had let herself be taught. "You'll marry him," Esme had told her. "Anyone who can teach you anything is worth keeping."

The hotel lobby was quiet. There were only the man behind the front desk and the humming overhead lights for company. Esme curled into the phone booth and cradled the phone in her hands.

"Mom's throwing a fit about not having the ceremony in a church. She says it's not a 'legitimate' wedding."

"Not surprising."

"Yeah, but I hoped she'd drop it. She's been huffing around, slamming cabinets, cleaning obsessively, like she's getting ready for . . ." Madeline's voice trailed off. She didn't have to say *Lily coming home*.

"Any updates?"

"Nick can't get anything. The FBI's here now. She's in the hospital."

Esme didn't push further. She didn't want to think about the girl being malnourished or sick or hurt. "Ten tiny fingers, ten tiny toes," her mother had whispered when Lily was born, gently pinching Lily's fingers and toes like a prayer.

"What can I do?" Esme changed the subject back to Madeline's wedding.

"Nothing." Madeline sounded relieved. They were playing a kind of pretend, but it was a pretend they were used to. "I just want it to be over, actually. I'm not having a shower because it's just another way to showcase how dysfunctional our family is. I can't think of anything worse than inviting everyone I know to watch me open presents with a hat made of gift bows on while Mom cries every time I open one and gives her 'if I hadn't married your father' narrative to all my law school friends. And that's if she shows up, because, you know, that's always a risk."

"Dad wouldn't let her not show up."

"Yeah, well, it might be better if she didn't. How sad is that?"

In another life, Esme would have been Madeline's maid of honor. She would have helped her mother plan a shower and then a bachelorette party, and they would have hot-glue gunned invitations and wedding favors. Now, Cerise couldn't even handle birthdays. Cerise would buy birthday cakes and light candles, but when it was time to sing, she'd find a reason to wash dishes or fill glasses with milk no one wanted because she couldn't stand life moving forward.

"You could've eloped."

"Yeah, well, part of me still wants a normal family. You're still coming, right?"

"Of course—why wouldn't I?" The accusation hung between them again. She would always be the one who'd snipped herself out of the equation and made a luxurious life for herself compared to living in Queens and helping their parents, but they were still sisters, and there would always be a part of Esme that wanted her family too.

"I don't know, Esme. I'm taking my bar exam in three weeks. I don't even want to think about this."

"But it's your wedding. You're only supposed to get married once. Why don't you just push the bar back? Or the wedding? What's the rush?"

Silence. Papers shuffled. Madeline didn't do anything spontaneously unless she . . .

"Oh, shit." Esme finally understood. "Does Mom know?"

"Of course not. You think I want to dump that on her too? She's got enough, and it's fine, really. After the wedding, it won't matter. Nathan wants to be a dad. He's excited about it. And don't even think about throwing me a baby shower, ever, because I can't imagine what a shit show Mom would be there. God."

"But what about you?" Madeline had always stepped in when their mother couldn't, spooning her ice chips when she was sick, showing her how to plot x and y on an axis, following library book instructions on how to make a Balanchine bun. She'd be a good mother, but how would Madeline try a case in the Supreme Court or be her own Darby Shaw if she had a baby?

"Do you want to be a mother?"

"Well, look," Madeline said finally. "It doesn't matter if it happened when I was ready. It happened, and now I have to be ready."

Esme felt guilty for sitting in a phone booth in Paris, for the bag of chèvre at her feet from the *fromagerie* and the croissant wrapped in paper. Her life was luxuriously selfish in comparison, despite how hard she'd worked for it.

"You were always so responsible," Esme said sadly.

"It would've been nice not to be a mom for a little longer." Madeline sighed. The relief in her voice was palpable now that she wasn't carrying a baby and a secret.

"How pregnant are you?"

"Six weeks or so. I'm not showing, just starting to feel sick. Everyone thinks it's stress."

Madeline, who had an answer for everything from some book she'd read once, who flicked the channel when kissing scenes came on, who hated ironing her father's shirts or folding his laundry, the same sister who said marriage was for people who didn't know what to do with themselves. Madeline, who'd watched *The Pelican Brief* seventeen times because she wanted her own conspiracy one day, was going to be a wife. She was going to be a mom.

"Madeline? Are you really in love?" She couldn't imagine perfect Madeline full of butterflies or anything less than composed, but Madeline must have felt something with Nathan, some shift in the energy around him that made her accept this new life. Or therapy. Hours of talking about the past had given her a decent shot at a normal future. *Please*, Esme hoped, *make a map for me*.

She wouldn't have Madeline all to herself anymore. She couldn't call at any time because there would be a husband and a baby, someone to question what was so important at two a.m. Madeline might not care what their parents said or did because she'd have in-laws to drive her nuts, and Esme wouldn't understand. Madeline would have her own family with whispered secrets and inside jokes. Their shared room so many years before would be obsolete, like a Walkman thrown in a drawer.

But worse, Madeline would disappear into her new life. It was already happening.

"Yes," Madeline said simply.

Esme wondered if her sister ever wanted to take the private world inside and spill it out, but she never did. Madeline's private life was much more intriguing because she kept it to herself. "You should have told me," she said.

Another sigh slipped through the line. Madeline's voice was only a whisper. "I just wanted a plan first." It hurt that Madeline took more comfort in planning, but Esme brushed the hurt away. This wasn't about her.

"You can tell me stuff now because I know. Who else knows?"

"Just Nathan."

Poor Nathan. He wouldn't understand. He was nice enough, serious minded with clean half-moon fingernails, tall and quiet and midwestern, patiently waiting for people to step off the subway before stepping on instead of pushing through. He knew things about soil from growing up on a farm and wanted to be a lawyer because he believed the law could protect people. He had a patience about him that Esme didn't understand, a cornfield quiet, she called it. He wouldn't understand why her parents acted the way they did when his probably slept with their doors unlocked. His painful stability would point out how deeply screwed up the rest of her family was in comparison.

A fly buzzed past, throwing itself over and over again into the glass. There were dancers outside now, smoking in the streetlight. She wanted to go before they drifted in. She didn't want to talk about the show tonight. It was too special to talk about. The silence on the other end of the line unnerved her.

"Madeline?"

"The news is on."

The volume blared, but Esme couldn't make out the words. She slid forward on her seat, crushing the bag at her feet by mistake. The phone booth filled with the smell of cheese. Esme pressed the phone against her ear.

"Fifty-seven-year-old Gloria Garcia," Madeline repeated distractedly. "Lived alone. Daughter and husband died in a car accident. Daughter was seven years old. The girl in the basement says she's the daughter. Searching for family members, other information. Blah, blah, blah. The neighbor says she was a nice lady, had a garden, looked after old people. Sounds like a real saint."

"What are they showing?"

"Her house."

"What does it look like?"

"It's white with a gray roof. Chain-link fence, hydrangeas. Nothing special."

Outside the phone booth, the concierge arranged red roses in a vase, added fresh water, snipped stems. **CHRISTOPHE**, the name tag on his red jacket said in blocky letters that didn't match his long, delicate lines. He caught Esme's eye and smiled. Being seen warmed her. He pulled one long rose from the vase and left it on the table. Red. Something stirred in Esme's memory, an unsettled feeling from long ago.

"Is there a tree house in the yard? Or a tree?"

"There's a tree."

"With red leaves?"

"I don't know, Es. It's August, and it just looks like a tree. They're not exactly zooming in on it. Please don't tell me you're thinking about that stupid psychic."

"Psychics take away hope where it should be and give hope where there's none." Wasn't that what the church-basement grief counselor had said? "Technically," she'd told him, "God does the same thing. What kind of God lets hundreds of people disappear every year? Explain that," she'd said before walking out. It had been a stupid idea anyway, meant to help her nightmares, but it had only made them worse the year she'd made SFB. She'd been the most tired she'd ever been in her entire life but hadn't been able to sleep. She'd tried Xanax instead.

Christophe moved the flowers to the lobby table. It hadn't been roses last time. It had been something purple. The roses were especially thorny, amplified in the curved glass vase. The buds curled into themselves, shocked to be in a hotel instead of the garden they came from. How could a woman who gave vegetables to her neighbors keep someone locked in a basement? It didn't make sense. The phone booth was too small. She was boxed in. The psychic was a stupid thing to hope for. It always had been, but still.

"It's just the weather now. I'll call you if they say anything else. Oh! And Esme?"

"Yeah?"

"Congratulations."

"For what?"

"You must have done really well tonight. You never say anything about the shows you're proud of."

"That's not true."

"Trust me—it is."

They said good night. It would be so nice to say good night to someone so close. She stepped out of the phone booth, thankful for the rush of fresh air. The first hint of a Charlie horse started under her arch. She needed an ice bath and to roll a tennis ball under her foot. Even the carpet felt like jagged rocks.

She was going to be an aunt. What did aunts do? Maybe being an aunt wasn't that different from being a big sister, but that . . . that . . .

Esme was back in her house again, the lock swinging on the front door. The pink sequined shoes were missing, without so much as a mark on the carpet, her mother's panicked voice to the 911 operator while spaghetti chilled on the table, drying on Lily's *Lion King* plate. No one would ever eat them.

Esme dropped the bag of cheese. It landed with a soft thud.

"Miss?"

Christophe stepped out from behind the desk. He was a charcoal sketch: dark eyebrows, dark hair that fell over his face in sharp, fresh-cut threads over cedar eyes. Long fingers on the keyboard, a coil of arms and legs, fixing the leaking tub in her room on her first night at the hotel. Christophe had two voices, the one he used with guests and another whispered into the phone when guests weren't checking in or out or tubs leaking or flowers waiting to be arranged. The dark lines around his eyes knit into shadows during those secret calls. He was about her age, maybe younger, too young to hide the wounded look when someone left change on the counter, a dismissal. Alternate versions of his own life swept in and out of the revolving door, but he was always here, trapped in his red-and-black uniform.

Truthfully, she was glad there was someone to call if she needed something stupid. There wasn't anyone else. He picked up the bag from the floor and handed it back to her. She didn't want it anymore but didn't say so. The red rose waited on the table.

"This came for you." He held out a small jeweler's box, wrapped in silver paper, tied with pink ribbon. No note. Her curiosity sparked the small space between them.

"Who's it from?" Other dancers had gotten gifts from fans, but this was her first. She had done well tonight; she knew it. The success scared her.

"I'm sorry," he said. "I don't know."

The phone rang. He slipped around the desk to answer it, eyeing her carefully beneath his lashes. The cord dangled. Hadn't there been an upside-down phone that night? Upended, dial tone beeping until it had gone silent?

She felt trapped, as boxed in as she had been in the phone booth. She wished she could curl into herself like a rosebud and stay nestled in her own safe self—or someone else's. Adam. She rounded the corner to his room and stopped.

Jennifer lingered outside Adam's door in a pair of electric-blue leggings and a shredded black T-shirt. It fell off her shoulder on one side. Her right foot rested against the inside of her left thigh. Tree pose, but instead of a calm forest tree, everything about Jennifer was electrified. Esme sensed she'd burn the whole place down just to find herself unscathed in the ashes, those blue eyes cold as ever.

She'd ignored Esme on that first day at the studio when everyone had introduced themselves, yawning theatrically when Adam had introduced his friend from school in a way that had made Esme feel like a mom of a childhood friend, someone who made really good meatballs and let kids play Nintendo all night or made waffles with ice cream for breakfast in dumpy mom jeans and a bleach-stained sweatshirt.

The Adam she knew would have hated someone like Jennifer, who'd probably had a stage mom and all kinds of stuff they'd never had. Adam's door closed behind Jennifer, but her presence lingered in the hallway, so strong and uninviting that Esme took a different staircase to her room. Where was the Adam who slid in beside her and shared peanut M&M'S, the "diet" kind? Or visited her last year in San Francisco just to see her first performance as a soloist? She was still the same Esme, still struggling for the next level, whatever that was.

Part of Esme was relieved. She didn't know how to be something more with Adam. The normal part of her that should've known what to do at nineteen didn't quite work. She could hide it well enough when she was doing normal Esme things, but when something new like Adam came along, she felt broken. The little box with silver paper reflected a blurry version of herself, dark haired and alone in the empty stairwell.

She waited until she reached her room before untying the ribbon and lifting the lid. A pale-pink seashell rested on a bed of white sand. She held it up to the light, admiring the gentle spiral of the thumb-size shell. It was perfect compared to the wildly uneven intersecting lines in her hand, her bitten-down fingernails. Everything about her was crude compared to the ethereal thing she was onstage.

She would be that kind of disappointing aunt, too, cool and traveling the world but missing birthdays and Christmases, too busy with her own life to be part of someone else's. She put the shell back in its box, knowing she'd never compare to what she was supposed to be. She hurried to the bathroom, closing the door between her and the shell, pushing away thoughts of Adam, the tree outside Mrs. Garcia's house, that book she used to read Lily about backsies. It was a bad deal, but there were no backsies. That was the bargain. Hadn't that character done OK in the end? She couldn't remember, and it hurt to try, so she emptied ice into the tub, anxious for the chill that would numb her thoughts, and slid inside.

Chapter Sixteen

Aunt Esme. It was her first thought in the hazy moment between awake and asleep. A new baby in the family, who didn't know what life was like *before*, would help. There'd be a reason to put up a Christmas tree, bake birthday cakes, or hide treats from the leprechaun on St. Patrick's Day. Cerise could make Halloween costumes for the baby. Her father would put the baby on his lap to "drive" in empty parking lots. They could do the things they'd had taken from them, kind of. The baby might make her want to go home again, and it would feel more like the home she remembered.

But eventually, they'd have to explain the embarrassing things: why Grandpa slept on the couch, why Grandma didn't get out of bed in October except to light candles at church, why Grandma had a birthday cake with a new candle every year on Lily's birthday for someone who wasn't there, why Uncle Nick didn't visit much.

Madeline would explain that Grandma and Grandpa acted strange because they'd once had a little girl named Lily, who would've been your aunt, but she disappeared one night and never came back. It made Grandma and Grandpa so sad. *But don't worry*, Madeline would lie, *Mommy won't let that happen to you.* The mysterious Aunt Lily would become a fairy-tale story, like Little Red Riding Hood being eaten by the wolf or the Gingerbread Man falling apart in the rain, a reason to be scared of things in the closet or under the bed because Grandma and Grandpa were proof that bad things could happen to real people.

Explaining these things was enough to make Esme wish Madeline wasn't pregnant so this little person would never have to understand.

If the girl in the basement was Lily, this was what she'd come home to, only worse because it was her fault somehow that they'd withered away without her, like Miss Havisham, whose heart had stopped at twenty to nine, who'd never taken off her wedding dress and let the cake rot on the table. Lily'd left them at the altar just by disappearing.

One day, the baby might ask why Aunt Esme was a dancer. *Because she loves dancing. Because it's a world different from this one.* She'd think back to trips home in the past few years, when she'd taken a taxi from the airport because her mother had forgotten what day her flight got in or had eaten dinner with a plate on her lap in front of the TV because her mother had gone to sleep as soon as she could and her father was working. Between bites of stale cereal on those trips, she'd realized that if she had guilt about leaving, she should remember that they'd abandoned her first.

The morning passed quietly. Esme wandered past her usual breakfast café on the corner, where a bookseller was laying out children's books on the sidewalk. On one of the covers, a turtle floated in the Seine, still and serene, while Paris swam around him in buildings and a sky of a million colors. Turtley. Hadn't Lily said once there weren't any books for turtles? *You were wrong*, Esme thought sadly, unfolding bills from her wallet and handing them to the woman. If not for Lily, maybe this would be the first little present she'd buy for Madeline's baby, even if the words were all in French. The paper bag tapped against her leg as she walked back to the hotel, curled up inside the phone booth, and wrapped the cord around her wrist, hoping no one would bang on the door or pace outside. She wanted time.

Madeline answered on the third ring. "No word," she said, sounding frazzled and a little annoyed. "Except that the girl's name is Liz, and the investigation is ongoing. And I'm postponing the wedding."

"What? Why?"

"Because I just want to wait. What difference does it make? It's city hall and a Chinese restaurant." Madeline's voice rushed out in an angry jumble that made Esme's cheeks burn. Was she waiting for Liz to be Lily, or was it regret?

"You can't do that, Madeline. 'We'll do Christmas next year, when things are better.'" She mimicked her mother from long ago.

"That's easy for you to say, Esme," Madeline snapped. "Because you're not here. Last night, Mom used all the centerpiece candles to make a vigil on the street. All of them. You had to see her down there, setting them up and relighting them every time they blew out."

Esme cringed. Her mother had become as embarrassing as Mrs. Rodriquez wearing her dead husband's clothes. After Lily, her parents were directionless. She'd promised herself not to be directionless and wouldn't let Madeline either.

"Madeline?"

Cabinet doors slammed shut. Plates rattled. Madeline was unloading the dishwasher, but Esme knew she was crying hot, silent tears, trying to hide it with busy hands. "You don't have to do any of this. If you don't want to get married, if you don't want to have the baby, we can figure something out."

The alternative wasn't great, but Madeline trapped in responsibility she wasn't ready for, for the second time in her life, was worse.

The rattling plates stopped. Esme pictured her sister tracing the outline of a dish with her finger. "You have choices, Madeline, even if it doesn't feel like it right now."

"What would that make me? This isn't exactly what I aspired for, but I have to live with it." There were probably dozens of dancers who'd had to choose, and many were back onstage, living for a dream. They'd beaten every statistic to be there. Ballet didn't let them do both, but that wasn't true for Madeline. For just a quick second, Esme was jealous of other people's balance.

"You could do both," Esme said quietly. "Mom would help you. She'd watch the baby so you could study and work. Lots of people do both."

"I really don't know how I feel about Mom watching the baby." Madeline was crying again, softly.

A memory flickered up, hazy and long forgotten, of her mother dipping the first beautiful wedding dress she'd made after Lily had disappeared into a bathtub of black dye. What did it mean? No one was innocent? Marriage was a death? It had been odd then. Now it was disturbing. What Cerise would do with a baby creeped Esme out, but another selfish part of her wished it would heal Cerise.

"Or maybe Uncle Nick will drop by, Esme, and I'll have to worry about my kid around him and a loaded gun. Let's add that to the equation too."

Nick. He'd never recovered, not really. It had probably never occurred to him that his silence had made them suspicious, but Nick was his own moon now, cold and orbiting his family in the same distant way they all were. Esme couldn't prove whether he'd done anything that night, but it didn't matter. He'd never be guilty or fully innocent, but he'd always be distant. Suspicion had forced him there. Occasional news that Nick was OK was enough.

"I'm so tired. All I want to do is sleep."

"That probably gets better," Esme said, wishing she knew more about pregnancy, enough to know how Madeline felt. "You also don't have to decide right now. What does Nathan say?"

"Nothing." Madeline's voice rose. "He says absolutely nothing."

"Then it's your choice, I guess."

"No." Madeline sighed. "I've already made it."

"Good," Esme said, the paper bag with the turtle book still on her lap. "I like the idea of being an aunt."

∼

Last night's rain evaporated in a fine mist. The sky was its own wide blue today. Watercolor blue. Rolling, sheep-cloud blue. Even the puddles reflected that beautiful sky, holding a tiny piece of it on the earth. Esme hated leaving it behind as she entered the studio, into tense, trapped air where people were probably gossiping. The reviews were in, and she was sure this group had their own opinions, as hidden and sticky as a spiderweb in the dark.

Someone was vomiting in the bathroom. The faint acidic smell hovered in the hallway. The retching stopped. She thought of her sister on the bathroom floor. Morning sickness must be daunting. That was what she'd heard in Madeline's voice: the dread of not knowing what to expect until even emptying the dishwasher was overwhelming. If she lived closer, she could let herself into Madeline's apartment with a spare key and sweep the kitchen while Madeline slept, put groceries in the fridge, water plants—small, stupid things to make her sister feel less alone. Esme sighed. For as long as she danced, she would never be near enough, and she wasn't sure how much she wanted to be.

The corps dressing room was a flurry of costumes. Clothes were thrown over garment racks. The whole room was a mess of hair spray. It stung the inside of her nose and tasted bitter. Her new dressing area was down the hall with the other soloists and much quieter. Clothes hung neatly on garment racks. Makeup and hairbrushes were stored on shelves. A small oscillating fan blew toward the door, carrying away the smell of hair spray. In a room this small, no one wanted to be the messy one.

"Am I in line?" Ashley asked, referring to her cheekbone and the height of her bun. "I can't get it right today."

"Too high," Esme said, slipping the elastic band from her hair. "Bring it down."

"I thought so." Ashley nodded in the mirror, her unmade eyes washed out by the rest of her made-up face. Esme settled into her seat and reached for her brush, secretly relieved that Jennifer's place by the vanity mirror was empty.

Esme sprayed her brush with hair spray and gathered her hair into a ponytail. It hung there while she dipped a sponge in pancake foundation and dabbed it over her face, closing her eyes and moving the sponge in small quick jabs. The vanity lights glowed yellow orange like tiny suns. Esme moved from foundation to white powder. She drew lines for her new eyes, making them bigger with eyeliner and pencils. The real Esme felt less touchable now, less bothered by what people were saying or not saying as she tucked herself away behind layers of makeup.

Esme thumbed through the costumes on the rack, looking for hers. It was where she'd left it, only there was a dark-brown coffee stain where it should have been smooth white. A puddle of spilled coffee spread on the floor, seeping into the pointe shoes she'd already sewed for tonight. Her stomach cramped. Jennifer's empty dressing table glared back at her. It was so immature, almost comical. Esme laughed.

Ashley startled. The eye pencil smeared across her face.

"Great." Esme fumbled with the hanger, threw the shoes into the trash, and huffed out of the room for another pair. She'd bring her costume to wardrobe. They'd do what they could.

Ashley followed Esme into the hallway. "What's wrong?" The concern in her voice sounded real enough, but who knew.

Esme kept walking. It didn't matter. It could have been anyone, on purpose or not. She picked through her box of pointe shoes for a pair and sat alone in the hallway, hoping Ashley would take the hint and leave, but Ashley hovered, half-dressed in her costume.

"Can I help you with something? Let me . . . maybe I could—"

"I'm fine," Esme shot back, harsher than she intended. Her chest burned. Her face felt like she was staring into a hair dryer. She thought of Madeline sitting on her kitchen floor, surrounded by open cabinets, watching a mess unfold from fatigue and uncertainty, trying to sort it out alone, pretending her life was still the same. Esme's spine rubbed against the wall painfully. The hot overconcentration of ignoring Ashley flamed in her cheeks. She just wanted to leave.

And then there was Liz, alone somewhere in protective custody, wearing borrowed clothes, being questioned by strangers. Esme imagined the pink sequins on Lily's shoes, her blue-and-teal-striped skirt, her tangle of messy hair. What would her little sister look like grown up? *If.* And the baby in Madeline's stomach, its own little universe of cells multiplying over and over again into a person. Everything was changing nauseatingly fast.

She thought of her mother turning down the sheets on Lily's bed beside her own and tucking in a twelve-year-old girl, pressing Turtley under her arm and whispering good night to a wide-eyed Liz in the darkness. Or worse, Cerise telling Madeline's baby that he couldn't sit on that little bed, not ever, because it was Lily's and always would be.

"Listen," Ashley said. "They're just jealous. You were great last night, really great."

Esme stabbed the needle through the satin and felt the first jab of a hot tear but wiped it away quickly. Her costume sat beside her in a heap. She wouldn't let whoever had done this have the satisfaction. They were watching from somewhere. Ashley shifted from foot to foot, then turned toward the dressing room, glancing back only once. Esme's back curled against the wall, her legs splayed, fingers working furiously at satin and ribbons, alone in the hallway, feeling much younger than nineteen. Maybe, Esme thought bitterly, this was how she should measure success. Had the seashell been a joke too?

And where was Adam? He was running around with stupid Jennifer and acting important because this was his show. She shouldn't have come. She should have stayed in San Francisco in her tiny apartment, where she could pretend that Adam was still her closest friend. Pretend, pretend, pretend. She was sick of it, but the truth was worse.

Ashley was back. She slid a newspaper to Esme and left it there. Esme stopped sewing and saw herself in the picture, head back, hands reaching toward the light. They were carrying her away. She wished someone could carry her away in real life. Then she could shed it all behind her—Lily, Liz, Madeline, the pressure of perfect—and just be white light. She only knew ballet French, but she recognized one word in the headline. *Étoile.* Star.

"I'm so sorry, Esme." Ashley sighed. Her tulle skirt swayed lightly around her ankles. The dressing room door creaked on its hinge as the breeze swelled through the hallway. "This is supposed to be fun, you know? And for me, well, I'm just here to remember why I loved dancing in the first place, but I guess that's not the case for everyone. I couldn't translate the whole thing," she said of the article. "But it says you were amazing, an unexpected surprise. You know how people get . . ." Her voice trailed off.

Esme watched Ashley from under her eyelashes. She looked lost and bright white in the fluorescent hallway. Ashley lifted Esme's crumpled costume gently, like a sleeping child, like someone had probably lifted Lily and carried her away that night, legs dangling, heavy with fatigue. There was nothing where the costume had been just a moment before.

"I'll take it to wardrobe," she whispered.

Esme jabbed the needle through the ribbon again and missed. A small red bead welled on her finger. It wasn't just about the coffee. She pushed the newspaper away. What if she couldn't do it again?

When Ashley was gone, she pulled the newspaper toward her and folded the article into a square. She'd send it to Amelia, another little glimmer of success for her wall, for her hopeful students. It would make Amelia happy too. *Think about that little girl,* Esme reminded herself, *the one dreaming about life when she made it.* Hadn't she read that jealous dancers let chickens loose onstage to ruin someone's performance? It was the funniest thing when she was twelve, chickens clucking onstage, pecking at tape lines. She and Adam had made a list of everyone they'd love to let chickens loose on but never would've done it. At least it wasn't chickens this time. *She's still in there,* Esme reminded herself. *You can still be that hopeful little person.*

~

Esme spun through the revolving door as Christophe was leaving with a motorcycle helmet tucked under one arm. He stopped when he saw her, smiled. From under the counter, he pulled another box with a silver ribbon.

"For you."

Her heart skipped an involuntary beat. She pulled off the ribbon. Inside, bits of broken beach glass in blues, greens, and frosted whites blended into something dreamlike. She reached inside and pulled out a sea-green piece with smooth edges. Esme traced her finger over a faded logo and the numbers 1947. "You really don't know who sent it?"

He shook his head.

She hadn't expected the answer to be yes. "Keep it." She pushed the little box toward him.

The elevator chimed down the hall. A woman laughed. Jennifer. Keys jangled, and a door opened and closed. It was probably Adam's door. Behind her, the phone hung in its booth like a sleeping zoo animal. She didn't want to see anyone tonight or call home. The memory of spilled coffee made that red-hot feeling creep back to her face. Her entire performance was a blur. Her stomach tightened. Her reflection bubbled back at her in the helmet, a stretched-out, lonely girl.

"Where are you going?" She forced a small, shy smile.

He motioned toward the revolving door, and she followed, the box of beach glass forgotten on the front desk.

His motorcycle was parked under a streetlamp; its obsidian head leaned to the left. It looked fast. He unstrapped a helmet from the seat and placed it on her head, adjusting the chin strap until it was snug and made her ears buzz. His fingers felt nice on her face, and she was thankful he'd done it for her because she didn't know how. She'd never been on a motorcycle, or a "donor cycle," as her brother called them. He'd flip if he knew she was about to speed off on one with a stranger.

God. She stared into the empty lobby, where someone new was already behind the desk, the little gift box cleared away. The place where

Esme had stood was empty beneath the fluorescent light. The front door of her childhood home clicked shut without a sound. It was that easy.

Someone might have reached for Lily's hand, and she'd closed hers around it as easily as Esme had let Christophe put a helmet on her head and adjust the chin strap.

Imaginary Lily was behind her now, a flash of sequined shoes in the streetlight. The helmet was heavy on Esme's head. It stopped her neck from turning quickly enough, but Lily's little voice was there too.

Take me with you, Lily whispered, too shy to ask with Christophe so close.

Of course, Esme thought. *You would show up tonight when I'm trying not to think about you.*

Lily giggled. It was a distant memory, distorted with time like talking through water, but it was enough to make Esme's breath catch before Imaginary Lily was gone again, just out of sight but close.

"Ready?" he asked, finding his place behind the handlebars. Its lights clicked on as Esme slid in behind him. Christophe pulled her arms around his waist and told her to hold on tight, to lean when he leaned. She buried her face into the back of his jacket. It smelled of warm leather. Her heart hammered. She couldn't imagine letting go.

"Where to?" he asked.

"The beach," she said. It was the first answer she thought of. She didn't even know if there was a beach in Paris.

"It's a long ride," he said.

Good, Esme thought. The farther, the better.

The engine sputtered. Christophe swept the kickstand back. This was a stupid idea. The worst. Sneaking off with someone she didn't know after midnight on a motorcycle. But then again, people went outside to make phone calls and never came back or disappeared on the way to school or work or from home, like Lily, on a night like any other. Maybe it didn't matter. The hotel blinked behind them and was gone as the bike rattled over uneven cobblestones. Esme wanted to scream like she would on a roller coaster just as it reached the calm place before dropping, but she didn't. She held on tighter instead, wishing he'd go faster so fear would make her stop thinking. Under her fingers, Christophe's stomach shook. He was laughing.

"What's so funny?" Esme shouted over the wind and the rush of swirling streetlights. Her voice echoed in the helmet.

"You are!" he shouted back. "Just relax."

Esme loosened her grip. She pulled her hair away from her mouth as the street moved beneath her feet. When it started to feel natural, she looked to the open sky. A woman rocked a sleeping baby in a window above. She buried her face into Christophe's back and let the obsidian bike carry them toward the shore.

Other dancers would be showering away sore muscles and layers of makeup; stripping damp second-skin costumes for loose, dry clothes; and crawling into bed. That world felt terribly far away. Esme enjoyed the miles that spread between her and the stage, wondering if her parents or sister had ever dared to ride away in the middle of the night with a stranger, giddy and drunk on escaping. She was proud to discover something they could never teach her.

The highway was empty. Streetlights blurred past. The bike revved and settled into its new speed. The ground rushed by in a sea of ink. If the bike slipped, her entire dance career would be over. She closed her eyes and focused on breathing, leaning when Christophe leaned into curves. Her hips did it naturally. She was in tune with the bike.

But if she was four years old and the ground was liquid fast beneath her dangling feet, would she cry inside her helmet, sounds lost in the wind as the gap between home and whatever came next stretched farther and farther, the relief of that first handhold fading? It was a dark thought that slipped between then and now. Imaginary Lily's hand balled the back of Esme's shirt into her fist and held on tight. Esme stared into a passing streetlight, so like the stage-light moon she'd reached for earlier.

If she reached her arms above her head now, she'd be nothing, no before or after. The thought was oddly comforting.

"We're almost there," Christophe shouted. The wind made it hard to speak. Her lips were dry. A sliver of moon rose in the sky. It didn't matter how long it took. Under the veil of darkened homes and shops, empty streets, and the rush of air around her, there wasn't much difference between a moment and a lifetime.

The motorcycle slowed to a stop. Everything was suddenly quiet, rushing wind replaced with the crashing and calm of the ocean. Her legs trembled as she stepped off the bike. The wooden boards creaked beneath their feet. Cafés and restaurants were closed along the strip. The beach was dotted with umbrellas rolled tightly shut. They quivered in the wind. The ocean was a mess of blackness and breaking waves. Esme tried to imagine what it would look like in full sun instead of just a tiny sliver of moonlight.

Is this where Mommy is? Lily might've asked her stranger. *We'll see*, her stranger might've said. She could almost see them, the outline of a tall, dark shape and Lily's skinny legs poking out beneath her red corduroy coat, her tangle of dark hair. Why, why did Madeline have to tell her about the girl in the basement? She should just be a woman looking at the ocean. She didn't want to think about all the horrible possibilities, one worse than the next. Imaginary Lily was a blank page. Esme could fill her in however she needed, but the girl in the basement was not.

"Come." Christophe pulled her toward the sand. He kicked off his shoes and carried them. They walked to an umbrella near the water.

"I've found beach glass here before," he said, uncoiling the rope around the umbrella. It sprang open into a canopy of blue-and-white stripes, a bathing screen. It looked like a tiny circus tent, out of place with only the moon for company. He swept the curtain aside and pinned it back, a window to the ocean.

The smell of seawater and tanning oil folded around her. Christophe spread his jacket over the sand. They sat together. The heat from his body burrowed through her jeans. The tent reminded her of childhood sheet forts held together with pillows and stuffed animals, but this one was sturdy, just as Christophe's thigh was beside hers or his arm around her shoulders, a secret place. When was the moment she'd realize it was wrong and couldn't undo what was happening? Christophe leaned his head toward hers.

"I used to come here as a kid," he said. "My brothers and I used to wade out as far as we could."

"How many brothers do you have?" A thin red string was tied around his wrist, frayed and faded.

"Four. They're all married and miserable." A sad smile pulled at his mouth. He shook his head as if the whole arrangement was inhumane. Esme felt a stab of guilt for her sister.

"And you?" Esme asked, curious about nonballet plans.

"Eventually." He sighed. "It happens to all of us eventually."

A crab skittered slowly along the sand, pale as moonlight, disappointed by their presence.

"It doesn't have to be," she said. "That doesn't have to be anybody's future."

His eyes met hers. "We can't all be prima ballerinas."

Her face reddened, followed by the familiar tinge of disappointment. She'd worked so hard and sacrificed so much, but no one saw it that way. She shifted away from him.

"I didn't mean it like that." Christophe's eyes narrowed with concern. "I didn't mean that toward you. I meant it more for me."

He reached for her feet and untied her laces. Esme squirmed, embarrassed by her gnarled feet. She didn't want him to see them, and yet as he untied her laces, she wanted him to see the toll dance had taken on one small part of her body, to see the scars she hid.

High tide was coming in. The waves crept closer, swallowing dry sand with every thirsty wash. Her shoe slipped off. Blisters, bandages, the callous on her heel, and the missing nail on her pinky toe fell under the moonlight. She was proud to arch her foot, an easy motion that had taken years to achieve. She waited for any trace of disgust or realization that her journey hadn't been easy. Instead, he ran his fingers over the calloused places. To her surprise, he lowered his face to her arch and kissed it. Her spine tingled.

"Tell me the story of the red string. Why do you wear it?"

Christophe looked at the string as if it were unfamiliar. His other hand reached for it and tugged, leaving a thin mark on his skin. He hesitated.

"It's a reminder." He wrapped his arm around her shoulder. His wrist and the red thread disappeared under her hair.

"Of what?"

"That"—Christophe sighed—"is a story for another time."

There was a disconnect between them, a forced intimacy. It didn't sit well, but the night ahead was too long for silence. The more she thought about it, the less she cared. She wished she was here with Adam, without the fresh snap of newness, so she could relax into their old comfortable place. She pushed the thought away.

That same hunched figure sat with Imaginary Lily in the distance. Had there been a moment when Gloria'd looked at the little girl babbling in the back seat through the rearview mirror and realized she couldn't undo what she'd done?

They sat quietly for a long time, listening to the sound of the ocean, following a trail of white dots in the sky. The world seemed impossibly small. And yet it could swallow someone here, bury them in the sand or wash them away with the ocean.

Esme felt oddly exposed. There was nothing to say. The wind shifted. Christophe traced small circles on her knee. His mouth found hers, a new mouth. Adam. The door closing behind Jennifer. This didn't feel right, but they were a jumble of hands and clothes, hot skin pressed against a warm summer night, lost in the ocean breeze, and Esme was not alone.

"I can see the moon," Lily had told the psychic, and Esme had been stupid enough to believe that she'd been in a canopy bed and not dumped on the side of the road like a thrown-away doll.

The first few tears spilled over. Christophe didn't notice, and Esme didn't care. Lily had shifted again from a *thing* that had happened to them and back to a little person. The weight of it was unbearable. Esme wiped her eyes with the backs of her hands. Sand scratched her face. *You're so fucked up inside, a symphony of misery.* She would never be normal. Everything she did would always drip with the mess of things Esme tried to hide. She'd never have a normal life without those awful thoughts, but neither would Lily. They were both caught in it, crawling on opposite sides of the same web, caught in a swelling tide of everything they'd lost.

~

Esme startled awake. The beach was alive in a new way. Seagulls and kites circled the sky in figure eights. Children splashed in the surf. A little girl ran past with a red plastic bucket, splashing water onto Esme's leg. Her feet had turned dark pink. The sand was gritty between her toes. The tent was as hot as a sun-drenched car with the windows rolled up. High tide had come and gone. Lily's memory was heavy and hollow.

"Oh my God." She sat up. The back of her neck was sticky from Christophe's arm. She shook him gently, controlling the urge to shake him harder. "Wake up."

He mumbled and sat up slowly, stretching, looking younger in the sun. The sand scratched the burn on her feet. Esme fumbled with her shoes, wondering how long it would take to get back, what time it was, how much rehearsal she'd missed, what Adam would say.

"Morning." He kissed her on the cheek.

She fought the urge to wipe it away. She had to leave this place. "Good morning," she said hastily, climbing to her feet. She touched her fingers to her face and was relieved it didn't feel raw and red like her feet. At least she hadn't burned her face.

"What's wrong?" He was already standing, eyes puffy, shoes in hand, shaking sand from his jacket.

"I'm late." It sounded stupid out loud. She looked away from the water, where Lily wasn't and never had been. "I can't be late."

Seagulls circled overhead. God, she was prey. Her stomach rumbled. Children were laughing, and a radio played in the distance. Christophe's guilt was as clear as the rush of water behind them. She'd ruined the moment, but the whole thing felt stupid in the sun. If he had been someone else, she might have liked waking up beside him, watching him sleep, maybe even swimming before leaving or sharing breakfast while the day rolled on without them, but he wasn't someone else, and the whole thing was wrong.

Christophe approached a family on a blanket near their tent, a young mother with an infant and a toddler, two little girls tossing sand into the wind. He asked for the time. Esme looked away.

"Nine," the woman answered with a smile. She must have been watching them sleep.

The panic in her chest momentarily subsided.

"We can be back in two hours, maybe a little longer." His voice was full of apology.

Esme thought of Lily disappearing beneath the water. The dream eased away. Sometimes she wondered if it was easier to live like her parents did, consumed with what they'd lost instead of trying to hack out a normal life. *Today is a new day.* She pressed her eyes closed and repeated the familiar words to herself. *And I'm happy to be here.*

"OK." She sighed, thinking of what she'd say to Adam. She wrapped her hair in a bun as a fruit cart rattled through the sand full of oranges and strawberries and the ocean rolled tirelessly back and forth beneath a sweating sun.

Chapter Seventeen

If she had not stolen Birdman's mail that day, her father wouldn't have made her take ballet at the YMCA. She would've bumped along, riding bikes up and down the street, circling back at the stop sign; played with sidewalk chalk; gone to school; looked over Madeline's shoulder when she read about chakras or Chinese horoscopes or whatever interesting thing Madeline was into and pretended not to be interested. That was scenario one.

Scenario two: She picked basketball or volleyball from the YMCA classes and went until her interest fizzled and her dad forgot the importance of constructive activities. She could've ditched the Y altogether and hung out on the handball courts or at McDonald's, pooling change for fries, laughing and carrying on in the ball pit until the manager kicked them out. Or she could have tried ballet at the Y and been terrible at it. That would've been the end of dance.

Scenario three: Lily had never gone missing. If nothing had changed, maybe she wouldn't have gone to San Francisco or she might've come home more because Lily getting taller and more grown up every time would've been weird. She would miss too much the longer she was gone and farther she was.

Scenario four: If Lily had gone missing but Amelia hadn't asked Esme to live with her. She would've been pulled away from dance eventually. It was too expensive, too far, or it was not right to dance because of Lily. Amelia had seen that.

"Why did you do it?" Esme'd asked Amelia years ago. "You didn't have to. No one expected you to."

They'd gone for coffee on one of Esme's rare, short trips back to New York just after she'd made SFB corps. She'd picked a coffee shop in Manhattan, a no-name place that wasn't Amelia's house or studio. There were too many memories there, too many associations with *then*.

"Well." Amelia had sighed. "Why wouldn't I water an orchid?"

"No, but really." She'd wanted an answer, not a metaphor.

"Yes, but really," Amelia had said. "You would've stopped dancing, and it would've destroyed you. To have that much potential . . . it broke my heart to think of you in a cubicle, thirty years old, surrounded by plastic ferns, wondering what you could've been. You already had one part of your life taken away. I couldn't let life take another . . ." Her voice had trailed off.

Esme mulled over the question of whether she would've been happier with or without dance. Life in a cubicle surrounded by paper clip chains and tape dispensers sounded terrifying. What would she use those tools for? What would the sum of her life be?

But it suited most people just fine. It might've suited her, too, had it not been for Lily. Lily had given her the push she needed to step away from home.

That was the last time she'd seen Amelia, but she wrote sometimes, sending postcards from places she'd traveled or programs from shows, knowing her life had started in that little house on the edge of a forest. Well, it was a park, but it had seemed like a forest then. Everything about Amelia had seemed bigger, an invitation into the next part of Esme's life. She could never really say thank you for that. She'd never know how.

Scenario five: If she hadn't met Adam at SFBS. They'd been singled out together, even if Esme suspected she wouldn't be as good without him. Once, after a particularly bad week without sleep, she'd searched the newly posted casting list for her name, but she hadn't been on it. Again. She'd dumped out her dresser drawers that night and shoved everything into her suitcase. The room had been blurry. She hadn't even bothered to turn on the lights. It hadn't mattered. She never wanted to see the shitty gray rug or her cardboard mattress or smell the lemon Pine-Sol stink of the hallway ever again. She would drive a taxi like her father if she had to, but she was done with dance. She'd left her dance stuff on her bed in a heap for whatever stupid dancer came next. And someone would fill her space, some other person who believed they'd be an exception to something impossible.

Adam had followed her down the hallway that night and out the front door, all the way to the bus station, where she'd bought a ticket to Sacramento because she'd only had a twenty-dollar bill in her pocket, but it was not here. Adam had bought one too even though she'd ignored him. He'd sat two rows behind her and stared out the window while she'd cried into her sleeve. If someone else couldn't cut it, they'd go back to their family and their bedrooms with New Kids on the Block posters and drawers of left-behind clothes. They'd watch TV and find other things to do instead, but not Esme. Going home was like crawling inside a shed cicada skin now. She couldn't do it, but there was nowhere else to go.

The moon outside the window had had a halo around it. When she'd finally calmed down and realized how stupid the whole thing was, Adam had slid into the seat beside her.

"You'll get there," he'd whispered. It had been the only thing he said for the rest of the night, but it had been enough to switch buses back to San Francisco. Esme had rested her head on Adam's shoulder as stars raced past the window. It was the first time she'd ever rested her head on a boy's shoulder, but she'd been too tired to feel awkward. It had struck Esme then that Adam hadn't had anywhere else to go either, and maybe he needed her too. The bus had rocked gently beneath them, and for the first time in days, she'd fallen asleep.

She ran through each scenario on the ride back to Paris, as she walked the long way to the studio, no longer concerned about missing rehearsal. In a few days, this would be over. She'd go back to San Francisco and lock her memories of Adam inside herself. They'd be safe there, packaged in whatever form she needed instead of what he'd become. Grown apart. She tossed the phrase around in her head, thinking of dandelion wisps huddled together until someone blew them apart, scattering seeds to make new plants before turning to seed and blowing away again. They were the same plant in new places. She was thinking about Adam, but it came back to Lily. It always came back to Lily.

~

"Es? I have news." Madeline didn't wait for a reply before rushing on. "Gloria Garcia's maiden name is Santos. Her brother is Anthony Santos."

The name was as familiar as a smell. Esme pressed the phone against her ear and waited for it to make sense. "Birdman."

"Yes," Madeline said, breathlessly. Any trace of her hysteria from the other night was gone. "The police contacted Mom and Dad and are running a DNA profile on Liz to see if she's a match for Lily. They said she roughly matches the age-progression images Mom has, and the time frame makes sense. Birdman was away when Lily went missing, but there was water in the plants, and the mail was gone. Maybe his sister was watching his place. She lived close enough."

Esme felt like someone had slid an ice cube down her spine. She sat up straighter. Her sinuses cleared, and her skin was covered in goose bumps. This could not be right. It could not all come together this quickly after eight years of nothing. She would not allow herself to even imagine it yet, but there had never been a connection this close. Imaginary Lily was outside the phone booth now running in little circles with her arms above her head. *Do not get excited*, Esme warned her. *It doesn't mean anything yet.* Imaginary Lily crawled under the table where the roses were still in their vase, only the petals had fallen and curled at the edges.

"How long does the DNA test take?"

Madeline inhaled sharply. "Well, that's where it gets tricky. Technically, it doesn't take more than a day, but labs usually run tests in batches because there's too many. So Mom tipped off the news, and the story went national, which hopefully puts more pressure on the lab to work faster.

"And you know I don't believe in this stuff, but when Mom went to church today, there was a lily on her usual pew. She thinks it's a sign."

They were too close this time, closer than any of the times before. The chances of finding Lily were still rare, less likely than being struck by lightning but not impossible. Anything she said or did might jinx it now. The thought of last night ruining anything was unbearable.

Four years ago, the police had found a tiny skeleton wrapped in a burlap sack on Long Island when a water main had broken. They'd roped off the backyard with yellow tape and dug up the soil in squares while the family looked on from bedroom windows. They were a nice family, two boys and one girl, a golden retriever who probably used to romp through the very same backyard that the police now pulled ribs and a skull from. The police had searched missing children's cases from the past ten years, and Lily's little file had been among them. There were thirty-two case files in total. Cerise had done thirty-two novenas, one for every child, every day. Father O'Brien had even given her a key to their church so she could come whenever she wanted. Her father had taken a baseball bat to the roof and beaten what was left of Birdman's coop to pieces. The splintered wood and chicken wire scattered across the checkerboard tar. Her brother had cleaned it up. Esme knew this because Madeline had told her. "At least you'd have an answer, closure," people had said, but they didn't understand. They'd always wonder why it had happened. There would always be pieces no one could answer, too scattered with time and silence and speculation and unfairness to ever bring any kind of peace.

The thought of comparing her life to her sister's was unbearable. If Lily were to come back, what would she think of Esme's life? It was easy to move on when she could pretend Lily would've wanted her to, but if she came back and felt that Esme hadn't done enough, hadn't been broken enough by the hole she'd left in her family's life—what then?

"I had a dream about her . . ." Esme interrupted. Her voice trailed off. She didn't want to talk about the beach or Christophe or how chaotic she felt now that everything was happening, but she needed someone to understand. "Do you remember when Nick was failing school, and Mom said he couldn't play baseball anymore, so Lily said the only team he could play for was the Tutors? She was only four. How could she be so sassy?"

"I don't know, Es. I always felt like you understood her better somehow, like you got how she ticked. I didn't get it. I still don't, and I hate how I was then . . . I keep thinking, if she comes back, what would she remember about me? That I was bitchy and annoyed all the time? That she bothered me?"

"You had your moments. But maybe it wouldn't matter. I don't remember much from when I was four—do you?"

"No." Madeline sighed. "But we'll always know what we were."

It was deeply and unfortunately true. Was that why her sister had stayed—to make up for whatever she thought she should've been?

"How're Mom and Dad?"

"Why don't you call them, Esme? How long has it been?"

"I can't, Madeline. I just can't. It's too much." Nothing had happened between them, and yet the more she traveled, the farther away she felt. It was hard to pretend she felt as close to them as she had before, well, before she'd left home, before Lily. Or she'd call, and they'd ask how she was and listen for thirty seconds before launching into a laundry list of everything they'd done that week—found a new forum, a new message board, reviewed the case file again—until Esme felt drained and defeated.

"Dad ripped the gate off the lot across the street and planted a million plants. I think he's lost his mind."

"Is that legal?"

"Of course not. But he did it, and all these people are coming to help him. They built raised beds, and someone bought a mulcher. The city will probably rip it down, but it's kind of nice for now, I guess. He promised me a tomato the other day. He was really excited about it."

She liked the idea of her father in a garden, surrounded by plants and neighbors.

"It's his kind of church." Madeline sighed again.

Esme thought of the studio, of the barre beneath her fingertips cuing her brain that it was time to focus. Her sunburn throbbed in hot waves under her tights. It was time to go.

"Tell them I said . . ." Esme paused. Tell them what?

"I'm not telling them anything," Madeline said. "They'd rather hear from you, Es."

"I know." Esme said goodbye and placed the phone in its cradle.

Sometimes she imagined that other life: coming home from school, backpack straps cutting through the padding on her coat, finding bolts of satin on the dining room table, smooth as a pearl, the TV on in the background. It was always Oprah at four p.m. Her mother nodded along behind the ironing board or the sewing machine, pins pressed between her lips. If she was quiet, she could do her homework on the coffee table and listen to Oprah too.

There were so many episodes about forgiveness. Esme imagined herself on that set over the years, Oprah's hand resting over hers as she told Birdman she was sorry they'd made him into a Boo Radley, sorry he'd lived up to it because everyone pushed him into being an outsider, sorry for naming him to the police and for the grief that had caused him. That should have been the moment Oprah's eyes welled up and Esme hugged Birdman, but it was not, because there was one more piece she could never get past.

I know it was you. The police couldn't prove it, and I'll never know for sure, but I'll always know it was you somehow, because who else could it be? She'd played it out over and over again at different stages in her life, and it didn't make sense any other way. It had to be him, and if he'd made Lily feel what Esme had felt that day in the hallway or worse, she'd never forgive him. Even if Oprah believed forgiving others was really a gift to ourselves, it didn't matter. She'd never forgive him.

And besides, Birdman was dead. He'd never have a chance to make things right. He hadn't wanted to. Or maybe he'd never done anything wrong, but Esme would never know. It had been an aneurism, quick and painless. The police had found him slumped at the table with a cup of tea and carried him out on a stretcher under a white sheet. What had happened to those doll parts on the table? That hair in the box?

Birdman never had been a former marine. He'd never eaten a poisoned orange, and he wasn't half-deaf. He'd been some kind of mannequin maker for storefronts, designing worlds behind glass windows, and he'd made them at home because he suffered from terrible anxiety, his sister had told Mrs. Rodriquez once, though she'd never said why.

Knowing hadn't comforted Esme. It disturbed her that any window display in the city could've been Birdman's take on freezing people in time, capturing life as people wanted it from the perspective of an old man with milk-bottle glasses and an empty pigeon coop on the roof, waiting for messages that never came.

"We tried," his sister had told Mrs. Rodriquez when she'd come to clean out his apartment, carrying one box after the next to the curb. "And I'm sorry," she'd said, "if he was a little odd. We did the best we could."

What a joke, Esme thought. *"The best you could" was keeping a girl locked in your basement.* What good had keeping someone from her family and taking her life away done? She hated them both, Birdman and his sister, whoever she was. She was glad they were both dead.

Esme closed the office door quietly behind her, winding her way down the hall to her dressing room, where she'd sew pointe shoes and put her makeup on as if the only important thing tonight was pretending to be someone else.

∼

"You're late." Adam hovered outside her empty dressing room, arms crossed. "And you missed rehearsal."

The mascara wand in Esme's hand stopped. "Yeah, I know."

"I looked everywhere and couldn't find you. I was really worried."

She'd covered her sunburn with layers of pancake and two layers of tights. The heat throbbed through them. The mesh fabric stung her skin. She busied herself with makeup, avoiding his reflection in the mirror.

"Do I have to ask you why?"

"I really don't have a good excuse."

"Well, maybe you should remind your new boyfriend that you have a commitment to this show. I asked you to be here, Esme, because I thought this was important to you, but now you've just embarrassed me, and everyone's whispering about it."

Esme spun in her chair. "Whispering about what exactly?"

"About you riding off with some guy and missing your shit, sneaking phone calls in the office. Think about how that looks."

Her half-finished makeup looked ridiculous, but she was too furious to care. "You don't know half of it."

"Well, if there's something more important than being here, maybe you should just go. It's unprofessional, and it makes me look bad."

"Oh," she pushed back, "but slutty Jennifer hanging around your room is fine, right? Because you can do whatever you want."

Esme shoved the newspaper in his face. *Étoile.* "And really? This makes you look bad? You should be thanking me, Adam. All of my 'unprofessional' shit got you this review. No, wait. You're not even mentioned. Maybe everyone's whispering about that too."

The words were hot and bitter in her mouth. She hated herself for saying them. She slammed the dressing room door in his face, but the door wasn't enough. Her fist opened and closed. She kicked the garbage can. It skittered across the room and knocked over Jennifer's chair. Then she reached for brushes and bottles. They cracked against the wall and pooled on the floor.

"Stop," Imaginary Lily said from the corner, eyes wide, face hidden behind the hair she wrapped around her thumb and stuck in her mouth. She wasn't supposed to suck her thumb. Lily knew that.

She was a liar, impersonating Lily's pain onstage, twisting it into some public thing she could use for herself, for the Waltz Girl, tapping into a cheap well of things she wasn't willing to think about or talk about unless it benefited her. This was the big sister Lily would come home to: someone who hadn't looked sorrowful or done any of the right mourning things, who'd skipped almost every memorial, every new search, because she was dancing and traveling while her sister lived in a basement. When they were little, she'd made up stories for Lily not just because Lily enjoyed them but because it made Lily easier to control. It kept the peace. The whole thing was a lie. She'd never worked hard for Lily to worship her. Four-year-old Lily couldn't see that, but real Lily would. Real Lily would see everything.

Go away, Esme prayed. *Go away, go away, go away.*

A light popped above the vanity and shattered on the floor. The other lights went out with it. She'd ruined this room. She'd ruined this show, her relationship with Adam, with Lily, her parents. She was a ghost in the darkened mirror, hair loose, tangled tutu. There wasn't anything she couldn't ruin. This was the lie Lily would come home to. *I missed you so much, but I lived my life anyway. I made you into a make-believe friend so everything I did or didn't do would be OK. I forgot you were ever a real person with real feelings, pain, dreams, because there wasn't room for you, Lily.*

Imaginary Lily crouched into a little ball in the corner. She was crying softly in a pile of broken things, but Esme didn't try to comfort her, because she wasn't real, and deep down, Esme suspected she also wasn't sorry.

She wished she could just leave, but there was nowhere else to go. The angry tears prickled over. Esme wrapped her arms around herself to settle the shaking, nauseous feeling in her stomach. She sat against the back of the door to keep it closed and shut off the lights. It felt better to hide in the darkness.

"Why did you even ask me here, Adam? What was the point?" Silence.

She bit her thumb, holding back tears so she could finish her makeup, aware of Adam's shadow in the thin line of light filtering through the bottom of the door. It was just unfair, all of it. Even if she'd wanted to explain, how could she? Yes, it was easier to ride away with someone on a motorcycle in the middle of the night and regret it afterward than it was to sit alone with eight years of grief, easier to push and push and push until her body was physically beat than to feel that missing piece of her life.

Why had she said yes to the Waltz Girl? She should've known it'd mess things up. It wasn't just another tragic female character: it was that day on the bathroom floor at the theater with Amelia when Lily wasn't coming back, only there was no more Amelia to lead her away anymore—or Adam.

Everything was changing. She'd been the one who'd left, and it comforted her somehow that at least they were all still there: Nick, Madeline, her parents. It was easy to pretend they were living the lives they'd lost if she didn't talk to them, even if it was screwed up. *This is why*, she thought bitterly, it was better to leave people behind before they disappointed her. *You can be left behind, or you can leave behind.* She'd chosen wrong with Adam.

"Why did you come?" he whispered back, knocking lightly on the door. Esme ignored him. She didn't know. She wished she could evaporate. *Let them whisper*, she thought, locking the dressing room door and flicking the light switch on. This wasn't her company. In a few days, she'd be gone. She slid into the vanity table and wiped away smudged makeup, starting over. She could always just start over.

~

Later, Esme lay on the stage floor and reached toward Adam. The painful longing was real. What the audience thought was just the Waltz

Girl's desperation was Esme's apology. Jennifer, the Dark Angel, hovered over them both.

"I'm sorry." It was only a whisper, lost in the orchestra, unnoticed by the audience, but she heard him. She didn't answer. If he'd wanted her to, he would have told her another time, not onstage before an audience, not under stage lights or before he was led offstage with covered eyes.

"I'm sorry too," Esme whispered, taking Adam's hand before the curtain call, waiting in the wings for their cue. He squeezed her hand gently over the sound of applause before pulling her onto the stage, where she handed him one red rose from a bouquet and all was forgiven.

~

"Shit," Ashley said, surveying the broken, scattered mess as Esme swept glass into a dustpan. "I take it you did this, or you wouldn't be cleaning it up."

That much was obvious, but Esme wasn't annoyed. The dustpan was full of dirt and glass. She would catch every last bit and make this room as right as she could.

"I know it's impossible not to take this stuff personally, but it's really not. They've done worse and probably would do worse to you if not for Adam, so . . ." Ashley's voice trailed off. "Someone put ink in my mascara once." She laughed. "It wasn't funny then, but I'm over it. You know what?" Ashley didn't wait for an answer. "You need a drink."

Ashley shimmied out of her tutu and into her robe. She started the shower, and Esme was thankful for the empty room.

"Take a walk with me," Ashley called over the running water. Esme wasn't sure if it was pity or not, but there was no one else. Even the hotel gave her the skeeves now, as she knew she might bump into Christophe.

~

"It's hard not to think about that," Ashley said. They were walking to the Palais Garnier, still smelling like Johnson & Johnson's baby shampoo from wiping away makeup. The smell reminded her of Lily. It always would, only now it was such a familiar part of her ballet life, too, so separate from the one that remembered baby shampoo at the edge of the bathtub at home.

"I heard it's true," Esme said, referring to *The Phantom*. "There was a fire in the eighteen hundreds. He was a composer or something who wrote music for one of the dancers. She died in the fire, and his face was messed up, and he missed her so much he decided to live under the theater."

Plates clattered on a café table. A cup wavered in its saucer. Esme was tempted to order something just to watch people pass on the street, arm in arm, strolling under a new moon from one fountain to the next, but she wanted to see the Palais Garnier lit up, surrounded by shops and street cafés with lingering patrons sipping wine into the blur between night and dawn.

Everything was suspended in time. If this was really Lily, and it might be, there'd be another line drawn through her life again. Lily before, without, with. She wanted to linger a little longer before the line was drawn.

"That's so sad." Ashley adjusted the bag on her shoulder. "It doesn't sound like she loved him back."

"No," Esme said, imagining dark tunnels dripping with dampness, rats, and roaches. It was the wrong place for a brilliant composer. Then she thought of the basement in New Jersey and shivered, wrapping her arms around herself to push the thought away. "If someone admired you that much from afar and did all these things for you, wouldn't it creep you out a little?" A couple rode past on a scooter, hidden in helmets, wrapped around each other and the bike, one entity instead of three.

Ashley studied Esme carefully. "Well," she said slowly, "I guess if I wasn't interested, I might feel that way, or I might not notice at all. Or maybe she just wasn't ready to see it."

"Maybe," Esme mused. It was easy to feel like a horse with blinders, aware of only the track ahead, heart pounding, the jockey pushing onward. It made her wonder what else she couldn't see, what was outside her own set of blinders.

A man dropped a coin. It glittered in the streetlight as it rolled along the sidewalk and into the gutter. "Merde," he mumbled, and Esme smiled.

"Maybe he was just nuts."

"Maybe," Ashley said. "We're probably all nuts."

The outline of the theater rose above the Rue de Mogador, glowing like a beacon over shops and tall steps. Esme wished she could go back to the 1800s and see the Palais Garnier without streetlights or the bleating of a siren in the distance or cars accelerating or slowing to a stop. She wanted to see it lit by candlelight, glowing at the end of the street like a new star in a galaxy all its own, calling people to a world of imagination that didn't exist anywhere else. Candlelit chandeliers and women dancing en pointe in daring ankle-length dresses had been magic then. What they did today could never compare to those early dancers. Everything they did now—especially in America, where ballet was still young—would always feel a little like children in dress-up clothes.

She would have liked to come here with Adam. It was the kind of thing they would've done before their lives had split. *This week must mean something*, Esme decided. There had to be a reason so much was happening at once, why so many threads of her life were tangling together after years apart.

"Wow." Ashley tipped her head to take it in. The names of famous composers hung above them. Rossini, Beethoven, Mozart. The steps were littered with people. A man played a guitar, strumming chords and singing softly in French, a song Esme didn't understand but wished she did, while others sipped from bottles in paper bags. No one on the steps was a dancer, but they were drawn here all the same. Esme's dance journey had started here, long before she was born, when ballet had been new and shocking.

This place was refreshing, a welcome pause from everything she'd still have to fix. It felt like a kind of mecca, a pilgrimage, and it gave her hope. If she could make it here, no matter how she'd gotten here, she could fix other things too.

"Wow is right." They stood in silence, staring at the building that had shaped so much of their lives from so far away. It didn't look nearly as big as she'd imagined, and yet it was bigger somehow.

"The sad part is"—Ashley sighed—"we'll never dance on that stage or the Mariinsky. They'd never want us."

"No," Esme said, "but that's OK. When I was dancing kid parts on some community college stage, this was unimaginable too."

"It never really stops, though, does it? It always feels like something's out of reach."

"A glass ceiling," Esme said.

"That's a good way to say it."

The guitar stopped and started again. Someone laughed as the traffic lights changed.

"Does Adam know?" Ashley asked.

Esme could pretend she didn't understand the question, but she did understand, and she was tired of pretending, tired of holding back, and relieved that someone else could see what she felt.

"No." She sighed.

"You should tell him how you feel," Ashley said. "You might be surprised."

The traffic light changed again, and the line of cars slid to a stop. Ashley yawned, stretching her arms above her head as the first wave of fatigue melted over Esme. Maybe Ashley was right. She took one last look at the Palais Garnier and its golden angels before following the same road home, aware of the light falling over her back, struck by the idea that sometimes great journeys ended in the same place they began.

Chapter Eighteen

From far away, a lily was a perfect white trumpet of petals. But up close, its inner petals were a clown's tongue of splattered pinks and yellows coupled with a funeral home smell, old and static, that made Esme's skin crawl. They had been everywhere after Lily had gone missing, part of a campaign her mother had come up with to raise money and awareness: Lilies for Lily. She'd sold them on the street, at church, at grocery store checkouts to make people remember. It was dangerous for people to forget, especially when it took only one small memory, a tiny detail, to splinter a cold case. It always pained Esme that lilies were so beautiful from far away and disturbing up close. There was nothing harder to look at than a lily in the light.

Tonight had been her final performance. After today, she'd be a soloist again. She'd leave Paris and Adam and go back to her regular life. She was exhausted. The weight of this week, of Christophe and Adam, Madeline, Liz and Lily—especially Lily—hung on her. Tonight she'd felt the crushing weight of falling on cue, forcing herself back up again. It hurt to push herself from the floor when all she wanted was to stay down, to accept that Adam would be led away with covered eyes, both onstage and off, that she was losing Madeline, that she'd already lost Lily and the person Lily was supposed to be. She was bone tired of falling and getting back up, of imagining Liz's life, of losing her north, her south, her east, her west and wandering alone. When they'd carried her tonight, the pressure of hands around her ankles and knowing they'd catch her if she actually fell had been a relief. The show ending was a relief. She'd leaned back one last time with her arms stretched above her head. The stage lights had warmed her face and made lights behind her eyes, reds and yellows, oranges and blues. One review said she was pain in motion, the pull between struggle and hope. She had been struggling, she realized, for eight years, ever since she'd seen *Serenade* with Amelia and it had given her pain a voice for the first time. The audience had seen all that compressed pain, the struggle between hoping and giving up. They'd come to see *Serenade*, but they'd seen Lily's story instead. They'd caught a glimmer of the harshness Esme lived in behind the ethereal thing she was supposed to be onstage. They'd seen all of the colors and imperfections of a lily.

Whether Liz was Lily or not, Esme was ready to let that story be carried away. She'd finally had a place to tell her story without words but with an audience to listen. Carrying it alone again would be unbearable, so she tucked the pain into all the old familiar places until she was just Esme again, pure white from a distance.

~

It was late but not late enough. She didn't want to go back to her hotel and risk seeing Christophe. It was too embarrassing, but disappearing wasn't the answer. She took a deep breath and spun through the revolving door. The hotel was quiet. The lobby wasn't the usual flurry of people whirling in and out like dust devils. Christophe was behind the counter reading something in the glow of the computer screen. He looked surprised to see her, as if she'd wandered into his make-believe world instead of hers.

Muse, she thought, *inspiring but superficial*. No, that wasn't right. *Escape* was the right word for riding away at night with a stranger. The world on the beach was its own isolated place, suspended in time like floating dust. It didn't belong here, with this Esme or this Christophe.

He took the little box of beach glass out from under the counter. "It was from me," he said. "The seashell too."

He closed her palm around it. The glass was cold against her skin. She hadn't suspected it would be Christophe. What else wasn't she seeing?

"I'm sorry," she started to say but stopped. For what exactly?

Christophe shook his head. "They have something in common, the shell and the glass. They've both been pushed around by the ocean. It doesn't make them any less beautiful or exciting to find, does it? Only more so." Christophe paused.

Esme was surprised by how insightful he was. She listened carefully, relieved, wondering if there was another message in his words like the lily on her mother's church pew.

"Last night was a beautiful surprise too," he said finally. "And I don't expect anything more."

The phone rang behind the desk. He smiled apologetically and reached down to answer it, stopping only to kiss Esme's hand, still closed around the beach glass. It eased away the tension in her shoulders, the disappointment in herself.

"Thank you," she whispered.

She left the little pile of beach glass in a nook beneath the phone booth seat. It seemed fitting to leave it there. The phone booth almost felt like an altar. The grooves in the wood, chiseled out by people listening to news from somewhere else, would be etched in her memory because of Lily. It might be the phone booth where she learned her sister was coming home. Or it might not, but she left the glass anyway, proof that she had been there. She wandered the hallways, too restless to sleep, following the floral pattern in the rug. It was worn thin from years of walking feet like hers.

Was she really so broken that other people could see it on her like a battered shell? She'd tried so hard to hide it, but letting it go onstage tonight had been a relief. Even hearing Christophe acknowledge it had been a relief. Maybe she wasn't such an ugly thing on the inside after all. And maybe this feeling was why her sister had gone to therapy, for this same temporary peace, acceptance. She finally understood, but Adam still nagged at her. She couldn't leave it like this, and maybe she didn't have to.

When they were students, Adam had gotten mono. His throat had been so swollen he couldn't speak, and all he'd wanted to do was sleep, but he'd been picked for a show, and Esme hadn't. Esme had put ice cubes in the blender and fed the ice chips to Adam. She'd brought him fresh orange juice with ginger and soups from the cafeteria. She'd done his homework so he could sleep between rehearsals. In those miserable moments between spoons of ice with a throbbing throat, Adam had reached for Esme's hand. "It'll be over soon," she'd whispered. Being needed had eased the sting of not being picked, lessened the line between them. After that final performance, Adam had given her his flowers, and she'd saved the petals. She wished there was something she could do now to bring them back together.

Adam's door was at the end of the hallway. Esme hesitated before knocking. The door was just like hers: white paint, thick molding, floral carpet. It smelled like cigarettes and sandalwood. She wanted him to open the door sleepy eyed and lost in a dream, unsure if she was really there. She knocked lightly and waited. Blood drained from her face, and her heart beat in her empty chest. It echoed in her ears. He might not be alone. She could always call Madeline or even her mother, who was probably rocking back and forth at the end of the couch, waiting for the phone to ring.

There was a shuffle inside. Fluorescent light spilled over Adam's face, his gray T-shirt and plaid pajama pants wrinkled from sleep. Esme wanted to cry. She just wanted someone to hold her.

"Esme? Are you OK?" His eyes narrowed with concern.

"Can I come in?"

He moved aside to let her pass, reaching for the light switch.

"I'm OK," she whispered back, kicking off her shoes. They landed in a heap at the foot of his bed. "I just need a place to sleep."

Adam didn't ask why. She lifted the covers and crawled into the space he'd left. The sheets were still warm and smelled like him, his honest smell. She breathed deeply, nestling her face into the pillow as he moved in beside her. He wrapped his arm around her. Her head rested on his chest. Esme blinked in the darkness, thankful she had a place to call home even if she'd have to explain in the morning.

"Good night, Esme," Adam whispered. He kissed the top of her head as if she were a child, and she was surprised by how familiar it felt.

"Good night," she whispered back. *Safe.* Esme rolled the word around in her head. For the first time in days, Esme dropped into a dreamless sleep.

~

The next morning, she woke to an empty bed. She stretched and yawned while water ran in the bathroom. It broke unevenly, splashing over Adam and the porcelain tub. The door was closed, but Esme could smell Adam's soap. Dove. Her chest swelled at the simplicity of Adam, but when the door opened, would he be upset that she was there? She hugged the blankets tighter, thankful for the extra warmth. She could always pretend to be asleep.

The other double bed was empty, neatly made. Adam had a stack of books next to his bed. Clean laundry in blues, grays, and whites was piled on the luggage rack. There was a comb on the dresser beside the TV, a four-inch bronze Eiffel Tower from a souvenir bin along the quay. There was nothing of Jennifer's, and Esme was relieved. She traced the creased spine of a book beside the bed, *A Moveable Feast.* The cover page rolled back from humidity, an invitation. "Then there was the bad weather," it said. Bad weather in Paris seemed unimaginable.

The bathroom door opened, and Esme jumped. Adam smiled, and the whole idea of fake sleeping felt stupid.

"Good morning." He beamed. "I hope you didn't have anywhere to be today."

It was 10:30 a.m. on Monday, and the show was over. She didn't have anywhere to be. The comb left ropy strands in Adam's hair. He moved the stack of laundry to the dresser and pulled two apples from the minifridge, sliced them, and spooned peanut butter on top. He was comfortable, or was it just pretend? Esme wasn't sure if the tension between them was gone. It felt more important to explain herself because he wasn't asking, but she wasn't sure how.

"One more day," he said, replacing the cap on the peanut butter. It was too long and not long enough. She didn't want to think about home. Shower steam lingered by the windows, collecting gold sunlight. It sparkled. Esme wanted to run her hand through it and watch it swirl. At home it would be just before five in the morning. She doubted her family was sleeping.

"Is there anything you want to see?" Adam sat beside her on the bed and put the plate between them. Esme wanted to rest her head in the place between his neck and shoulder again, where his pulse throbbed and sent waves of heat across her face, but she sat up and took an apple slice instead.

"I don't know," she said, thinking of Christophe, embarrassment making her mouth taste like pennies. "I think I've seen enough."

The apple was crisp on her tongue, refreshingly cold.

"That's silly," he said between bites. "There's so much here."

"Aren't you going to the studio?"

He was wearing jeans even though the sun was warming through the window, sandals, and a crisp white T-shirt. Normal clothes.

"Nope. I want to see stuff."

"Like what?"

"Like Hemingway's house."

"He lived here?" She wished she had something interesting to add.

He pointed to *A Moveable Feast*. "It's about his time in Paris. The first few sections are about this area. I wanted to find them. Want to come?"

This was the old Adam. He slid an apple through a smear of peanut butter, carefully not looking at her. Was he nervous? His cheeks were flushed. Esme felt suddenly shy. He was asking her on a date, kind of. He must have decided in the short moments before she was awake, mouthing the idea in the steamed mirror, unsure if she'd still be there when he came out.

"I'd like to." Esme wavered. She didn't want to scare away the peace between them, but what if the police had news today, if Madeline called and couldn't reach her? Disappointment bloomed on Adam's face. She wanted to go. She'd spent a lifetime waiting for Lily, hoping for the family they used to be. This time could be different, or it might not, and Adam was here only for one more day.

"Do you have a cell phone?"

Adam looked up, confused. "Yeah, why?"

Esme sat up a little farther, towing the blanket with her. "Is it OK if I give someone your number, just in case? I've been waiting for news about something."

"Everything OK?" Adam's brow wrinkled. Esme wanted to smooth the wrinkle with her finger.

"Yes," she said, deciding to tell him the simplest version. It felt strange to say it out loud. The words were dry on her tongue and hung in the air. "They found a girl and think she might be my sister. She's been missing for eight years."

Adam stared at her for a minute. Esme tried to read his expression, to control her own as Adam pieced it together slowly.

Do you understand now? She prayed, thinking of all the secret phone calls, how much she hadn't wanted to be the Waltz Girl, of all of the resistance she'd felt but couldn't express. Lily would always be there, lingering just under the surface, waiting for just the right reminder, just the right little girl holding hands with a grown-up, a mess of brown hair blurring the years that had passed and the exactness of Lily. She couldn't pluck her out like a splinter or tuck her away in her memory. She'd always find a way out, and that was OK. She'd loved that about Lily, that innocent invasiveness, and it was the same then as it was now, Esme realized. If she let Lily out in small doses, found her in a flower or a pair of tiny shoes in a window, Lily wouldn't crash through at the beach or a nightmare or any of the places Esme didn't want her to be. *She just wants to be remembered,* Esme thought, realizing that this would only work if Liz wasn't Lily. If she was, well, she still didn't have an answer for that.

"Holy shit," Adam said softly.

"Yeah," Esme said. She laughed at the idea of it, at the improbability, the possible miracle, the impossible. "Holy shit."

"Of course," he said, scribbling the number on a piece of paper. "Of course."

His hand covered hers, warming her skin and the bones beneath it, anchoring her to shore.

~

There were no messages for her at the front desk. She dialed Madeline's number and left Adam's on the answering machine. Then she showered and changed into a summer dress, one her mother had made especially for this trip, probably hoping some Paris designer would see it and plaster it on magazine covers. Esme pulled the dress over her head. At first it was baggy and shapeless. She pulled at the waist and shifted the shoulder straps until it settled. What her mother had done slowly dawned on her.

It was the dress Anna Pavlova wore in Esme's favorite photograph, the one where she was sitting on the lawn with a swan on her lap. The dress was barely visible in the picture, but her mother must have studied it closely, approximating the pleats in the front, how the top would flow over the bottom. It was a pale green, Esme's color. Inside the pocket was a string of costume pearls. Esme stared at herself in the mirror, thinking of her mother at her sewing machine, studying the picture, a glimmer of the mother she'd been before, sewing costumes. Sewing herself into Esme's dream.

Esme fastened the pearls around her neck and ran her hands down the skirt. She didn't know how to say thank you. Her mother probably wasn't expecting it either, but she would find a way.

She brushed her hair and patted lotion onto her face until she looked bright and fresh. That was it. No makeup today, just her own face. She was tired of hiding.

Adam was waiting in the lobby. Christophe was gone, thankfully. It was just the two of them. The dress swished when she walked, light as air around her knees. It made her feel ready. The roses on the table were leaning toward the door, where the sun made a triangle on the carpet.

"Hey," he called, flipping his phone shut. He smiled and shifted from one foot to the other. The hazy comfort from their morning together dissipated. He had changed into a button-up shirt. Was this a date?

The same teenage Esme who'd bought Hostess cupcakes from the vending machine and eaten them in teeny bites, saving half for the next week, could not be on a date with Adam. The same Adam who'd once spliced the *Home Alone* kid into Sleeping Beauty so Macaulay Culkin would scream in the mirror when Aurora woke up could not be on a date with Esme. He lived in New York. She lived in San Francisco. There was an entire country of rolling mountains and flat plains between them and, of course, ballet—but still.

"It's a date," Imaginary Lily whispered from the phone booth, followed by smoochy kisses. "Adam and Esme sitting in a tree . . ." Lily's voice trailed off when Esme narrowed her eyes, wishing she could feel annoyed at real Lily again just once and take it for granted all over again.

They stepped quietly from the lobby to the street. The fountain bubbled. Around it, people sat with sandwiches in waxed paper, balancing paper-bag plates and textbooks on their laps. The university crowd, a group Esme might have been part of had she not done ballet. They watched the summer students carefully, aware of how different their choices had been.

"All right," Adam said. "The Latin Quarter is pretty cool, but there's Montmartre or the river, Notre Dame, the Eiffel Tower. I'm down for whatever."

"Me too," Esme said. "Let's do it all."

"We won't have time for all of it." Adam laughed.

"Obviously," Esme agreed. "Let's start with the Latin Quarter and wander. I want to see Hemingway's house."

She should see everything, for Lily's sake. Maybe one day they'd sit together and talk about things to see, like cotton candy fog and San Francisco.

They crossed big streets that reminded Esme of New York. She couldn't wait to get away from the noise and places too familiar to be interesting. It was only when they found the winding cobblestoned streets that Esme relaxed.

"So," Esme asked, "want to know why it's called the Latin Quarter?"

"Churches?"

"Universities," Esme said, proudly remembering Madeline's facts. "They taught classes in Latin, hence . . ." She pointed to the neighborhood around them. "My sister told me there's a pantheon. Parthenon? I get them confused, but there's one here, and a coliseum. It's a park, but they used to flood it with water to race boats and have gladiator battles."

"Where did you learn that?" Adam asked, amused.

"My sister, living vicariously."

They rounded a curve. A small plaque marked Hemingway's house above a shop with spools of colored yarn in the window.

It wasn't the view she'd expected. Trash bins lined the narrow street. A children's clothing store sat below. She tried to imagine what he'd seen through that small window years before, writing through a haze of cigar smoke and early-afternoon alcohol.

"Herds of goats came up this street every morning. The shepherd rang a bell so people would know he was coming. They waited outside with buckets for milk. Imagine?" he asked. "His Paris must have been so different."

The back of Esme's hand brushed Adam's as they tipped their heads to look at the window above. A motorcycle passed behind them, kicking up the breeze and rustling Esme's dress. Fabric tickled the backs of her knees and sent a shiver up her spine. Something was different about today. If she pressed her hand to her chest, her heart might beat backward or a paper cut would bleed blue. The phone in Adam's pocket was silent, but she sensed it the same way animals sensed storms. Esme didn't want to burrow. She wanted to live a little longer.

Adam handed his camera to a passing woman and asked her to take a picture.

The air rushed out of her lungs as Adam lifted her to his shoulder. It was a move they'd practiced a million times together in the studio, but it took Esme by surprise on the street. She adjusted her dress and crossed her ankles, finding her balance before lifting her arm to point to the sign. She smiled at the camera, aware of the sweat forming under Adam's fringe of pale-blond hair.

"Say *fromage!*"

Today could be the day. Something could be happening right now while Esme sat on Adam's shoulder, enjoying the familiar pressure of his hand against the small of her back under the shadow of Hemingway's past. Adam carefully set her down. Esme was thankful for the sidewalk beneath her feet. She lifted onto her tiptoes and kissed Adam's cheek softly, thankful for the view down the winding street, for imaginary herds of goats.

Adam fumbled for his pocket. The phone was ringing. Esme held her breath. If it was one o'clock here, it was ten a.m. there. Adam turned the screen toward Esme. She knew the number. It was the first she'd ever learned. Her heart was quiet in its cage of bones. Adam held her elbow tightly as he handed her the phone. She flipped the phone open, suddenly aware of how much effort it took to stand, and lowered herself to the sidewalk, her legs fragile against the cobblestones. It was her mother.

"She's coming home." Cerise sobbed, painfully happy sobs. "Lily is coming home."

Esme pressed her hand to her mouth. Her skin electrified, and when she opened her mouth to speak, she cried instead. Adam's hand was on her shoulder; he was unsure what to do. When Esme looked up, he was blurry. For a quick second, she mistook him for her brother.

"Say a prayer and thank God," Cerise said. "This is our miracle."

Esme didn't remember hanging up. She didn't remember handing Adam back the phone or lifting herself from the sidewalk to her own two feet.

"My sister is alive," she told him. She wanted to scream it, but her voice was only a whisper. She laughed and wiped her eyes with the back of her hand. For as much as she'd feared this, it didn't matter now. When she looked at Adam, he was joy, too, her joy, behind his wide eyes and big smile, as if he'd been waiting for eight years with her. Esme lifted herself onto her tiptoes and circled her arms around Adam, burying her face into the warmth of his neck. He wove his fingers through her hair. Esme pulled away finally, laughing and crying but clear eyed enough to see the glint of a prism in the window overhead throwing tiny rainbows on the street around them.

Chapter Nineteen

"Hey." Adam stood in the doorway holding a water bottle. The hallway lights glowed behind him like a fluorescent halo, making him look more shadowlike than person. She was cross-legged on the floor, folding clothes into her suitcase. The outfit she'd worn to the beach was crumpled behind the door. "Can I come in?"

"Sure."

Adam sat on the bed, then lowered to the floor beside her. His face was level with hers. "What's next?" he asked, gesturing toward everything piled at her feet.

"Home." She sighed. "Then back to San Francisco, I guess."

She'd been up all night thinking about what it would be like to meet Lily, the looking-glass version of the sister she'd imagined for so long. She hoped the bond of being sisters would undo the years apart, painfully aware that living across the country would limit the slow building her mother said they'd have to do. It was hard to believe that something unfolding for eight years, that had shaped so much of her young life, could finally come together in less than a week.

He nodded slowly, uncapped the bottle, and took a sip. "Are you happy there?"

They'd never talked about happiness before, whether all the dreams they'd had as students had been what they'd expected, how happiness came in temporary waves.

"It's what I worked for, right?" She shrugged, tossing a T-shirt into the open suitcase.

"Well, let me ask you this . . ." He stared out the window at rows of wrought iron windows and trellises on the limestone building across the street, carefully choosing words. The sweater she was folding rested in her lap.

"I got offered a place in Boston. I'd dance, but I'd also choreograph."

"Boston?" She'd been only once, early on as a corps member. She didn't remember much. The reality of Adam moving even farther away sat in her stomach like a pit, so heavy it grounded her to the floor. At least when he was in New York, she could picture him walking streets she knew from her childhood, her early life connecting to his present life, but that would end when he moved to Boston. The sweater she was holding felt slimy under her fingers. She pushed it away.

"They asked about you." Adam's eyes were nearly turquoise in the light through the window, an indescribable color she could only call Adam. He swirled the water in the bottle until a funnel spiraled on its own. "As a soloist with some principal roles."

She was ready. The Waltz Girl had proved that. Boston was four hours from New York, closer than San Francisco, closer to Lily. It meant she'd be with Adam. They could leave shows together and find warm, yeasty pizzerias on cold nights or walk along the Charles. Was that really what he was offering?

"All the best colleges are there. You could even think about school."

"I think—" Esme started and stopped, unsure if this moment and whatever answer she gave would unroll the next section of her life, if she'd regret it or look back and know she'd made the right choice, but there was Lily. "Can I think about it?"

"Of course," he said. "I only promised I'd talk to you. I'll give you his number if you're interested."

"Who runs it?"

"Paul Katzman."

Esme laughed in shock. "Amelia's Paul?"

It would be a kind of homecoming, a circle from where she'd started. It couldn't be a coincidence that everything had happened this week.

"He has a soft spot for very stunning Waltz Girl performances." Adam winked.

Construction drills started outside the window. Hammers banged. They were building a scaffold across the street and a web of nets to swallow a building. It sat there without protest, vines swaying from the trellises.

Adam sighed. "I botched this week, Esme. I know I did. I should've . . ." His voice trailed off. He shifted his weight and ran a finger over a folded shirt as if he were petting a kitten. Esme wished it were her hand instead.

"I just keep thinking about who I was in San Francisco, how hopeful I was, how focused. Maybe I was too focused, because we all were, but most of my memories have you in them. I just thought that maybe this summer I could reconnect with who I was, and I thought you being here would help, but I wasn't thinking about how much changed since then. I don't know . . ." Adam rubbed his forehead between his hands. "I'm not even making sense." He laughed, a bitter sound, filled with regret. "I probably sound nuts."

Esme crawled closer and rested her hand over his. "You don't sound nuts."

His hand relaxed under hers.

Esme sighed, releasing all the questions she had about her own life, what it meant. The weight of it huffed out in one long breath. "That summer, when we first met, I felt so free. Everything I did was important. I was allowed to be happy, but I didn't have time to be—or really, I wouldn't let myself because I thought I had to work harder. Every time I got a role or a nice compliment, I worked harder to keep deserving everything because there was a goal at the end, especially after . . . well, it was easy to leave everything behind and ignore whatever I felt about Lily or my family because I had something else instead."

Esme paused to gather her thoughts. The ice machine in the hall-way rattled as a nameless person filled a bucket and walked heavily along the carpet.

"After she went missing, one of the things I made myself believe was that she was in a children's book somewhere, like Narnia or *Where the Wild Things Are*—you know, one of those books where kids slip between worlds. She was just on a journey, and I was on mine. Ballet let me believe it. It made it realer somehow.

"I did what I wanted to do," she said finally. "I found my Narnia, but it never felt like enough. And truthfully, I was so afraid of 'the end,' when I'd have to stop and see the things I didn't want to." She thought back to her mother's shadow behind the trailer curtain, of the manne-quin under the sheet, long forgotten.

"And then to find out she was so close the whole time, Adam, just across the Hudson, and we couldn't find her. I can't imagine what her life's been or how any of this could've happened."

A tool dropped outside and bounced against metal. Surrounded by the floral wallpaper in her room, it sounded especially strange. The sea-shell sat on its bed of sand next to her bed, a battered piece of the ocean.

"We've nestled ourselves into this world because the rest is too scary."

Adam held up his hand to protest, but Esme shook her head.

"I keep dancing and reading books and pretending it's normal not to see my family. You know"—she laughed—"I can't even talk to my parents without . . . without . . . well, have you ever seen something reflected in a spoon? It's all distorted and bloated and not the right version of itself anymore, and the more I talk to them, the more I feel that everything's just wrong. And is it fixed because she's back now? Of course not. I know that, but I always thought that if she came back, then it would be. I never wanted to accept that it wouldn't be right no matter what.

"And now she's coming home, and I'm truly happy, but it's so confusing, Adam. Look at my life. What kind of straws did we draw? I keep thinking about this time she packed a suitcase to go to the moon. Or the time I was sick, and she listened to my heart with a Fisher-Price stethoscope, but I have no idea who she is now or what she's been through."

The words she'd been holding in for years spilled out. She felt cleaner somehow, happy to leave them behind in a hotel room. These four walls had probably seen a lot, and maybe this was what they'd remember about her: she was finally honest.

"You'll get there," he said, resting his hand over hers.

"Yeah." She sighed. "But I don't even know what 'there' is. No one does."

"No one knew what was through the wardrobe door either."

Silence fell around them both like a blanket. She wished she could stop time to keep them this way.

"You know," he said, staring at the ceiling, "I did something today I never thought I'd do." Adam took a breath. "I called my father."

Construction workers shouted outside the window as Esme pieced together the little she knew about Adam's family, his mother in Cuba, his journey on a raft.

"I hadn't spoken to him since the day some ship picked us up. My mother pushed us away on that raft, and the plan was never that I was supposed to live with my father when we got here, no . . ." Adam shook his head sadly. "My mother had a sister here, and that's where I was going. She couldn't take me herself because she wasn't well, but I didn't know that then. I didn't know anything. And I'd always blamed him for it, figured it was his idea somehow and he'd talked her into it because why else would she send me away? A better life, yes, but I wouldn't have known anything different. But the thing is, I am happy here. I am lucky to be here, and I thanked him for making the journey with me. I doubt we'll have another reason to talk again, but it brought me a lot of peace to tell him that, and I think he was surprised. The point is we don't have to live with our pain, Esme. It's a choice. And you might not agree, but hear me out. Do you remember that day we wanted to burn driftwood to see if it burned blue?"

"Yeah."

"Why did it matter so much?"

Esme laughed, remembering how important it'd been at the time to prove such a thing was possible, but she didn't have an answer.

"It wasn't, but we made it seem important by wanting it so much. If it's true for the driftwood, it's true for other things too. Come to Boston, Esme. Let's start over." He rested his head against the top of hers. She breathed in his smell of clean soap, the spicy smell of his deodorant. "I wanted you here because you know the version of me I most want to be. Does that make sense?"

Esme nodded, remembering her own younger face pressed against the window of a taxi, riding over the Golden Gate Bridge, an eleven-year-old girl brave enough to leave home and chase a dream, too young to realize that one decision would unfold her future so quickly she wouldn't even question it. She was filled with longing for that unwritten life, that same foolish bravery. That girl was gone, so far removed in space and time, so she turned to Adam instead and kissed him. Like the little girl she once was, she'd deal with the consequences later and just take joy in the moment, pure, uncomplicated joy.

Adam kissed her back. His hands framed her face and made her feel protected. Her heart hammered in her chest unapologetically, a reminder that she was alive, with a future she couldn't yet see. She slid onto Adam's lap and let him hold her like a child. He wrapped his arms around her, and they stayed silent and still, lost in thought. Outside, construction workers struck hammers against wood. Someone dropped a board. Men shouted to each other in French, but they sounded happy. She leaned into Adam, knowing she'd have to decide, or the world would move on without her. Madeline would get married. She'd have her baby. A new generation would begin while Lily's life was rewinding and fast-forwarding at the same time. Esme didn't know where she'd fit in with either of her sisters' new lives, but she wanted to be part of them.

"Yes," she whispered, overwhelmed by second chances she'd never expected. "I'll talk to Paul, but I have to meet my sister first."

Adam squeezed her tighter and let go. "I'm glad," he said. "Is there anything you'd like to do? Any last thing you'd like to see?"

Esme laughed, surprised by how much she wanted to go home. "I feel like I've seen it all. More than I could have asked for." She slid off Adam's lap and settled back on the floor beside him.

"I know what you mean," he said. His blue eyes stared into hers. Fatigue etched around them. He might be the only person who actually did.

He lifted a stray shirt from the floor and folded it. Together they packed the last of her things until all that was left were the two of them and her suitcase. This room would be someone else's soon. She wondered if Lily would think of the past eight years that way, a place that was and wasn't hers, a bizarre memory she could tuck away after she figured out where she belonged. Esme leaned the suitcase against the wall. She was ready to find out. She hoped her sister was too.

PART THREE
TODAY

Chapter Twenty

The living room furniture was still the same. The sewing machine was still in the corner, the mannequin beside it. There was a layer of dust over the TV and different shoes by the door, but the bin with Lily's toys was still under the window. Even after everyone else had moved out, the bin had stayed. *A Bargain for Frances* peeked out from the top. Everyone was here now, except Lily. The police had sent Detective Molina and a social worker, Nancy, to discuss what they'd found and what came next. They were both female, young with kind faces, and Esme was glad. That would make Lily feel safer.

The basement Lily had lived in had a bathroom, a small refrigerator, and a TV without cable. There were lots of videotapes—family videos with the real Elizabeth and Disney movies in thick plastic cases. There were shelves full of books and a neatly made bed. The floor was covered in rubber play mats with roads where a child could drive toy cars and trucks. It would have looked like any other playroom if there hadn't been a padlock on the door. Only Gloria Santos could lock or unlock it. They'd found the key on her person.

Gloria Santos had been a nurse. She'd worked four days a week at NewYork-Presbyterian Hospital in the trauma ward. Her colleagues said she was quick on her toes and even tempered no matter what came through the door. The administration had had concerns about her ability to work in trauma after her family's accident, but she'd begged to stay. If her family had come to her ER, she'd said, they would've had a better chance. "Let me do that for someone else's family," she'd told them. "It's all I have left."

The police believed Gloria Santos had suffered a heart attack and couldn't reach the phone. Esme smiled sadly at the irony: after all the pain she'd experienced and caused others, her heart had quit.

Lily didn't remember the night she'd been taken. There was no one to ask now and no one to punish. They'd have to live with the unknown, the injustice of it, but that was nothing new. It paled in comparison to the work they'd start with Lily soon, and Esme was almost relieved there wouldn't be a long, drawn-out trial, that Gloria Santos wasn't alive with a parole date looming. She could never contact Lily again. It was over.

Gloria Santos was not cruel, Detective Molina and Nancy explained. She was mentally ill. Lily replaced the child she had lost. There was no indication of physical abuse.

"But you have to remember"—Nancy paused—"Lily thought Gloria Santos was her mother for eight years. She thought she was Elizabeth Santos. When we found her, she was very upset. She knew something had happened to Gloria, but she couldn't do anything to help.

"And she also knew," Nancy said slowly, "that she wasn't supposed to leave the house. She alluded to 'consequences' and was very upset at the idea of it, but we haven't established the extent of what that means yet."

Esme's father stiffened. He was holding Cerise's hand, moving his thumb in small circles, but it stopped now. Esme couldn't remember the last time they'd held hands without Cerise pushing him away. It didn't have the ease it once had, but it was a start. Cerise rested her chin on her hand. She'd waited eight years for today, and now she was crying softly for Lily, still here but different from the person she would've been if she hadn't been taken. Esme watched her parents carefully to see what they felt. Their emotions seemed more nameable than the things she was feeling.

"We do believe Gloria was sorry for what she'd done." Detective Molina paused again. They were talking so slowly, Esme realized, giving her family time to process. "There were videotapes of ballets and newspaper articles." She met Esme's eye. "About you. We think she wanted Lily to have some connection to her family, even if Lily didn't know who you were."

The psychic's words from long ago echoed. "She'll know you," she'd said. "She'll know you without knowing you." Hadn't she always hoped Lily might be in the audience? Gloria Santos had gone to and from work, collecting newspaper articles and videotapes to feel better about what she'd done. It couldn't have been too terrible, she must have decided, if Esme had done all right. Esme wanted to feel sorry for Gloria, who'd lost her family and snapped, but Gloria had known what the hole of losing someone was and had done it to them anyway. It made the whole thing worse somehow, unforgivable. She'd always hate her, Esme decided, but she'd never show it because Gloria had meant something to Lily. She wouldn't let it come between them.

And Lily was here, all ten fingers and all ten toes. She hadn't been physically abused. It would take a long time to unravel the psychological trauma, but at least they'd have the chance to do so. Lily was still here.

"We're giving Lily time to process and warm up to the idea of meeting you all. You have to remember she doesn't have much social experience. Gloria was her only means of social interaction, plus whatever media she was exposed to, but beyond that . . . nothing. Talking to us has been overwhelming for her. She's very quiet, but we think she'll open up as time goes on."

"Could we . . ." Cerise's voice was only a whisper. "Could we see a picture?"

They would meet in a week, if Lily was up for it, but that felt like forever. Detective Molina pulled a picture from a file. They'd skipped eight years, but it was Lily. A strand of wild dark hair fell over the long, slender nose she shared with her siblings. Her skin was the same color as the inside of an apple. She had Esme's hazel eyes and long lashes, only Lily's were red rimmed, cheeks puffy. She'd been crying. Her four-year-old self would've curled her hair around her thumb to hide her face. This Lily was too old for that. She'd had no one but Gloria for eight years. For as often as Esme had felt alone, there had been other people. Madeline's hand found hers. There was paint on Lily's hands and jeans. An artist. Esme smiled. At least they'd have that in common.

Cerise held the picture gently, moving it closer to her face and then away again. Andre watched over her shoulder. It was delivery room–like to watch her parents meet their baby after eight years of wondering, only instead of being young and fresh faced, amazed by the little person they'd created, they were both lost in something personal, together but not, the part of their lives that had created Lily so deeply shattered now because of her. Her father might never move from the couch back to his bed. The house was partitioned with invisible barriers because it somehow kept them going. The thought of Lily climbing over and under the emotional labyrinth her parents had built, if she managed to at all, was unbearable. Esme prayed there was enough of four-year-old Lily left to trample through the rules they'd made for themselves and didn't need anymore, if they could only admit it.

Nick sat on the floor against their father's old recliner, waiting for Cerise to pass the picture he'd probably seen at the station, but there was something about her brother, an unacknowledged relief. Her mother's voice from long ago echoed, begging Nick to admit something he hadn't done. Esme couldn't imagine how it had haunted Nick, but now Gloria was the shadow shape lurking in every "what happened" scenario and in every "why." Esme was sorry she'd ever doubted him. It was too late now to undo, even if Gloria had proved him innocent, but she would try. She would call him to see if he wanted to get coffee in a diner after a shift for him and a show for her, when they were bone tired from serving their audiences, him in his costume, Esme in hers. If they could play those roles every day, then maybe, eventually, they could play brother and sister too.

Cerise passed the picture to Esme. The water glass on the table caught the light just right and cast a blue shadow on Lily's hand. It wasn't tiny rainbows like the psychic had suggested, but she hadn't been entirely wrong. Esme stared at the blue light on Lily's hand. They were that light, split and fractured, scattered by one event. Would Madeline have studied law if not for Lily or Nick become a cop, or would Esme have pushed herself to dance, forcing herself into a make-believe world and a language without words to hide in? And what would Lily be now? But no matter what had happened to them, whatever statistically improbable event had shattered their lives, they still came from the same place. That part, Esme realized, could not be taken from them.

"Does she remember us?" Cerise inched forward on her chair. "Does she understand what happened?"

Detective Molina and Nancy exchanged a quick look.

"Well"—Nancy sighed—"trauma influences memory. Whatever memories she has are mixed with what Gloria taught her, and the two might not jibe. It's going to take time," Nancy said softly. "Healing takes time."

Detective Molina and Nancy left with photo albums and pictures of her family. It was a safe way to meet before seeing each other in person. Esme wished she could just sit with Lily. They didn't have to talk, just sit side by side so Lily would know she was safe, accepted however she was. Nancy said that once the questioning was over, they could make a plan for Lily's long-term psychological care. They left brochures for reunification programs they could attend as a family. One had a horse on the cover with a smiling family around it. Equine therapy. Lily might feel more comfortable with animals at first. Lily used to like animals, and Esme sensed she still would. She smiled to herself, thinking of Lily watching her dance. Did she like ballet? Her face warmed, and her chest felt feather light. Maybe this was the answer to why she danced. It had saved her after Lily had disappeared, and now it would bring them back together again.

~

Esme paid the cab driver and stepped into the sunlight, into the watery stretch between home and Amelia's studio where the orange thing had been years before. It was gone now, washed away with water and time, but Esme imagined Lily leaning over her lap on the Long Island Rail Road, pink sequined shoes glimmering in the sun, peering through her tangle of hair for her fish named Marley, who could go to the store for mint chocolate chip ice cream if it wanted to or swim with whales. For Marley, anything was possible.

She dropped a letter in the mailbox, a postcard from Paris of the Eiffel Tower in the mist. *A wise woman once told me that if I could dance through the hardest part of my life, I could dance through anything. She was right.* She had put the newspaper article from Paris and one about Lily in the envelope too. It was one small thank-you.

The water was quiet. Later, it would be alive with boats. Esme spread her blanket over the grass, still damp from morning dew. A sprinkler clicked on across the street. The rise and fall of cicadas stirred Esme's thoughts. Everything smelled like mowed grass and salt water, so unlike their real neighborhood, which Nancy had recommended against meeting Lily in for the first time. A neutral place would be best, one that was new and safe for everyone, but it didn't have to be an office or the police station, and Esme was glad.

Lily had told Nancy she'd like to see water, like a lake or an ocean, because she'd never seen one before. It wasn't true, Esme thought sadly, thinking of all the times they'd gone to the beach and pressed sand into buckets to make sandcastles, decorating sand turrets with seashells. But it didn't matter if Lily remembered or not, Esme reminded herself. They were starting over.

This place had been Esme's idea. She'd found an article in the newspaper about a small town by the bay that had a dibble stick gathering every year. Kids dressed as mermaids and pirates to dive for Popsicle sticks in the bay. It was only a small event and might be a good distraction if they needed one. Even Cerise hadn't protested. It didn't matter, Cerise had said, not after this long. Not when Lily was finally coming home. She'd given the article to Nancy to show Lily. It was just a small event, Esme had promised, only a handful of people, and the grassy stretch along the water's edge was big enough that they could watch from far away if it was too much for Lily. Nancy had suggested taking Lily there beforehand to familiarize her with the place and make sure it was OK. Lily had said yes.

She didn't expect Lily to remember anything about Marley or this place, but it seemed fitting, an overdue apology from Esme's eleven-year-old self to her little sister, a promise to finish a story that had started a long time ago, if Lily still wanted to know.

In all the years her train had rolled past this watery stretch, she'd never actually been here. It was only rolling water and sky and marsh grass through the rectangular window, quiet and scentless. But here, wind rushed past her ears. Her skin warmed in the sun, then chilled suddenly when clouds rolled in. Everything smelled like salt water and cut grass. It was alive in a way she couldn't have imagined through the window, different from the tidy rectangle of scenery she remembered. Lily might be like that, too, she thought, reminding herself that the little girl she remembered was now twelve.

It was a perfect August day. The leaves were beginning to yellow. So many summers like this had already passed without Lily. She traced the outline of the Throgs Neck Bridge with her eyes open and then closed, imagining details to settle her nerves. The sound of the bay washing over the rocks echoed in her ears. Nick and Madeline would be here soon, her parents too. Most importantly, Lily would be here. She set out a cluster of bananas, sliced oranges, berries, and apples on the blanket. It didn't look like enough, but Detective Molina said Lily liked fruit. And reading. Of course, Esme had thought. Reading had been her world outside the basement. Esme pressed her eyes closed, pushing away all the places she'd been and how much she hadn't always appreciated them. Those places would have meant so much to Lily. The unfairness of it all made her shake. She didn't want to talk about books with Lily, who might say how much she'd like to see Paris or London or San Francisco or some other place she'd read about but couldn't really imagine, and Esme would hate herself for having been there and the line it drew between them. She wasn't ready for this. It wasn't too late to leave.

She stood up. The urge to run was so strong, but water splashed behind her. Imaginary Lily hovered at the water's edge, cupping her hands with water and letting it pour back into the bay.

"It's OK, Esme," she said.

"No, it isn't," Esme whispered back. "It's never going to be OK."

"Why can't I hold the water?" Imaginary Lily asked. It poured through her fingers. Sunlight bounced off Lily's white sundress. Lily stepped into the water, and the bay wet the hem of her dress. Her hair was still reddish in the sun, and her little shoulders had been rubbed with sunscreen. Would there still be an Imaginary Lily now that the real Lily was back? Esme took one last look at the little girl crouched at the water's edge in glittery jellies, her little round belly, a white star in the sun.

"I don't need you anymore," Esme whispered. Her voice broke, but Imaginary Lily was watching something in the distance.

"Look!" Imaginary Lily called from the water's edge. "He's here!"

Esme could not see what Lily saw. Lily walked into the water. Her sundress pooled around her knees. She smiled back at Esme, twirling gently from side to side. A fin popped up from the water, orange and white, and Esme knew it was her fish named Marley.

A car pulled to the curb behind her. Imaginary Lily sang into the wind, and the sound was lost in gentle waves and the murmur of traffic in the distance, and then she was gone. *But she was never really there*, Esme thought sadly, wiping at her face with the backs of her hands. She'd only wanted her to be.

"Keep it."

Esme recognized Madeline's voice. The car door slammed, and Madeline climbed the waist-high metal divider to Esme. She was wearing a knee-length skirt under a loose blouse and thick-strapped leather sandals, carrying an oversize tote bag stuffed with loose papers and books. Madeline sagged under its weight. She'd chopped her long, thick hair into an uneven bob. Madeline already looked like a lawyer.

"Good morning." Madeline dropped her bag on the blanket and rummaged through it for a bottle of sunscreen. The thought of leaving seemed ridiculous now.

"He got lost on the way here." Madeline furiously rubbed SPF 50 over her face and chest. It smelled like coconut and gave her skin a waxy look, exaggerating the delicate new freckles on Madeline's nose and cheeks. Pregnant freckles. A small sign that there was a new part of their family growing and changing under Madeline's baggy clothes.

"It didn't help that it was the same cab Dad drove, and I kept thinking about that car circling the block over and over again after . . . well . . ." Madeline's voice trailed off, but Esme understood. Esme looked toward the water where Imaginary Lily had been. They would all be in their private places today.

"And don't say anything about my hair. I did it last night and immediately regretted it."

Esme thought of the pile of tried-on clothes in the corner of her hotel room. Nothing had been right, not even the jean shorts and gray T-shirt she'd eventually settled on.

Esme reached for the bottle and spread some over her skin to keep her hands busy. Bringing sunscreen was a mom thing to do. Madeline unpacked paper plates and utensils, plastic cups, stacking them in neat piles. Her stomach was still flat, hiding the little cells inside that would eventually morph into Esme's niece or nephew. Lily would be an aunt too. The thought made Esme queasy. She was too young to be something so adult.

"I got up so early thinking we were going to Long Island, you know? And I mapped the whole thing out for him, but he still got lost." Madeline's eyes were rimmed with dark circles. "It took forever."

"Yeah," Esme said. This place had always felt so far away when she was ten, eleven. Eight years. Would Lily remember? Were all those years of bedtime stories and make-believe games stored up in her somewhere, or was it all just gone? Esme bit her lower lip until it turned numb. She'd been Lily's favorite once, but that was different now. Would Lily like her real family, or would she wish for Gloria instead? The thought had kept her up all night. She pushed it away to focus on Madeline. These were the last few minutes before a new line was drawn through their lives again.

Madeline looked the same, except for the freckles, but there was a glow about her that Esme couldn't explain. She thought of her sister as a kid, reading on the roof in someone's old lawn chair, finishing books in a day while the 7 train rolled past, how she'd come back to their room smelling like outside dust and too much sun.

"Stop smiling at me like that—you're gonna give it away."

"I can't help it. Can I touch it?"

"There's really nothing to feel yet." But Madeline let Esme put her hand on her stomach.

"Hello," Esme whispered to the little person inside. "I'm your aunt Esme, and I knew about you before anyone else."

Nick's Jeep pulled up beside the curb. Esme pulled her hand away.

The car idled for a long time before the engine turned off and the car settled into place. Esme tried not to look at the outline in the driver's seat because she couldn't tell if he was looking at her. The thought unnerved her. Nick was cocooned in there, in the same spot he drove to and from work in, ate meals in at odd hours, maybe even slept in sometimes, but Esme suspected he was rewinding time back to that night on the fire escape, holding a cigarette, feeling that nicotine buzz wash over him strongly because it was a secret. He was staring at the sky and just Nick, however he wanted to be, instead of Nick the disappointment, still young and stupid on that fire escape, not the man he'd be forced to become in less than an hour. No, they hadn't grown up that night. There was still a lot of unfinished work there, but their childhoods had ended, suddenly and without warning. If Nick was on that fire escape, she was in her bedroom, dreaming of San Francisco and her beautiful red bridge in the fog.

Her brother stepped out, not the scrawny one hidden in dark hoodies bouncing tennis balls against his bedroom wall but a tall weight lifter version in an NYPD T-shirt and sweatpants. He looked like he'd just finished a run, only he was still moving. Restless energy. He always had been. His arms and legs reached and grabbed until the car was empty. He was like those physics diagrams with a ball balanced on top of a ramp. Potential and kinetic. Everything was both. Nick was both. She waved, and Nick gave her a half smile. Amazing, she thought. He could carry a gun and hunt down criminals at all hours of the day and night, but meeting a twelve-year-old girl was terrifying.

When her parents pulled up, it made being here realer. She bit her lip, quelling the swell in her stomach.

Her father stepped out first, circling the car to help Cerise from the passenger side. They moved slowly, dazed, feet shuffling over the grass slope. Her father was so devoted, Esme thought sadly. This fragile woman wasn't the woman he'd married. He hadn't expected to be cast out onto the sofa, blamed until he withered, and it struck Esme then that maybe her father had been trying to make up for that night ever since. *It's over*, she wanted to tell him. *We forgive you. You were never to blame.* But it wouldn't matter. There would always be a part of him stuck in that taxi, circling the block night after night looking for anything to make things right.

Cerise's short hair was blown out and curled into feathery wisps. She was wearing an old black dress with coral calla lilies, the one she'd worn to their first Communions, and even from a distance, Esme knew her mother was wearing Tabu. Cerise carried a pink frosted cake on a glass plate, the one they only used for birthdays. Esme felt a stone catch in her throat. Life was starting again, and yet part of her would always wish her mother hadn't packed away the moon after Lily but had kept making frosted cakes on that special glass plate for her or Nick or Madeline, because they'd always been in reach. They'd been colored invisible instead. The left behind.

There was a formality about her parents that struck Esme as odd. The parents. Honest people who'd tried to raise their kids right. They were so dressed up, dressed for an occasion or a trial where nice clothes from the back of the closet made them worthy instead of parents who'd failed somehow. Did her parents love each other anymore? Maybe not in the way they had when they'd first met, but they would try now, for Lily, because she deserved and needed them. They'd moved beyond husband and wife a long time ago. They were parents, and for Lily's sake, that was what they would be.

"Good morning." Andre stood beside the blanket. His shirt was so strongly starched that it barely moved in the breeze. Esme stifled a giggle. He rolled his eyes and shook his head, making eyes at Cerise, who was now rearranging food on the blanket, moving watermelon to the middle and a plate of cookies to the outside, correcting the spacing between plates, asking Madeline why she'd brought only paper plates instead of something nicer.

"It's a picnic, Mom," Madeline said, but Cerise ignored her.

Andre studied the bay, absorbing the tall wisps of marsh grass, the slow, snaking line of cars on the other side of the glimmering water, white dots of sleeping sailboats anchored to mud below the surface.

He looked to the sky and back to the water. Sunlight flickered on its surface. He held his arm over his stomach like a brace, and despite the lines and shadows that had deepened over the years, Andre looked like he had so many years before: lost and stumbling through life with only his mother's cross to guide him.

Then the lines and shadows lightened. His arm fell away from his stomach, and he looked toward the sky again. This time he was smiling.

"Would you look at that?" he mused, nodding with appreciation at the open sky before turning to Esme. "You picked the perfect place." Andre's eyes watered, and tears rolled down his face. "Who even knew this was here? Thank you."

She hadn't realized she'd been waiting for approval until he planted a kiss on her cheek. Tears sprang up behind her eyelids. Seagrass with gold wisps touched the sky, swaying as a breeze cut through the humidity. Sailboats moved silently along the water. Waves brushed moss-covered rocks at her feet. The silhouette of a horseshoe crab wandered beneath the surface. When she looked at it all together, it was as beautifully choreographed as any of the dances she'd ever performed. She lifted her head to the sky as her father had and whispered, "Thank you."

For a long time no one spoke. Madeline lay back on the blanket and watched this new world. She blinked and held her arm over her eyes as if she wasn't sure it was real. Nick sat on the edge of the blanket beside Madeline, toying with a blade of grass. Esme tried to pretend that picnics with her family were normal, only they weren't. It felt better not to talk, where everyone could wander through their secret places, the ones they'd built after Lily, before the walls had come down.

Andre placed his hand over Cerise's. It was a measured gesture, and the thought of Cerise pushing it away today was terrible, but she didn't.

Cerise, remember Orchard Beach? Esme wished her father would say so her mother would look up, surprised, from the plates on the blanket. A daze would cross her father's face and settle on them all. Cerise would smile, not the careful smile she'd had since Lily, but a real one.

Her parents would be lost in something personal, a secret from before, rewinding time, and it would make Esme feel ten years old again, her world as small as a bird nest, padded with feathers and high above everything that could ever go wrong.

Cerise closed her hand around Andre's. Despite whatever they felt for each other, Esme suspected they needed each other today because no one else would understand.

They heard the car coming before they saw it. Esme searched the tinted windows for any sign of the person inside, for the outline of her head, the shape of her shoulders, reminding herself that Lily was not four years old anymore, dressed in her blue-and-teal-striped skirt and polka-dot tights. She wouldn't wrap her hair around her finger and suck her thumb or smell like strawberry detangler and baby soap. It took a long time for the car door to open. Esme wondered if Lily was studying them behind the tinted glass, comparing the family before her with the one she'd imagined. She tried to see them as Lily would, her parents sitting beside one another, Madeline's uneven hair, the marks on her legs from sitting in the grass.

Lily stepped out of the car, so different from the girl in the picture. She was tall, wearing a pink T-shirt and paint-splattered jeans rolled up to her ankle, where her skin was a pale cream. Her hair was a mess of long, wild brown curls, red in the sun. A strand blew across her face and hid her eyes, but Lily didn't brush it away. She watched them carefully from beneath it, almost like she was preparing to draw the people before her. She was so serious, so unlike the snake charmer who turned dirty tights into dancing cobras or once squeezed a tube of toothpaste onto the floor so she could paint a heart.

This was the same Lily who'd once packed a suitcase and waited by the front door to go to the moon, only she looked the same way Esme remembered herself at twelve years old, a quiet watcher, full of secrets. "She may or may not remember her life before," Nancy had warned.

The world around them felt lost now, held together by a girl in a pink T-shirt and jeans.

Cerise walked forward first, measuring her steps to a slow walk, fighting the urge to run.

"I—we—never stopped looking for you," she said, voice breaking.

Lily searched her mother's face. Esme's breath caught. It was the same curious look she'd seen on her brother and sister, an expression they were born with no matter how many years they'd spent apart. And then it was gone, swallowed in the folds of Cerise's dress as she pulled her closer. Lily's arms circled back, pale against the dark pattern on her mother's dress. One broken nail. These were not the little hands Esme remembered, tucked into her own to cross the street, or the same little ones that made turkey handprints before Thanksgiving, baby soft and warm. Andre closed around them. Eight years of tears and hope held them together under a smear of blue sky.

They couldn't have found her, Esme thought suddenly. No amount of searching would have led them to Gloria's basement. Cerise buried her face in Lily's hair. The sun shifted behind a cloud. The memory of Cerise's sewing machine whirled through her head, making costume after costume to pay for Esme's ballet classes, wedding dresses to make rent and food. *I'm sorry*, Esme wanted to tell her mother, who'd always found a way to fix everything except this one thing, and Esme hadn't realized she'd been blaming her. It wasn't her fault. It wasn't anyone's fault.

Madeline's arms were wrapped around her stomach. She was shaking. That old script must be running through her head. *Life would be better without you.* Esme's own words echoed. *Later—I'll tell you later.* They hadn't known everything would cut off midsentence, how much everything would matter later.

"Come on." Esme pulled Madeline by the wrist. They folded around Lily, one living, breathing unit. Lily was all angles, shoulders and elbows, not the doughy little girl Esme had once carried on her hip. That girl was gone; she always would be, replaced by the fast-forwarded version instead. Esme put her hand over Lily's to preserve time for just a little longer, tracing the long fingers beneath her own. Esme leaned her head against Lily's. Lily's hair pushed back. The ground was uneven under her feet. No, they were swaying, rocking from side to side. Esme prayed they wouldn't terrify the girl at its center.

Lily was crying soft tears. She looked from her mother to her father, to Nancy leaning against the car that could take Lily away if she was overwhelmed. "Are you OK?" Nancy mouthed, and Lily nodded. Nancy smiled encouragingly. It was OK. This was OK if Nancy was smiling and Lily was still here.

Cerise pulled back and wiped her eyes. Lily's hand fell away from Esme's, and already it felt like a memory, a dream. Cerise ran one hand through Lily's hair, smoothing stray wisps and the places they'd held her too tightly. Her hand found Lily's and pulled her toward the picnic blanket. She was Mom again, already in motion, passing plates and opening containers. She handed Madeline a bottle of white wine and a corkscrew. Madeline raised an eyebrow.

"What? We're celebrating. Just open it."

Cerise filled plates with potato salad and sandwiches. Esme stared into the pile of irregularly chopped potato salad, wishing she could squeeze herself between Madeline and Nick, to sit so close their legs overlapped until she couldn't tell where one started or ended, before pulling Lily into their tangle under the same shining sun. Did they want that, too, to let go of all the barriers they'd built, the grown-ups they'd become?

"Eat," Cerise told them.

Esme picked at her food. Andre scraped his plate with the side of his fork, ready for seconds. Esme couldn't remember the last time her father had looked so happy.

Lily pushed her food around, unsure how to respond to Cerise staring or pushing away strands of hair that blew across her face, asking if Lily wanted sunscreen. She'd thought someone else was her mother for eight years, and that woman was gone. Esme wondered whether staying with Amelia longer would have caused the same confusion. How overwhelming this must be, being here with a family she didn't remember. Lily toyed with a blade of grass.

Esme caught Lily's eye. "Want to see pictures?"

She pulled a photo album from her bag, and Lily crept closer. Together they flipped through pictures of Lily coloring on the living room floor, in the bathtub with floating boats and a kicking scuba diver, riding her tricycle with flying streamers, tucked in beside Esme with *A Bargain for Frances*, a tiara, and a Strawberry Shortcake nightgown. What struck Esme most as Lily flipped through pages, lingering on some longer than others, was all the pictures that weren't there and never would be. The loss felt as great as the joy of Lily being here now.

"It must be weird"—Esme paused, afraid to ask the question she'd been wondering since they'd found her—"to find out you're someone else."

Lily stared at the pages in front of her. They were up to one of Nick's birthdays now, a bike party in the park. They were wrapping crepe paper around the spokes, some kind of silly game.

"Like a dream," she said. "But I'm not sure which one feels more real yet."

"Yeah," Esme said, thinking of her time in Amelia's house, of the cardinal in the bush. "It might feel that way for a while."

Lily nodded. Esme ignored the glassy drop that fell on the photo album, and the second, before handing her sister a napkin. *She just needs to find her closet full of costumes.* Esme thought of that night at Amelia's. *Something that pushes her from the world she knows into the one that comes next. I'll help you find it*, she promised silently. *We'll all help you find it.*

Chapter Twenty-One

At noon, a fire truck wailed mournfully in the distance. A front door opened, and a woman in an electric-blue evening gown waved from the porch, her dress spreading around her like a meadow of taffeta. Cerise wrinkled her nose at the sparkles and trail of ribbon.

The woman walked toward the water and adjusted her crown, made of Popsicle sticks. As if she'd summoned them, children gathered from neighboring homes dressed as mermaids and pirates, tickled with excitement. The Dibble Queen of the Dibble Stick Parade summoned her tiny group closer.

"Come on," Madeline whispered. They left their blanket and followed the woman in blue, Nick leading Andre by the elbow. Both looked amused.

"Is this the thing from the newspaper?" Lily whispered. Nancy crept closer, just in case.

"I think so." Esme smiled, fighting the pinprick feeling in her chest that Lily had chosen her to whisper to. "Let's find out."

"Ladies and gentlemen, merpeople large and small, pirates of the sea, and all that is divine, we gather here today for the twentieth anniversary of the Dibble Stick Parade, the day the bay opens its waters and welcomes us home for our age-old celebration of dibble diving."

Children giggled and poked at the ground with water-shoe toes. A breeze rustled the train on the evening gown and sent a web of ribbons flying like blue lightning. The Dibble Queen lifted the crown from her head for the crowd to see.

"And now for the rules." The queen paused, the crown still held high above her head. Esme eyed Lily nervously. Was this OK? Lily's head was tipped toward her shoulder, eyes narrowed. How strange this must be for her, but maybe there was something familiar about it, too, something booklike.

"Rule number one: all dibblers will enter the water on a count of three and swim for the dock. All swimmers must touch the dock before diving for dibble sticks. Rule two: after successfully finding a stick, you must yell *dibble* at the surface." The crown lowered, and the queen broke it apart stick by stick.

Nick nudged Esme. "Did you bring your bathing suit?"

"Did you?"

Nick winked.

The Dibble Queen handed sticks to mermaids. They ran to the water's edge, dragging silver tails behind them, and threw them into the water.

"And the final rule." The Dibble Queen's voice rose higher. "No matter your age, today we are all young at heart." The Dibble Queen placed her hand over her chest. The queen must have been one of the mermaids once, shivering with excitement as some other queen spoke the same rules in another beautiful dress.

"Dibblers, on your marks." Pirate hats and mermaid tails shook to the ground until it was a mess of sequins, felt, and feathers. Nick took his shoes off.

"What are you doing?" Madeline stared at her brother.

"I'm going in." Nick's voice was muffled as he pulled his shirt over his head.

Madeline covered her mouth and laughed. "You're not serious."

Children lined the water's edge.

"I'm getting a damn stick." Nick smirked, his eyes fixed on the water.

"He'll get it." Andre shook his head. "Look at him. He already decided."

"Three!" the Dibble Queen yelled from her place on the dock. Nick was in his underwear. Esme kicked off her sandals. She giggled, and Nick reached his hand toward Esme's. Without thinking, Esme linked her hand through Lily's.

"Oh, for God's sake." Madeline undid the straps on her sandals. "There's fecal coliform in there."

"There's what?" Cerise asked.

"Shit." Madeline frowned. "Human shit."

"What about your clothes?" Cerise held Nick's clothes over her arm and reached for Madeline's.

"It's this or nothing." Nick snorted.

"Two and a half!"

Madeline's hand found Nick's. They were a chain of four again.

They ran for the bay. Grass clung to their heels as Nick splashed into the water and swam for the dock. Madeline and Esme waited for Lily to take off her shoes and roll the bottoms of her jeans. Then they waded through the shallow spots, catching stones and water plants with their feet. The sun made red streaks in Lily's hair. Lily tipped her face toward the sun and closed her eyes. It was a private moment, a wished-for, imagined dream.

But instead of racing for sticks, Nick dove for the bottom. Air bubbles raced to the surface. For just a moment, Esme forgot the years that separated him from the other swimmers. She wished briefly for that feeling of kicking toward the surface, watching light bend through the water in angular shards, lungs filling with air as she spit salt water from her mouth, a long-ago kid feeling.

"Dibble!" Nick screamed, grabbing a floating stick.

"You didn't touch the dock!" the queen shouted back. Parents laughed, and just as the others broke the surface, treading water beneath them, holding sticks high above their heads, Esme saw her father smile. "Maybe next year!" The queen blew Nick a kiss.

Lily sat at the water's edge. Four-year-old Lily would have raced as fast as any of the other kids, laughing and glowing in the ripples of light shining from the water, but now she toyed with blades of grass. The sky was full of wispy clouds. Esme watched the boundary between the water and the sky where Lily was too. It was hard to tell if Lily liked her new family, the world she'd stumbled out of and into again.

"I wonder if she wears the same dress every year," Lily said. The queen sipped from a Coors Light can.

Her parents watched from the blanket, waiting like they would have when they were young.

"We could find out," Madeline said, chasing a ripple with her toe. "We could come back next year."

Next year, there'd be a new little baby here too. Esme smiled at the secret.

She nodded and turned back toward the water. Kids would play for hours, until just before the sun went down, pretending they weren't nearly as cold as their shriveled fingers and toes would suggest, running into sun-warmed towels when their parents called them home.

"Who won?" Nick called to the queen.

She threw her head back and laughed. "Who knows? Everyone thinks they're the first one up. Better that way."

Esme found a place in the sun beside Lily. They sat quietly for a long time, watching the gentle waves and listening to children laughing. Esme wished she could go back to her childhood bedroom and lift Lily to the bed, holding her under her arms so she could trace the thick cables on the Golden Gate Bridge and imagine that fog tasted like marshmallows or Lucky Charms.

But Lily was too big for that now. She was twelve, tightrope walking the line between her past and future, trying not to fall. How much of Esme's twelve-year-old life had felt that way? And yet she'd always known who she was. She wanted to put her arm around Lily's shoulders but didn't. They watched the water together. *Little sister*, Esme thought, filled with wonder. *This is my sister.*

She would call Paul. She would accept his offer and move to Boston. Then she'd buy bowls of New England clam chowder and take long walks along the Charles with Adam. She would have an extra bed for Lily if she wanted to come for the weekend, and Esme would buy every kind of curly-hair shampoo so Lily could try them all, and she'd buy every fruit in the supermarket for Lily too. She didn't want there to be anything Lily might need, anything she might not know to ask for. She wanted Lily to feel welcome. They could try everything until Lily knew what she liked. She'd help Lily paint the room she used to share with Madeline any way she wanted. They'd rip down all the old posters and all the old stuff until it was Lily's room, officially. And Esme would get ballet tickets so Lily could see shows, if she wanted, and they could talk about the ones she'd already seen until things were easy between them again. She would be close to Lily, to Adam, her parents and Nick, Madeline and the baby, and she couldn't imagine it any other way.

"Hey, Dibble Queen!" a little girl shouted from the platform. Water dripped down her skinny legs and pooled around her feet. "You chicken?"

The queen straightened to full height and put one hand on her hip. "You know I'm not."

"Then jump!" the little girl yelled, her voice bending and tumbling through wind and water.

"Jump!" Nick called. "Jump! Jump! Jump!" A chorus of dripping children blended with the call of birds above and the hum of cars behind them as the queen, gown and all, joined them in the water. Lily smiled at the tulle lily pad floating on the surface, ribbons streaming. Esme tried to see the world as Lily saw it: new and breathing in every shade of sunlight.

Chapter Twenty-Two

An anonymous someone donated two weeks at the reunification program of their choice. It would be two weeks in a new place, with therapists teaching them techniques to use when there were too many feelings or too much tension, easing them back into the life they should've had. It would be a break from the phone calls from reporters, from writers offering to author Lily's biography about her life in captivity. They hired a spokesperson to tell people repeatedly that they were thrilled to have their daughter back and would appreciate peace and privacy.

They decided on an equine therapy ranch in New Mexico because Lily liked the idea of horses. Before leaving, Cerise spun through every convenience store at least once per day because Lily might need Dramamine for the flight, and she'd definitely need sunscreen when they were outside. She was so fair. Or antacids in case the food didn't agree with her and electrolyte tabs in case the heat was too much or aloe vera in case the sunscreen wore off too soon, calamine lotion in case she touched something she wasn't used to, and bug spray because didn't horses carry ticks?

"Mom," Madeline whined after the fourth trip, "they said to only bring clothes and toiletries. They have everything else."

"Yes, but what is *everything*? They can't have everything."

"It's a miracle she hasn't bought rattlesnake antivenin yet," Madeline mumbled.

"Only because she didn't think of it," Esme whispered back.

Cerise hadn't gone away in years. She folded and refolded clothes before putting them into the suitcase, switched sleeveless shirts for T-shirts, sweatshirts for jackets, and reread the packing list again and again. It was hopeless: preparing for something nothing could prepare them for, not really, so they let her spin in and out of the house with plastic shopping bags and send Andre to the grocery store for snacks in case Lily didn't like the food until there was no room left in the suitcases and no time left to shop.

Cerise looked relieved to finally leave her suitcase on the baggage scale at the airport and close her eyes on the flight. They were flying together, except for Lily, who'd flown ahead earlier with her therapist to start one-on-one work before everyone else arrived. Her parents had driven Lily to the airport and guided her through the maze of terminals, promising Lily they'd be there soon. As Lily had slung her new backpack over her shoulder and tightened the straps, Esme had wondered if her strange new family was any comfort for someone who'd spent most of her life alone. Lily didn't always answer to Lily. Watching Cerise shape the name Liz on her tongue was a reminder of everything they were up against. As hard as it had been to put Lily on that flight alone, she was sure there was relief too.

Esme sat alone on the plane because they hadn't been able to find five seats together. Nick had taken one at the front of the plane, and Esme had worried he'd bolt before they closed the hatch, but he'd stuffed his duffel bag into the overhead bin and slammed it shut, popping headphones into his ears and squeezing into his seat, where his legs jutted into the aisle, proof enough that the rest of him was still there. Equine therapy was supposed to help them see each other in a new light, outside the norm of regular life, and Esme hoped it would be true. It was time, after so many years, to see Nick not just as the teenager he hadn't been for a long time.

~

The sun came up slowly over the ranch in the morning, warming the sandy desert soil from lunar cold to scorching in only minutes. Esme woke up early and slipped out the back door. Her cottage sat behind the corral, where they would meet the horses, and next to the vegetable garden, where they would pick things for breakfast, lunch, and dinner. There was a small chicken coop near the garden, too, with hens tucked inside, nestled against each other for warmth. "Explore. Find your special places," their therapist, Diana, had told them last night. "Those will be the places you'll go if you need to take a break."

But the places she'd explored last night had faded in the afternoon sun to shadow shapes in the darkness beneath an endless sky of stars. In the morning, they were dusty and sun scorched, washed out under the bright white of the sun. She was glad they were here. They would all look different in this new place. It was refreshing not to be in their cramped apartment in Queens, cluttered with memories. She rounded the corner between rows of raised beds full of plants and found Lily, crouched in the soil, picking orange bell peppers, cradling a folded list in her lap. Someone had braided her hair, but it had come undone and covered her face. Or she'd braided it herself. Esme shouldn't assume Lily could or couldn't do things.

"Can I help?"

"No," Lily answered without looking up. Esme swallowed away the lump in her throat, unsure if she should leave or stay while Lily twisted the stem of a pepper until it popped free. Esme sat on the edge of the next bed of mint and sage and herbs. She pulled a sprig of mint and traced the jagged leaf with her fingers. The moon was a sliver in the sky, fading slowly. The pepper plant rustled as Lily worked. Esme'd read something once about introducing pets through a closed door for the first time so they could become familiar with the other's scent. This wasn't the same, but if it took time for animals, it would take time for them too.

Esme busied herself picking sprigs of mint and cucumbers. She would slice them later in the kitchen, hopefully alongside Lily, and make them cucumber water for breakfast. The sun was warm on her shoulders, and as she worked, she stole glances at the curve of Lily's back, the way she sat with her legs folded under her, ankles crossed, filling her basket with peppers and tomatoes. There were thin white lines on Lily's ankles, long healed, but they had not been there before. Esme could not ask how she'd gotten them. The smell of mint was suddenly too strong, and Esme realized she'd crushed the leaves in her hands, ground them into a paste that left a green line under her fingernails. She forced herself to take a deep breath and let the anger pass.

Light fell unevenly over the taller plants, throwing shadows into the space between beds. Lily abandoned her basket and watched a shadow on the ground, tracing her finger through the soil to mark the shape of it.

The sun would move in an hour and make a new shadow somewhere else, but Lily's sketch was proof that it had been there at all. It struck Esme then that Lily had seen only the same shadows from the light through the barred window in the basement. It'd been a long time since Esme had watched a shadow. There were so many things Esme hoped to show Lily, but she hadn't considered that Lily might have things to show her, too, even if Lily didn't have words for them yet.

Lily smelled a purple eggplant and then a bright-yellow squash flower. If Esme was not mistaken, she was whispering something to it. Esme wished her father was here to see this and imagined he would wake Lily up before the sun when they got home and invite Lily to join him in the garden across the street, where he would show her how to plant bulbs, pull weeds, clip herbs, and hang them to dry in the sun. Talking to plants might help them grow, but Esme suspected it would help Lily grow, too, whispering secrets in the garden. Esme pushed away the part of herself that wished Lily would whisper secrets to her. If Lily wasn't ready to talk, at least she'd know Esme was there, patient and still as a shadow until the sun traced her somewhere else.

~

"Hold the reins." Josie slipped the leather strap into Lily's hand and drew a line in the sand with her toe, marking the end with an *x*. "When you're ready, you can walk Diamond from here to here. The rule is you can do it however you want, but no one else can help you, Lily, unless you ask. Understood?"

Lily nodded. For as much as Lily's new size still shocked Esme, she only reached the middle of Diamond's speckled gray chest. Thick veins ran through Diamond's neck beneath her shiny coat. Ropy muscles laced through her skinny legs, making Lily look painfully fragile. Lily's face was already sunburned. The straw hat Josie had given her to block the sun left checkered light squares on her face and hid her eyes. Diamond toed at the ground and flared her nostrils. The rein tightened in Lily's hand, but it was hard to tell what Lily thought about this whole experience.

"Give it a go." Josie stepped back. Lily tugged. Diamond stayed put.

"Keep trying," Josie called.

Lily switched hands and made a clicking sound. Diamond followed Lily's lead until she realized there was nothing to eat in Lily's closed fist.

Just walk, Esme prayed. That was all this horse had to do to make everyone clap and cheer for Lily, but she wouldn't do it. Lily dropped the reins and turned toward the exit. Andre stepped forward, but Josie held up one hand.

"Lily, why not try again?"

"I don't care if it walks." She scooped a handful of dirt and threw it at the ground. It scattered in the breeze.

"I can see that you're frustrated," Josie said. "Why not ask for help?" She walked toward Nick and placed a sugar cube in his hand. "Nick has something that will help now."

Lily stared toward the cabins, where the shades were drawn to keep the heat out. The air conditioners hummed in the distance.

"Let's try one more time, Lily, but this time, Nick will help."

"I'll help too." She was the old Cerise again, determined to move that horse for Lily's sake, but Josie stopped her with a smile.

"Lily, would you mind?"

Lily stared at the uneven dirt in the arena and shook her head.

"OK, let's try again. Tell them where to stand and what to do."

Lily pointed to the *x* Josie had drawn. Nick took his place.

"And what should Cerise do?"

Lily sat down in the dirt. The hat slipped to one side, but Lily let it fall. Maybe this was too much. There were too many new choices. It was hot as hell, and Esme's mouth was parched. Water wouldn't even help. She needed to be away from it, in a cool room, alone, where she could close her eyes and recharge. If that was how she felt, how much more overwhelmed was Lily? She handed Lily a water bottle, but Lily only held it between her hands.

"Just hold the horse," Lily mumbled, pushing her hat into place.

The brochure said families would try new experiences in the gentle presence of a horse, but it did not mention the unbearable heat or that the gentle presence of a horse might not want to budge. How would moving a horse make a difference when Lily moved into Madeline and Esme's old bedroom, in a new bed with blank walls, listening to the unfamiliar sounds of her parents getting dressed in the morning or making coffee when they would have stayed strangers if the police had not found her in time? How would these things work when Lily had to eat at the dinner table or go to school or make friends? Was this something she wanted? The girl under the straw hat was a blank unknown, even after a week at this place.

You weren't the Waltz Girl overnight, Esme reminded herself. If she'd known at her first ballet class how long it would take, she probably would have quit. The unknown had saved her then. The comparison should've been comforting, but it was unsettling.

Cerise and Nick waited for instructions on opposite ends of the sandy line, holding their piece of Lily's puzzle, but Cerise was focused on Nick. He looked small in the middle of the corral, surrounded by sand and an endless blue sky, his olive skin pale in comparison to how bright the sun was overhead. Sweat dotted his upper lip, but hours of training, of running and lifting weights and keeping odd hours, had left Nick the most collected in this odd environment. He'd been so quiet on the plane ride or at dinner when the chef had given him things to chop or pick from the garden, silently going about whatever had been asked of him. Now, standing at the end of a line drawn in dirt with a sugar cube outstretched in his hand, it felt like an apology for something he'd never done.

Some of the old hardness fell away from Cerise. She stepped forward, and the horse followed in her footsteps as Cerise walked toward her only son. She wrapped her arms around Nick's shoulders, lifting onto her tiptoes to reach him. He rested his head on top of hers, and Esme held back a sob. She couldn't hear what they were saying, but the emotion of it shivered through her.

"You're going to have obstacles," Josie said to Lily. "And that's OK. It's OK to ask for help."

Esme leaned against the fence near her father, watching her brother and mother sway in the dusty breeze. Madeline offered Lily a hand and helped her up from the ground. Together they walked Diamond back to the stalls, one on either side.

"I never doubted him," Andre said quietly.

"It was easy to," Esme whispered.

"Yeah, well . . ." Andre sighed. "He didn't make it easy. Even she . . ." Andre looked away. Esme found her father's hand, calloused from so much time in his garden. Madeline and Lily walked back from the stables without Diamond, but something small and orange squirmed in Lily's arms, and for a quick second, Esme thought of her fish named Marley.

"Is this going to work, Dad? Any of this? It just feels . . ." Her voice trailed off. The sun was hot on her face and shoulders.

"It has to," he said finally. Esme nodded. He was right. There was no other option.

"She found it," Madeline explained, "under a pile of blankets in a stall, and I think she'd very much like to keep it."

The kitten purred against Lily's chest. It closed its eyes as she rubbed her pointer finger over its forehead. Cerise looked to Andre, her face still red and bleary, and it took a minute for the smile to break between them, a resigned laugh that said if after all this, Lily wanted a cat, of course the answer was yes.

"What's its name?" Andre asked.

"Does it need one?" Lily asked. She traced her finger over the delicate line of its ear, but there was an edge in her voice that hadn't been there before.

"Of course it needs one," Cerise said. "If it's going to be part of our family, then it has to have a name."

Lily blanched and just as quickly lowered the kitten down to the ground, where it stood on four wobbly legs, its tail as straight as a pin.

"What's wrong, Lily?" Cerise asked.

"Maybe it doesn't want to go," Lily mumbled. Dust kicked up behind Lily as she walked to her cabin alone, head down, hands hanging at her sides, empty where the kitten had been. The cabin door opened and closed.

Madeline scooped the kitten into the crook of her elbow.

"Let's go inside too," she whispered.

Esme closed her eyes, and the sun blinked yellow and black behind her lids. *Please let her love us*, she prayed, *however long it takes*—because the thought of keeping her captive again was worse than losing her the first time.

~

Madeline set the kitten up with bowls of milk and water and a nest of towels outside Lily's door. A little while later, it disappeared inside.

"Because it's cold at night," Lily explained at breakfast the next day. "And there might be bigger animals outside, but I left the window open in case it wanted to go outside, but it didn't. It slept on my pillow all night by my head."

The cat squirmed in Lily's lap, walking in a circle until it found the right spot. Lily fed it a piece of egg from her plate.

"He likes you," Cerise said. "He feels safe with you."

"Maybe," Lily said, her fingers sticky with yolk.

Esme hoped the same would eventually be true for Lily.

~

They left a week later without the kitten. Lily had named it Garfield and changed its water and milk bowls and left the pillow from her bed outside on the porch for him. It seemed fitting that Lily would leave him here, under so much sky and with so many places to explore, instead of bringing him home to Queens, where he'd be an indoor cat, confined to their small apartment, forced to live in an unfamiliar place.

They came home to the same kind of street altar people had built years before with teddy bears and balloons, candles, posters that welcomed Lily home, and flowers, especially lilies. The community needed to heal, too, Esme realized, because what had happened to them could have happened to anyone, anywhere, but it had been here.

"They made this for you," Cerise explained to Lily, "because the whole world was hoping and praying you'd come home safe, but no one prayed as much as we did."

Lily picked one of the flowers from the street. If they weighed everything left on the sidewalk, it would outweigh Lily. The enormity of it sat on Lily's shoulders. She fumbled with the petals of a lily until her fingers were covered with yellow pollen and the edges withered. It must be so overwhelming, Esme thought sadly, for a girl who'd known almost no one for her entire life to suddenly be so known.

"We could donate everything," Esme suggested, "to children's hospitals. They might like the toys. Or we could put some of the flowers in a vase for your room."

Lily gathered the boldest pink and orange flowers.

Birdman's old window was covered with jelly stickers of little hearts and stars. The new family had put Styrofoam grow cups full of overflowing clover on the window ledge. He was gone, and yet it still felt like he was watching, presiding over what their lives had become. Four-year-old Lily would've loved a new cast of stuffed animals, but now she studied the glittery letters on the welcome-home posters, the side-by-side pictures of herself at four and herself today.

"Your favorite color was hot pink," Cerise said sadly as the bouquet in Lily's hands grew.

"It still is," Lily said finally. Clouds rolled in over the 7 train tracks, low and heavy. Esme caught her mother's eye and smiled. At least that hadn't changed.

Nick and Andre were waiting by the front door with the pile of mismatched luggage. On any other day, they would've been quick to go upstairs, change into sweatpants, and click the TV on, but today they lingered by the mailboxes, waiting for Lily to come home.

When they stepped through the lobby, Esme hoped Lily would recognize the mailboxes they'd checked for birthday cards every day when Lily was too young to understand that her birthday only happened once per year, but she didn't. She waited as someone else pushed the elevator button to their floor, even though it used to be her favorite job. Lily carried her backpack over one shoulder, her hair loose from her ponytail, studying the green-gray hallway and the dim lights as Cerise narrated their journey from the lobby to their front door. *This is where the trash goes, these are the stairs we use sometimes, this is the good elevator*, as if Lily had never been here before.

Andre handed Lily a new set of house keys with a key chain that looked like her horse, Diamond, and on the back, he'd etched Lily's name with a pin in imperfect script. Esme's eyes flooded. He'd bought her a souvenir as if they'd been on vacation, and in a way, they had been. It was a journey. Lily put her new keys in her pocket.

They stepped inside. Esme realized, as Cerise shifted from foot to foot and fumbled with her fingers, that she was not the only one waiting for Lily to recognize the faded rug or the crocheted blankets on the couch, the bin of toys under the window, the boxes of cereal on the table. She did not remember to take her shoes off by the front door or hang her jacket in the closet. She stood in the middle of the living room, studying the doors that opened to other rooms, the faded pictures on the walls, as if it were the first time seeing these things her parents had spent so long preserving just for this moment.

The disappointment in the room was palpable. They had all been hoping that this was the moment Lily would remember, but she didn't.

"Right," Cerise said. "Let's give you the tour."

But Nick was already punching in a number on the phone. The cord dangled at his side.

"Hey," he said to Lily. "Pepperoni or mushrooms?"

It was a kind of test: she'd hated mushrooms and picked the "slugs" off her food. Lily slid her backpack to the floor and rested it against the couch. Lily looked from Esme to Madeline and to her parents, unused to making choices.

"Pepperoni," she said at last. Nick gave her a thumbs-up, and Esme was thrilled. Even Cerise smiled.

"Come on," Cerise said. "Let's show you home."

Esme watched as Cerise handed Lily a pile of clean, folded towels and led her from room to room, showing her where the forks and glasses were in the kitchen, which bed she'd sleep in.

"We'll fix this room," Cerise promised, eyeing the old posters and the furniture in Madeline and Esme's room. "We'll make it however you want, and I'm sorry we didn't do it before you got here, but we were waiting for you."

And on that, her voice caught. They'd always been waiting. Soon, Lily's alarm clock would blare from her new room, and she'd sleep through it like a teenager and take long showers and fill the bathtub ledge with her shampoos and conditioners. Cerise would buy snacks again from the supermarket and teach Lily how to do laundry or set the table for dinner each night. Esme hoped Lily would fold into the fabric of their lives so much that they'd forget sometimes that she'd ever been gone at all.

But for now, Esme was struck by her sister sitting at the edge of her old bed in the same striped sheets Esme had slept on when she was her age and lived in this room last when her future hadn't yet popped open before her.

"Come on," Esme said, smiling at Lily as she led her teary mother from her old bedroom. "Let's let Lily get changed."

Esme met her mother's eye. "She's not going anywhere tonight."

"No." Cerise laughed and dabbed the corners of her eyes. "Thank God."

And for the first time in many years, Esme thanked him or her too.

Chapter Twenty-Three

Esme pressed her eyes closed as they passed the watery blue stretch under a cloudless sky. Marsh grass reached for that same blue as the train rolled past. At home, Lily's new bedroom walls were drying. They'd spent the morning pulling apart Madeline and Esme's old bedroom furniture, emptying drawers of clothes no one remembered wearing, and painting the bedroom Lily's winter-morning blue until the whole room felt like it was breathing. If only because she'd spent so much time sifting through the relics of the person she'd been and what she'd left behind, Esme felt drawn to the studio in a way she hadn't felt since she was eleven years old. "Do you want to come?" she'd asked Lily. "It's a special place for me." Lily hadn't answered, but she'd pulled herself up from the floor and found her shoes. Esme took that as a yes.

"Is this . . . ?" Lily asked, trailing off.

"It is." Esme pointed past the marsh grass. "That's where we had our picnic."

Lily's hands were still in her lap, not fidgeting like they often did. She was hard to read. Sometimes she pulled into herself and was quiet for hours, fumbling with the hem on her shirt or pulling at her cuticles, staring out the window at nothing in particular. Esme imagined it was from spending hours and hours alone. Esme fought the urge to put her arm around Lily because it didn't feel natural yet. Was there a part of her sister who remembered these eleven train stops?

They stepped off the train and crossed the parking lot, where most of the boutique shops had changed but the glass windows still glinted back over the parked cars. The sign on the studio door said CLOSED, but Amelia was inside waiting. She'd been so excited over the phone, and Esme couldn't wait to see her, to see her first studio. Without thinking, she reached for Lily's hand and then felt the momentary panic when Lily's warm skin touched hers. Lily wasn't big on touching. *Boundaries*, Esme reminded herself, but while Lily didn't hold Esme's hand back, she hadn't pulled away either. Esme took that as one hopeful step before letting go to push the studio door open.

The waiting area was dark, but that same grapefruit smell folded around her. The old broom leaned against the wall in the corner behind Amelia's desk. A Chopin nocturne was playing inside, and those first few notes were enough to make Esme dizzy. Light spilled through the open door to the studio, throwing a triangle of sunlight over the floor and chairs where Cerise and Lily used to wait, making kissing-booth signs and sewing costumes.

"This—" Esme tried to explain, but her voice caught, and her eyes welled. She was eleven years old again, staring at those newspaper articles of other famous dancers on the wall while Lily crawled on the floor in her red corduroy coat, scratching away with crayons while Esme danced into her future, oblivious to all that would come next. And now Lily was here, too, just beside her, nearly the same age Esme had been when Lily had been here last.

Amelia filled the doorway, and even in the dim light, Esme could feel her smile.

"Esme," she said, full of all the old tenderness, if not more.

Esme snapped to attention.

"I'm so happy you're here. Both of you," she said.

She led them to the newest framed photo above her desk, where Esme was leaning back in a bath of blue light, being carried into the empty space beyond the stage. She took the frame off the wall and handed it to Lily, who traced her finger over Esme's tiny shape.

"Brava," Amelia whispered. "Brava."

Esme nodded, too choked up to say anything more, and suddenly the whole day was completely overwhelming and complete in a way Esme couldn't have imagined. She felt tired enough to sleep for a thousand years, but she should tell Lily about living with Amelia at some point because they'd both been somewhere else once that had recharted their course.

"Come," Amelia said, guiding them both toward the open studio. "I can't have you out of practice when you get to Boston."

Esme slipped out of her shoes and pulled a pair of leg warmers over her leggings, laced her pointe shoes, and watched out of the corner of her eye as Lily left her own sneakers against the wall.

"May I?" Amelia asked, gesturing toward Lily's hair. She began braiding it into a rope that swept the stray curls from Lily's face.

"Is this OK?" Esme asked Lily.

Lily looked up from under her lashes, nodding only slightly as Amelia braided the last few inches and tied it with an elastic band.

"She'll tell us if it's not, won't she?" Amelia said with as much authority as Esme remembered. It was just as comforting now as it had been then. Even Lily seemed to find it reassuring. She followed Amelia to the mirror, where Amelia positioned one of Lily's hands on the barre, adjusted her shoulders, and tipped her chin just a bit higher than it already was. Esme found her place behind Lily as she moved from first position to second and third under Amelia's guidance.

They were back at the beginning again. Esme watched her sister in the mirror, her loose gray T-shirt spotted with sky-blue paint over Esme's leggings. When Lily was still, Esme could almost see herself in the length of Lily's arms, her side profile in the mirror, the soundless nods and eagerness to hold Amelia's gentle corrections, only Esme had come so far from that little girl in the mirror, full of promise. She was beyond Amelia's corrections now as she traced her own patterns in the mirror across the floor, showing off everything she'd become in the past eight years because she'd had to—but also because she'd always hoped Lily would be watching, and now she was. Amelia clapped to keep time as she always had and taught Lily a waltz so Lily could cross the floor, so to speak, all on her own.

EPILOGUE

By October, Esme had settled into Boston. She spent the mornings taking classes, learning new choreography, and her favorite, choreograph-
ing with Adam, the two of them puffing and spiking through bursts
of inspiration, finishing where the other left off. She'd signed up for a
creative writing class at Boston University, and when she was feeling
brave, she read her short stories aloud at night while she and Adam
soaked their feet in ice baths. Sometimes her stories were about dance,
but mostly, they were about kids who slipped between worlds.

In the morning, she woke to cinnamon oatmeal simmering in the
Crock-Pot, a smell that reminded her of Amelia every time she lifted
the lid. But best of all, she woke to Adam curled on the pillow next to
hers under a tangle of blond hair. Esme never felt like the day had truly
begun until his blue eyes opened, bluer than the sky through their window. Her other life had been dreamlike. It would never quite feel as real
as Adam's ankle draped over hers in the morning or at night before they
fell asleep. Next month, he was coming home with her for Madeline's
wedding, and for the first time, Adam's thread in her life would cross
with her family. The whole idea was thrilling.

Lily's room had started something for her parents. They'd bought
a new leather couch and painted the living room bright white. Andre
wanted to fix the kitchen up next because they were growing so much
nice food in the garden; they should have a beautiful kitchen to cook

together like they'd had in New Mexico. Cerise couldn't believe it'd only taken a few tomatoes to change the olive-green countertops she'd always hated. Sometime between Lily's bedroom and the living room, Andre's pile of folded sheets and blankets had disappeared from the living room.

They had plans to turn Nick's room into a sewing room for Cerise, but Esme suspected that would change when Madeline told them about the baby. Madeline was just starting to show but keeping the baby a secret until after the wedding. Even though it hadn't happened in the "right" order, Madeline insisted, she could still tell them in the logical order.

Esme went home as often as she could, taking the bus to New York for a night or two with Lily. They took the train to Central Park and climbed sparkling black rocks in silence, sat by the pond to watch frogs and turtles. Quiet time was just as important as talking time, Lily's therapist had said. It built the comfortable space between them.

On one of those trips home, Lily woke Esme before dawn. The light outside the window was a smoky gray. It was too early for birds, and the house was silent.

"Will you take me somewhere?" Lily whispered.

Esme found her shoes and left a quick note for her parents. She followed Lily to the garden and waited while she picked the last of the lavender and tied it into a bundle. Lily locked the gate when she was finished. It still startled Esme when Lily did little normal things that made her part of their fabric, locking a gate, pouring a bowl of cereal, opening her old bedroom door, sleepy eyed.

There was still dirt on her hands as they walked to the subway and waited for the 7. The sun came up behind the platform, red orange through the smog. They took the train to Long Island City, where Gloria was buried with her family. Esme waited under a pine tree while Lily knelt in the freshly turned soil, tucking flowers against the marker where a new stone would be but wasn't yet. Esme wondered who Lily was praying to behind her mess of dark curls, if she was saying goodbye to Gloria or Liz, the person she'd thought she was for eight years.

Lily was quiet on the ride home, her shoulder touching Esme's when the train jolted forward.

"Look." Lily pointed.

An old advertisement for *Swan Lake* hung above them on the subway. Esme looked for Adam, but he wasn't in it, or he was too small to see. She never did understand how Prince Siegfried could confuse Odette with Odile, the black swan for the white. Liz for Lily. *How easy it is*, Esme mused, *to be enchanted by what we want to see.*

"Have you seen that one?" Esme asked, and Lily nodded.

The doors opened. It was unseasonably warm, the last few days of an Indian summer rebelling against the start of fall. In a few hours, Esme would be on a bus back to Boston, where she'd roll the past few hours around in her head. She wouldn't tell her parents where they'd been unless Lily wanted them to know. Esme pulled out the tiny pinecone she'd taken from the cemetery and tucked it into Lily's palm. If they'd been kids, she would've told Lily to hold it in her hand until it sprouted into a tree and grew and grew until Lily could climb it like in "Jack and the Beanstalk," but Lily wasn't that little girl anymore, and neither was Esme. Lily's hand closed around the pinecone as sunlight splintered through the windows.

Different, Esme thought, remembering what Amelia had told her that day at her house. Life would be different—not necessarily better, but different. The skyline was a maze of glass and concrete. The sun rose above the tallest buildings. Home. She put her arm around Lily's shoulders and let it rest there as the train carried them home.

BOOK CLUB QUESTIONS

1. Considering Nick, Madeline, Esme, and Lily's relationships to one another at the beginning of the novel, how do they understand or misunderstand each other? Imagine it's ten years after Lily returns: How have these relationships changed?

2. What was your reaction to the psychic? Did you believe her?

3. If Esme were your child, would you have allowed her to live with Amelia?

4. Tragedies often cast doubt and blame on those most impacted. In what ways does this happen to Esme's family? In what ways does Esme cast doubt on her own family?

5. Each of the family members processed Lily's disappearance in their own way. Discuss the ways in which they coped and how those coping strategies contributed to the recovery work they've begun at the end of the novel.

6. Esme's imaginary world is often the only relief from the reality of what's happened to her sister. How does Esme's imaginary world change as the novel progresses? What is the relationship between Esme's imaginary world and her life as a dancer?

7. Discuss Gloria Santos's choice to take Lily. How do you feel Esme's family members' feelings toward Gloria will change over time? How do you feel Lily's feelings will change toward Gloria?

8. When Esme receives an offer from Paul Katzman, she considers how her life has come full circle. In what ways has Esme's life truly come full circle, and in what ways will it never be the same?

9. Imagine that Lily had never been kidnapped: How do you think Esme's life as a dancer would have been different or the same?

10. How does the title of the novel, *A Lily in the Light*, reflect the main themes of the story?

ACKNOWLEDGMENTS

To my amazing agent, Rachel Eckstrom: for a writer with a ninety-thousand-word novel, I don't have enough words to thank you, not least for introducing me to the fantastic Alicia Clancy and the Lake Union team. Thank you, Alicia, for loving this book so much, rolling the dice on a new author, and advocating for this book through and through.

Thank you to Heather, Sophie, Julia, and the many talented Sackett Street Writers who coddled this story in its early infancy and steered it into a manuscript. To Natalia and Robyn, my friends and beta readers, whose brutal honesty made this thing real.

To Martha McPhee, who took me under her wing and taught me that writing is rewriting. And for Barbara, who came to the first reading I gave as a nervous new writer and offered endless encouragement.

To Mom and Dad, Michael, Jenna, and Emma: these pages are full of our story too. When we were throwing LEGO houses down the stairs to see whose house was strongest, we did not know what we'd grow up to be or how we'd inspire each other.

And Rob, for not only coming without protest to Lincoln Center and the Palais Garnier and reading countless drafts of this book but for understanding the need behind all those nights and weekends alone in another world. Your belief in me pushed me through both the doubt and inspiration to bring this idea to a book. I couldn't have done this without you, truly.

ABOUT THE AUTHOR

Kristin Fields grew up in Queens, which she likes to think of as a small town next to a big city. Fields studied writing at Hofstra University, where she received the Eugene Schneider Fiction Award. After college, Fields found herself working on a historic farm, teaching high school English, and designing museum education programs. She is currently leading an initiative to bring gardens to New York City public schools. She lives in Brooklyn with her husband.